The Reapers MC, Ravenswood Series

Reaper's Revenge

Book Four

Harley Raige

To Karen
Thankyou
for being
a part of this
journey
with me
Harley
Raige

For updates on my upcoming releases please
follow me
www.tiktok.com/@harleyraige

www.instagram.com/harleyraige

www.facebook.com/harleyraige
Join our group
www.facebook.com/groups/the.rebels.of.raige
Become a Rebel of Raige and join the Rebellion!

Authors Note

The author is British. This story does contain
British spellings and phrases. This book also contains
possible triggers, including but not limited to murder,
self harm, torture, questionable cheating, shock
pregnancy, dub-con and kidnapping. It also contains
explicit sexual situations, strong violence, taboo
subjects, a shit tonne of offensive language and
mature topics, some dark content,
plus, M/M, F/M and F/F
18+

Dedication

To every one of you knobheads who have stayed this far.
I couldn't have done this without your support.
This ones for you!

Contents:

Steel

As I'm led into the police station for processing, my mind is racing. What the fuck is happening? Where's Ray? I need to find her. I need to remain calm throughout this situation, or I'll never get out. This isn't my first rodeo, so I remain calm and appear relaxed on the outside while the inner me is crawling, nails scraping down the inside of my brain, demanding to be listened to and to be let out.

They record my vital information, take my mugshot, empty my pockets, and shit, this looks bad. They remove mine and Ray's phones and her rings, along with my keys and my wallet. Shit, shit, shit. They're covered in blood, and someone is called to take swabs. They confiscate my clothing, which also has blood on it, but whose? I'm sent for fingerprinting and a full-body search, which is fun—not! They check for warrants, carry out a health check, and then give me my phone call. I call Ares, but he doesn't pick up, so I leave a message. They throw me in a cell.

My mind is still racing. I'm unable to quieten it. This is what it must feel like to be insane. I feel like the inner me is screaming, throwing himself against the walls, dragging blunt fingernails down his face, tearing skin, and all I can do is sit and wait and wait some more.

It's a good fifteen hours later when Scar and Ares arrive. I'm going out of my mind. They lead me into a room to talk to my counsel, and they're both there. Ares looks terrified; it is not a good look on him, and although they both look stoic to anyone who doesn't know them, Scar looks fit to hurl.

"What the fuck's going on?" I whisper.

"It's a shitshow, Brother." Ares shakes his head. "She played us. She fucking played us all," Ares spits, "I fucking knew she was too good to be true. I'm sorry, Steel."

I look over at Scar, and she hangs her head, "Tell me everything!" I bark at her, causing her to flinch.

"Please, I don't believe it. I think... I don't... this can't be real... "

"Scar!" I snap, I'm literally going out of my mind, and I need answers.

A steely mask slides over her features, like she's detaching herself from the situation. She takes a deep breath before speaking.

"The initial charges were the murder of Lewis Carlisle and kidnapping and potential murder of Ray. The second charges have been dropped." She pauses.

"That means she's okay. They found Ray?" I say with a hopeful tone.

"She came forward, apparently." Ares scoffs. "We were fucking raided by the FBI, Steel. That's why

I didn't answer my phone. About thirty minutes after you left, they burst through the fucking doors into the clubhouse and ransacked everything. They even raided the old gun locker. They ripped everything apart; they seized all the computers. Luckily, they didn't find anything and won't find anything on them. She shafted us, Brother."

Scar flicks him a glare like she can't quite believe it. "Apparently." She flicks a glare to Ares, which I read as "shut the fuck up," and looks back at me. "Apparently, she turned up and has been placed in protective custody."

I scoff a laugh and shake my head. Ray has never needed protecting. "So what's happening?"

"There was a witness at the security offices. They saw you shoot Mr Carlisle, then drag Ray from the car by her hair, snatch her rings from her fingers, throw her in your truck and drive away. Then you came back minutes later alone, and that's when the police turned up. Apparently, Ray said she got away from you. You lost it when you found out she was having an affair with Mr Carlisle."

"What? Affair? What the fuck are you talking about?" My mind is reeling. It's overloaded with shit slamming around up there. I can't slow my thoughts. Affair? That's why she didn't want kids? Was she leaving me?

"Yes! They were having an affair, and a few people from the ball confirmed that they were a couple."

I rub at my face, unable to process anything more. "What does this mean?"

"You're being charged with murder. They found the murder weapon in your truck, Ray's blood on you and in the truck, the rings and the phone in your possession. Steel, this is fucking bad, we're lucky they didn't find anything at home, or we would all be locked up. She's testifying against you. That's why she's in custody. She's confirmed you killed him."

I close my eyes, and my head sinks into my hands, and a stray tear runs down my cheek. I look at Scar, and all I can think is, "She never loved me, did she?"

"Steel." Scar reaches forward and places a hand on mine. "I don't... I can't... I won't believe this till I hear it from her lips myself. This isn't real. Ray wouldn't do this. You're her universe. She wasn't even living till she met you. We're trying to get hold of Dane, Dice, Bran and Demi, but they're all away for the weekend, and Bernie and Cade aren't answering. We will get to the bottom of this, Steel, I promise!"

As I'm being led back to my cell, I fracture inside. I thought I was a strong man, a mountain of a man, and when I met her, I became the strongest I'd ever been. Now, I'm a shell, I'm empty, I feel everything yet nothing. I swallow down the lump that forms in my throat as I try to... I don't know what to try to do. My heart stutters in my chest, my breathing becomes pained, there's a tingling sensation in my fingers, and nausea rolls over me. The dizziness takes me by surprise as I stumble into the wall. I'm gasping for breath as I slide down the wall. A buzzer goes off as I'm dragged down the corridor.

I'm aware of chaos inside me, and as I focus outwardly, I'm in a medical room.

"It was just a panic attack. Vitals are good; you can take him back to his cell," A woman in a lab coat says to the guards in the corner. Panic attack? What the fuck?

Ares

I'm pacing in the bar. Scar has her laptop out in our booth and is doing fuck knows what. I'm doing even less. There's a sombre feel to the place. We've been betrayed; we all loved her, and she stabbed every single one of us through the heart.

Scar is in denial; the boys and Demi are all AWOL, and so are Bernie and Cade, which just adds to her guilt for me. Are they all in on it? What's real anymore?

Scars getting ready for court, and she's called her dad to move here sooner as she's out of her depth on this one. Steel's arraignment is scheduled for tomorrow, so we need to be ready.

As I'm pacing back and forth, the door opens, and laughter rings out as Dane and Dice stroll in. I lose my fucking shit. "Did you fucking know?" I reach Dane and punch him straight in the face, knocking him back a step. Dice steps in front of him as Dane rubs at his jaw.

"What the fuck, man?" Dice spits at me as he holds me back while I try to get to Dane again.

"Ask him where fucking Ray is."

6

"What the fuck, Ares? I don't know. I've not been here for two days." He rubs his jaw again, looking around the place. "What's going on?"

I turn and stomp away as Scar gets up. "Can I talk to you guys outside?" They nod and leave. I pick up a bottle off the bar, fuck knows what it is, and launch it across the room, smashing it against the fireplace. I'm fucking livid, and right now, everyone is public enemy number one. My best friend, my brother, has just lost everything; his whole fucking world has come crashing down and for what? A fucking woman. Bitch!

Scar walks back in alone, and as I look at her, I see the strain on her face as she sadly smiles at me and goes back to the laptop.

"Dice will be back in ten minutes. I've asked him to trawl all the footage he can find and background search this Carlisle guy. I don't believe for one minute Ray was having an affair with this guy."

"You're trying to prove her innocence? Scar, are you fucking kidding me right now?"

"Woah, wait! I'm trying to prove a lack of motive. It's all based on this so-called affair. If I can prove they never met before the ball, it might be a chance, Ares." She whimpers at me, and fuck, I'm tired, so she must fucking be.

"Sorry, princess. I don't know what to do."

"Maybe we could do with some sleep? I've asked Dane to keep trying Bran, Bernie and Cade." She grimaces as she looks back at the laptop.

"Are you serious? You think I trust him?"

7

"Look, if you don't trust him, it will keep him out of the way, okay?" She sounds pissy now, so I nod. I'm so fucking tired.

"Fucking hell, man." Dice throws his arms around me. "How is he?"

"Fucking broken, Dice, how do you think? She was your best friend. Did she say anything, anything at all?"

"Nothing, man. Honestly, I'm as blindsided as everyone else. Could we be missing something?" He shrugs. "It just doesn't sound like Ray's style. If she wanted to take us down, she could have done so more efficiently than this. She knew the guns weren't in the old facility. She could have shown them so much."

"Don't, Dice! I can't take anything else. We've got the feds sniffing around now. We're on their radar, so we need to be smart." I tap him on the shoulder. "See what you can find. The feds took all the computers in the tech room and all visible tech we had."

"Yeah, no worries, man. They won't find anything. It's all deleted, stored somewhere they'll never find it. I'm gonna go back to the apartment and sort Hades out. Does anyone know if he's been fed or out?"

"Yeah, we've been making sure he's taken care of." Scar nods.

"Even if we believe everything, she wouldn't have left him." Dice looks between us both, and I grimace because a few days ago, I wouldn't have

8

believed any of this, and now I don't know what to think.

I think it's fair to say that the swinging brick she often referred to as her heart wasn't metaphorical or swinging. "Scar, come on, Let's get some sleep, we've got a big day tomorrow." Scar nods, closes her laptop and follows me to our room.

Dane

"Mum, where's Dad and Pa?"

"Hey sweetheart, they're at that convention upstate they should be back in… about an hour or so, why?"

"Have you seen Ray?" I breathe deep and try to sound nonchalant, but it comes out slightly panicked.

"No, she had that job on Friday, so I haven't seen her since before then."

"Have you heard from Dad while he's been away? I can't get hold of him or Pa."

"No, in fact, I haven't been able to either. I hoped they were just in a dead spot?"

"Mum, can you get Dad and Pa to call as soon as they get home? It's really important. And if you hear from Ray, let me know."

"Dane, what's going on?"

"I don't know, Mum, just get them to call, okay? Love you." I hang up and pace before heading out with Hades. "Come on, boy, let's take a little look around her office to see if we can't find anything."

As I get to the bottom of the stairs, Dice is coming towards me with his head hanging and

10

shoulders low. "Hey, I'm gonna take the dog out. How did it go?"

"Dane, everything's fucked. What the fuck has she done?"

"Wait? Hang on. You don't believe this? Ray wouldn't. Dice, fucking hell, she's your best friend!"

"Dane, I just don't know what to think. I mean, come on, it looks real fucking bad. What am I supposed to think?"

"Dice, I can't right now. Seriously? What are you meant to think? Who the fuck are you? You're her best friend. She stood by you when no one else knew the real you. She came to get you when you got kidnapped, fucking hell, man. She loves you! She loves them all, and you've all fucking convicted her already!" I shake my head. "I'm gonna head to the office. When I get back I think I'll go to my mum's. I'm clearly not trusted or wanted here."

"Dane, wait… it's just… come on, it looks bad."

"It looks impossible is what it looks like, Dice, but when it's all over, and she's back, she'll be glad to know who her true family were." I turn and head away as fuck him and fuck them all! I may love them too, but seriously, to condemn her without even seeing her, talking to her… "Fuck!" I shout at no one in particular.

The office is dead, and so I head up to Bran's place. It's empty, so I leave a note in the kitchen. Why does no fucker lock their doors? I call at Tank's to see Skye. It turns out no one told her anything, and now I've just opened my mouth. "I'm sorry, Tank. I didn't know she didn't know."

"I don't believe it!" Skye crosses her arms across her chest and leans against the counter. "After everything she's done for me, I won't speak for anyone else, but she wouldn't do this to me. She wouldn't leave me or the baby. She promised me she would look after us before I got married, and when I did, she told me I would always be her family. That's what I believe! Until she tells me herself differently, then I'm not listening to anything else." She hugs me as I leave.

"I'm going back to Mum's, they"—I point in the direction of the club—"don't want me here. Whatever's going on, Ares thinks I'm in on it, and Dice already thinks she's guilty." I head back to the apartment.

I grab my backpack and pack up the stuff for Hades as I load him in the truck. Dice shouts me from the top of the stairs. "Dane, wait... don't go."

I turn to look at him. "Do you honestly think she did all this? Do you think she had an affair, killed the guy, framed Steel, set the FBI on you all, and went into witness protection?"

"When you put it like that, it seems a little far-fetched, but you can't argue with the evidence, Dane."

"Evidence? What fucking evidence? Have you seen any? Because I certainly haven't." I shake my head, "Try and clear Steel. If you find anything useful, please send it to me. I'm going to try and find my sister. People seem to be forgetting she's missing!"

I climb in the truck, and me and Hades head to Mum's.

Dad and Pa come through the door, shoving and pushing each other, laughing, and me and Mum give them a look. I've told her everything, and she's as confused and gutted as I am.

"What are you doing here, kiddo?" Dad pulls me in for a hug.

"We've all been trying to get hold of you. What's wrong with your phones?"

"I didn't know anything was." They both pull them out of their pockets, and I grab mine and dial Dad's. Nothing. Then Pa's. Nothing. Holding my hands out, I take the phones off them and head to the kitchen table. I've got my laptop set up. Pulling out the sim and taking the back off the phone, I strip them all down.

"Fuck! Look at this." I show them all. There's an extra chip in them. "Mum, pass me yours."
Taking hers apart, I see hers hasn't got one. I remove them all and plug the phones in. Checking them over, I find some military-grade software embedded into an app and a tracker, among other spyware, these aren't even their proper phones they've obviously been cloned.

"I think we should all get new phones, whoever's done this is as good as me, and that's fucking scary!"

I call Tank from the landline and tell him the situation. "Tank is gonna tell Dice and Ares about the phones, and they'll sort them out on their end, and Skye is gonna send Demi and Bran straight here when they get back tomorrow morning. You might wanna sit down for this next bit!" I say to my dad and

Pa. After I've done telling them everything and the twenty minutes of what can only be described as an adult tantrum they both have, they flop down.

"Fuck, what do we do now?" Pa asks.

"We wait for Bran, then we go to the base, and we do our own investigation like we would if it was a paying customer! We work together and don't let anyone know, and we find Ray. Only she can tell us what's really going on. Also, one of us needs to go see Steel. It's his arraignment tomorrow."

Bran and Demi turn up, and I check their phones. Demi's is clean, but Bran's has got the same crap on it as ours do. Dad and Pa head out and grab new phones while we start dinner. Hades looks out of place. He doesn't know what's happening and why he's not at home.

"Hey, buddy." I sit beside his bed, and he whines, putting his head on my leg. "You're gonna stay here for a bit. Mum's gonna look after you while we're away. I promise we will find her and bring them both home, okay?" He licks my hand and closes his eyes as he whines again. I sit with him till they're back and dinner is ready. Then we head to bed. It's gonna be a while before we sleep properly after tonight.

Steel

I'm sitting in court waiting for my arraignment to start. Scar and her dad are with me. Her dad flew in yesterday, and Scar has brought him up to speed with everything. I'm asked to plead, and I plead not guilty. The prosecution argues that Ray won't be safe if I'm let out on bail, and the judge agrees.

I'm about to jump out of my seat when David, Scar's dad, places a hand on my knee. "Pick your battles, son. We're gonna need to play smart. This doesn't add up, so I need you to stay quiet, out of trouble and keep your head down. This is gonna get so much worse before we find the truth. Don't give up on her. She wouldn't you! Whatever's going on, until we see her, it's all hearsay!"

I nod. I mean, I know that's what I need to do, but my heart's already broken. I'm already ruined, and I don't think I will ever be the same. She destroyed me when all I ever wanted was her. I'll never be able to trust another woman. I don't even think I could bring myself to be intimate with another woman. She was it for me.

15

There's another hearing set for four weeks. Apparently, the Evidentiary Hearing is where everything's laid out, and Ray will give evidence. I need to look her in the eye when she says these lies. I need to see the look on her face when she rips my beating heart out of my chest and squeezes the life out of it for good. I know it won't beat again after that. Either way, I will die, whether it be at her hand or if I'm in prison. I remember the day I asked for a divorce, and she told me that I could put myself in a body bag or she would do it for me! That feels like my only option now, too.

Seeing as I'm refused bail as my wife is so terrified of me; she fears for her life and is in protective custody, I'm taken back to jail.

The seconds tick by so slowly, eventually turning to minutes painstakingly pitifully dragged out to what feels like an eternity, before finally turning into hours, stalling, stuttering, and backtracking, barely making it into days.

Scar and David came to see me. They informed me the footage at the bar to prove I was there had been erased, and so had all the footage two hours either side of me being arrested outside the security offices. There's no footage of the ball.

Apparently, Bernie sent two teams of two guys undercover with Ray after what happened before. But that's all the information Scar could get as Bernie, Cade, Bran and Dane have disappeared. And no one's been able to locate the security guys since, making everything look more suspicious. The blood on Ray's phone and rings was hers, so it fits with her version of events.

Her fabricated version of events are that she had left me for this Carlisle guy, they had moved in together, well they were staying at a hotel, they'd gone to the ball, had a lovely evening and stopped off at the security office for Ray to pick up some paperwork. I had been following them and shot the guy, the driver had run off, never to be seen again. I kidnapped and hurt Ray before leaving her tied up in a warehouse.

Then I'd gone back to the crime scene to plant the phone, shoes and rings on his body to make it look like he had hurt her and she'd killed him, I mean, you couldn't make this shit up, but apparently, my fucking wife could and did or has. The person who had called the police and said they saw me shoot him had given all our names and descriptions and said we were arguing outside the security office about the affair as I dragged her from the vehicle by her hair. Once I was locked up, Ray managed to get herself free and to the police station and was immediately taken into protective custody. I mean, it wouldn't make a best seller, but someone has a right imagination.

Scar and David say although the murder weapon was found in my truck, there was no gunshot residue on my hands, and my fingerprints weren't on the gun. Scar says it's circumstantial at best, which isn't reassuring when it's fabricated anyway. The person who called the police hasn't been found.

So I spend my seconds hoping they turn into minutes quicker than they did the minutes before. And hope the hours don't drag longer than the hours before that. I've counted the bricks in each wall, the bars in my cell and every thought somehow reverts back to her. Every time my eyes close, she's there reaching for me, and every time I reach back, she slips through my fingers. I wake in a panic, a cold sweat, panting for breath, and when I wake from my nightmares, I realise I'm still in them, and there's no way out.

I try to keep my head down in here, but I'm a big motherfucker, and someone's always trying to cause shit. They know why I'm in here; they think I did it and taunt me over the fact my wife left me for a rich dude. I try to keep calm and try and tune it all out, but I'm worried I'm gonna snap before I get to the hearing, and then they will just throw the book at me, lock me up and throw away the key.

The only thing going my way is that I haven't had another panic attack as in here that would be fatal. I would be seen as weak and picked off, and I'm getting verbal lashings, but a glare and my sheer size and height keep them all at arm's length. No one's really sure what I'm capable of, and no one's willing to test it just yet, but if that happened, I would be fair game. It's not that I can't take care of myself. I mean, I'm the fucking Lieutenant for the Reapers, for Christ's sake! But at the minute, I'm broken.

I try not to think of her, but she consumes me. I try to distract myself, but she devours me. The slightest thing reminds me of her, and in that moment, my emotions flair. I want so bad to strangle her, to wring the life out of her, and as I picture myself doing it, that's when the heat slides in, my heart starts to pound, then my dick throbs and I remember the feel of my hand around her throat as I slid inside her. I can feel her everywhere; her touch still lingers, and I want to rip off the skin or caress it. I can't make up my mind. I'm in such a quandary and wound tighter than a two-dollar watch.

I'm fractured. Half of me forgives her, loves her, still wants her, can't live without her and the other half of me... well, he just wants to wring the life out of her and possibly bury his dick in her at the same time. I'm so confused.

Scar

I'm tired. No, I'm exhausted, emotionally, physically, mentally. I don't believe this, I can't, and until I see her in that witness stand, I won't, but the case against her is damning. Dice has found nothing. There is no CCTV, no street cams, and no footage of any sort of the limo, the ball or the aftermath. Someone's covering their tracks, and I know Ray isn't capable of doing that, but she has so many contacts… they have so many contacts that it looks bad, it looks so bad.

If my dad wasn't here championing for her in my ear, I'm afraid I would be with Ares on this one. She's destroyed us all. Ares hates her with a vengeance; he was teetering before over The Armoury stuff, but this has tipped him over the edge. I think if he can get to her in court, he will rip her to shreds, and I half think she deserves it. I've not found any evidence to support her story, but there's also none to support Steel's. What we do have is a dead guy, a murder weapon and a giant fucking mess.

The guys are out trawling the streets trying to find any small shop owner or homeowner that has security footage to help our case, but we're coming up empty. Dice got a message from Tank telling us they found chips in all their phones, and Dice checked ours, and we had them too, so we've all had new phones. The FBI found nothing on the computers they seized, but Dice said they wouldn't, and they turned every inch of this area over and found nothing. The only rooms they didn't find were the secret basement here and in the barn.

I'm running on fumes as the door swings open to the law firm, and in walks Beauty. She only works around the corner, and she has coffee and pastries, and I walk over and hug her. "Shit, I'm glad to see you." I sag into her.

"That bad, huh?"

I just nod, steal some coffee, and slump back into my chair.

"There must be something, Scar. I don't believe this. I know it looks bad, but after everything she did to save the boys when they got taken... I know you've known her forever, but I won't believe it till I see her."

"I wish it were that simple, Beauty, but she's left a right fucking trail of destruction, and sifting through the wreckage, all I'm finding is empty, devastated, and broken hearts. I don't know if anything is salvageable. It's like with her gone, everything's falling apart."

"Hey, let's go for a walk, get some fresh air, go and sit on the bench in the square."

"Beauty, I can't. I'm going through her witness statement and— "

"And nothing!" She slams her hand down on top of the folder. "A break for thirty minutes, and then we'll go through it together. Deal?"

"Deal." I sigh because I really do need a break. I'm overwhelmed and emotional over it all. I can't believe what's happening, and I feel numb. I stand and grab Beauty's hand, and we head out to the bench.

I plonk myself down and relax my head back, staring up at the sky. I've never felt this alone since before I met Ray. I can't imagine my life without her. She's my reason for being, my reason for living and right at this moment, my heart is breaking. I close my eyes and feel the warmth of the sun on my skin. I feel a single tear streak down my face, and I try to hold it in, to draw it back. I try to will it to disappear, and then I feel Beauty pull me in, and I sob. I let all those unshed tears that I've held for weeks flow; my heart breaks at losing my other half, my soul shatters at losing its twin, and I break.

It's harsh, desperate, all-consuming and devastating, finally admitting to myself that I've lost the thing that holds me together, that built me into what I am today and will destroy me if I let her. I can't let her. I can't let Steel down. "I'm done!" I breathe out. "I'm fucking done!" I rise from the bench, I swipe at my face, I'm gonna make her regret this. Every. Single. Lie. I start to walk back with Beauty beside me.

"That's my girl!" She grins, and she takes my hand. Smiling up at me not realising my inner turmoil.

"Thanks, Beauty." I turn and kiss her on her cheek. "I really needed that."

"Now, let's go and see how we can destroy this evidence."

I laugh at that. As I walk back into the office, leaving my emotions at the door as they can fuck right off. I need my laser-focused head on for this. My heart can finish breaking when I get Steel out of prison.

Sitting at my desk, Beauty perches on it beside me. "Hit me with it!" She says as she worries at her lip, her fiery hair catching the light and distracting me for a second. Before bringing my gaze towards her bright blue eyes, she's fucking stunning. "What? Do I have something on my face?"

I shake my head, "No, you're just... beautiful." I stand in front of her and slide my hand against her cheek, sliding my thumb across her lip. I bite my own, wishing it was hers. At this moment, I just wanna feel something, anything but this. I take a step closer and cup her face as I stare into her eyes. My breathing is heavy, my heart pounding in my chest as my fingers trail across her jaw and down her neck to the sweetheart neck of the sundress she's wearing.

I trail my fingers along the swell of her breast and caress my thumb over her nipple, feeling it pebble under my touch as she gasps on an inhale. Her eyes shoot to mine, but she doesn't stop me, her hands gripping the table on either side of her. My other hand slides up her thigh, and she freezes, and my fingers trail softly up her velvety soft skin. As I slide my fingers against her inner thigh, she gasps again, and I can feel the heat. I can feel the humid moisture pooling, and I stare into her eyes. What's happening right now?

There's nothing in her gaze that feels like she wants me to stop. Her pupils are blown, her breathing a rapid pant, and her creamy skin is flushed as I run my fingers along the damp fabric of her pants. She stutters a breath. But nothing, she doesn't move, doesn't stop me, so I slide my fingers around the fabric and brush one tip against her lips.

She closes her eyes, and her head drops back. I lean forward and gently kiss her neck. She groans, and I can feel her hips twitch toward me, so I kiss her again and gently press my fingertip along where her lips touch. She gasps and grinds against me, trying to get closer. I kiss along her neck to her collarbone, and as she takes a deep breath, I slide my finger between her lips and slide through her soft, inviting warmth from back to front till I meet her clit. I slide my finger across it, causing her to buck against me.

I pull back slightly, taking in her flushed cheeks, her head back, exposing her neck to me and pounce. I devour her, slamming my lips against her as I thrust my finger inside her. She shudders under my initial kiss before parting her lips and sliding her tongue into my mouth, causing me to groan. I slide my hand into the front of her dress and roll my thumb over her nipple, cupping and kneading her breast with the rest of my hand.

I slide in another finger as she grinds against my hand while I pinch her nipple. She's gasping and writhing against me as I devour her kiss, nipping at her lip and tugging, causing a filthy moan to slip from

24

her mouth into my own. I smile against her lips, and she smiles back, and I plunge in another finger. Her head lolls back away from me, so I bite down on her neck. Kissing my way up towards her ear as I circle her clit with my thumb while pumping my fingers in and out of her, her come sliding down them towards my palm. She's soaked.

She gasps and shudders as I feel her pussy clench against me, and I tilt my fingers, finding that sweet spot and focusing my attention there and on her clit. She gasps and grabs my wrist, holding it in place as she grinds shamelessly against it. I grin against her neck and bite down again. She moans and writhes as she gasps, panting for breath. Grinding against my hand, I flick her nipple before reaching my hand into her hair and slamming my mouth against hers as she comes all over my other hand and my desk, shuddering against me, my wrist in her vice-like grip as she rides out the last pulses of her orgasm against it. Her hand releases mine as she leans forward and kisses me gently before leaning back on the desk and trying to relax her breathing.

"Beauty, I'm… " I trail off as she puts her breast back into her bra. I take a step back, allowing her to slide off the desk and right her underwear and skirt. We're both just staring at each other as I take a breath to speak, the bell of the door rings, and I step back further, gasping as I turn to see a flustered Dozer standing there with his hands in his pockets and a hard dick pressing against his jeans I flick up to meet his gaze, and he looks away.

"Ladies." His voice sounds raspy and strained as he stays by the door. "The girl at the shop told me you were here. I thought we could go for lunch?"

Beauty looks between us as I'm sure he can see the flush of my cheeks and puffiness of my lips from our kisses. She nods and places her hand on my shoulder. "You okay?"

"Yeah." I let out a shaky breath, trying to slow my racing heart. "I'm good." She leans in and gives me a chaste kiss on the lips, and as she pulls back, she whispers. "Don't worry, he'll be fine."

I nod as she heads over to Dozer, and she leans up and presses a kiss to his cheek. I don't know when he started staring at me, but his gaze doesn't falter until Beauty cuts in. "Ready?"

"Yeah." He nods at her without breaking eye contact as she steps around him to the door. His face is impassive, his eyes never leaving mine, burning into me before he turns on his heel and follows her out of the door. I sag into my chair and scrub my hands down my face, but then I'm hit with the smell of her, and I groan.

After washing my hands and taking a deep breath, I pull out the witness statement from Ray, gritting my teeth, determined to get through this. As I read through it, my heart clenches. I've heard Steel's side. I know hers isn't true, as the timeline doesn't add up, but reading it, my heart clenches. This would have been awful to go through if it had actually happened. She paints Steel as an aggressive, overbearing, ruthless, abusive husband who forced her into a marriage she didn't want but was too afraid to say no, too scared of the repercussions if she didn't go along with his every demand.

She talks of the love she and Carlisle shared, and how he was tender and gentle with her, and when she finally plucked up the courage to leave Steel, he took it badly and went after her in a rampage, killing Carlisle, then beating her and kidnapping her before going to "clean up her mess", as she says he kept calling the situation.

"Fuck," this is some hard-hitting stuff and totally fabricated although we don't have any evidence to discredit her testimony, they don't have any either to prove it. The evidence in question is limited, circumstantial at best, but also, there are no photos of Ray's so-called injuries, just he said, she said. The evidence she claimed she had, which instigated the raid on the club, came up with diddly squat for them. The only thing we can do now is wait till the Evidentiary Hearing and hope we can find a way to get Steel out of this.

Steel

Just another day in paradise, eat, shit, sleep, repeat and so on and so forth. My seconds are consumed with trying not to think about her, causing me to think about her, then berating myself for thinking about her, causing me to think about her even more.

We're outside in the yard. A young, wiry, gangly thing walks over to me. I'm leaning against the wall so no one can sneak up on me. I've got eyes on everyone from here and watch every move they make.

"Hey, I'm Cyrus." He smiles at me.

I continue to glare at him, "What do you want, kid?" No one's talked to me since I came here, not even tried. I've been taunted and ridiculed, but talk, nope, no one has.

"I've been asked to give you a message!" He lunges at me. I see it coming, but I'm not quick enough. The shank hits me in my side, going in about an inch. "Ray sends her regards!" I grab his wrist and crush it, causing him to drop to his knees. Screaming out as I twist, snapping his wrist like a fucking twig. I

28

grab his throat with my other hand. But I'm ripped off of him by the guards. He laughs as he's carted off to solitary, and I'm escorted to the medical room.

My mind is reeling. Ray... Ray did this? Why? I don't understand. I'm livid and broken, and I can't fathom it. Ray sends her regards; what the hell does that mean? As I'm taken into the medical room, I'm so angry. I've still got the shank sticking out of me, and as I'm led to the bed, the doctor says something. "What?" I bark out, the last ten minutes just playing round and round in my head on a loop.

"Take a seat and lie back. You can leave, gentlemen. We'll be fine," she assures the guards. "I'll buzz when he's ready to be collected. Can you send up a full set of clothes? I'm going to have to cut these off."

They grumble as they leave, and the doctor sets about cutting the overalls off. "Just pull it out, Doc. It's not in far." I grab and pull the shank out, tossing it on her table as she gasps at me.

"Well, you might as well stand up and take your overalls and T-shirt off so I can stitch you up!"

As I remove my clothes, I can see her watching me. She's not unattractive, but she's definitely not my type. As I sit back, she cleans up the blood that's running down my leg, wiping slowly though, more sensual than I would have expected. She starts to stitch me up when there's a knock on the door.

"Put them over there," she informs the guy who's brought me new clothes. He drops them on the chair and leaves while she continues stitching. Once she's finished, she cleans me up again, her fingers lingering longer than professionally acceptable. "You know I've always wanted to have sex with an inmate." She walks over to the door and locks it, leaning her back against it, "I've never found one I like… till now." She takes a step forward. "What would you say to… helping a lady out?" She takes another step forward.

"Sorry, I'm not interested. I'm married."

"Is that to the woman who just sent you that little message?" She points at my injury.

"What the fuck do you know about it?" I snarl.

"You just seem really angry, and maybe I could help you out, too… you could fuck me and get back at her. You could pretend it's her if you like and make her pay."

"I'd be careful what you wish for," I say as I step forward, grabbing her around the throat. The thought of Ray passes through my mind, and I could totally stick one to her while sticking one to the good doctor here.

I shove her back a few steps till she hits her desk, then I reach down and grab her hips, twisting her round so she faces the desk. I rip her skirt up, and at the same time, I bend her over. I grab the gusset of her tights and rip it out, yanking her pants to the side. I step closer behind her. I engulf her, head in one hand, forcing it against the table before pulling my dick out and driving it into her without warning. I slam into her again. Harder this time, smashing her against the desk. As she whimpers, I push against her head and slam into her again. With every thrust, I hope to feel something. With every slam of my hips, I want to disappear; this feels wrong and awful, and as she comes around me, I can't bring myself to release; I mean, my body's trying. I'm still slamming into her, but there's nothing happening. I just don't feel anything. I grit my teeth as I slam again, and her whimpering continues. I slide my hand to the back of her neck and push her harder into the desk.

"Please, please stop. I can't... please." She gasps. I release her and yank myself out of her, growling, and she pants against the desk. Her legs sag, and it's a good job she's laid on the table. I rip my boxers off and put all the new clothes on, snatching a large mesh bandage off the side and slapping it over the wound that's now seeping.

"Buzz them," I snarl at her, and she tries to stand, wobbling as she tries to right herself. She buzzes and then slumps in her chair, gasping for breath.

As I'm left in my cell, I stagger to the bed and drop onto it. A sudden wave of nausea floods me. What the fuck have I done? I'm painfully aware that whatever is happening with Ray and me, what I've just done has smashed the final nail into the coffin. That was her deal breaker, and as the cold sweats kick in, the nausea rings out again. I scramble off the bed and drag myself to the toilet as I puke my guts up, I can feel her on me, on my dick, and it's making me feel sick again. I puke again, then drag myself up and scrub at myself. I need to get her off me.

As I slide down the wall, so I'm sitting half against the wall, half against the toilet, a sob spills out of me, and tears streak my face. Ray was the only woman I'd ever gone bare with until now. I don't know if I was hoping we would get back together. Maybe it's all a mistake, maybe… but now I know it's over whatever else has happened. Those few minutes have destroyed my life, and she'll never forgive me for this. My breaths start to stutter again, and my mouth waters as I heave again; there's nothing left, but with how I feel over what I've just done, there's no going back now.

Scar

Me and Pops head over to the prison to visit Steel. He got shanked yesterday, and we need to check to make sure he's okay. He says he's fine. A few stitches, and the guy who did it is in solitary. I need to go through a few things anyway. I need to check his testimony and make sure he still wants to plead not guilty. We need to check her story and find the holes. Pops reassures me that we've got this, but I'm not so sure this is Ray after all.

Steel walks in, sits down, and says it's not major, and he's keeping his head down, keeping out of trouble and trying to stay positive and alive. Although there's something on his mind, I can tell. "What's the matter, Steel? What's going on?" I ask him, and he just hangs his head. "Steel, come on, you can tell me."

He shakes his head. "I fucked up, Scar! I've seriously fucked up everything. Whatever happens now, it's over, done."

"What do you mean, done? What did you do? Steel, come on, tell me what's happening?"

He slides his hands over his face, then reaches up, tugging at his hair, he says, "I fucked her. I fucked the doctor."

I gasp and shake my head. "It was already fucked, Steel. You've not made it any worse. She deserves it. She doesn't deserve you to wait for her. She doesn't deserve you to be the man you are. She doesn't deserve you at all."

"Scar, that's not fair, and neither of you have seen Ray. Neither of you knows the full situation. You've written her off already. What happened to innocent until proven guilty? You've already hung, drawn and quartered her without even seeing her!" Dad scolds us both. "And if you wanted to break her heart, Steel, you have succeeded. Now, let's get down to it."

We go through Ray's testimony, and we go through Steel's testimony. We go through the evidence or lack of it. The hearing is in three days. Steel's been in here for weeks, far too long. It should never have come to this. It's a total farce. Hopefully, when the judge sees the lack of evidence in a few days, we will be able to take Steel home. Ray, she can rot in hell for all I care, I don't know what she's trying to prove, but seriously, the bitch has got issues.

I take in Steel's dishevelled look, the anguish on his face, and the defeat in his eyes. "You still love her, don't you?" He looks at us and nods.

"She's… my everything, but I know what I've done… she'll never let me near her again. Scar, I'm so confused."

"Steel!" Dad's voice breaks through our thoughts, and we glance at him. "Just stay safe, son. We'll get you out of here and sort everything out." We rise and leave Steel sitting there with his head in his hands. She's really done a number on him.

When I get back to the clubhouse, Ares meets me and sweeps me in for a kiss. Dad's gone back to the office. "What's that for?" I grin into his kiss.

"It's a thank you for not being a total bitch and screwing us all over like your sister."

"She's no sister of mine, Ares. The witness statement is way, way out of line. The only truth in it is her name. Steel's in a mess because he fucked the doctor in prison." I shrug.

"He what?"

"He got shanked and ended up in the med room and ended up fucking the doctor."

"Good on him. Hopefully, he will forget that toxic pussy and find a nice girl."

"Hey, Scar," Dice says from behind me.

"Hey, Dice, have you heard from Dane?" He shakes his head. All this shit has broken them up, too. Dice took Steel's side, and Dane took Ray's, surprise. "Don't worry, when it all comes out at the hearing in a few days, he will realise his mistake and come back with his tail between his legs."

"Ya think?" He smiles at me, and I don't fucking know, but I smile back. Someone should have some fucking hope in this situation.

We sit around and have a drink, and the rest of the Psycho Six turn up. The drunker they get, the more it turns into Ray bashing all except Priest, who left when it all started, and Tank, who keeps his mouth shut, and when it starts to get really bad, he makes his excuses and leaves.

"What's his problem?" I slur a little.

"He's team Ray, him and Skye and Priest. They don't believe a single word of it and say they won't till they see the words come from her mouth."

I shrug. "Well, they'll have a shock when she tosses them aside with the rest of us!" I'm wallowing now. I know I am. I feel like the one person who had my back through everything has now stabbed a knife in it. I feel hurt and betrayed. "I'm going to bed!" I stand and stomp off, angry at myself that I'm bothered. I have so much anger for her for fucking everything up and anger at the world that my ride-or-die rode off into the sunset and fucking left me behind.

It's the day of the Evidentiary Hearing. The whole inner circle is there with Ares. Steel's wearing the suit he wore for the wedding. He wanted to make a statement. I'm not sure what that statement is, but anyway, here we are. We go through the hearing submitting evidence or lack of it, and we listen to Steel's side of the story. As the judge calls for Ray to take the stand, we look away. I turn my back on her as she walks in; we all do. It's a show of unity against whatever shit she's selling, as we ain't buying it!

"Who the fuck's that?" Tank barks out. Leaping from his seat, he says, "That's not fucking Ray!"

"Order! Order! Sir, take your seat. If you do not, you will be held in contempt of court!"

As I look up at the young woman on the stand, Dad is already approaching the bench. I rush over after him.

"Your Honour, I thought you were calling Ray Steel to the stand?"

"Yes, counsel."

"Your Honour, I've known Ray since she was fourteen. This is not her!"

He waves the prosecution over. "Who is this woman?"

"Mrs Ray Steel, Your Honour."

"That is not Ray!" I snap as I go back to the table, grab my phone from my bag, and turn it on, sliding through the photos. I pull the wedding photos up. "Your Honour, this is Ray Steel."

"Bayliff, can you escort erm... Mrs Steel to holding, council I'll see you in my chambers."

After speaking with the judge, they've agreed to do a DNA test on the imposter. If it comes back, she's not Ray, then Steel can be released, and the case dropped as there's no evidence now. This whole thing has been a shit show from start to finish, and when they take Steel back to prison pending the DNA test, there's only one thing he says, and it breaks my heart.

"Where's Ray...?"

And now, if everything is a lie, I turned my back on my sister; I left her out there alone... we all did. She has no one!

An embrace pulls me in. "Don't worry, this is Ray. She'll be okay." My dad says against my ear as he holds me tight.

"She may be okay, Dad, but... will we? I gave up on her. I believed it all. And now... now, I feel like I've made the biggest mistake of my life. She'll never forgive me for this. It's the one thing we always had ... each other! And I abandoned her, K.F.D. She did that for me. When the time came for me to do it for her, I left her alone." I'm sobbing now uncontrollably. I hate myself. How the fuck am I ever gonna make this up to her?

Dice

When we get back from court, we all go to the bar and start drinking. I think we are drowning our sorrows, not celebrating.

She was my best friend, the only person who knew the real me for a long time. She protected my secret till I was ready to tell everyone. She knew we were in trouble and rescued us before anyone else even realised we were up shit creek without a paddle. She was my ride-or-die.

This whole time she's been missing, we believed everything that was said, no questions. The only people who believed Ray wouldn't do any of this were Tank, Skye, Demi, Dozer, Beauty, Priest and Barbie. Apart from Dane and Bran and their dads, we all believed it. We believed everything they told us. Even fucking Steel.

I give up drinking, pull up my phone and call Dane. Voicemail. "Fuck!... Dane, it's me. Can you call me back? It's urgent!"

Shit, I really need to talk to him, so I call Bran, then Bernie, then Cade and the same, straight to voicemail.

Fuck it! I head out and jump in the truck. I probably shouldn't ride my bike since I've been drinking.

I pull up outside the house, and the lights are off, but I knock on the door anyway. It takes a few minutes, but Marie comes to the door. "Dice? What are you doing here?"

"Sorry to bother you, Marie, I need to see them."

"Dice… they're not here. They left when Ray went missing; they haven't been back since."

"Shit!" I tell her everything that happened in court today and send her a picture of the woman who turned up that I hacked into the court system for.

"Dice, I'll let you know if they find her. They're tracking down leads. They're relentless. They will search till they find her and bring her home.

"Thanks, Marie. If you do hear from them, can you get Dane to call me…? I think I owe him an apology."

"Night, Dice." She takes a step back into the house and clicks the door shut.

Why does it feel like my heart is breaking? Like I've lost them all? The way Marie looked at me and spoke to me was cold and detached. I know she'll know what's going on. She's so intelligent, and while she comes across as an apple pie sweet, friendly neighbourhood woman, she helped raise Ray, Bran and Dane, and she's been around those men for years. I know she knows more than she says.

As I get back to the clubhouse, the wake is still going strong. That's what it feels like a wake. It feels like we're mourning the loss of someone we love. I bypass it and head straight to my room. I need to start looking for her. I need to bring her home, and I need to make her forgive me.

Steel gets released the next day. When the court officials went to the holding cell to take the DNA sample from the imposter, she was dead; it looked like she had taken some poison or something. She was on the floor, contorted at weird angles, eyes bulging and foaming at the mouth. We never got any answers, so they had to release Steel.

We're all waiting outside as Ares pulls up in the truck with Steel and Scar. We all hug Steel and welcome him home. He steps back, taking us all in.

"Fuck I've missed you all. Someone please tell me you know where she is?"

We all glance around and then shake our heads.

"Fuck!" he bellows as he kicks the wooden post of the railing around the deck at the front of the clubhouse, splintering it into a million pieces, scattering pieces of wood all over the decking and leaving the railing hanging limp, unsupported. That's what Ray must feel like.

"I'm looking through all the footage, what little there is. I've tried to contact the guys, but no one's returning my calls. Marie says they left as soon as Ray went missing, and they haven't been back since."

"So what, she just vanished? Show me. Show me everything!" He pushes past and barges into the clubhouse, glaring over his shoulder. "Fucking now, Dice!" he barks as he continues toward the rooms.

Steel is already pacing when I walk into the tech room with Ares, Viking, Tank, Blade, Priest and Dozer. "Five fucking weeks, she's been gone five fucking weeks, and no one was even looking for her? Fuck! What have we done? What the fuck have I done?" He slams his back against the wall and bangs his head back into it a few times before sliding down and crumpling to the floor. Cupping his face in his hands, he goes silent. The only noise in the room is his ragged breaths, and as he looks up, his eyes are red and glazed, and tears have tracked down his face.

"I fucked the doctor while I was in prison," he mumbles out. "I thought Ray was behind everything. The guy that shanked me said, 'Ray sends her regards!' as he plunged the shank into my side, so I fucked the doctor, and she'll never forgive me for that. She's off god knows where, and I was getting my dick wet, wanting to hurt her for what I thought she was doing."

"Hey! We've all let her down!" Ares crouches beside him with his hand on his shoulder.

"Speak for yourself!" Tank spits. "I told you! I told you all! And not one of you believed she wouldn't do this. If we don't find her, it's on all of your heads." He points at us all except Dozer and Priest and spits again, "This! This is on you if she doesn't come back!" He turns, slamming the door and leaves.

"I'll go after him," Priest says as he leaves too.

42

"He's right!" Ares says softer than I've ever heard him speak. His voice, normally so restrained and authoritative, is now barely a whisper. "I was the worst! I saw what I wanted to see even before she went. I didn't trust her over The Armoury thing, I was a twat! Now, let's find our girl. The sooner we do, the sooner the grovelling can start."

I fire up the computers, and we start from scratch. We find footage I couldn't before, now whether that's because I didn't look hard enough or it was hidden I can't be sure. We follow her as she leaves in the limo. We have footage of her leaving, and we track them till just before they get to the ball, and then the footage is cut. I backtrack, having an idea. "Who sent the limo?"

"It was one Bernie arranged. That's why it picked Ray up first, then they picked that guy... what's his name, up before heading to the ball."

I track the vehicle again, concentrating on the driver. When I get a clear enough shot of him, I pull a screen grab, download it into my facial rec programme, and leave it running in the background.

"What was the name of the hotel?" I ask. I know the footage was wiped, though.

"The Grosvenor." Steel informs me, still from his position on the floor. "I thought everything was wiped?"

"It was! What was the ball for? Was it a charity? I'm gonna check social media. I bet people recorded and took photos. Maybe shared them on the hotel's page, the charity's page? It's worth a shot."

Steel shows me all the details he has, and I start searching. "Steel, why don't you get to bed? You look dead on your feet, and you're no good to us like this. I'll keep looking. We'll wake you if we find anything, okay?"

"No, I wanna stay."

"Steel!" Ares grits. "Come on, man, let's get you some rest. We'll have somewhere to start when you wake, okay." He leans down and pulls Steel up and into his arms. "It's fucking good to have you back, Brother. Now fuck off and go to bed."

Steel leaves looking as depressed and dejected as the rest of us feel. "You guys might as well go too. I'll call you if I find anything."

The siren sounds before we have a chance to do anything, and I dive up and chase my brothers out of the door. Steel's just pushing out the main doors as we come barrelling through to the bar, and we all rush out together. There's a black van with screeching tyres, making a quick exit out the gates in front of the garage, and there's a big duffle bag in the middle of the parking lot.

"What the fuck's that?" I point over while we all hang back.

Tank comes running around the corner, out of breath as Ares takes a step forward. "Stay back, guys. Fuck knows what it is, but let me have a look first, yeah?" Ares cautiously steps towards the bag. It's not moving or ticking from what we can see and hear, so that's a good sign, I suppose.

Ares makes it to the bag and nudges it with his foot, "Bleurgh! The smell, I think it's a dead animal or

44

something?" He bends down and grabs the zip, slowly tugging while he covers his nose and mouth with his other hand.

"Fuck!" he screams. "Call a fucking ambulance. It's Ray!"

We all rush forward, and Tank yells, "Get her in my truck. She should go to the clinic... NOW!" He sets off running to fetch his truck.

We stop just before we get to her, and I hold my arms out when I see into the bag. She's covered in dried blood and god knows what else. She looks naked; she's nearly emaciated. Ares cradles her head as he brings it out of the bag. She's alive, barely.

I look around, and Steel is on his knees in front of the clubhouse, his hands in his hair just rocking. Tank pulls up and drags a blanket out of the back of the truck and wraps it around her as he lifts her so gently out of the bag and lays her across his back seat. He doesn't say a word to any of us. He just climbs in his truck and pulls off.

"Steel!" I bellow. "Pull your shit together, we need to go after Tank!"

We all start running for the bikes.

We pull up outside the clinic, and Tank opens the back doors as Ares is barking orders at the doctors while they bring a stretcher out, load her up and take her away.

I pull my phone out and call the one person I need to see right now! "Dane, fuck answerphone! Dane, it's me. You need to get down to that clinic. We found Ray, she's... she's not good, Dane!" I hang up and call through the rest of them. Then I call Demi, and when she answers, I give her the info, and she promises that she'll get in touch with the family. We all pile into the waiting room and pace and sit. "Fuck!"

We've been there about an hour or so when the doors fly open, and they walk in dressed in combat gear, like dark avenging angels. They all look older, somehow deadlier; they all have beards now, longer hair, darker skin, not in a fashion statement way, more in a I-haven't-got-time-for-menial-tasks-like-shaving-and-hair-cutting kind of way.

They don't even spare us a glance as they push straight into the clinic through the doors we've been told to stop at. We all rise from our seats, but they don't even look back.

Steel pushes through the door after them and shouts down the corridor.

"Not the time, son!" Bernie barks back as the others keep walking.

He keeps walking behind them regardless, leaving us all waiting, wondering, and hoping.

Steel

As I push through the doors behind her family, I suddenly feel dread as I get closer to the door at the end of the corridor where there's a nurse's station, and they jump as soon as they see us walk through.

"Sirs." One of the nurses steps from behind the desk. "This way, please. She's still in surgery, but the doctor will be through as soon as possible."

We're taken into a smaller room and left to sit and wait more. As she closes the door, Bernie asks, "You look good, son. When did you get back?"

"Today." I rasp out. I can't look at any of them; I'm filled with shame and regret, so I just sit staring at my hands.

"Where did you find her?" Cade sits forward. His voice sounds gruff, almost like from lack of use.

"We didn't." I look up at them. "A van drove through the compound and threw a duffel bag out of the back as it went." I choke down the bile as I try to say the next words. "She... Ray, she was in the... bag." I swallow the lump as my eyes burn.

47

Bernie stands and grips my shoulder. "She'll be okay, son, it's Ray." It's the only comfort he offers as he sits back down, and we just wait. No one talks. They look exhausted. It feels like hours pass until the doctors come in.

"She's through the worst. Most of her injuries seem superficial. She did suffer a ruptured spleen, and we've carried out a partial splenectomy. She should be fine to leave in a few days, and recovery time is from three to twelve weeks. We've cleaned and dressed most of her wounds; she's in recovery, and we'll bring her through as soon as she wakes."

He walks out of the room, not asking if we have any questions, and we just sit and wait. One of the nurses fetches us through. "You can see her now, but not for long. She needs her rest."

As we walk into the room, she's hooked up to machines. It doesn't look like her. She's black and blue and a manner of other colours ranging from yellow to black. Her face is swollen, and her right eye is bandaged. Her arms on the bed look thin, really thin, like she's not been fed in a while. I hang back near the door as the others crowd the bed. Her eyes open, and she scans everyone's face, giving them the slightest curl of the corner of her lip.

"I'm fine." She grimaces. "I've been worse." No one says anything. She looks over at me, and the slight smile drops. "Can you give us a minute?"

They all nod and leave the room. I stay leaning on the wall near the door. After a moment, she sighs and says, "I don't want an argument!"

"Why the fuck would I want an argument?" I jump in defensively.

"Look, we both know what you did. I'm not mad... I'm done!"

"What? Ray?"

"Don't, Steel. It was my deal breaker! So consider it deal broken, okay?"

"Ray, you don't understand. It didn't—"

"Steel, don't. Whether it meant anything or not, it doesn't matter. The lovely establishment I stayed in had 24-hour footage of every single one of you, my so-called family, my so-called brothers, you!" She shakes her head. "I've heard everything, seen everything. I know what you all think of me. I know what was said, and I had the pleasure of seeing you pound into that fucking doctor for five days straight on a loop full volume. When I saw a video of you, a woman with her lips wrapped around your dick, I knew something was wrong. I came for you. I brought you home. Someone told you I said something, and you all believed them, so much so that you fucked the good doctor. Not one of you even attempted to look for me, Steel. No one came for me, and I'm only here now because he's done with me for the moment, so I'm tired, and I'm going to say this only once: we're done, you, me, them, done. I don't want to see any of you again! Now please leave."

"Ray—"

"Leave!"

Cade walks in. "You heard her son. Time to go." I look down as I walk past them all and back out into the waiting room with my brothers.

"What's happening?" are Ares' first words as I walk through.

"She's done, we need to leave." I walk past them without another word.

"Don't be a fool, Brother." Ares grabs my arm. I stare down at his hand and back up at him.

"She's done. Have you ever known her not to know what she wants? It's fucking over."

"You didn't walk away when you first met; don't make that mistake now. Fight for her; we all need to. You'll regret it if you walk away and don't try."

I slam myself into the chair and bang my head back on the wall. "She's right, though. How can she ever forgive any of us? We believed the lies, and no one tried to save her; no one even looked. Whoever had her showed her footage of everything."

"What do you mean?" Dice looks confused.

"Whoever it was had cameras everywhere. Everything that was said about her she knew, even me fucking that doctor. She saw it. She heard it all."

"Shit!" Dice shakes his head. "We need to check everywhere."

"We will. But there's no rush. We stay here till she's released. When we go back, we can worry about the cameras. We stay by her side," Ares insists.

The door swings open and her pas, Bran, and Dane walk out, heading for the exit. "You're leaving?"

"Yeah son, she needs rest. Just leave her be, okay?" Cade says as they push through the doors and walk out.

"What the fuck? I can't believe they're leaving her." I push through the doors back to the family room we were in before, which is across the hall from her room. "If I'm staying, I'm staying close," I say to my brothers as we all pile into the room and open the blinds so we can see her room at all times. I will fight for her. I just know I can't live without her.

I grab the doctor as he walks past to ask him about the extent of her injuries. He tells me she's suffered a lot of physical trauma, possible torture with the marks that will now mar her skin forever. Her face was cut, not dissimilar to mine, and she's going to need a lot of therapy. Yeah, right, he'll be lucky if she actually has the bed rest he's ordered, but I know her, and the clinic has done well to keep her in bed for as long as they have.

For the rest of the three days they're keeping her, we keep a vigil, wearily watching doctors and nurses go in and out. She doesn't let any of us in to visit, but we stay all the same. It's getting late, and she refuses to let Scar anywhere near her. Her pas don't even come back, and Marie never shows. She should be released sometime tomorrow. We hang out, we hover, and we just wait. It's getting late in the day when David turns up. After he comes out of seeing her, he's the only one she's let in. He comes to see us.

"She's up to something. Keep an eye on her."

"What do you mean?"

"She's just said goodbye to me, like never see me again goodbye, wherever she's going, whatever she's doing, she doesn't plan on coming back, for any of us."

51

"Shit!" I start pacing. I mean, what the fuck am I supposed to do with that knowledge?

Ray

The door opens, and Pops walks in, his lips pressed into a sad smile, and I sigh. "Come on in."

"I wasn't sure if you'd see me."

"Pops, you know I love you, and I know you've gone to bat for me, which I appreciate, but I won't put you in a place that makes you choose between me and Scar. She's your daughter. I understand."

"And so are you, Ray. I would never choose between you, you know that, and Scar's—"

"Don't, Pops. I know what she thinks of me. He has the clubhouse bugged, and there's a 24-hour video feed. He made me watch everything, even at the prison. I saw everything, Pops, what was said, what Steel did, I saw it all, and I saw her say I deserved it. Don't do this. I'm done. I'm walking away. I hope you understand. I will always love you. And I thank you for everything you've done for me over the years." I let out another sigh. "This is the end for us all, Pops. Just remember that what happens from here on out, I love you, and I always will."

"Ray…"

"It's okay. I'll be okay. Just look after them all and yourself."

"Ray, you make it sound like I'll never see you again."

I shrug. What else can I say to that? I don't actually think I'll ever see any of them again.

"Ray, don't do anything stupid. I love you, and I'll support you whatever. You know that, right?"

"Goodbye, Pops." I turn away from him.

"Ray, please."

I just shake my head but refuse to look at him. I can't; it's breaking my heart to lose him, but I know it's for the best.

As he leaves, the tears flow. I don't make a sound, though. I know I'll lose them all after this. Either way, I'm on my own.

The nurse comes in for the final check before bed. "Do you have it all?"

She nods. Pulling out the duffel bag from under the drugs cart, she asks, "You'll send the money?"

"You know who I am?" She nods. "You know I'm good for it. You'll get it within the week."

She nods and leaves the room. I start on my preparations, gritting my teeth and pushing through the pain.

Once I've "set" the room, cleaned and changed, I slide out of the window. It's only a two-storey building, and even though I'm weaker than normal, I'm able to scale the side of it before panting under the window as I hit the floor, pulling out the phone the nurse left.

"Hi, I'm out. Is it ready?"

"Yes."

"Thank you."

"Ray…?"

"Don't… please!"

"I love you, baby girl. Please come home to me."

"I love you!"

Fuck. I jog across the parking lot to the van that is stashed in the darkest corner. Sliding my hand along the front wheel, I find the keys and climb in, tossing my bag on to the passenger seat.

I head to the MC, I use the back road that comes in near the lodges, and I set to work. Once I've got everything sorted, I head to my apartment. It's so empty with no one here. I don't like it. I wish things could be different; I wish I could have the life I want, but I never get what I want. I don't think I deserve it. I've been a questionable human being at best. I drag the mattress off the bed and throw it over the balcony. I grab my cut and head for the stairs, pulling out the phone and dialling.

"Send the texts."

"You sure?"

"Just do it."

"See you on the other side."

"K.F.D!"

"K.F.D. Come back to us!"

I hang up and wait. The next thing I know, there are bikes and trucks everywhere, and the whole place looks like it's being evacuated. As the stragglers leave, I head into the clubhouse and through to the rooms. I make short work of what I need to, and I leave. As I get outside the headlights of a lone bike arrive, and I hide in the shadows.

The figure heads towards the front of the bar, then his phone chimes, and he reaches into his pocket before heading back to his bike and then up the dirt track towards the barn. I run back into the clubhouse as best I can and set everything in motion, jogging out of the back door and up to the barn. I catch my breath before I walk in, and he's inside.

"Miss me, motherfucker?"

"Ray?" He gasps. "You're… you're…?"

"Alive? Yes! … here? Yes! Pissed? Double yes! You played me!" I point at him as I stalk into the barn. "You helped torture me for five fucking weeks, and you're gonna fucking pay. I thought you were my brother? But the whole time, you were working against us, against them. Any last requests?"

"Ray, don't do this you don't understand. I had no choice."

"Funny, because you had a choice when you sliced my arm every day so I'd know how many days no one gave a shit about me, or from the white-hot screwdriver you forced into my underarm arm every time that I wouldn't tell him what he wanted to know, or what about the times you pulled my finger nails out with pliers because I wouldn't submit and say I would join him? Or what about my fucking eye? My face? I'm lucky I'm not blind, and that's only because you were such a fucking pussy that you failed, or what about the times you punched me when you couldn't get it up while I was tied down just to feel like a fucking man? So let's go. Let's see how long you can be a man while I'm untied."

"You don't want to do this, Ray. He'll come for you."

"Oh, I'm counting on it." I stalk towards him and punch him straight in the face. He drops to the floor, wailing like a little bitch. "Is that it? Is that all you've fucking got, you snivelling piece of shit?"

I kick him while he's down and walk over to the scanner on the back wall, opening up my office. I kick him in the face, and he's about out of it. "Well, you're as disappointing as your fucking name. They couldn't have chosen a more fucking fitting name."

I drag him down the stairs and lock him in the cell, then I end this, setting everything off. There's no going back from here. They will either hate me and forget about me or hate me and hunt me. I'm fine with either. I've made my peace with it all. I've had five weeks to plan, and this will end my life as I know it. Whether I come back from it is a different matter entirely.

Before making my exit, I take one last look at the place I thought would be my forever home before turning my back on it and walking back to the van. As the flames start to lick the buildings, I can already hear the fire trucks coming, so I disappear, leaving my world behind me, burn world burn! I'm going down in a blaze of glory, and this time, I've got a one-way ticket to hell.

Pulling out the phone as I drive away, I say, "It's done! There's a little something for you in the office. Make that fucker squeal. Let me know if you find

57

anything useful. Emergency contact retro, see you on the other side, Brother!"

"Love you, Ray, make him fucking pay!"

I hang up and just drive. I've left them a nice little reminder of what they've done and what I'm capable of. Hopefully, they'll heed my warning and stay away.

I head north to regroup, rebuild and replay my plan, I'm burning the world down, and I'm taking every fucker with me who stands in my way. You want to rebrand yourself as Dante fucking Crane? Well, whatever you want to call yourself, you just lit the match on my fuse. I'm going to ground and regain my strength, but Hades help you when I come back!

Steel

There's a knock on the door to our waiting room. Ares steps forward and opens it to a nurse standing there, "Gentleman," she greets. "There's a group of... men to see you in the outer waiting room."

"What?" Ares barks at her. It's the middle of the fucking night, and our brothers and Scar are sleeping. There's only me and Ares awake.

"Come on, let's see what's happening," I say as I stretch out of the seat. We follow the nurse, and as we walk into the outer waiting room, the rest of the club is there.

"What the fuck are you all doing here?" Ares spits clearly snappy from the sleep deprivation we all have.

Savage waves his phone. "You messaged us all and told us to get our asses here now. We thought something might be wrong with Ray."

"I didn't fucking message anyone, who's on guard?"

"No one. You told us all to come, lock up and leave, so here we are." they all look around at each other and back at us.

Me and Ares look at each other. "Shit, Ray!" I gasp, and we turn and run straight to her room. As we sling the door open and fly through it, I stop dead in my tracks, and Ares slams into my back, sending us both skidding along through the door.

"What the fuck?" He gasps, shocked at the state of the room. And I freeze. The bedclothes are stripped back, there's blood all over the sheets, and the table that slides over the bed has a bloody piece of paper on it with two lumps of what looks like bloody fabric or something with a scalpel stabbed into the paper. He puts his hand on my chest. "Let me look, mate. Just give me a second, okay?"

I nod. I don't think I'm processing anything at the minute, and all I can stare at is the blood. It's all over. There's so much of it.

"What's going on?" Tank walks into the room behind me. "Holy fuck, what the hell? Where is she? Is she okay?"

"Shit," Ares breathes out. "It's her tattoos."

"What do you mean, it's her tattoos?" I step forward. He's taken the scalpel out of the paper, and he's using it to spread out what I thought was fabric. Looking over his shoulder, I retch. "Shit."

"That's fucked up." Tank chokes out with his fist against his mouth.

Ares spreads out her 'Reapers' tattoo from her hip and her 'Steel' tattoo from her chest.

I pull the paper off the table, my hand shaking and my voice not much better as I read it out loud…

60

Ares,

Blood in, blood out! I hope this is enough. Consider it my resignation. If not, go fuck yourself for the rest!

Steel,

Consider this notice of our impending divorce. Papers are waiting at the clubhouse with the bike and cut! Enjoy your newfound freedom. You can fuck all the doctors you like now! Hope your dick falls off!

To everyone else who failed me, I'd like to say it's been a pleasure, but you can all suck my dick and rot in hell instead!
Hate, from

Reaper!

"Jesus, she doesn't beat around the bush, does she?" Tank shakes his head. "Where is—"

His phone rings, cutting him off. He glances down and mouths. "It's Skye. Hey, love, can I call… wait, wait… calm down, love… we're on our way… get away from there… I'm coming." He hangs up. "We need to go now. The clubhouse and lodges are on fire!"

We don't have time for anything else. I grab the tattoos in the paper I have in my hand. Don't ask me

61

why; I just couldn't bear leaving a part of her behind again, and we run, shouting to the others to get back to the clubhouse as we thunder down the corridor.

It's chaos; fire trucks are everywhere, and the parking lot is closed. We have to abandon the bikes out on the road, and as we run into the grounds, the fire crews are milling around. There doesn't seem to be any fire now.

"What the fuck happened?" Ares barks as the fire crews spin to see what's going on. There's an ambulance parked in front of the garage, and I can see Demi, Skye and Beauty in the back. Me, Ares, Dozer and Tank run over to them. Tank sweeps Skye into his arms.

"Are you okay, love?" She nods, although wearing an oxygen mask.

I grab Demi. "Are you hurt? What happened?" They all look at each other and shake their heads. "Demi, what happened?" She shakes her head again. "Did Ray do this?" Demi looks away.

"I will fucking kill her!" Ares spits. "Do you see it now? Do you? She's a fucking parasite! I will fucking—"

"You'll what?" Skye rips the mask off her face. "You'll what, eh, Ares? Abandon her? Leave her alone? Turn on her? Spew hate every second of every day? Too fucking late! You fucking did that already! She left you a message! You've made your fucking beds, now lie in them! Not once did she ever abandon any of her brothers! We"—she gestured to the girls—"were never in any danger. Check the damage, Ares, because I believe she went easy on

62

each and every one of you that turned your fucking backs on her!"

"Love, you could have been hurt, the baby!" Tank tries to reason.

"If she wanted to have hurt anyone, she could have. She made sure you were all safe and away from here!" Skye stands and throws the blankets off her. "She made her point! And she made sure we were safe while she did it. I even fucking watched because of what you did to her." She jabs her fingers at Ares and me because Tank and Dozer always were on her side, and in that moment, I know she's right. She's pushing us away now, so it doesn't hurt her. She's trying to make us feel justified in hating her. "You fucking deserve what you got!" She steps down from the ambulance. "Tank, can you take me home, please?"

"Love, the fires, is there anywhere left to go?"

She huffs and shakes her head. "Ray loves me, you and our baby. Do you honestly think she would do anything to hurt us?"

Tank shakes his head, takes her hand and leads her away from the chaos.

"Let's go home!" Dozer slides his arm around Beauty, and they walk off.

"You don't even know if you've got a home to go to. You think she left you safe?" Ares spits after them.

"I know she did!" Dozer shouts back, and they carry on walking.

I sigh. Is there any damage to the coffee shop? Your lodge?" I ask Demi, and she shakes her head.

"She didn't set fire to the apartment. She wouldn't risk our businesses to get one over on you." She walks away. "Even if you deserve it!" she mutters under her breath.

We walk over to the front of the clubhouse, and all the guys are surrounding something. "What's going on?" Ares shoves through. Ray's bike has her cut laid across the fuel tank with some papers laid on it, flapping in the slight breeze, and a knife up to the hilt stabbed straight through them into the fuel tank. Her badges have been ripped off her cut. In white spray paint on the parking lot next to her bike, it says, "You've made your beds. Now lie in them!" As I walk over to the bike, the papers are my divorce papers. I rip the knife out, slide it in my boot, and read them, then turn and walk towards the bikes.

"Where the fuck you going?" Ares spits.

"She's filed for divorce. I've got till lunch to contest it. But I have to do it in person at this law firm that's almost 500 miles away."

"If you ride like a bat out of hell, you'll never make it. Why the fuck would you want to?" Ares spits again.

"Don't you fucking see, you're doing it again! You're fucking blaming her for it all when it was us, Ares. We left her, we failed her, we fucking abandoned her, and I fucking cheated on her. We're lucky she didn't burn the clubhouse down around us. She's pushing us away, so we can't hurt her any more than we already have. But I won't leave her again; no matter what she does, I will always have her back whether she wants me or not! I won't let her down

64

again, Ares! You do what you want, Brother, but that's my fucking wife, and I will not let anyone take her away from me or talk bad about her again! Do. You. Fucking. Hear. Me?"

I turn and stalk away. I need to get there. I need to stop this. There's only one way I can do it.

Barbie

We're finally allowed back into the clubhouse. Ares is fuming, he and Steel have just had a right go at each other, and I've never seen them like that. I'm dejected, though. I understand why Ray did what she did, I do, and I listened to what they said. I heard what Steel did, but I never thought I would be someone she would hurt. But I suppose with something like this, it has to be all or nothing. As we walk into the clubhouse, she's smashed all the liquor and carved up all the tables and seats in the booths.

"I don't know what mess we're gonna find in our rooms, so just be careful, guys, okay? Apparently, Steel's apartment is okay, so whoever can't stay in their room, go there. We'll get some shut-eye and regroup later!"

I follow the boys down the corridor. They open doors to smoke and ash, their beds have been set alight, and the ceilings are plastered with thick smoke. I guess she meant it literally. *You've made your beds now lie in them.*

I sigh as I push through my door. When I get inside, there is nothing, no smoke, no damage. I look around, but there's no smell of accelerant or anything. I hear guys grumbling and trudging down the corridors around me, but my room is fine. I sigh and throw myself down on the bed; there's a weird crumpling noise and I pull the covers back.

A piece of paper is folded in half with my name on it.

Barbie

Thank you for everything, for believing in me and trusting my character. I will never forget you. Just know that I love you, and although I probably won't see you again in this life, I hope we meet in the next. I will miss you so much!

Love, Ray xx

I hold the note against my chest. "I love you, Ray, I always will," I whisper to the room. Tears roll down my face, and I realise none of us will ever be the same again without her. And it's all their fault. They only have themselves to blame.

I walk towards my wardrobe and pull out my rucksack and saddlebags. I load up with everything I have. I don't have much. I've never needed much, but I can't stay here now. I thought this place was a brotherhood, and it turns out that it is, just that if Ray had been a guy, they never would have doubted her. I drag my stuff out through the bar.

"What the fuck, Barbie? You don't have to bring everything, just enough to get by till we're sorted."

"She didn't touch my room! But I can't stay. I thought what we were was something special. We had each other's backs, looked out for each other, and loved each other, but this isn't what I signed up for. When she needed us, no one was there for her. I'm ashamed to be a part of a brotherhood that abandoned its sister! You wouldn't have treated her like you did if she was one of the guys."

I drop my cut on the floor and walk out. I don't look back. I don't want to be a part of that if she's not a part of it with me. She made life so much more beautiful. I've never felt so alive and loved as I have with her there. If she's not here, then I refuse to be too. I take another look around, slide everything onto my bike and ride off. Who knows where I'll go, but I don't care as long as it's not here.

Steel

I knock at the door. Marie answers, and I push my way in without waiting to be asked. Bernie, Cade, Bran and Dane are sitting on the sofa. "I need your help." Marie comes and stands at the side of me. "I need a chopper, now!"

"Look, son, you can't come in here demanding things. That's not how life works," Bernie informs me like I haven't just had life right royally fuck me in the ass and like I didn't figure that out myself.

"You looked for me for years. You made a promise to my dad that you would look after me and treat me as your own. Well, if Bran or Dane stood up now and needed a chopper, you'd get one here, so I'm asking. Can you get me a chopper?"

"No!" Cade shakes his head. "Yeah, we promised your dad these things, but now with Ray…"

"Is she your daughter? Your biological daughter, I mean?"

He nods. "So you'll take her side over mine? I thought you didn't take sides. Would you take Bran's side over Dane's? Am I not family now I've fucked up? Is that it?" I shake my head. "I made a mistake. I

69

need to make it right. Will you get me a chopper or not?"

"No!" Cade stands and folds his arms across his chest.

"You haven't even asked what I need it for."

Bernie stands, too. "It doesn't matter, son. We can't help you."

"Can't, or won't?"

"Steel. Just go!" Bernie insists.

Before I know what I'm doing, I reach into my waistband and grab my gun. I slide to the side, wrap my arm around Marie's chest, and slide behind her, pressing the gun to her temple.

"I won't ask again. Get. Me. A. Fucking. Chopper!" I grip her tighter to my chest. "If I can't keep my wife, you don't get to keep yours. I will blow her fucking head off!"

Bernie takes a step towards me, and I push the gun harder against her temple. "Do not test me, Bernie. I will burn the world down to get her back! Now, when will the chopper be here?"

Bernie moves, and I drag Marie back a step. "Chill, son. I'm grabbing my phone."

"She's coming with me. I'll let her go once we get back."

"You're not taking her anywhere, son!" he spits at me." Bran and Dane are twitching but trying to remain calm.

"Bernie, with respect, I'm not letting her go till I stop this divorce. Then I will deliver her back unmarked and safe."

Marie starts to turn in my grip. She looks up at me and slides her hand up to cup my face. My eyes close, and a tear runs down it.

"Get him the chopper, Bernie."

"Marie, I'm not taking sides. If Ray finds out we helped him… "

"Bernie, did she specifically ask you not to help him?"

"No, but…"

"No but nothing. If we're ever gonna get her back, she'll need him." She turns back again and pushes the gun down, and I hang my head in shame. I can't believe I've held Marie at gunpoint. My in-laws are so gonna want this divorce to go through now. "Now let me get my coat, Bernie. Get us the chopper, Steel; listen to me, okay?" I glance up at her and nod. "You can't ever let her down again. If we get her back, you'll have to make sure you don't. Do you hear me, son?"

I nod again and pull her into a hug. "I'm sorry, Marie, I'm so sorry, I just… I can't think straight without her. I need her. I need to stop this."

She just nods and takes a step back. "Give me a second, okay? Bernard Walker, I don't hear a phone call being made ordering us a chopper. Make it happen!"

Cade takes a step forward. "Don't!" That's all Marie says before she walks away. Bernie orders the chopper, taking a step towards me.

"I'll go with you too, son." Bernie walks towards me, and I just stand there. He wraps his arms around me, pulling me against him. "Pull a stunt like this again, and I will kill you myself, you understand?"

"I'm sorry, Bernie, I just… "

"I know, son, let's get you sorted, come on."

Fifteen minutes later, we're being dropped off in a random field near their house as the chopper lands in front of us.

"Do you know where she is?" We've been flying for a good hour, none of us speaking till I break the tension.

"No, son!"

"Is she okay?"

"No, son!"

"Is she safe?"

"No, son!"

After a while longer. "Bernie, will you help me find her?"

"No, son!"

"Bernie?"

"Look, Steel, I'm not being awkward. She specifically asked that we don't step in and that we don't interfere. She has a mission that only she can do, but we need to let her deal with it on her own. I don't like it, but I have to respect it!"

I make it to the solicitors and contest the divorce. I make it with an hour to spare; once I've put a stop to the divorce, I now have to find Ray.

I'm gonna have to be smart about this. I will have to be brave and strong, and most of all, I will have to prove that I won't let her down ever again. I don't know what's going on. Bernie and Marie won't tell me, but I know they know! I know they know everything while I know nothing, so I'm gonna have to get help from my brothers. I just wonder if any of them still want to help after she set fire to everything. I can't blame her, though, in the end. "We did make our beds, and we should lie in them."

Well, we could if she hadn't burnt them all. I do wonder how much damage she really wanted to do though I suspect she got everyone out safely and I know she kept the girls safe, so I need to speak to them. They obviously had some interaction with her while she was there. Did she plan that, or was she caught? Also, if she wanted to burn the clubhouse down, she could have done it. I didn't even go and look at the damage. I didn't care enough, but I need to check everything out when I get back.

I make it back to the clubhouse, and the bike's still in the centre of the parking lot with her cut laid across it, the stab mark straight into the tank. I walk over and glide my fingers across the supple leather. Leaning down, I pick up her badges, the "Enforcer" one and "Reaper", and slide them into my pocket. I take the cut in my hands and bring it up to my face. Closing my eyes, I smell it. It smells like petrol and citrus and something woodsy, just like her. Breathing her in, I don't know how long I stay like that.

"You okay?" I turn, and Dice is standing a few feet away.

I shrug. "Fuck knows, Dice?" I look over at the parking lot to the big white lettering. "How bad is it in there?"

"She set fire to everyone's bed! Well, everyone who doubted her, some she left untouched and Barbie's left."

"What do you mean?"

"She didn't touch his room, but he said we were supposed to be a brotherhood, and if Ray was 'one of the boys', she wouldn't have been doubted. He didn't want to stay in a place where we could turn on our own. He left his cut, took his stuff and left." He shrugs, "Everything's so fucked up. Most of the guys are in your apartment. She dragged your mattress out, threw it off the balcony, and set fire to that, but the rest of the place is fine."

"We really screwed her over, huh?"

"Fucking understatement, Brother! You and me hurt her the worst. I know it, you know it, so what the fuck are we gonna do about it?" He just stands there, waiting like I have all the answers. I know fuck all.

"Let's try and find her. I'm gonna need your skills. Bernie won't help; he says he can't. I've managed to stop the divorce, so it's a start."

"If nothing else, that's gonna piss her the fuck off. Hopefully, she'll come back to try and kill you. At least we will see her that way."

"Erm, thanks, man. Let's hope she comes back but not to try and kill me. That would totally suck. Come on, let's get that computer fired up!"

As we walk into the clubhouse, I take in all the damage. Actually, she was very strategic, almost like she wanted to prove a point without actually destroying everything. I wonder how much of this was for revenge and how much was to piss us off so we would leave her alone and turn us against her. Dice shows me his room, and the hose from the fire service did the most damage. She'd only set the beds on fire. I suppose the message outside makes perfect sense now. The rooms are filled with smoke damage, but the water caused the most issues. Fuck, what is she thinking? I hope I can get her back.

We walk into the tech room, and Dice fires up the computer. "Where shall we start?"

"Can you hack the clinic? I wanna know what damage she sustained and what they put her through. Do we know who took her and what happened yet?"

"We don't know anything. I'll start with the clinic, though, and I'll set up an alert in case they access her records for anything else."

After a few minutes, he shakes his head, "What's up?"

"I don't know if you really wanna know."

"Show me!"

"Here, all toe and fingernails ripped out, multiple deep lacerations across her left forearm over 150, multiple deep burns caused by a screwdriver heated up and forced deep into the skin in her left underarm, two fractured ribs, multiple minor lacerations bruising throughout and an 'X' carved through her Reapers and your name tattoo. Her right leg has multiple deep lacerations and puncture wounds from the heated screwdriver, a deep laceration from her temple across her right eye and down to her cheek. It says here she's lucky to have kept her vision. Well, at least that's a good thing." Then he lets out a shaky breath. "Fuck... that's some fucked-up shit. Who the fuck would do that to her? And to what end then to toss her aside?"

"Maybe they got what they wanted?" I sigh.

"Let's hope not!" If it's information on us, it could bury us. If it's information on The Armoury, then maybe we'll all be fucked anyway!"

"Right, print out that report, then let's start back at the beginning and track her from leaving here on the night she was taken." We followed the limo and got the photo of the driver already. Dice prints it out again, and I pin it to the wall along with the clinic's report. "Right, you said this guy's driving licence was fake. What makes you say that?"

"I searched for death certificates in his name and got one, so we stopped there."

"Okay, so what if we search for his name, the fake licence name? If it's a name he picked or an identity he stole, he might know the real guy. There might be a connection."

Dice searches and searches before coming back with his name. "Right, the fake name is Timothy Spent."

"Okay, print out the fake driving licence."

"What for?"

"I want to see everything all together, so find and print his death certificate, then run a google search on the name and let's see what it comes up with."

I pace and pace while Dice taps out over the keys. Occasionally, a page will print, and I grab it and pin it to the wall in an order that makes sense to me.

"Shit, look at this!" Dice hisses out.

"What am I looking at?"

"It's a news article about Timothy Spent's death. He and two others were murdered, and their house burnt down. They were drug dealers... in the UK. That's not all. Look at the dates. It says here a woman was questioned in connection with the murders but was released."

"Yeah?"

"Have you heard the story about Ray's back tattoo?"

"Kind of."

"Right, three guys kidnapped her and stabbed her to get to her brother. He didn't give a shit, so her pa, I don't know which one, traded Bas's life for hers. They killed her brother, and she went to the hospital anyway. Fast forward to before she came here. She killed them, the three guys. Timothy Spent was one of those guys."

"So she didn't kill him. When did he come here?"

"That's the thing. He entered the country about three to three and a half years ago but hasn't left, or I can't find any record of him leaving, but she killed him a couple months before she came here."

"So she didn't kill him."

"Steel, do you honestly think Ray would confuse killing him? No, I think she did kill him, but someone had already used his identity to come over here."

"So, how has he stayed here so long?" I ask, confused as fuck.

"He's married!"

"Can we find out about his wife?"

"Yeah, just pulling up her driving licence... holy fucking shit!" Dice gasps.

"Fuck! That's her! That's the woman who pretended to be Ray and killed herself at the court."

"Fuck, so whoever the driver is, is definitely linked to you and Ray somehow." Dice prints the woman's driving licence out, and I add it to my wall.

"So this guy stole Timothy Spent's ID and came here, then got married, then three years later, kidnaps Ray and frames me?"

"Yep!"

"Well, I'm more confused than ever." I shrug. "I think I need to sleep on this and start fresh tomorrow. My head is a mess."

"I've set a few scans running to track her vehicle when she left here after the fire, and I'm downloading all our footage."

"Wait, did anyone ever check this place for hidden cameras and bugs?"

"Shit, no, there's just been so much going on. Come on. We should do that first."

"Wait, can we check to see if those cameras are working? Can we find the signal and tap into their footage now we know they exist?"

"Maybe... let me see if I can find an external signal being transmitted and any footage while that's running. What else should we be looking for?

"I don't know, man, everything, no matter how small a connection or even if we think it's no connection, we should check everything and go from there!"

"Wait… I've got a signal. I'm downloading all the data. Shit, these files are massive. How long have they been recording? I've hacked in through the back door, so I should be undetected for now. I should be good to save everything and then dump the whole lot. That way, we'll be the only ones with a copy. I'll leave it running while we start trying to find the cameras. Once we've got the footage, we can check the angles and see if we've missed any."

We head upstairs. And start at one end of the building, going through every room. Each room has a camera, and Dice removes them all. There's one in each corner of the bar and two behind it. We scan the building, find another ten, and head to the apartment. "We'll have to check the garage and coffee shop tomorrow. I'm beat." Me and Dice head upstairs, and there are bodies everywhere. "Come on, we'll kip in my room. We'll have to stay on the floor, as I think she totalled the mattress!"

Dice

Waking up the next morning, I startle. Fuck… I forgot where I was for a minute. I head out of the room and into the kitchen, flicking the coffee machine on as I head to the bathroom. Once I've showered, I take a coffee into Steel.

"Morning."

"Ah, thanks, man, you'll make someone a good wife one day."

"Fuck you, asshole." I chuckle. "Come on, let's get cracking. We need to check the rest of this place, lodges, everywhere and then get back to the tech room to see what my searches have found."

Once we're dressed, we head out to the living room, and Steel sighs. Fuck, we need to sort this out. He wakes everyone up. "Right, motherfuckers, where's Ares?"

"They went to stay at Scar's dad's place." Viking grimaces as he sits up off the sofa where he's been awkwardly laid all night. "Shit. I'm gonna head back to Carmen's tonight, fuck sleeping here."

"Well, before you do, I want you all to strip out the rooms and everything that's damaged and throw it

80

into a pile in the parking lot. We need to start cleaning up this shit hole. Me and Dice are going bug hunting, so get moving, dickheads."

There are multiple groans, but they all get up and start heading for the bathrooms as we head up to the lodges.

Steel knocks on Demi's door first, "Hey." He gives a sad smile as she opens it. She crosses her arms and leans on the door frame.

"Hey." It's all she says in return, nothing else.

"Look, I know you're…" He starts.

"Disappointed, disgusted, ashamed, would you like me to go on?" She interrupts.

"Fuck, Dem, I know I screwed up." He shakes his head.

"Screwed up, seriously? Screwed up is when you forget to take the meat out of the freezer the night before or when you lock yourself out, but this"—she steps forward and jabs him in the chest—"this, big brother, is the most epic fuck up of all fuck ups. You literally burnt her world to the ground and kicked the ash in her fucking face."

Jesus, Demi never swears, like ever, and right now, in front of us, we see a fire in her we've never seen before. The hurt and anger, all trying to make their intentions known.

"Demi, I'm gonna get her back, I'm gonna bring her home, I'm gonna fix it. Don't worry." Steel tries to reason.

She takes a step back and goes to shut the door. He steps up, holding it open as the tears start to flow.

81

"You're never gonna get her back. She'll never come home. You can't fix this."

"I can, Demi, and I will." He tries again.

"Don't you see? She's said her goodbyes, she's not coming back... ever!"

"What do you mean?" I butt in.

"I mean, whatever she's doing, she doesn't intend to make it out alive. She's gone, and she's not coming back. She said her goodbyes to us before she burnt everything. When she set the fires, what was left of Ray went up in smoke with it; there was only Reaper left, but there was something else creeping in, trying to take hold, something not natural, something dark. She's letting it in, and soon, there won't even be any Reaper left. She's gonna burn the world to the ground, and she's gonna destroy herself achieving it. You lost. You handed her the torch. She's gone. It's too late."

I step forward. "Demi! What did she say exactly?"

"What she said was for the people she trusts, the people who didn't let her down. What she said is irrelevant to anyone else. If she wanted to say it to you, she would have. Now, what do you want? I'm just heading to the coffee shop."

I tell her what we need, and she leaves us to it so she doesn't have to look at us for a minute longer than she has to, apparently. She tells Steel she loves him and she always will, but right now, she just needs to mourn the loss of her sister.

"You okay?"

He just shakes his head. "Let's get this over with. We need to find her before she does all the stupid things. Fuck... if she makes it out alive, I'm gonna fucking kill her."

We check all the lodges and get just as friendly a welcome at Skye's. However, we only find bugs and cameras in Ares's and my lodge. We head to the barn and the gym, where we find more bugs and cameras, before heading back to the tech room.

Ares joins us as we're scrolling through the footage leading up to her coming back here from the hospital.

She parks up near the fishing office, and we pick her up on our cameras. She flips off in every shot, but she flips off at the wrong angle for our cameras,

"Fuck, look! She's flipping off all the cameras we removed. She's flipping off whoever was recording us. What the fuck does that mean?"

Steel and Ares are shaking their heads; it makes no sense.

We see her tear through the place, waiting in the shadows as a bike approaches, and one of the brothers turns up and heads towards the clubhouse before checking his phone and heading to the barn.

"Who the fuck is that? Everyone was at the hospital."

"It's fucking Roach. What's he doing back? I thought he was on an assignment for you?" Steel says to Ares.

"No, he told me he needed to be with Tali and was staying there for a bit."

"So where the fucking hell has he been?" I spit at them both.

We watch Ray head to the barn, and then, after a while, she leaves on her own.

"What the fuck. Where's Roach? He doesn't come out, look. We fast forward through the footage but don't see him leave.

"Is there a dead spot? Could he have slipped out, and we missed it?" Steel's pacing now. "I thought Roach and her were close. She wouldn't hurt him, would she?" Ares pulls out his phone and calls him, but nothing. "What if he's in the kill room?"

"Fuck, can we get in there? Steel asks.

"Dane," I whisper. "Fuck, Dane can get in."

Steel's already pulling out his phone and putting it on speaker.

"Dane, it's Steel!

"Yeah, I know! What do you want, Steel?"

Just hearing his voice makes my heart race, my mouth goes dry, my palms sweat...

"We need to get into Ray's office. We think Roach is down there." Steel barks.

"Yeah. No, you don't need to go down there." Dane replies with no emotion.

"Dane, if he's been down there all this time with no food, no water, what if—"

"Steel, don't worry about Roach. He's getting what he deserves. That's all you need to know."

"What the fuck is that supposed to mean...? Dane...? Dane." Steel snaps.

The line goes dead. "Fuck, we need to get in there. I never really thought she would really hurt one of us." Ares paces.

"Can you hack into the cameras down there?" Steel asks me, and I shake my head. She has them on her own network; Dane designed it. It's higher security than Fort Knox. Fuck, he's a fucking genius, that man.

"Wait. Skye. She had the app on her phone. She had the app when ya know…" Then Steel storms out of the place and heads towards Skye's.

He hammers on her door. "Skye, Skye. It's Steel, Skye."

Opening the door, she crosses her arms before we can say anything. Steels storming in. "I need your phone. We need to see the footage of the office you can get in, right? You still have it on your phone. Tell me you still have it."

"Woah, woah, what the fuck?" Tank comes out of the bedroom and stops Steel dead in his tracks.

"We think she has Roach in the office." Steel tries to reason. "We need eyes in there, Skye. Do you still have the app?"

Skye nods but crosses her arms.

"Skye, we need to check Roach is okay."

Skye looks away from us all.

"Skye?" Tank touches her arm. "We need to see."

She shakes her head.

"What the fuck do you mean, no? He's a brother. We need to make sure he's okay," Ares spits, and Tank steps between them.

"Don't fucking talk to her like that." Tank turns and holds her by her shoulders. "Skye, if he's down there... if he's hurt."

She shakes her head again and takes a deep breath. "He's not. Not any more anyway now I'd like you to leave."

"Skye, where is he?"

She just shrugs.

"Maybe you should go." Tank moves us towards the door and shuts it before we hear the click of the lock.

That says it all: we never lock our doors, and now we're locking each other out. Things are really fucked up.

"So now what?" I ask.

"Back to the tech room. Let's see what else we can find." Ares storms off, and we follow behind him, things making less and less sense the more we find.

Skye

Tank pushes them out the door, shuts it and locks it. Stepping back towards me, I burst into tears. "Love, it's okay. I won't allow them to treat you like that. But I will ask, can you get in touch with Ray?"

I nod.

"Love, I need to see her." He pulls me to him and holds me tight, "For me, not them. I need you to ask her if she will meet me, okay?"

I nod against him. "I can't lose her. She's the only parental figure I've ever had, and if it wasn't for her…"

"I know love, I know." Tank rubs my back and holds me close.

"I need to go to bed." I lean up and kiss him and head to the bedroom, where I cry myself to sleep.

Waking the next day, I head out to the kitchen. Tank is already up cooking bacon, shirtless, and as I proceed to drool, he grins. "Morning, love, how are you feeling?"

"Better, now my two favourite things are in the kitchen."

"Ah yeah, and what are they?" he grins at me

"You and bacon." I grin at him. "Definitely in that order!"

Smiling, he pulls me against him for a knee-trembling kiss before turning me and slapping my ass and pushing me to the table. "Eat, then we need to contact Ray, okay?"

I nod. What else can I do? This man never asks me for anything, and I'm the only one able to contact her, but she trusted me to only contact her in an emergency, but there is another way. I don't want to use the phone she left me. I don't want it to be known that it's that easy. So, I'm going to use the "retro route", as she called it.

After breakfast, we head into Ravenswood. There's a free ads in the local paper, so we go to their offices, and I fill out the little card to place my ad. Tank reads it before I hand it to the clerk.

"This is why you've been having the free ads delivered to the club?"

I nod.

"This makes no sense!"

"It will… to her!" I pull him in for a hug. "And now we wait."

"You sure?"

"I'm sure. The free ads will be printed tomorrow and distributed the following day, so it could be a couple of weeks before we hear anything. It depends on when she reads it, so we need to check every one from now on to make sure it's right and wait for the reply."

"What if it was an emergency? This doesn't seem a very productive way to get in touch when it's life or death."

I look away from my husband. I won't lie to him if he asks, but there's some information that's not mine to share.

He nods. "She left you a better way, but you didn't want to burn the bridge when it wasn't life of death?"

I grin up at him. Fuck, I love him so much. I pull him in for a kiss, my bump that's no longer hidden pushing against us. "Wow!"

"Ow!"

Tank rests his hands on my stomach. "Bean, take it easy on your momma." He chuckles as we both take a kick to the ribs. I rub my stomach and receive another one for good measure. He laughs out the sexiest laugh, and my heart melts for this man. He's truly gonna love this little one to the moon and back.

"I want to name him after her," I mutter.

A quick flash of hurt flicks to his face before he turns his features neutral. "That's a lovely idea, love."

"I also want to honour your family tradition." He gives me a puzzled look. "Tray?" I smile at him, "I was thinking we could call him Tray?" I chew at my lip. We've not really spoken about names, so for me to just hit him with this, I know he might need some time.

"Tray Pershing? I fucking love it." He picks me up and spins me around, and we both laugh as we get another kick. Placing me down, he rubs my stomach. "Bean's gonna be an all-star football player,

I think." He laughs again, which causes another kick. Our little bean, Tray, loves his daddy's laugh, and honestly, so do I.

We head back to the clubhouse, and as we get out of the truck, Steel's just coming down the steps.

"Great," I mutter under my breath. I love him as much as I love Ray. He took me in, and he's the only father figure I've been able to rely on. My own dad never hung around, and the ones that followed, well, we know how that story ended, but he hurt her, which hurt me, and I don't know if I can forgive him yet.

My lip trembles as I look at him, and he walks straight over to me. I stop dead in my tracks; my heart pounds, and he pulls me in for a hug, and I break. I sob against him, and he wraps me tighter in his arms.

"I'm sorry," he mumbles above me. "I know I hurt her, I hurt you, and I didn't want to hurt either of you. I'm sorry. I miss you." He leans down and kisses me on the top of my head, and my arms tighten around him.

"I'll leave you two to talk. I'll be in the bar when you're done, love." I nod against Steel, and I feel Tank rub my back before walking away.

I just hold onto Steel and sob. I'm so emotional right now, and with everything going on, I feel so lost, so alone. I know I'm not. It's just... Ray's such a big presence all the time, to then just be gone... my heart aches and breaks once more that I might never get a chance to see her again, and she might never get a chance to meet Tray.

"You want to go to the coffee shop?"

"Will you buy me cake?"

90

He laughs down at me. "Yeah, I'll buy you a cake." He kisses me on my head again and then releases me, taking my hand and pulling me along to the coffee shop just as we walk in. I get another boot to the ribs, which makes me gasp and double over, resting my hands on my knees and taking a few deep breaths.

"Shit, Skye, you okay? Is the baby okay?"

I stand up, straightening my back. "Yeah, he's trying out for the NFL today!" I grimace and rub my stomach. "Wanna feel?"

"Can I?"

I nod, and he tentatively moves his hand towards my stomach. I thought Tank had big hands, but Steels are on another level. I take his hand and pull it towards my stomach, and we wait, nothing. "Give him a... oof." Steel laughs, and he kicks again. "He likes it when his daddy laughs, too."

Steel grins down at me. "That's the first time I've ever felt anything like that." He pulls me in and hugs me, and when I pull back, his eyes shine with unshed tears, and I frown at him.

"What's wrong?"

"If I don't get her back, I'll never have a chance to be a dad. She's my everything... I can't live in a world without her." He pulls me tighter again, and I just hug him back as I truly know how he feels.

Viking

I'm back at Carmen's, and she's been distant, to say the least. She's barely spoken to me. She claims she's "busy", but we both know she's pissed at me about Ray. Tali is withdrawn, too, and walks around sobbing. She won't talk, and I can't for the life of me get near either one of them. I wonder if being here is just too hard for both of them. I might head back to the club if I can't talk to either of them today... My phone rings, and it's Ares.

"Hey, Brother!"

"Hey, is Roach with you?" he asks.

"No, he's still out on assignment."

"What did he tell you?"

"What do you mean?"

"Turns out, when Ray burnt the place to shit, she trapped Roach in the office. Skye says he's not there now, and she and Dane have said not to worry about him. He's getting what he deserves, but we can't find him and don't know where he is. His phone isn't even ringing."

"Fuck... how long's he been missing?"

"We saw him on the footage from the night of the fire, but that's it. He went into the barn and never came out, but we can't get eyes down there. Skye says he's not in there."

"How the fuck would Skye know?"

"Apparently, when Ray had her step dad down there, she gave her access to the cameras. She said he wasn't down there long, but Dice cant find any footage of him leaving, so we're assuming Dane's involved as he also said not to worry about Roach."

"Fuck. Leave it with me. I will have a word with Carmen and get back to you."

"Thanks, Brother."

Fuck… what the hell is going on? I walk into the pool area, and Carmen's working on her laptop at the table.

"Hey, can we talk?"

Closing the laptop, she looks up at me. "Sure." Although the warmth seems to have disappeared. I feel like she is done with me.

"Are you done?"

"No, I still have a few hours of work left. I should be finished later, well, for today, anyway."

"No, I mean with me." I sit down at the table across from her and look at my hands before looking back at her. "Are you done with me?"

"Viking…"

"I knew it." I get up and start pacing. "I knew it was too good to be true. There's no way someone like you would actually like someone like me. Was I just a fuck? Shit, I thought it was more. I thought you loved me. I know I love you, shit; it was just a fuck, wasn't

93

it? I can't believe I was so fucking stupid, I thought I'd found my forever, but I was just a fucking fuck."

I kick the chair I was sitting on, and it skittles across the tiles before hitting one of the other tables.

"Viking! Can you please fetch that chair and sit down?"

Feeling like a scolded child, I snatch the chair and sit back down. Carmen rises from her chair and comes to stand in front of me. She grips my jaw in her hand and lifts my chin to meet her gaze. "I love you." A whoosh of breath flies from my mouth as my shoulders sag. "I love you, Viking, you're not just a fuck, you could be my forever. I just have a hell of a lot going on, and I'm distracted. I'm sorry."

"What about Tali? What's wrong with her? Is it Ray?"

"She shakes her head but then says. "Partly, but she and Roach broke up."

"Do you know where he is?"

She shrugs.

"Carmen, he's missing. Ares has just said he went into the barn. Ray followed him, and only she came out."

Carmen shrugs again, which is a weird reply for a woman in charge of a cartel. She's got nothing.

"Have you seen Ray?"

"Viking, I need to get on. I'm so busy. Can we talk later?"

"Carmen, what the hell is going on?"

"Wherever Roach is, I'm sure he's getting what he deserves, and that's all I need to say, so we will talk later, okay?"

Fuck. I storm back into the villa and pull out my phone. "Ares, something sketchy is going on. Carmen says Tali and Roach broke up. I told her he was missing, and she didn't care, then said she's sure he's getting what he deserves. What the fuck does that mean?"

"Brother, that's what Dane and Skye said... What the fuck did he do?"

"While Carmen's distracted, I'm gonna talk to Tali and see if I can't come up with something. Keep me in the loop, Brother."

"Will do. Be careful, okay? We both know what Carmen's capable of. Don't go kicking the hornet's nest."

I hang up and head to Tali's room, knocking on the door.

"Come in." I push into the room, leaving the door open. "Viking?" she gasps and pushes off the bed and stands to the side of it.

"Hey, kiddo, can we talk?" She nods and sits back on the bed. I walk into her room and take a seat at her desk. I don't want her to feel uncomfortable. "Your mom is a little distracted at the minute, and I know you and Roach broke up. I just wanted to make sure you were okay."

She nods.

"Did he tell you where he was going?"

She glances over to the window and places her hands in her lap, looking down at them, and shakes her head.

"Tali, did you know he was missing?"

She just shrugs. What the fuck is going on with all these women and the fucking shrugging all of a sudden.

"Tali, if you know something, can you tell me?"

She looks out of the window again.

"Have you seen Ray?" She looks down at her hands but doesn't say anything. "She came here, didn't she?" She still doesn't say anything. "After the fire. She came to see you? What did she say, Tali? We're worried about her."

"Seems you're more worried about Roach, but he's where he belongs."

"What did he do, Tali?"

"You saw Ray! You saw what he did!"

"You're saying Roach did that?" She just looks away again. "Tali, please, I need to find my sister. I know I fucked up, but I love her, and I just want her to be safe, okay?"

"Safe?" She huffs. "No one can save her, Viking. She's gone."

"Tell your mom I'm sorry. I'm going back to the MC. I'm going to find Ray and bring her home, and if your mom will forgive me, I will come back, then and only then." I pull her to me and hug her. "I love you both, okay? Take care of yourselves, and call me if you need me."

I walk out of that villa and don't look back. This is so fucked up. If Roach did this to Ray, then he can rot where he is, but my sister needs me more than ever, whether she'll ever admit it or not!

96

Dice

We're getting nowhere. It's so fucked up, we can't find any info on anything, everything's a dead end. I'm so stressed and not sleeping, and on top of all the Ray shit, Dane won't even talk to me. I can't live without them both. I need to take a step back and regroup to see if I can't find a way to get them both back permanently.

I jump on my bike and head into Ravenswood. I park up in the centre, and as I'm about to take my helmet off, I see Dane at the other end of the parking lot, heading this way, waving. He's wearing sexy as fuck ripped jeans with a wife-beater tucked in and a pale blue short-sleeved shirt unbuttoned over the top. His jeans are tight and stuffed into military boots. He's still got the messy longer hair and short beard, and fuck my life, if he doesn't look smoking hot. I'm just about to wave as a guy in a fucking suit, of all things, heads past me, waving.

I leave my helmet on, and when they meet, they hug and Dane gives him a kiss on the cheek before stepping back, stuffing his hands in his pockets and kicking at the floor. He looks... is he nervous? Are they on a fucking date? Are you fucking kidding me right now? The suit guy reaches and takes his hand, and walks towards the coffee shop.

"Dane." I hadn't realised I was off my bike and jogging over to him. "Dane. What the fuck, man?"

He spins round, and I see him mouth, "Fuck!"

As I reach him, I slow down. "What the fuck? Your sister's missing, and you're fucking out on a date? Are you shitting me right now?"

"Dice, I say this with the utmost respect; it's fuck all to do with you." He turns to walk away again, still holding the suit guy's hand.

"Dane, seriously." I reach out and grab his shoulder. He spins and drops the suit guy's hand.

"What the fuck is wrong with you, Dice?" He pushes me a step back. "What the actual fuck are you trying to prove?" He gets in my face, and I can see pure hatred, and it breaks my heart.

"Dane?" I run my hand up his chest and settle over his heart. I can feel his heart pounding and his eyes dilate, and I breathe against him, taking half a step closer so my hand is wedged between us.

"Erm, I'm just gonna go…" I vaguely hear the suit guy say, but we can't take our eyes off each other.

I slide my other hand up to his face, and his eyes close.

I make the most of the opportunity, and I gently kiss him, running my tongue against his lips. He opens up and lets me in as he pulls me to him. I slide my hand around his neck, fisting the back of his hair and holding him to me. The kiss isn't frenzied; it's slow, steady, almost loving. I breathe him in and

98

cherish every second as our tongues caress across each other. I pull him closer, hold him tighter, and melt into him. I plough all my feelings, fears, and regrets into the kiss.

As I feel him start to pull away, I whisper, "Come home?" I pull him tighter. "Please come back to me, I can't live without you." He rests his head against mine.

"Dice," he breathes out.

"Please, Dane?" I kiss him again, and he melts against me. This time, it starts to heat, and as it does, he pulls away, and I start to panic. He's cutting me off, and I can't let him walk away. In this moment, I have to do everything it takes to win him back, no matter the cost, "I'll do whatever you want! Whatever you need, just please don't leave me again." I fist my hand in his shirt and my other in the back of his hair, and I pull him to me. Our mouths smash together, teeth clash, he bites down on my lip, and I groan into him. I feel him smile against my lips, and I smile back as we battle for emotional release. I pour everything into this moment, and it feels like he does too. When he pulls away again, I let him, panting for breath as our chests skim against each other with every passing breath.

He looks into my eyes, really looks, and I don't know what he sees, but he cups my cheek. "Dice, I love you, I really do." My eyes widen at that statement. Fuck... I love him, too. "But—"

"Don't, please don't." I take a step back. I can feel my lip start to quiver and my eyes well. "Please? Dane?"

He pulls me in for a hug. "I'm sorry, Dice. I don't know how to do this with you."

"Just try, let's just try, please, Dane. I will literally do anything, anything at all."

"Dice…"

"Please?" A stutter of breath rushes from me as I feel him slipping away.

"I'm sorry." He turns to walk away. As he gets to the buildings I can't let him leave, so I do what I do best. I antagonise the situation. Dane likes rough. He likes an edge, so that's what I give him. I slam my hands into his back, thrusting him forward.

"You fucking wanker!"

As he turns, I grab his throat and slam his back into the wall. "You think you can just toss me aside? You think we're done? We'll never be done. You are fucking mine." I slam my mouth into him in a frenzy. I tighten my grip, and he moans against me. "Mine." I kiss him again, I can taste blood, and I know it's his. I lick along his lips, causing a shudder to run through him. "Mine." I push him against the wall with my whole body as he grinds himself against me. Maybe it's not healthy, maybe it's wrong, maybe we're just two twisted souls trying to find each other. I reach between us and rub his dick through his jeans; he's solid, hard as fuck, and my mouth waters. He moans against me as I rub into him harder with the heel of my hand.

"Dice," he murmurs against me, but I don't allow him more than that. I devour him, his scent, the new sensation of his beard, the new length of his hair. I can run my fingers through it and grip the back tightly

100

till he winces as he moans against me. I take everything I can because I won't allow him to leave me; he's it for me, my one shot at happiness, life, love, everything. "Dice," he murmurs again, and I'm punishingly forcing him into the wall. I'm grinding the palm of my hand into his dick, and he groans again against me, and his hips start to move, chasing my hand, chasing his release.

He stutters a breath against my lips, and I drink him in as his hand slides into my hair, and his other grips my ass in a vice-like grip as he thrusts against me, gasping.

His head lolls back, pulling away from the kiss as I grind my hand into him again, I bite down on his neck, causing a grunt from him and suck it into my mouth marking him as mine, and I groan as I taste the blood, I've clearly broken the skin, and he just grinds into me again his breathings all over the place his eyes are rolling closed, and I continue to push into him, grind into him, bite and suck against his neck, I'm making a mess, I know I am, and I can't stop. The thought of him covered in marks from me makes my dick go harder than ever, and as he pulls me harder against him as he shudders his release into his own jeans, he stays trapped against me and the wall, and I smile against his neck.

"You wanker!" He gasps at me. "Take me fucking home."

I glance back at him, smiling. "Where's your truck?"

"At my dad's," he pants, and I don't wait to be told twice. I grab his hand and drag him towards the bike. I'm taking him home, and I can't stop the grin that spreads across my face.

Dragging him to the bike, I thrust the helmet at him, and he pushes it back. "You're the one that needs to see where you're going, knobhead."

"Fine." I shove the helmet on and slide onto the bike.

Dane climbs on behind me and painstakingly slides his arms around me, causing me to shudder. Pulling off, once we get free of the town centre, I slide my hand down to rest over his, and then he slides one hand further down, cupping my dick. I groan as I speed up, and I can feel the rumble of his chuckle through my back. Fuck, why does he have such an effect on me? He languidly rubs at my dick all the way home. I'm breathing heavily by the time I pull up at the MC.

Pulling up right at the bottom of the steps to the apartment I now call home, I slide off the bike and grab his hand, dragging him up the stairs. I can feel him chuckling at my desperation, and I don't give a shit. I storm through the apartment straight to the bedroom and push him inside. As he turns to talk to me, I'm on him, clashing mouths as I push him back while fumbling with his jeans.

Dane normally likes to take control, and I'm down, but today is my day. Today is about me showing him I'm it, I'm his everything, and making sure he doesn't leave ever again. I break the kiss to push his jeans down. He's commando, and I groan as his dick springs free, signs of his earlier release everywhere as he's stumbling back with his jeans

102

around his calves. He's ripping his shirt off and his wife-beater over his head. As the back of his legs hit the bed, I thrust my hands against his chest, knocking him back onto it. I rip my own top over my head and kick my boots off, shoving my jeans and boxers down and kicking them off. He rises up onto his elbows, and I bend further down and slide between his legs, licking up his length.

"Fuck, I've missed the taste of you." I flick my tongue over the head and slide my hand around his thick, pulsing shaft. He groans, and as he drops onto his back, he struggles to rid himself of his jeans while I devour his dick, making sure I lick every single inch, which causes me to smile. Ray once said, "I licked it, so it's mine." And fuck, if that isn't the way I feel right about now.

I rub my hand over his dick as I pop it out of my mouth and slide up his rigid, form, mouth-wateringly sexy, ripped, fucking delicious body, pulling his leg with me. I spit into my hand and rub it into his cheeks, forcing them apart and sliding a finger straight in.

"Fuck." He gasps at the intrusion as I pump twice before removing my finger and replacing it with my throbbing dick. I feel the resistance, I relax, and when I feel the give, I push my way in straight up to the hilt.

"Hades, Dice, fuck's sake," he gasps. I give him a second while he adjusts. As a feral grin spreads across my face, I pull back before slamming into him, wrapping my arm under his thigh and lifting higher as I thrust into him again. He lets out the fucking filthiest groan as I crash into him. Reaching up, he pulls me against his mouth, crushing mine to his and his to mine in an almost angry fight for dominance. Well, not right now, beautiful. I'm in fucking charge. I bite down on his lip, and as he gasps, I thrust my tongue in, mirroring my punishing rhythm. I slam into him, and the illicit groans and moans filling the room are like my personal symphony.

"Fuck, Dice." He grinds against me and reaches down to pleasure himself. I slap his hand away. I don't want him blowing his load. I want to feel him fuck me senseless once I've ravaged him, and that makes me groan. Fuck, I wish he could pound into me from behind right now. I slam into him again, and he reaches up and pinches my nipples, twisting them in his grip, and I shudder.

"Fucker."

He laughs, and Jesus, the shudder it causes to go through my whole body only makes him laugh even more. As I screw my eyes shut and thrust again, he cups my face.

"You gonna come?" he rasps, and I nod. "Look at me," he commands from beneath me, and I can't do anything but what I'm told in that second. The power he has over me is exhilarating as I stare down to meet those beautiful hazel eyes. I can't help but fall over the edge, pulsing inside him. He bites down on his own lip, never taking his eyes off mine. He shudders and tightens against me. I thrash, falling out of rhythm as I chase my high.

"Fuck," I grunt out, and I spill inside of him, gasping for breath and function of any other part of my body that I seem to have lost. He clenches against me. I groan and drop onto him. "Fuck, you're gonna be the death of me... I can't wait." He leans up and kisses me as he groans into my mouth. I grind my hips against him, twitching at the sensitive spasms it sends through me.

As I come down from the high, I can feel his own dick pulsing and throbbing between us, and he smiles at me. "My fucking turn." His smile changes to a vicious smirk, and fuck me, if I don't nearly come again from that look alone. I pull out of him steadily and try to stand on wobbly legs as he slides off the bed.

"Hands and knees motherfucker, and hold on tight." He grins at me.

Fuck, this is gonna be wild. I feel the bed dip behind me as I feel his limbs slide into place. He reaches around to grab my come that's leaking out of him, and I groan at how filthy that is. Slicking his own hand and returning the favour, sliding a finger in, causing me to groan and shudder. He nudges at my legs, kneeing them further apart as he removes his finger and pushes his tip against me. As he pushes against me, he slaps my ass.

"Relax, let me in," he grunts from behind, and as I relax, he fully takes advantage and steadily forces his way in. I groan and drop my head as his grip tightens on my hips, becoming almost painful, and he holds me in place. Once he's fully seated, he shudders. "Fuck, I've missed you!" he mumbles, and I groan as he pulls back slowly and bottoms out again. When he pulls out, he slowly slides back in and shudders. "Fuck, you feel so good. You were made for me."

I shudder at his words. I can hear his smile around the next "Fuck," that slides out of his mouth. I drop down onto my elbows, and as he shoves inside me again, I groan. I hear the door click open.

"Fuck." I clench.

"Hades," Dane mutters with a moan at the sensation.

"Holy shit… fuck!" Steel mumbles from the doorway. "So… you're back?"

I try to pull away as Dane grips me tighter, holding me to him. I look through the gap between our legs. I can see Steel resting on the doorframe with his arms crossed with what looks like anger etched across his face, but it's hard to tell if he's upside down or I am. I think the blood is rushing to my head as I feel Dane's dick pulse harder inside me. Fuck is he getting off on Steel seeing us like this?

"Steel, as much as I would love to chat… I'm a little busy being balls deep in my boyfriend right now, so unless you wanna watch and offer words of encouragement, which, can I add, I'm totally down for or if you wanna join in, I'm down for that too." I can hear the grin in his words, making me shudder, and he slaps my ass. "Wait," he grumbles at me, but I'm mortified, hoping the ground will swallow me and hide me from embarrassment. But he just clenches my hips harder, holding me in place.

"As much as I appreciate the offer, I'm gonna have to decline, but by all means, carry on. It's not like there's anything more important going on right now."

"Thanks, Brother! So is that a no to the joining in or a no to the watching?" Dane pokes.

"Fuck you." Steel turns and walks away, leaving the door wide open.

"Fuck's sake, let me get the door!"

"No fucking chance. I'm not pulling out till we're done. Now, where the fuck were we?" He pulls back and slams into me, causing us both to shudder and groan.

"Fuck, you got so hard when he walked in. Does he turn you on more than me?" *Whack*. I get a crack across the ass cheek, and I yelp, "The fuck was that for?"

"You deserved it. Yes, he's hot. Yes, he's sexy."

"Okay."

"But he's not you. I just like to be watched." He shrugs. "Now shut the fuck up while I rock my boyfriend's world." He pulls out and slams into me so hard I would have face-planted if his grip wasn't so vice-like. And I can't help but smile. *Boyfriend*. That's twice he's said it, and if it doesn't make my toes curl like a schoolgirl with a crush.

He slams into me again, but this time, he keeps pushing, shoving me flat as he crashes onto my back. His frenzy steadies, and he grinds into me slower, groaning. He grabs the back of my hair and yanks my head back as he bites down on my shoulder, marking me like I did him.

"Fuck, I love being inside you. You make me so fucking hard all the time."

I groan as he pulls back harder, and the bite against my scalp contradicts his slow, grinding thrusts.

He bites against my neck and grinds into me again. "Marry me?" he grumbles as he shudders with his thrusts.

"What?" Did I just hear that right? Fucking marry him? *Nah, I must be dick drunk worse than I thought.*

"You fucking heard me! Marry me. Fucking marry me and be mine forever, this life is too short. I want it to mean something, so marry me?"

He grinds again. "Dane," I gasp out. "You fucking serious? Stop a minute."

"Yeah, serious, and not sorry, not stopping. It feels too good, so if you're not gonna say yes, just shut the fuck up."

He bites down on my shoulder, and as he sucks it into his mouth and grinds against me, my body starts to shudder. Fuck how can he make me feel like this? So out of it totally, dick drunk, him drunk, the whole world seems fuzzy and floaty when he's around, and I can't think of a reason to say no, so as he next bottoms out, I groan out, "Yes."

"Yes?"

"Yeah, I'll fucking marry you, dipshit. Now fuck me like you own me."

He bites at my neck and laughs. "Be careful what you wish for, babe." He pulls back and slams into me, ramping the pace back up as he tugs on my hair, and all I can do is groan into it. Fuck, I love this man.

Waking up in a sweaty, sticky mess with an ache all over, I smile and reach over to pull him to me, but the bed is empty. I startle and sit up; no, no, no. Don't do this. *Fuck.* I grab my clothes and throw them on, running out into the living area to stop dead in my tracks as Steel has Dane around the throat against the door, snarling at him. I come to a halt. They both turn to glare at me, stepping away from each other.

"What the fuck's going on?"

"Nothing, babe. I just came to make you breakfast."

"Steel?" I glance between them both, and he shakes his head and storms into his room.

"Dane, what's going on?"

"He wants me to help find Ray."

"Will you?"

"She's not lost, Dice, we know exactly where she is."

"What the fuck? Why won't you tell him? Us? Why won't you tell us?"

"Not my call, Dice. She doesn't want to be found."

"Is she okay?"

"No."

"And you're gonna leave her out there alone, not okay?"

"It's what she wants."

"Dane, please. She needs us; she might not know it, but she does. She needs us all. We have to help her."

"Dice, don't, it's not my call."

"Dane?"

109

"Dice, don't. I don't have to like it; I just have to support her."

"Dane?"

He glares at me briefly, then heads into the kitchen. "Okay, what do you want for breakfast?"

"Seriously?"

"Yeah, seriously. I'll make you whatever you want."

"No, seriously, you're just gonna change the subject and not even tell us where Ray is? Dane, she was in a fucking state when we all saw her last."

My phone bings with a text, and when I look down, it's from Ares.

Pres: Church, thirty minutes.

"Fuck!"

Ares

"So, boys, the shit has hit the metaphorical fan. Viking's been informed that Roach is the one behind Ray's injuries. We don't think he kidnapped her alone, and we don't know why, but all the information we have relating to her injuries he caused them all." There's uproar as people start shouting over each other.

"That fucking snake."

"She had that kid's back; this is how he repays her?"

"I'll kill the fucking bastard."

"Cunt!"

"Guys, guys, calm down. This isn't getting us anywhere. Dice, what do you have for us?"

"Honestly, Pres, not much. Dane's back, and he won't help; some kind of fucked-up loyalty thing to Ray. They know where she is but won't tell us. He did take me up to the barn to prove Roach wasn't in the office. It's empty. Dane said he looped the cameras, and they came and got Roach within twenty-four hours. They say he's alive, but that's all they'll say. They're 'questioning' him!"

111

"Who the fuck's this 'they' you keep referring to?" Tatts butts in.

"The Armoury." Ares shakes his head. "The Armoury have Roach. Fuck, we're gonna get nothing from him, then that's useless. What else have we found?"

Dice cuts in again, "There was a guy that Ray killed before she came here. His identity was stolen, and whoever was pretending to be this Tim guy arrived in the country before Ray even killed the real guy. He got married, and he was the limo driver, and his wife was the girl who pretended to be Ray to frame Steel. The 'infidelity' in prison was also a set-up."

"Clearly," Steel deadpans.

"So, what do we know?" I ask as the room falls silent. "So, fucking nothing, then?"

"Well, if someone got his boyfriend's dick out of his ass and cracked on with the surveillance footage, maybe we could find a lead," Steel snipes at Dice.

"Maybe if you didn't put your dick in someone else, she would be fucking here now," he spits back, and they both push from the chairs and have to be restrained from punching each other.

"Guys, this isn't helping. We could all take part of the blame for why she isn't here. We all let her down. Dice, do you think you could have another look?"

"Yeah, there's still some stuff to go through. Tank, could you take Dane back to his dad's to grab his stuff? He's moving back in."

"Sure. We done here?"

"Yeah, Tank, we're done."

I sigh and drop into my chair as I bang the gavel. "Right, everyone, fuck off. Let me know if you see, hear or fucking smell anything."

The remaining Psycho Six, Dozer, Steel and myself stay behind.

"Tank, see if you can find anything out. You and Dozer are the only ones they like. Sweet talk them, whatever the fuck it takes, just find something. Dice, you're back in with Dane. Use that to find whatever you can—"

"No!"

"What the fuck, Dice?"

"I'll find what I can, Pres, but I'm not using my relationship with Dane to exploit him. I've only just got him back. I'm not losing him again."

"Dice, this is Ray."

"Yeah, and if we ever do get her back and she finds out I used him, she'll kill me anyway. So I will find what I can on my own, and I will ask for help, but that's it. I'm not using our relationship against him. Final answer!"

He rises from his chair. "Thanks for taking Dane. Tank, tell him to come get me from the tech room when he's back!"

Dice strides out of the room and heads to the tech room.

"I'm going to look for her." Steel stands.

"And where the fuck you gonna start? She could be anywhere."

"North, she's gone north."

"Steel, how the fuck do you even know that?" I bark at him as he's being fucking ridiculous.

"When she filed for divorce, she did it as far south as she could, to get me as far away from her as possible. She'll stay remote but somewhere near the coast, it's less obvious you don't belong. Coastlines always attract strangers. Tourists."

"That's your whole fucking theory? 'She'll go north because she sent me south?' Steel, do you know how fucking stupid you sound?"

He shrugs. "Maybe, but fuck, it beats hanging around here just fucking waiting. I need to look into where I'm gonna search, so I'll be around for the rest of the week, then I'm going to find my wife."

"Fucking hell, everyone's gone mental."

"Dozer, do you think Beauty will call in at Scar's? She's still staying at the law office."

"Seriously?" He shakes his head. "After what she fucking pulled last time?"

"Fucking hell Dozer. I can't right now, just ask. We can be butthurt and jealous all we fucking like once we have Ray back. Until then, I'm choosing to see it as an error in judgement on both sides. So just drop it, yeah? I've got enough to contend with. Scar's working fucking stupid hours, she's not eating, she's a right state, and all I can do is try and get her sister back, *our* sister back. Please, guys, this club is falling apart without her. It's like a hand grenade went off, and I've been given a fucking paintbrush to clean it all up with, so please help me?"

They all clap me on the shoulder and assure me they've got my back, but fuck, she's like water seeping into a crack in a rock, freezing, expanding, and smashing the fucking rock. How the fuck am I supposed to keep all those goddamned pieces together?

I follow Dice to the tech room and pace behind him, feeling fucking useless. "So, what's the connection between fake Tim and fake Ray, and Ray and Steel? And what's Roach's connection, and why did Roach get the Hellhounds to kidnap Catalina?"

"Pres, I know you're trying to help, but I need to concentrate on Ray for now. Can we look at Catalina later? I'm sure Carmen has people on that."

"Yeah, but why would Roach kidnap his girlfriend?"

"I don't fucking know."

"Well, maybe, if we find that out, we can find out who Roach is or was working with."

Dice spins in his chair. "Actually, that makes sense. So Ray was kidnapped. Initially, they thought she was Scar."

"Yeah, so what's that got to do with this?"

"It was the Hellhounds who were working with Miguel, so Ray escapes and hands Miguel over to Carmen, then declares war on the Hellhounds for their part in the human trafficking. Roach knew that, so why would he want the Hellhounds to take Catalina? The Hellhounds were already on Ray's radar. Was it to have her killed in the process?" Dice turns back to his computer and types out a few lines of code.

"What if he was setting the Hellhounds up? What if he and whoever he works with are in competition and played Ray and the Hellhounds against each other, knowing she would take them out?"

Dice turns to glare at me. "How would they know that Ray was capable of taking them out?"

"Dude, it's fucking Ray. Anyone who has ever met her regrets it in some way or another."

"Pres, not fair."

"Yeah, yeah, sorry. So, who stood to gain if the Hellhounds were taken out?"

"Well, nobody is as big as The Armoury, and although there are a few smaller fish in this area, including us, there's nothing to rival them. So, if anyone was trying to get too big for their boots, The Armoury would take them out. So, who's been making waves?"

"Dante fucking Crane," we both spit.

"That's who kidnapped me, Steel and Dozer. He was the one who pretended to be The Armoury. So, was he trying to take over, or was he trying to discredit them?"

"Dice, see if you can find any information about him other than what we already have. See if we can get a picture, or at least a fucking description, so we know who we're looking for."

Dice puts the feelers out through all his contacts and over the dark web, and then we call it a night. "Let's keep this between me and you for now, Dice." Hopefully, tomorrow will shed some light on this guy. "What if Roach is working for him? That would give us the connection to Miguel and the Hellhounds. Fuck, let's hope we get something."

Tank

Dane climbs in the truck. "Thanks, man. I appreciate you dropping me off."

"No problem, anytime."

As we pull out the gates of the club and head for Heighton, Dane turns in his seat. "Tank, when you see her tomorrow, don't be too hard on her, okay?"

"What?"

"Ray told me she's meeting you and Skye tomorrow. Just go easy on her, yeah? She's not all together at the minute. She's… broken!"

"Dane, I'm going to see her because I love her and want to make sure she's okay. I won't force her to come back or hurt or upset her. Honestly, I just wanna give her a hug, hold her in my arms and hope I can help."

"You can't right now, but she'll appreciate it." He sighs. "If I give you a letter for her, will you give it to her for me? She's off-grid, so we have to be cautious how we contact her."

"Sure, man." I smile at him. "Of course I will."

As we pull up at Bernie's, I say, "Do you need a hand taking your shit back?"

"Nah, I'm good, man, thanks. I'll just grab you the letter, okay?" He climbs down from the truck and heads inside. The front door opens. Cade comes out. He has stayed away from the club since Ray disappeared. The only one who's been near is Bran, and I'm classing driving past as he heads to the lodge he shares with Demi. He hasn't set foot in the clubhouse, and neither has Demi; it's a whole weird vibe. She's definitely had an effect on everyone.

"Hey Cade, how's things?" He climbs in the truck beside me.

He shakes his head. "Can you do me a favour, Tank? I need you to give her a message."

"So you're all in contact with her, huh?"

"Not really. Just that night we visited her in the hospital."

"Yeah, you didn't really hang around to see the aftermath of that departure. She certainly knows how to make an exit."

He chuckles, but there's no humour in it. "Yeah, you have no idea. She's always been... shall we say... creative?"

"Dude, she cut off her own tattoos as her resignation and impending divorce."

"Like I say, creative."

"It certainly got her point across, so what do you need me to tell her?"

"Can you give her this?" He hands me a letter. "You need to make sure no one follows you. You need to make sure she's safe, Tank. She's gonna need someone in her corner when shit goes sideways, and it will. She'll need to know no matter what, she can turn to you, Priest and Dozer. She has no one else at the club. If she makes it out of this alive, she's gonna be destroyed."

"Cade, what the fuck's going on? You're all talking about impending doom and devastation. What's the alternative? What's the good side to aim for?"

"Tank, that is the good side. The bad is she's dead."

"So you're telling me she either ends up a shell or dead? Nothing else?"

"Pretty much." He grabs the handle to step out. "Just make sure no one follows you. For her to do what she needs to, she needs time. She's doing this to protect you all from him."

"Cade? Who's she protecting us from?"

"She'll either tell you or she won't. Either way, that's for her to decide."

He steps out of the truck as Dane comes back out of the house.

"Thanks, Tank. Here, give her this and tell her I miss her."

"Dane, please tell me. Can I save her?"

He shakes his head. "No one can. Tell her I love her, okay?"

I nod as he closes the door. Fuck, what the hell is going on? These guys are always so confident; they all have an aura around them, they have confidence and big dick energy on steroids, and Ray is that ramped up; she's got the biggest dick of all. They're all such a force, but seeing them like this doesn't fill me with confidence for a best-case scenario. Now, all I'm feeling is my sister's gonna die, and no one can do anything to stop it. I can't lose her, and I can't let Skye lose her either. She's never had a real family till Ray saved her. It will destroy my new family if anything happens to her, but I also know I can't tell my brothers. I have to keep the meeting tomorrow a secret from everyone.

I've booked Skye an appointment at the clinic, so we're going there first as a cover in case we're followed. I just need to stay vigilant. It's a fair drive to meet Ray, so before heading back to the club, I head to Walmart, get snacks, blankets, pillows and drinks and hide it all in the back of the truck. That way, no one will be suspicious when we leave. Fuck knows what a mess we're gonna find when we finally make it. Ray… Fuck, I hope she's okay.

Waking up, I shower and then wake Skye. My life has changed so much over the last year. I've met the most amazing women. I gained a sister—well, three really, Ray, Demi and Scar—I found the love of my life, the reason for my heart to beat in Skye and Bean. I can't believe I'm gonna be a father. I can't wait to meet my little boy, and I'm scared Ray's gonna miss it. We're not that far away now. Skye is glowing, and he'll be here in a couple of months. I've never been so ready for anything as I am to meet this little boy.

While I'm making breakfast, Skye steps up behind me, wrapping her arms around my waist, and I chuckle. She smiles and kisses my back. "You think it's funny, do you?"

"I think it's adorably funny." I turn off the stove and turn in her arms, pulling her to my front. I always cook her breakfast shirtless. She always slides in behind me, wraps her arms around me, and kisses my back, but recently, her hands barely reach, resting on my sides when she crushes our bump against me. I kiss her forehead, "How are you feeling?"

"Hungry, nervous?" She grins up at me.

"Come on then, let's get this day started." We eat breakfast and head out. I've kept myself distant from the boys so as not to arouse suspicion, and as we head past the clubhouse, Steel is just heading across from the apartment.

As I slow, Skye glances at me. "What the hell are you doing? Keep going."

"Skye, chill. If I don't stop, he will think something's wrong. Just relax, okay?"

Slowing and pulling to a stop, I roll my window down. "Hey, guys, where you off to so early?" Steel leans in the cab.

"Clinic, Skye's got an appointment, then we're off looking for baby stuff, gonna make a day of it. What you up to?"

"Just finalising details for the trip."

"Trip?" I question. Who the hell has time to go on a trip?

"Yeah, sounds better than a suicide mission to find my wife and drag her back from the fires of hell, kicking and screaming till she forgives me."

"Ah, trip." I smile. "Yeah, that does sound less intimidating and more achievable."

"When are you leaving?"

"Couple of days."

Nodding, I say, "Catch ya later."

He taps the top of the cab as he walks away, and Skye lets out a big whoosh of breath, panting, "Shit, that was so scary."

"Calm down, love, you'll make yourself ill. We've got a long day, and I can't have you on edge for all of it, okay? Think of Bean."

Smiling down, she rubs at her round, neat stomach, and I reach over and put my hand on it. "It's gonna be okay. Just relax."

She nods, and we set off again. Pulling up at the clinic. We head in.

An hour later, we're heading back to the truck. As Skye climbs in, I grab the supplies out and hand them to her, adjusting pillows and blankets around her to make her comfortable and handing her all the drinks and snacks to stash in the footwell. We've got a good three to four-hour drive ahead of us. Steel was right when he said Ray would head north and stay along the coast. I feel bad for not telling him, but I can't risk losing or scaring her off. I need her to know she can trust me, and until I see her for myself, I'm keeping my lips sealed.

Pulling up at the diner, we're half an hour early, and I lost Skye a good two hours ago; she's been so tired that I think the steady motion of the truck lulled her to sleep. I'm just about to lean over and wake her as a hooded figure comes to stand in front of the truck. Shit, it's Ray. She shakes her head and lifts her finger to her lips. I slowly take the handle and open the door, shutting it with the softest click I can. Before rounding the truck, I don't slow. I don't stop in front of her. I just scoop her into my arms and hug her. She feels so tiny. I feel her body shake against mine, and although no sound comes from her, I can tell she's sobbing. As the tears roll down my cheeks, I do the only thing I can at that moment and hold her tighter.

When we pull away, I look into her red puffy eyes. "Fuck, you look like shit."

"Missed you too, Brother." She half smiles, not a real one, more of a placating one.

I cup her face, and she closes her eyes. I run my thumb down the angry red scar through her eye.

"It looks worse than it is."

"How are you?"

"Straight in with the tough questions, huh?"

"Ray?" She doesn't even look like herself right now, and she's certainly not acting like herself. She's barely a person at this moment in time. I can feel the darkness, the emptiness staring back from her eyes, their sparkle gone, her light gone. She's almost a shell right now. I don't know if she's gonna come back from whatever this is, but I pull her in for another hug as I can't bear to not feel her in my arms. At least if she's in my arms, I know where she is, I know she's safe, and no one can hurt her. The minute she steps away, I will lose that feeling.

"Ray!" The scream comes as the truck door flies open, and Skye comes running at us. Ray turns as she runs into her, wrapping her arms around her and sobbing into her chest. I take a step forward and hold them both as tight as I can.

"Shit, kiddo, you cooking a lineman in there?"

We all share a laugh, and all I wanna do is bottle this moment and save it forever. The only thing is I know it's gotta end. I can't for the life of me bring myself to let them go.

This moment right here is what I need to fight for, getting us all back together. Once Skye's sobs steady, we all take a step back. "Come on, we should go inside." Stepping through the doors, Ray checks the place over and chooses a booth in the corner near the restroom, like she hasn't already surveilled the place and has fifteen escape routes planned and a gun taped under the table.

We place our order, and Ray smiles across at Skye. "So, how's married life treating you both?"

"Oh my god, Ray, it's the best; he cooks shirtless, like all the time, and it's the best thing, and then there's the sex. I did all the things—"

"Woah, maybe I should go to the bathroom while you girls talk about... stuff!"

"Oh sure, sorry." Skye blushes, and it's the sweetest thing ever. I know with all her issues, Ray had been helping Skye out in that department, and I know I've thanked god on more than one occasion for the "things" she learnt, but fuck, I don't want to hear them talk about it.

I lean in and kiss her on the cheek. I slide the envelopes across the table to Ray before smiling at them both and leaving. I give them a good few minutes before returning.

When I get back, the food has just arrived, and we eat in almost silence. Ray picks at hers, which is worrying. It's not like her. She's still so slim. She's put some weight back on, but she's not back to herself and clearly not interested in food, which is a big red flag on its own. Ray not interested in food is a thought I never thought I'd think.

Once we've finished eating, Skye blurts out, "We've picked a baby name."

"You have?"

Skye nods. "So Tank has this family tradition where all the boys' names start with a 'T'..." she trails off.

I nudge her and nod. "Carry on, love."

"I wanted to name him after you and honour Tank's tradition, so we picked Tray."

"Seriously?" Ray gives an actual smile, like old Ray would have almost, and a single tear rolls down her cheek, which she swats away.

"I couldn't think of anything better than honouring the two people I love most in this world who, without you, I wouldn't be here."

"Kiddo, that's beautiful. I'm honoured."

125

"Would he be someone you would come back for? Would you come back for him?"

"Skye, you think I wouldn't come back for you? You think you wouldn't be reason enough for me to come back?"

She shakes her head, and it breaks my heart a little that she thinks Ray doesn't love her enough to stay just for her.

"Skye, I need you to listen, okay? No matter how shit things would be between the club and Steel, you alone are enough for me to stay, and then there's this knucklehead." She nods over to me.

I smile at her. Fuck. I really do love her.

"I'm telling you this so you understand, not to make you feel guilty. I need you to know if I had a choice, I would be with you. Fuck the rest of them, and especially fuck Steel. You are more than enough. The reason I'm not with you is to protect you. All your lives were threatened, and I know he will gladly kill you all to spite me, so I'm laying low till I can take him out. I'm staying away, and I'm keeping the promise that I made to you. I will always protect you, or I will die trying. I'm doing this so... Tray can have a future with both parents in a place that's safe."

"Ray, just tell us what's going on. I can help."

"Tank, I love you, and I know you think that, but he will kill you if he knows I'm in contact. He won't hesitate, and I'm not strong enough at the minute. I'm still healing. I need to lay low for now. I need you to keep her safe, to keep them safe. That's the one thing you can do for me. I will trust you with that."

"Ray, who is coming for us?"

126

"Don't you worry about that. I'm gonna make sure he doesn't get anywhere near any of you. I just need to get fit and well, then give him what he wants. For now, I need to go inside his organisation and destroy him. I can't have anyone escape, and I don't know enough about his organisation yet to destroy it."

"Ray, if we know who's coming, we will know who to look for, who to be wary of."

"Tank, he's worn so many faces over the years that you would never see him coming. I never saw him coming. For that, I am truly sorry, but I'm the only one who can get close, the only one he will let in and the only one he will trust. You just need to give me time, okay?"

"Why you, Ray?" I shake my head. "What does he want with you?"

"He wants me to join him, and he wants to take out The Armoury."

"Fuck, Ray, you can't. It's a fucking suicide mission going up against The Armoury, you know damn well it is."

"Which is why I probably won't be coming back. I've already said too much. I just need you to be careful, stay together and don't let anyone you don't know anywhere fucking near the club, okay? Till I'm either back or dead! And if I'm dead, Tank, promise me you will run. Leave the club and never look back."

"Ray, don't say shit like that. We can take him down together."

"Tank, if he gets wind that I haven't cut myself off from all of you, he will raze the club to the ground. He's fucking powerful and cautious. For now, I have to go undercover and really be what he wants. I need to make a deal with the devil. If I make it out alive, I will come back for you, okay?" She reaches across the table and takes both our hands. "Both of you and Tray, if I don't, I've left you everything, the money, the shares in the businesses, it's all yours. You're the nearest thing I have to a kid, Skye. I couldn't love you any more if you were mine."

It's weird they have this mother-daughter relationship, yet Ray is younger than Skye, Ray and Steel are the only parental figures Skye's ever known.

"I will give it all up to keep you. I don't want the money, Ray. You left me more than enough when you set the fires. I just need you."

I keep quiet. I feel I'm missing information here, but this is something between them, so I hold her hand tighter and just listen.

"David has my will, accounts, everything. Just please take care of each other and trust no one!" She stands from the table. "I've stayed too long already. If I don't see you again in this life, I will wait for you all in the next. I love you, Brother. Take care of them. Skye, I'm so proud of the person you're becoming. You're gonna be the best mum ever, and I just hope I get to see it. But if I don't, I need you to know I love you, and I'm sorry I failed you."

She walks away and leaves us sitting there, shell-shocked. It really sounds like she's never coming back. Skye's shaking, tears rolling down her face as I wrap my arms around her. She sobs against me.

"Shall we go home?" Skye nods against me. Once we get in the truck, I get Skye all settled in and comfy, and I climb behind the wheel.

"When you said Ray left you enough, what did she leave you, love?"

"She told me everything was going to shit, and she gave me a holdall and told me to trust my instincts. If it didn't feel right, to run far and run fast. When she left, I opened it up. There was a new identity, new documents for me and you, and the number of a guy who could help me with documents for the baby if we'd already had him by that time. I checked the bag. It was full of cash. A gun and a letter in it said it was untraceable and legit, so I could spend it freely without worrying about being found."

"Fuck, I need to see the bag when we get home."

She nods. "It's safe, I hid it."

"Good girl, now rest. It's been a fucking long day, love." I rest my hand on her leg as I drive us back to the MC.

Steel

Pulling the truck to the bottom of the stairs, Dice helps me down with my stuff. "You sure this is a good idea?"

"Nope, but it's the only one I have. She's been gone for weeks. I'm gonna find her or die trying."

Dice hasn't been much help since he got back with Dane. Whatever he knows, he's not sharing, and he's barely trying to find her now, and without him behind the computer, we actually have nothing. But I have my gut, and I know my wife. Whatever she's running from… or to, I'm gonna find her. Since I've been unable to rely on Dice, I've used the old-fashioned way of tracking a person, and after a million dead ends, I got three confirmed sightings.

Yes, it was painstakingly mind-numbing, but it paid off. I sat with my phone and laptop in my room for days. I searched every gas station north of here, then called every single one. I told them she was my sister escaping an abusive relationship, and I needed to save her. Most people shut me down, but three confirmed she had passed through. Some people are stupid, really—catch them off guard, and they will spill what you need. I mean, if they actually thought about what I'd asked, why would you say yes to someone over the phone? I mean, I could be the abuser, but I'm not one to pick. It has given me my area to start.

I could have asked Dice to check out their cameras, but I'm not sure he wouldn't have told Dane, and I'm pretty sure Dane knows where she is, so he would have told her, and I would have lost my advantage. As I'm loading the truck, my brothers come to say goodbye. I don't know how long I will be gone for or if I will ever come back.

I've vowed I won't come back till I find her. I don't want to be here without her. The apartment doesn't smell like her anymore; she's a ghost on everything I touch. I sometimes sit in the dressing room and just sniff her clothes like a fucking psycho, but even that's fading. The bed doesn't smell like her anymore, and Hades is gone, too. I'm lonely, and it's worse since Dane and Dice are back together. He has his Ray. I want mine fucking back. I'm not giving in till I at least see her, speak to her, explain to her, beg her, whatever it takes.

Once everyone's left, I head around to the coffee shop. "Hey, I'm leaving, just wanted to say... goodbye."

"Leaving?" Demi steps out from behind the counter. "Where are you going?"

"I'm gonna find her or die trying. I can't stay here without her, and I've let everyone down. I can't forgive myself till she forgives me, and she isn't going to do that while I sit here and do nothing. I'm sorry I let you down, Demi. I truly am. I love you."

"Steel."

"Don't, just hug me and pretend you don't hate me for a second, at least till I've left, okay?"

"I don't hate you, Colby. You're my brother. I'm hurt and upset for Ray, but I don't hate you. I'm sorry if I made you think that. Be careful, okay?"

"Love ya, Dem. See you soon."

I turn my back on the only place that has ever felt like home because it's just some walls in a room with a door that I can't stay behind without her. I want my home back, and that's her.

So, I trust my instincts. I head north, and I drive to the first sighting. It's a couple of hours away, and when I arrive, I grab my phone and the picture I have of Ray. It's the most recent one I have of her, without the scar that she now sports, which is too much like my own to be a coincidence. Fuck, if I ever see Roach again, I will kill the bastard.

As I enter the gas station, it's an older woman working. I give her my sob story, and she has no idea what I'm talking about. "I spoke to someone called Lee."

She shakes her head. "That's my son. He will be in tomorrow. You can come back then."

Sighing, I ask, "Okay, what time?"

I head out to the truck. I'm only two hours away from home and already at a dead end. Pulling out the laptop, I start researching my next move, and then I start searching for the guy from the gas station. *Bingo*. I love kids and their social media. A few clicks, and I've found where he lives, so rather than wait, I'm gonna pay Lee a visit. See if I can't shake the little shit for some information.

As I pull up to the little shit's house, I know I'm gonna have to get creative. I pull the screen back and knock on the door. I wait patiently for him to answer it. As it opens slowly, the smell of weed hits me, and I almost choke on it. Damn kid's stoned to fuck.

I pull out my wallet and flash him my driving licence. "Police, son. I have some questions for you regarding a woman who passed through here a few weeks ago."

"Whoa." He grabs onto the door frame as he tries to focus, grinning up at me.

"You're so, so... tall." he grins again, fuck stoned people are stupid.

"I've just called at the gas station and spoke to your mom. She said you would take me back there after closing to access your security footage."

He just nods and grins again. "Get the keys to the gas station. We're going out now."

I push him back into the house and follow him to his room, which is even worse. I fling open the window as this twat's never gonna be able to access a fucking key, let alone a security system. The gas station closes in an hour. I steer him to find his keys, then his shoes, then his wallet. Fucking kid's out of it, then I drag him out to the truck and drive the long way back to the gas station. As we pull up, the lights are still on.

I make him wait till the main lights go out and his mom drives off. I purposely didn't remind him to bring his phone so he can't be tracked. As we head into the office, the struggle is real right now. Kid can barely focus, so he gives me the password, and I log in. I sit him in the chair with a bag of Funyuns I grabbed as we walked through. As I scroll through the footage, it takes a while to figure it out, as he's about as much use as a chocolate ashtray.

Then, I find her. Fuck, she looks rough. She almost looks fucking homeless as she stalks in, pays for her gas, and grabs some supplies. Once I have the time stamp, I check the other cameras and check the vehicle she's driving. I know she won't have stolen it as she won't want it flagged up, but if I can get the tag, at least I know what I'm looking for.

"Gotcha! 2004 Toyota Camry in silver, how very unassuming of you, wife."

Writing down the details, I check for every bit of footage. I take photos as I go of the car, of her. This is the closest I've been to her in a long time, and I can almost feel her near.

I check the forecourt cams and see the direction she drove off in, and fuck if my dick doesn't stir seeing her as she stalks across to the car. She's wearing black jeans, combat boots and a black hoodie. She has the hood pulled up, but in the light of the shop, you can clearly see it's her, and her face is still bruised, and the scar is angry and red with a scab running through it. It looks horrific at that moment. I can't believe he carved up her fucking face. I wonder what drove him to do what he did to her? I hope someone's making him pay somewhere.

When I'm done, getting everything I can, the lad's passed out in the chair, I lock the door. I leave, sliding out of the back emergency exit, making sure it shuts behind me.

At least I have a direction. You may be the motherfucking Reaper, but you are mine, and I will track you to the ends of the earth or die trying. I'm coming for you. Let's hope we don't burn the world to the ground and everything in it when I finally find you.

Climbing in the truck, I feel hopeful. I head to the next sighting, northeast of where I am. If I know my wife, she's gonna zigzag all over the fucking place to try and throw me off. The thing is, when I want something, I'm like a dog with a bone. Nothing will stand in my way. Not even her.

Pulling up at my next destination, it's dark out, everywhere's closed. I pull around the back and sleep. I want to be ready when they open. I hope I'm as successful as I was yesterday. Yeah, I'm taking that as the win. I had eyes on her for the first time in weeks. I know which direction she went; although it's only a slight piece of information, I'm running with it.

When the gas station opens, I'm waiting. I head inside and talk to the bubble-blowing mean girl behind the counter. I'm gonna have to think on my feet and flirt a little. Everyone loves a bad boy, right?

"If you show me the footage, I'll come back at the weekend on my Harley and take you out."

"Ew, gross, you're old enough to be a grandpa. I'm so not down with that. It would be like the most gross idea for a date like ever."

"Fine!" I turn and storm out. Little bitch didn't need to be so fucking rude!

I wait around till she leaves and scope out the next attendant on duty. Fuck, it's an older dude. What angle can I work to get him to show me the footage? Winging it is pretty much all I've got at the minute. I head inside. "Look, man, my wife left me as I fucked up and did some dumb shit and fucked someone else, now she's fucked off and left my sorry ass, and I'm trying to find her. Yes, I'm pussy-whipped. Yes, I'm a dick. I just need a break and a lead!"

Fucking awesome dude lets me troll through all the footage, and I find her again nearly a week later than the last place, so she's clearly not moving very fast; hoping the zigzagging is enough to throw me off. Thanking the guy and leaving him a massive tip, I head on to the next place. She's heading northwest this time. I just hope I'm closing in.

The next place is a bust. I sit back and do some more research, calling gas stations non-stop for days, but nothing. It's quiet, no sign of her. What if I'm wrong? What if she doubled back? After a few days, I'm frustrated, and I can't find anything. I give in and call Dice.

"Dice, I need your help."

"Steel?" his voice rasps back.

"Yeah! Dice, I'm drowning. I can't find her. I don't know what to do or where to go from here. It's been weeks since I've found anything. I'm just bumbling around now with nothing. Dice, please?"

"Give me a couple of hours, and I will see what I can find. I'm not promising, though, Steel. I can't go too deep."

"I understand, Dice. Thank you, Brother!"

I wrap myself in the blankets and just nod in and out of sleep. She's everywhere in my dreams. I feel her short breath against my skin, a chaste kiss on my cheek, a caress of skin, a flash of desire in her eyes, and then there's the blood. I startle, thrusting up from my reclined position, sweat pooling on my brow, deep, panicked breaths stuttering from my lungs as I clutch at my pounding chest. That's how they all end now. My dreams turn into nightmares, her face contorted in agony covered in blood, her blood and startled screams ring through my thoughts. I wake in a pool of sweat and regret.

Steadying my breath, I pull out the map with all my chicken scratch etchings on it. I've marked every place I've been, searched and eliminated. I'm going in circles, losing my mind, and my heart breaks every day, leaving me feeling empty, hollow and broken.

The text breaks me from my pity party. It's a set of coordinates from Dice. No explanation, no nothing. I scribble them down, and delete the message. He clearly didn't find them himself, and I'm grateful.

Pulling into the store to grab some supplies before I head up the mountain, I've been informed she's in a cabin halfway up. There's about an hour's trek from the bottom. She's been there a few weeks, but no one other than the delivery guy has seen her since the first day she arrived. She places her order, the delivery guy meets her at the bottom of the mountain, and she pays and leaves. The last delivery was four days ago; she's not due for another one for three more days. I'm hoping she's still here. It's fucking freezing, and there's snow on the mountain. Everywhere in this godforsaken place is freezing and wet and depressing. It's time to get my girl and take her home.

I drive to the bottom of the mountain and park up, grabbing the supplies and wrapping myself in a blanket. I don't really have clothes for this weather. I start my trek. The only saving grace is I came in the truck rather than on my bike. As I start trudging, the higher I get, the thicker the snow becomes. It's fucking rough up here. The trees are thick, and although they provide cover from the blizzard, which is pouring down from above, they also don't let much sun, light or heat in, so the snow that's getting blown around is just staying, and it's fucking miserable. Why the fuck would she come here? It's cold, damp, dark, depressing, and if you're not in the best frame of mind, I can imagine it would just give you a swift kick to the nuts over the edge.

I can see the smoke from the fire she must have going, but I can't work out where it's coming from, so I just keep trudging straight. By the time I can see the

138

cabin, my fingers are about to fall off, my toes will definitely be left in my boots when I remove them, and my dick has retreated so far up inside myself right now that I could pass for an actual girl.

The closer I get, the slower I walk. It's not because I don't want to see her; I'm now panicking that she's not gonna want to see me. As I get closer and closer, the cabin is small and basic. It has logs stacked at the side of the door with an axe next to it. She's clearly strong enough now to cut the wood for herself, so that's something.

After seeing her in the hospital, it was heartbreaking how frail she looked. But if she's chopping her own wood, that's a good thing, right? Or what if she's not chopping her own wood? What if she's not alone? What if she's met someone else? Fuck, I hadn't even though of that till right this minute. What if I've been replaced? I hang back behind a tree in knee-deep snow and wait, and wait a little longer before convincing myself if she's in there fucking someone, they're not gonna come out, so I just need to go in.

I decide not to take any chances. I have my gun in the back of my jeans, which are now wet to the thigh and frozen to the knee. I can see every shaky breath I'm taking in the air in front of me, lingering and taunting me like the pussy I am. I don't want to take my gun out if I don't have to, basically, because it's too fucking cold to grab it, so I sneak my way closer to the cabin and grab the axe.

Resting my hand on the door handle, I push my way slowly inside, holding the axe in a death grip. To the left, the fire's roaring, and there's a small two-seater couch with a coffee table. Straight in front of me is the bed, and there's a small room on the back right wall, which must be the bathroom. I shut the door behind me. I'm in the middle of the cabin, which has the kitchen-type area.

There's no one here, the bed's made, the place is clean, the fire's roaring and the bathroom door is slightly open. I step one step in the direction of the bathroom as she shouts, "You best have taken your fucking boots off, arsehole!"

"Fuck." I mutter. My pounding heart is now slamming against my ribcage.

I let out a shaky breath and take a step back, removing my boots, then looking down at myself and my sodden jeans, so I remove them too, then the wet blanket and my leather jacket. Fuck it, my T-shirt is piss wet, too, so I take that off, leaving it all in a pile in front of the door. I'm in my boxers, and even they're wet. I step towards the bathroom again.

"Don't just leave the fucking wet stuff on the floor, dick. There's an airer behind the door. Put the stuff in front of the fire to dry, fuck's sake," she grumbles.

Well, we're off to a good start. She hasn't shot me yet, although I then realise I haven't spoken. Does she know it's me, or is she waiting for the new boyfriend that I'm pretty sure is a total figment of my imagination. Anything's possible. I place everything on the airer in front of the fire and tentatively step towards the bathroom,

I knock on the door. "Ray, baby, it's Steel. Can I come in?"

I hear her sigh a disappointed sigh before answering with, "Sure."

Now my mind's racing. She sounds disappointed, like maybe she was expecting someone else, and if she was, then how long do I have before he returns? "Well, are you fucking coming in, or are we carrying on this scintillating conversation through. The. Fucking. Door?"

I take a deep breath and step inside, clicking the door shut behind me. "Hey."

"You came all this way to say hey?"

"No!" I snap.

"Good conversation," she mumbles.

She's in the bath, submerged in bubbles, and the heat in here is stifling. The back of her head is resting on the tub, and her hair is wet, but hanging out of the tub and down to the floor, the top of her head is to me, and she hasn't moved to look at me or see if I'm alone. She has her left leg on the side of the tub, and I can see a lot of red, angry scars all over it. Fuck, Roach really did a number on her.

Stepping further in, I make my way to the toilet, the lids down so I sit on it and rest my elbows on my knees. "Are you ok?"

"Fucking peachy! What do you want, Steel?"

"I want my wife to come home."

"We're not fucking married anymore, dickhead," she spits.

This causes a smile from me, the first I think I've smiled in weeks. "Yeah, about that…"

"Don't…! Don't you dare fucking say we're still married!" She sits up in the tub, and I can see even now, she still has faint bruising, and the scar down her face is raised and angry. Her left arm is gripping the tub, and it's a fucking mess. There are scars all over it, and there are a few along her collarbones and chest, too.

"Yeah, we're still married!" I smile again.

"What the fuck did you do?"

"They didn't tell you…? Not my finest moment, but let's just say I did what I had to!"

"Ah, so you fucked someone… great." She lazes back into the tub, resting her head on the back and closing her eyes. "What do you want, Steel? I thought you would have snatched my hand off at being out of this shit show." She gestures back and forth between us. "I gave you an out. Why the fuck would you want to stay married? You clearly didn't want to be married, or you wouldn't have stuck your dick in that doctor. I'm exhausted, Steel. Just say what you came for, then fuck off!"

"Ray." Great, I came here on a wing and a prayer with a plan to track her to the ends of the earth to find her or die trying, to dedicate my life to seeking her out, and after a few weeks, I find her, she's here right in front of me, and I got nothing, no grand gestures, no life-altering declarations, zip. Nada. I got zilch!

After what seems like an hour, she stands from the tub, and I get to see the full extent of her injuries. I mean, the skin she removed where her Reapers tattoo and the tattoo of my name are pink and uneven, angry and raised. Her left arm is sliced in neat lines all along her forearm. There must be hundreds, and her left underarm has raised round lumps from the burns from the screwdriver, but they're all in neat rows; they really took their time. Her right leg is the same, almost like tally marks in straight, neat rows.

She turns and heads towards the door, pulling a robe from the back of it. I can't help but notice there's not one mark on any of her tattoos. Why preserve them and wreck every other piece of skin?

As she slides the robe on, she glances back over her shoulder. "Water's still warm if you wanna warm up. I can hear your teeth chattering from here. When your clothes are dry, you can head back to whatever fresh hell you came from, marriage or not. You're no longer my responsibility."

She steps through the door and clicks it shut behind her. Taking a deep, shaky breath, I close my eyes and wipe the tear away from my cheek. I slide into the bath and hope I don't lose my toes and that I grow a pair of balls to deal with Ray when I leave the sanctuary of the bathroom.

I step out of the bathroom with a towel wrapped around my waist and my boxers in my hand. She's curled up on the sofa with a mug in her hand, and there's another steaming one on the table in front of her. I smile and walk across, throwing my boxers on the airer. I pick up the mug and sit down on the table right in front of her.

"Thanks."

She just picks up her own mug and takes a drink, and we sit in silence.

After the drinks are gone, the air is certifiably uncomfortable. "You wanna talk?"

She just looks through me. "I think applying for divorce about sums up what I needed to say, but clearly, you've got something to say, or you wouldn't be here, so let's just get it over and done with, shall we?"

She just stares at me and waits and fucking waits. This is why she's our Enforcer. She leaves it till it's that uncomfortable, you'll tell her whatever she wants to stop the fucking awkward silence.

"I'm sorry, Ray." I shake my head. "I don't know what I was thinking…"

"Yeah, you do."

"What?"

"You know exactly what you were thinking. You believed what you were told because I've been so disloyal and such a terrible wife, then when you were given a so-called message from me and ended up in the medical wing and the doctor flashed her eyes and offered to flash you her stinking vag, you took it. You wanted to hurt me. Check. You wanted to punish me. Check. You wanted me to feel how betrayed you felt, how hurt you felt, and how alone you felt. Check, check, fucking check!" She shakes her head. "Did I miss anything about how fucking bad I made you feel? Huh?"

"Ray!"

"Nothing more to add? I think we're done here, Steel. I hope you find someone you truly deserve, and both of you can fuck till your dick falls off. Now I'm tired, so you should go!"

"Ray."

"Steel, pleasure as always. Don't let the door hit you in the arse on the way out."

She stands, throwing some more logs on the fire, then walks over to the bed, removes her robe and slides between the covers, leaving her back to me. Fuck. I start shaking my clothes out, and I'm just about to get dressed, and I feel like I hear the tiniest noise, the tiniest exhale, sniffle, whimper, something. I fucking hear something. I drop my clothes and climb into bed at the side of her, pulling her body as close to mine as I can get, and I wrap my arms around her and hug her so tight I wouldn't be surprised if she couldn't actually breathe.

I can feel her crying, although barely a sound comes from her. I can feel the way her body moves that she's trying to hold it in. She takes a deep breath.

"You were supposed to be mine."

"I know!"

"You were supposed to be my forever."

"I know!"

"I only asked for two things, and you couldn't do them!"

"I know!"

She stills and takes a breath. "You're off the hook."

"What?"

"I forgive you, we're done here. You can leave now, conscience clear, game over, no repercussions, just over. That's what you came for, right?"

"No, I came to apologise. I came to grovel and plead my case. I came to win you back and take you home. I can't live without you, Ray. I fucked up. The whole situation was fucked up, and everything you said was right. But I love you. I need you to come back with me. I need you to come home, Ray."

"My home's not there anymore, Steel. Even my own sister turned her back on me and believed I would screw you all over. What does that actually say about me, that the people I would die for think so little of me?"

"Baby."

"I'm not your baby anymore, Steel. I'm no one's anything, you should go before it gets dark. Otherwise, you'll get lost on the mountain. It did take you nearly two hours to get here."

"How do you know that?"

"You think I haven't protected myself?" She shakes her head at me. "Does anyone even fucking know me at all?" She turns to push me away to get out of bed, but as she rolls towards me, I back up so she drops on to her back. She brings her hands to my chest to push me off as I slide my body over hers. Grabbing her wrists, I slide them up above her head.

"Steel! What the actual fuck are you doing? Get the fuck off me!"

She tries to buck me off, and I groan against her.

"Steel!" she barks out at me.

And I grin down at her. "Come on, baby, you know I like it when you play hard to get."

"Fuck you, you arsehole, get off me!"

I have her pinned under me, and I slide my leg between hers, widening them so I can slide in between. I groan as I feel her wet heat against the front of my dick.

"Steel, I swear to fucking Hades himself, if your disease-ridden dick comes anywhere fucking near me, I will rip it off and beat you to death with the soggy fucking end!"

She thrashes against me, but that just causes me to groan more and her to shudder as my dick tries to force its way home.

Putting both her hands in one of mine, I lean up, pinning them above her head. I smile down at her. "You're gonna be a good girl and let me slide in without a fight."

She tries to snap at me with her teeth, trying to bite me, but I manage to pull away in time, causing me to laugh, which causes her to groan underneath me. I smile again. I still have an effect on her. Good to know, and she's wet fucking through. She can deny it all she likes, but we both know she's missed me, too. I reach down between us, and she starts thrashing again.

"Steel!" She tries to rip her hands away from me, but I have them in my giant, meaty hand and have them crushed together in a vice-like grip.

"I'm fucking warning you...! Steel...! You fucki—" And then she groans.

I slide straight in, right up to the hilt, balls deep, and I groan as my eyes roll back. "Fuck, baby, there's nothing feels as good as you."

"Get the fuck out of me, you bastard!"

I rock against her. "Be a good girl, and let me make you come."

"Fuck you, arsehole!" The venom in her voice as she spits in my face shocks me, but as I pull out slowly and slam back in, I feel her shudder underneath me, and as I'm fully seated, I grind my hips and make her whimper.

"Are you gonna play nice if I let your hands go?" She relaxes, and I release my grip just enough for her to pull one hand free, and she punches me in the ribs. "Naughty wife!" I flick her nipple as I reach up and wrangle her hand again, sliding it in with the other. She can't be trusted, so she stays as she is. I pull out again and slide painfully slow back in, and as I hit home again, I slide myself up over her clit, and she gasps.

"Motherfucker!"

"I've missed you so much!"

"I fucking hate you!" she spits again or tries to, but it comes out more of a breathy moan.

"Love you too, baby." I use my free hand to slide over her breast. She's gained some weight back, but it looks like she's been training hard. She was always ripped but had a feminine shape to her. Now, she's just hard-edged; that softness has gone, but it's still her; she's still my Ray.

She gasps for me, and I pick up my pace.

"Fuck! Steel."

I grind against her again, and she thrusts up against me, gasping again. Her gaze shoots to mine as I catch her just right, and she's gonna come; I can feel it. She's trying to thrash, to buck me off, but I've

148

got her hips pinned now, dragging myself up and down against her clit, giving her no room to escape or move from the orgasm that she's trying to fight. I grind into her again. I lean down and kiss her neck; that's the only mistake I make as she turns and tries to rip my throat out with her teeth. I can feel the blood run down my neck, and I laugh as I grind into her relentlessly, overstimulating her clit and rubbing my body against her as I slide in again, and there she goes, screaming my name like old times. I try to ride it out, but the sound of her coming tips me over the edge, and I can't help but crash over with her.

Both our breaths are coming in short, and as we gaze into each other's eyes, panting for breath, I don't ease up on the wrists, though once bitten twice shy and all that. As our heart beats start to slow and my dick softens, she lets out a dirty moan and grinds against me, and I know how much this turns her on, so I grind back.

"This changes nothing. I still fucking hate you!"

"I know." I grind slowly again as her hips come up to meet mine. I release my hold on her wrists, and she wraps her arms around me and pulls me in for a kiss that says, "I still love you, but you hurt me. I still want to be with you but can't allow myself to, and I will always love you." I take what she allows me to as she fists into the back of my hair, and my come slides around her thighs as she grinds against me,

"I love you," I whisper against her lips as I grind into her again, and a tear rolls across her cheek. "I love you," I tell her again.

I know it's not enough, I know this doesn't make it right. and I know she won't forgive me easily for a long time, but having her in my arms is all I can hope for right now. So I pour all my emotions into each kiss, each thrust and grind against her body, and each pound of our hearts against each others. I want her heart back, and I want to make sure nothing, including me, ever breaks it again. I pour my heart and soul into making love to her, hoping she feels how sorry I am, how much I love her, and how I will spend the rest of my life trying to make it up to her. The thing with the doctor was not me wanting to be with another woman, it was pure spite and hurt, and I know I fucked up. I hoped it would make me feel better in that moment, but all it did was break me, too.

It broke me that I could do that to the woman I love so fiercely. It broke me that I went in bare, something I've only ever done with Ray without thinking. Maybe if I'd thought about it, it never would have happened. As she shudders her release against me, I devour everything she gives me. I cherish her and hope to whatever gods out there that I can get her to forgive me, or at least try.

When I wake, it's with a smile on my face. I'm happy and content. I have my woman back, and although things are far from good, I know I can win her back. I know I have to try. As my eyes flutter open, the smile fades. She's not with me. She's not in bed. I rush to the bathroom.

"Ray? … Ray?" There's nowhere else she could be. I turn and rush to the door, flinging it open. It's stopped snowing, but fuck, it's cold, but its almost like I don't realise as I step onto the deck, shouting her name into the empty forest.

"Ray!" I take another step, "Ray, please."

Nothing. That's when I see the boot prints heading up the mountain.

"Fuck!" I roar to the sky as I rush inside. My clothes are folded neatly on the couch, but her knife, her favourite knife that she never goes anywhere without, her favourite knife that's always in her boot, is stabbed into the thick wood of the mantle over the top of the roaring fire, holding a letter to it. I just stare at it. I can't move. I can't will myself towards it. I don't want to know what it says. I just freeze, staring at it, not moving, not breathing, just nothing. I hear the crunching of snow outside and realise I've left the cabin door open. I turn. I can hear male voices, familiar male voices, then stomping and chattering.

I pull on my boxers as they push the door open. Ares, Dice and Tank. Ares walks straight over to me and pulls me in for a hug. "Fuck, Brother, I'm so, so sorry!"

I look between the other two, and their sombre, solemn faces say things I don't want to hear.

"What are you doing here?"

Dice closes the door, and Tank steps forward. "We got your message, we came straight away."

"Message… I didn't send a message."

Ares pulls out his phone and passes it to me.

Steel: She's gone, she's dead. (pinned location)

"We're sorry, Brother. I can't believe she's gone!" Tank steps forward and pulls me into a hug.

"She's not gone. I didn't send this. She was here last night. She was here. We made love all night and passed out… When I woke up, she was gone. She's not dead. She's gone to get wood. Yeah, she must have gone to get wood. Check the axe. I bet the axe is gone. She's just collecting wood, she's fine, dead, she's not dead, she's just —"

"Steel!" Ares snaps at me. "Brother, you're rambling. I got this message from you last night."

"I didn't send it, I didn't."

I turn towards the fireplace, and my hand shakes as I pull the knife out of the note and hold it to my chest. I try to steady my shaking hand to read it, my eyes fill with tears at the thought of her being gone.

Steel,
I know you're sorry. I am, too. I want you to know I forgive you.
We didn't manage to get it right in this lifetime. You're my one regret, regret that I wasn't enough, didn't deserve you, and couldn't change enough for you to fully love me for myself.

152

I will always love you. I'm leaving my heart with you. It belongs to you now and always will. I won't need it where I'm going!
Be good to yourself. I won't see you again, but I Know I will look for you in the next life, maybe just maybe, we'll get a second chance then.
Love, forever and always, Ray xx

"No! No! No!"

I start to grab my clothes, and I drop to my knees when I see them. Her rings. Her fucking god damned wedding rings, laying there on the pile of clothing she's taken off the airer and folded for me. Fucking hell. It breaks me, and I can't function for a single second longer. As far as I knew, they were still at the police station. They wouldn't let me have them back even though they were in my belongings. They were confirmed as hers, so she must have gone and collected them just to break my heart and give them back.

"Steel." Tank rests his hand on my shoulder. "Come on, get dressed. We need to go look for her. We can't leave her out there in this weather. We need to go before it starts snowing again."

Standing, I get dressed and slide her rings in my pocket. I grab the blanket, throwing it around me, and we head up the mountain, following her tracks. If it wasn't for the snow, we'd have no idea where she was, but as we trudge further and further, we reach the peak of the mountain. I drop to my knees and scream at the world. I can't bring myself to go to the edge. I can't bring myself to go any closer. There's a pile of clothes on the floor spelling out K.F.D with the 'D' underlined with sticks. Her favourite New Rock boots are at the ledge at the top of the cliff, and she may have left me behind, but I'd bet my life she wouldn't leave the knife and boots behind, so if she has no use for them, she also has no use for me either.

Ares takes a tentative step towards the edge while Dice pulls out his phone and starts taking pictures. "Are you fucking serious right now, Dice?" I scream at him.

"Steel, I need to see everything so I can find some clues to figure out where she's gone. I just need to document everything and take it back with me so I can find her.

"It's fucking obvious, isn't it?" Ares spits. "She went over the fucking edge." As he peers down, he points. "Look, there!"

We rush to the edge and, in the water, crashing into the rocks, are some more clothes. "She fucking jumped. It's fucking obvious. There's nowhere else for her to go. Below, it's just water and rocks and a cold, harsh death, and she'd sooner take that than sort things out with us. Well, the bitch can fuck off. I'm done playing her games. Good fucking riddance!"

"Argh!" I run and throw myself at him. "You lousy motherfucker, you never wanted her here!" I punch him in the face, and as his head whips around, he fires a shot back.

"She was like a motherfucking disease. She ripped through my club like a fucking tsunami, wrecking us all and leaving us gasping for breath

154

hanging on to driftwood for dear life; she's a fucking plague!"

I punch him again, throwing him onto the ground as we flail and punch and thrash at each other as Tank and Dice try to separate us.

"Stop, she wouldn't have wanted this," Tank tries to reason.

"Fuck what she would or wouldn't have wanted. She can fuck right off. She's fucking dead to me!" Ares shrieks.

"You take that back!" Dice spits and turns on Ares, punching him as I jump back, knocking Tank to his ass to get to Ares. The three of us are going hell for leather now, and I don't think anything will stop us. We're rolling around on the floor, and we're all just punching wildly in a complete frenzy. After a few minutes, a giant ball of snow is launched on our heads, and it dazes us as we fall back.

"What the fuck, Tank?" Ares spits.

"You're a fucking embarrassment. In fact, you all are. Just fucking look at the state of you all. You didn't deserve her. She was too good for all of you! This"—he gestures to the area and to the three of us—"is on you! She's gone again! And this is all on you!" He turns on his heels and starts to storm back down the mountain.

Dice pulls himself to his feet. "He's fucking right, we've fucking this up for the final time, and nothing we can do will make this better. I need to go home. I need to tell my boyfriend I couldn't save his sister, again."

He shakes his head and storms down the mountain, too. I'm fixated on the little specks of red on

155

the white canvas of the snow and how they are going in and out of focus before I realise I'm crying again.

"How could I have fucked this up so badly that she would toss herself off a mountain?"

"You had help, Brother, we're all to blame." Ares pulls me to my feet. "I'm so sorry, I didn't mean what I said, it's just…"

"She got under your skin, and you love her too!"

"Yeah, man. I fucking love that girl almost as much as Scar. She makes me angry and pushes my buttons and taunts me, but she makes me a better me."

"She made you a better you!" I drop to my knees and scrub my hands over my face, rubbing them into my hair. "She's really gone this time, isn't she?"

"I don't see any other outcome, Brother. There are no other tracks away. There's no other way out. She just didn't have enough fight left. We broke her; we all did. What do we do now?" Ares wraps his arms around me as silent tears roll down his face.

"We do what I do best. We find out who took her with Roach and burn his world to the ground with him in it. I'm gonna enjoy spending time in that office with whoever's responsible. I will be the motherfucking Reaper, and I will raze the city to the ground till I find the fucker."

I push up from the ground and wipe my face. I have a newfound purpose, revenge, and it will be the sweetest yet. I will not lose her in vain. I will earn my place by her side once again. She said she will wait for me in the next life. Well, I'm gonna burn what's left of this one down and take every fucker that ever hurt her with me.

"Till we meet again, my love!" I whisper to the wind, and I turn and make my way down the mountain, a hollow shell of the man I was when I started up it. But hollow will serve me well. I have nothing else, nothing in my life to distract me from my goal, and that's to make it back to her.

Some may call it a death wish. I call it a purpose. I will take that motherfucker out. Now, I need to find out who he is.

We make our way to the cabin in silence. Once I get there, I toss the place, take any scrap of anything that was hers or smells like her, and torch the place. This is the last place I was happy, even just for a moment, when I had her with me, under me, buried between her thighs, hearing her moan and feeling her come undone against me, knowing I'll never have that again. I burn it to the ground. If I can't be happy here, no one else will.

We make it back to the bottom of the mountain, and Ares' truck is gone. Clearly, Tank and Dice were done with our bullshit. We've barely spoken since the fight, and I'm still reeling at the things he said. I know he lashes out at her when he's hurt by her actions, and I know he doesn't mean it, but fuck, that shit hurts. I love that woman with everything I am.

"I'm sorry, Brother! I'm truly sorry. I didn't mean anything I said. I do actually... love her. I just don't know how to process what she makes me feel. With Scar, it's different. There's the fucking, and it makes sense. With Ray... there's none of that, but it feels similar, and I don't know what to do with all these fucking feelings."

"You wanna fuck Ray?"

"No! God, no." He shakes his head. "It's just… I don't know… Big!"

"Big?"

"Yeah, with her, everything feels big and important, and it confuses me."

"Come on, let's go home. I need to start burning the world down. I've got stuff to find out."

We drive back in silence, and I get Ares to drive straight to Bernie's. I tell them what's happened, and Marie breaks, but Bernie and Cade are stoic and just nod.

"Thanks for letting us know, son!" Bernie claps me on the shoulder and steers me towards the door.

"Wait, that's it? No questions, no nothing, just thanks for letting us fucking know?"

"Yeah, we already said our goodbyes, son. We just need to process. Thanks again." The door clicks shut behind me.

Ares gets out of the truck. "That was quick, how did it go?"

"Felt like they didn't give a shit, to be fair. They'd already said their goodbyes and just needed to process it. I need to see Bran and Demi."

Once we've seen them, I'm reeling. I mean, show some compassion. Demi breaks, and I cry, and we hug.

Bran just stands there. "Thanks for letting us know." He pulls Demi from my arms and closes the door on me. Ares just stares, as confused as me.

"What the fuck? Is that the same response you got from Cade and Bernie?"

"Yep, exactly the same, no emotion, no nothing, just thanks for letting us know!"

"Fuck!"

"Yep, I'm gonna get some sleep. I'm exhausted, and then tomorrow, I'm gonna hit the ground running. I need to see if Dice is gonna help me or if I need to find another tech guy."

As we walk to the apartment, Ares stops and turns to me. "Whatever it takes, Brother, I'm with you. I'll help however I can."

I nod and head up the stairs. As I walk in, Dane and Dice are sitting on the couch, not talking. Clearly, there's an atmosphere.

"Dane, I'm sorry, I…"

He waves a hand at me, "It's fine, Steel. Ray was her own person. She knew what she was doing. It's on her, no one else." He rises from the couch. "Thanks for letting me know." He walks off towards his room.

"What the fuck was all that? He's shown no emotion or anything. When I told him, he said the same. 'Thanks for letting me know.' That's it. I mean, what the fuck?" Dice is now pacing the living room.

"I got exactly the same from the others. Demi and Marie lost it, but Bran, Bernie and Cade, not a fucking flicker, like she means nothing. I mean, he's already talking past tense. Well, fuck that. She's still with me. She's still here. I can feel it." I walk over to him and hug him. "Dice, will you help me find him? I know you didn't want to get involved when I asked for

159

help to find her, but you came through in the end. Will you help me now? I'm gonna kill that motherfucker, and I need access to the office."

"Yeah, man, I'll help, let's burn his world to the fucking ground."

I hug him hard. "I love you, Dice. Now, let's get some rest. Tomorrow, I wanna start following Roach's last moves. See if the slimy fucker can lead me anywhere."

As my head hits the pillow, her scent surrounds me from the sheet I tore off the bed to bring back with me, and I cry myself to sleep and sleep like the dead.

Scar

Ares walks into my dad's, and I wasn't expecting him home. He'd rushed off in the night after a text from Steel. He hadn't said what he wanted, just that Steel needed him. It must be nice to be needed by someone. I was once her ride-or-die, her sister from another mister, then she ruined it all, and now I'm paying for it. She abandoned me, promised to always have my back, and when I went to the hospital to see her, she wouldn't even let me in. She wouldn't even look at me; I just wanted to explain, but she wouldn't even see me.

"Scar, did you hear me?" Ares's voice cuts through my rambling mind. That's all that seems to happen lately. She consumes my every thought. I'm so angry at her for what she did to Steel, and then I remember she didn't do anything, and then I'm angry at her for disappearing, then I remember she was kidnapped and tortured, and then I'm angry that I didn't know. I went to see her at the hospital and remember she wouldn't see me, so I'm even angrier at her. She always had my back, but this time, she's just left me flailing in her wake alone.

"Scar, princess."

My eyes snap to his, and I smile. "Hey, when did you get back?"

"Scar, I've been standing here for ten minutes. Are you okay?"

I wave my hand at him. "Yeah, just a long day. I'm gonna go for a bath, then have an early night."

"Scar, I need to talk to you? Did you hear anything I just said?"

"Yeah."

"Scar, I need you to sit back down."

I sit back at the table.

"It's Ray."

"I don't want to talk about her. I'm still angry at her for everything she's done. I'm not ready to forgive her yet. When she apologises, then I'll think about it."

"Scarlett!" My dad shouts. My dad never shouts. My eyes shoot to him. "Scar, it's Ray… she's gone."

"I know, and she can stay gone till she wants to apologise. Then I will listen. Till then, Dad, I'm not interested."

I push from my seat and head towards the bathroom. Clicking the door shut behind me, I can hear them talking. It sounds heated, but I don't care. I don't care about anything anymore. She did this to me: she draws you in and makes you think you're her everything, then you do one thing she doesn't like, and she tosses you aside. She hasn't been anywhere near since she got out of hospital and made a mess of the club. She set it on fire. I mean, what kind of person does that to her family?

162

I can't get over the things she's done. But what I can't get over really is the fact that I know none of it's true, and I hate myself, so I'm manifesting it on her, and I can't bring myself to drop it and apologise because if it was me, if I screwed this up and hurt her, I know I can't come back from that.

I sob as I slide down the door and crumple to the floor. I let it all out, and I break. It was me. I let her down. I thought the worst when I should have known better. She would never do the things she was accused of and she wouldn't have hidden away while doing it, either. If she thought we deserved it, she would have shouted it from the rooftops while she destroyed us all. How could I have been swept so far off track that I betrayed and abandoned my sister, my heart and soul?

She's the reason I'm still breathing. I need to make this right.

There's a knock on the door. "Scar, princess, can I come in?"

"Yeah." I breathe on a stutter as I scoot away from the door, still crumpled on the floor.

"Princess." The tone says it all as he bends down and scoops me into his arms, sliding his body under mine so I'm cradled against him in his lap, and I sob into his chest.

"It's my fault she's gone." I sob. "We always had each other's back, and the only time she's ever truly needed me, I turned on her. I need to make it right. I need to see her. Can you help me?"

I feel him shaking his head against mine. "Princess, she's gone, she's dead. I'm so sorry we didn't get there in time."

"You saw her…?"

"No. We followed her tracks to the edge of a cliff. She had taken her clothes off and spelt out K.F.D and underlined the D with sticks, then the footprints led to the end of the cliff, and there were some clothes in the water, she went over the edge, princess. I'm sorry."

I scramble from his lap, slamming my back against the wall. "No, no, no, she wouldn't. She would never, not to herself."

"Princess, it's not your fault. It's on us all. We all turned on her and let her down. We were all wrong!"

He stands and takes a step towards me, but I rush out of the door. Dad's sat at the table, his head in his hands, sobbing into them as I rush into the room. "Dad, say it isn't true, she's not, she wouldn't, you know she wouldn't. She wouldn't do that, she wouldn't, Dad. Please tell him, tell him it's not true, tell him, Dad. Tell him, tell him!"

My dad just shakes his head and cries into his hands, sobbing out, "She's gone, Scarlett, it's too late!"

"No!" I bellow at him. "No!" I run out of the apartment and into the square, screaming at the top of my lungs as my legs give way. I crumple to the floor. She can't be gone. She can't leave me. I need her. I've always needed her. Everything's so fucked up. I can't go on without her. I can't.

164

I startle as arms wrap around me and lift me to my feet, my shaking legs barely supporting me. "It's okay, princess. I've got you. I will always have you."

"But you're not her!"

"I know, princess, and I'm sorry, but I'm here, and I will always be here."

I push at his chest. "You can't promise that; she promised that and left me. She chose to leave me. You can't promise that, no one can!" I push to leave, but he pulls me closer.

"Princess?"

"Don't, Ares, you can't fix this, no one can. She's my heart, and she's gone, and now I'm... I'm... I'm nothing." I push him again. "I just wanna be alone!"

I know I'm taking it out on him. I know I'm not being fair, and I know I will have to apologise at some point, but in all honesty, I couldn't give a flying fuck at the minute. I'm devastated and lashing out, and that's exactly what I did to Ray. Now, she's gone, and I can never make it right. My knees buckle. I drop to the floor again. I've barely made it half a dozen steps from him, and all I can do is sob. "Ares, I'm sorry. I'm so sorry." I shake my head. "I'm doing it again. I'm blaming you, I blamed her, and soon I will have no one. What's wrong with me?"

"You're grieving, princess, and I will always love you. You're my world, my everything. I know I'm not her, and it's not the same, but I promise I'm not gonna choose to leave you, ever!" He drops to the floor and cradles me in his arms while I sob.

Dice

I wake up wrapped in his arms, and I hold as still as possible while I take in every line, every freckle. He's kept the beard, and fuck, I thought he was hot before, but now, I mean, I've always been good looking, I've always known I was. I'm not big-headed about it, it's just a fact, and I've never had any trouble with the guys, but him... well, fuck. He's on a different level. I'm in awe, and as I'm taking in every slight feature, the corner of his mouth ticks up, and my eyes fly to his, but he keeps them closed.

"You're staring, creeper!"

"How the hell did you know I was staring? You haven't even opened your eyes."

"I'm a trained assassin. I knew you were awake before you did."

I bark out a laugh. "You're ridiculous!" Then I school my features, and my heart breaks a little. I used to say that to her. He reminds me so much of her.

"You're thinking about her, aren't you?"

"Yeah, you wanna talk about her?"

"Nah, I'm good. Let me take your mind off things."

"I'm not sure you can."

But he's pulling the covers off and already sliding down my body and lying between my legs. His hands skate up my thighs as his breath tickles the inside of my leg.

"Dane."

He grins up at me as he takes my dick in his hand and strokes up the length before licking my shaft and sliding his tongue around my head, causing an illicit groan to come from me as he slides his other hand up to cup my balls. His sex drive is insatiable. I suppose that's what I get for falling in love with a guy ten years younger than me. Fuck.

He licks and nips at my dick as he slides the head around his mouth as he takes me all in. I groan, and he chuckles, causing me to groan again.

As he deepthroats me again, the door flies open.

"Time to get up, Dice. We need to get started."

"Fuck…! Steel, I love you, but you really need to start to knock, and Dane, please stop sucking my dick like a pornstar when Steel's in the room." Dane chuckles around my dick but carries on, and I throw my arm over my face, groaning. "Steel, can you give us half an hour?"

"You can have five minutes, Dane. Work your magic fast. We need to go!"

Dane removes the hand cupping my balls and gives Steel a thumbs-up while he deepthroats me again.

"Seriously?" I groan and moan and gasp at the same time. This man is going to be the death of me. Death by dicking, that's what it's gonna say on my tombstone. "Here lies Dice, Dicked to Death by Dane!"

My dick pops out of his mouth as he laughs, surprising me before I realise I said that out loud, and groan again. He goes straight back to sliding his tongue around me, and I stutter my breath. "Fuck!" He nips at the tip before sliding me back inside his mouth. He chuckles and sucks harder as I come down his throat before popping my dick out of his mouth, sliding up my body, and giving me the filthiest kiss. Why is it so hot tasting myself on him?

After he breaks the kiss, he checks his watch, "New record. Steel will be impressed." He shoves me over and slaps my arse before climbing off the bed and walking out of the room, totally naked.

I groan. "Fuck my life!"

As I grab my shit and head to the shower, Dane is just coming out with a towel wrapped around his waist. He kisses me as I walk past. I grab the towel and spank his ass, leaving him to walk back to the room naked.

"Fucking hell. I've seen far too much of your dicks and asses to last me a lifetime. I think I'm gonna need to bleach my eyeballs."

"Start fucking knocking then."

"Touche! Now hurry the fuck up. We've got a Roach to exterminate!"

When I come back from the shower, Dane is sitting at the counter with his laptop open, and Steel is

168

handing him breakfast and setting mine beside his. "Dane, come on. Don't be a dick. You know we can find the stuff easier if you help us with your big fancy computers at the base."

"Steel, I love you, but I'm not interfering. I promised Ray."

"Dane, she's gone. We need to destroy the cocksucker that helped Roach. We need to find him, and we need to destroy him."

"Steel, just stay away from it all, okay? There are still things going on that need to be dealt with, and you two playing fucking Lone Ranger and Tonto is only gonna make matters worse!" He shakes his head. "Please listen to me when I ask you to leave this alone."

"But—"

"Steel, nope." I get a kiss on the head as he scoops up his laptop, throws it under his arm, grabs his breakfast, and is out the door.

"Shall we follow him?"

"No, Steel, we're not following him. Let's go have a snoop and see what we can find on Roach."

As we head into the tech room, Viking and Blade join us. "Why aren't you at Carmen's?" Steel asks.

"Told her I wasn't going back till I find Ray." He shrugs. "Now I can't bring myself to go back till I've found the fucker that caused all this. How can I hold my head up and say I can protect Car if I can't find this fucker?"

"So, have we decided who it is?" Blade asks. He has his butterfly knife in his hand, rolling it around through his fingers and back over his thumb. It's a distraction for him when he's feeling more than he wants to. He's been doing a lot more lately.

"Dante fucking Crane!" I spit. "It has to be him. If it walks like a fucking duck, quacks like a fucking duck, then my bet is it's that motherfucker, but I'm missing something I can't place: why Ray?"

"There's no connection?" Steel asks. We keep going over this, and we're at a loss.

"I'll be fucked if I can find one other than him wanting to take over The Armoury, but he hasn't gone after any of the others that we know of, not like Ray."

"So where the fuck do we go from here? Do we even know what this motherfucker looks like?" Viking asks, and it's a valid question. It's just no, we don't. No one who has had dealings with him seems to be breathing.

I start tapping on the keys. "We're gonna start at the end and work backwards. The night Ray lured Roach here and kicked his ass."

We track him and trail, and lots of footage has already been recorded over. A few places have everything backed up, so we run a map and a timeline, and as it's starting to get dark, we notice a pattern, "There's an area here." I mark it on the map. "He disappears for hours on end. That must mean something."

"This whole area here seems to be rundown, condemned, virtually derelict buildings. That must be where they're either running their gang from, or that's where they had Ray. I'm printing the maps off and giving you all an area, we need to search every building. Take note of everything in them, no matter how small."

I start the printouts.

"So what's in that area? Why's it so run down?" Viking leans in closer.

I start running some searches. "It's like it's a whole town, fucking area is a good ten blocks, maybe twelve. The buildings all belong to... fuck knows, they're hiding behind shell corporations. It's gonna take a bit, but they were purchased for regeneration around twenty-three years ago. There's a thirty-year hold on them. They can't regenerate the area till the thirty years have expired. It seems they bought all the properties within a year or so, and then nothing, just sitting there decaying."

"What's the name of the company?"

"Hang on. I'm working on it!"

With our plans in our hands, we decide to divide up the area so we can cover it more efficiently. Texting all the guys, we sort ourselves into pairs: Steel and Ares, me and Priest, Tank and Viking, Blade and Dozer. We have an area of about two to three blocks each. We decide to call it a night and head out at first light.

"Wait, I've got it ... It's SCYLLA."

"Scylla? What the fuck kind of name's that?" Blade asks.

"I fucking knew it!" Steel blurts out, "Everything comes back to them fuckers." He starts to pace, fists clenched.

"Steel, who the fuck are they?"

"It's the fucking pas. The fucking Armoury, the fucking bastard family, my fucking in-laws. How the fuck does everything keep coming back to them? This is all twisted."

"How do you know that?"

"When we went to sort out the banking after the wedding with them, they started telling Demi and me everything, but it was all too much. The money, the organisations, the companies, the businesses, everything... so they said they would tell us later, then everything went to shit, and it never happened, but Scylla was one of the names they mentioned. It just didn't mean anything to me back then. This is all to do with them, but why? It all seems too personal. We were kidnapped, and the girls were sent those videos. That's not business-related. Then locking me up and pitting me against Ray. It's as if someone's trying to break us up, like someone didn't want us together, but then they're going after The Armoury too, so they've clearly fucked someone over, and now they're going back after them." Steel shakes his head and scrubs his hand through his hair.

"So if Cade and Bernie are Scylla, that means Dane, Bran, and Ray must be too. And now you and Demi. Do you know how to access any of their companies or businesses? Can you get us behind the curtain?"

"Not that I know of. They've handed over our legit accounts, but everything else is still in trust."

I tap a few more keys. "So we search tomorrow for any signs of where Roach had been visiting, and we go from there. Leave me with the Scylla thing and The Armoury, and I'll see what I can find out."

"Wait, do you feel that?" Blade asks, stepping to the window and opening it. "Listen."

"Fucking helicopters, multiple, what the fuck they doing here?" I storm out the door and head to the back of the clubhouse. As we stand on the field, our apartment door flies open.

Dane's running this way, dressed in full tactical gear, gas masks gripped in his hand. As he runs past us, he shouts over, "I love you, the shit's hit the fan. I'll be back when I can!"

"Dane, what the fucks happening?"

"Dante, he's trying to bring us down. He's hit one of our bases. Be careful and stay away from all this."

He stops when he gets onto the field, and as the helicopter comes over, it tosses a ladder down, which he grabs onto. Before he's climbed more than a few rungs, they lift off and head north, Dane climbing as they fly.

"Fuck, if I wasn't scared out of my mind right now, that would have been sexy as fucking hell!"

Steel slings his arm around me. "Don't worry, he can take care of himself. I'm starting to realise just how naive we've been when it comes to them and their capabilities. Come on, let's get some food and go to bed. We have a busy day tomorrow."

Tank

I wake up and make Skye breakfast. As I take it into her, she tries to sit up too fast and grabs at her head. Placing the breakfast on the bedside table, I sit beside her.

"You need to slow down." I rest my hand on our bump. She's so big now. He could be here anytime. She's due next month. With everything going on, she's been more stressed than normal, and the whole Ray situation is really taking its toll. She's struggling to come to terms with her loss. Well, actually, she's not struggling, more refusing. She believes Ray's still alive and wouldn't toss herself off a cliff "like a pussy," Skye's words, not mine. But I'm inclined to agree with her. The Ray we saw that night wasn't giving up. She's up to something, and whatever it is, it's gonna get messy, and she wants us as far away from it as possible, so we're ignoring the fact that we don't think she's dead and just going along with the general consensus that she topped herself.

I rub at her tummy for her as the heat from my hands settles Tray and soothes her too. "You gonna be okay while I'm gone, love? I can get Demi or

Beauty to come and sit with you if you don't wanna be alone?"

"I'll be fine. Just be careful, okay?"

She lets out a shaky breath as she tries to sit up. "Just really uncomfortable." She tries to stretch her back out but sighs. "I'm fine, honestly. I'll call if I need anything, promise."

"I love ya both."

She smiles at me, and I pull the covers back and start to slide in. "What are you doing? I thought you had to go?"

"I do, but then you smiled at me like that, and I think I need to show you how much I love you before I leave."

"Ah, you do, do you?"

"Uh-huh, and I think it may make you more comfortable."

"Really?" She cocks a brow at me, and I grin at her.

I slide my hand under her stomach and into her sleep shorts, and she whimpers as my finger slides across her clit and into her soaking pussy.

Groaning, she tightens around my finger. I start to pump it gently, and she whimpers again. "You want me to stop, love?"

"Fuck no. I need you inside me now. Tank, please," she rasps.

I gently roll her onto her side and slide her shorts down while she removes her vest top. Her tits are full, her nipples hard, and I remove my clothes and slide in behind her. Her stomach's too big to go any other way now. Fuck, fuck... I just love the feel of her body against mine, no matter how I can get it. I slide one arm under her neck and wrap it around her to tease her nipples, and she gasps.

"Too much?"

"Yeah!" she gasps. "Don't stop!" I chuckle as my other hand roams over her stomach, caressing every inch. I never understood when I heard men say they loved their woman barefoot and pregnant till recently, and fuck, I've got to say, she's glorious. As I slide my hand down between her legs, I gently guide myself to her. "Tank, fuck, just hurry up."

"So impatient, love." I chuckle into her neck as I nip down against it. She rocks back, trying to slide my dick in herself, but I hold steady before applying pressure with only the tip.

"Jesus, Tank. Please, I need you!"

"Anything for you, love."

I gently push in, and she winces, so I stop. Then, when she relaxes, I push again, and this time, I'm met with a sag against me and a satisfied exhale. "Tank," she gasps as she starts trying to rock her hips, and I adjust my position before sliding out and back in again gently. She quivers around me. "Yeah, like that, just like that." She's biting down on her lip, and I nip at the skin on her shoulder.

"How's that, love?"

"Fuck, Tank, yeah, like that."

I slide out and gently back in as her hand slides down to her clit. I rest my hand over hers and apply a little more pressure to her fingers as she rubs across the tight little nub. She shudders at the contact, and I grin into her neck. She's totally at my mercy, or I'm

176

totally at hers; I haven't quite figured it out yet, but I rock back and forth, and she shudders and quivers against me. I can feel her tightening, and she picks up the pace with the fingers, so I pick up my pace with my hips, hitting just a little harder than before. She gasps and pushes back, and that's all the encouragement I need to pick up the pace again. She gasps, and I back off.

"Don't stop, please, I'm so close."

Grinning against her, I pull out altogether and tug her onto her back as she groans with disappointment. Sliding down, I clamp my mouth over her clit and suck it into my mouth, sliding in two fingers and rubbing her g-spot. "Fuck, Tank."

She gasps as I grin into her pussy and bite down on her clit as her back arches off the bed. She starts to gasp for breath, and as she stiffens and holds her breath, biting her lip, I lick and nip till over the edge she goes. As she comes into my mouth, I groan. She tastes so sweet, and I keep sucking as she quivers against me, lapping till I taste every last drop of her. Once her breathing steadies, I lift one leg and push her back onto her side. I slide in over her and enter her still-pulsing opening. Groaning, I pull out and push back in, and she tightens her grip on the covers.

"Harder," she gasps. "Just a little harder."

I oblige because the look of sheer ecstasy across her face is addictive. I keep pushing, and when she gasps, it turns into a moan. I know that's the spot, and I pick up my pace, and she grips down on me. I shudder as I feel myself start to come. She gasps as she feels it, too. Filling her up till I collapse beside her, still buried deep.

I kiss her shoulder. "How was that, love?"

"Fucking perfect." She grins as she kisses my hand that's resting across her. "Fucking perfect!"

Kissing her again, I say, "Let me get you cleaned up."

"No...! Don't. I want to stay like this. It's the most perfect I've felt in days, please?"

"Whatever you want, my love." As I pull out of her, she groans, and I slide my fingers up her inner thigh, finding my come seeping onto them and slide it back in. She shudders against me.

"Can you manage another?" I smile against her shoulder as I rub my come into her clit.

Biting down on her lip, she nods, and I start pumping my fingers as I rub over her clit. She grinds back into me as she chases another release. Once she comes, she sags against me, and her breath relaxes and evens out. I can feel her falling back to sleep, so I slide out from behind her and let her rest.

As I arrive at the clubhouse, everyone's there already. We head out to the area on the map. It's a place we've never heard of, but as there's nothing and no one here, it's hardly surprising. It's like a ghost town, so our teams split into the four corners and arrange to meet in the middle. Me and Viking search the houses that are all boarded up, with graffiti everywhere. Clearly, kids have been using these places to drink and get high. As we go from house to house, searching every room, we find nothing.

We go from house to house, street to street and so on. When we arrive at an industrial area near the town centre, we stop to take a drink and call the others.

"Anything?"

"Nope!" Steel answers.

"Nothing this end either," Priest says.

"Nah, man, nothing. We're nearly at the industrial area, so we'll see you soon. Stay safe, brothers." Dozer hangs up.

"Fuck, I hoped we would find something, anything"

"Hey." Viking bumps my shoulder. "We're not finished yet. There's still time."

"Viking, we've been out here most of the day."

"Then let's get a move on so we're done before it gets dark."

As we enter the industrial area, there's what looks like a small strip mall with an old pharmacy, a doctor's office, a mini market, a hardware store and a coffee shop.

"You see what I see?" Viking asks, and I nod because all the shop fronts are grimy, filthy really, with torn paper covering the windows, but although the doctor's office still looks a mess, it almost looks … cleaner. The newspaper over the windows is newer, less discoloured and torn.

Texting the group, I pull my gun as Viking does the same, and we head towards the door.

"See that?" I nod to the camera above the door.

Viking nods.

I text the group again. The door's locked. I check the door to the pharmacy next door, and it's open. The guys text back to wait. and we'll all go in together, so we drop a pin and wait. It's only five minutes or so till they all arrive, and Steel kicks the door in as we all take cover; as fuck knows what we're gonna find in there.

We split up and search every room. There's clear evidence someone's been here more recently than anywhere else in this shit hole of a town but nothing that says Ray was even here. Dice pulls his phone out and starts typing. We clear the place, and just before we make a move to leave, Dice stops us. "Here, on the floor plans. This place has a basement."

"Fuck. Everyone, search again, search the floors, walls for secret doors, fucking anything. Take this place apart if we have to!" Ares barks as we all scatter again.

"Here!" I yell. "There's a push panel under the stairs in the back of the cupboard." Pushing the panel, the door springs forward, and the smell that hits makes me gag. "Fuck… it smells like something's died down there!"

"We can't all go in. Guys, form a perimeter around the building, heads on a swivel in case they are watching the cameras. Steel, stay here with Dice. I'm going in alone."

"Wait, I need to go. I need to see!" Steel gasps.

"Just let me check it first, okay?" Ares nods to him, and his shoulders sag, but he nods back. We all turn and exit the building, leaving Ares to go in and Dice and Steel waiting by the door. I step into the fresh air. I take my first real breath since finding the door.

Ares

I pull my shirt up over my face as Tank wasn't wrong when he said it smelt like someone had died here.

I use the light on my phone, but as I step to the top of the stairs, there's a light switch. Maybe if they've been using this space, there will be electricity, so I flick the switch, and the lights flicker on with an amber glow, filling the room from the fluorescent bulbs. I gasp. It's a dirtier version of Ray's kill room. The room itself is filthy, to say the least. There's a table like you'd find in the morgue with leather straps attached to it. It's got dried blood, among other things, on it. I mean, a lot of blood and stuff. It's disgusting. There's a table at the side of it with tools, knives, and scalpels, some clearly new, others rusty but all bloodied.

There's a wall full of screens. Ray said she'd heard and watched everything, and in front of it is a high-back chair with leather straps on it, too. It looks like she was strapped into the chair and made to watch everything. There's a small table at the side with some clamps. They look like the sort that keep your eyes open. Looks like she couldn't even close her eyes to get away from everything. There's blood, and shit literally everywhere. It doesn't look like there was anywhere clean or anywhere for her to sleep.

I take a deep breath and regret it immediately. It smells like death in here. There's a wall with photos pinned to it, and as I look over them, they're of us. Someone's been following us for months, maybe longer. There's another wall that just has photos of Ray, and the ones that have other people in their faces are scratched out over and over again.

Someone clearly had an obsession with Ray. "You can come down!" I say as I close my eyes and take another breath that I immediately regret again.

As Steel and Dice reach the bottom of the steps, they say, "Fucking hell!"

Dice gags, but Steel pushes forward straight to the wall with Ray's pictures and runs his fingers over them, "She looked so happy here. With me, with us all." He caresses every photo as if it's her, here in person.

"She was." I remind him that she was made for our club and us, and I'm regretful of the part I took in pushing her away. I miss my sister, the bane of my existence, as she was down in my phone, but I miss her terribly. How the fuck are any of us gonna be the same again without her? Especially Steel, he's riding on a death wish, and that's never gonna end well.

"Don't move anything yet. Let me just take some photos. We can check the finer details at home." We take a step back to the bottom of the stairs while Dice takes pictures of everything, even the blank floor and wall space. He takes close-ups of all the leather straps, and then he pulls a load of plastic bags from his rucksack. "I need to collect everything up. We're taking as much as we can carry." Dice informs us. "Steel?" Dice hands him some bags. "Can you check those filing cabinets over there? Bag anything up you can find and label which drawer they came from." He hands him a Sharpie.

"Ares, can you help me remove these straps? I've got a guy who can run DNA on them and see who else touched them. Put these on." He hands us both some latex gloves, and we get to work.

We take everything down off the walls and bag it. That's when Dice finds the camera. It's tiny, it's so small that if you didn't know what you were looking for, you'd miss it. "The sick fuck was recording everything they did to her, watching her every move!"

"Can you find the footage?" It's a long shot, I know, but if we can catch a glimpse of Dante, we will know who we're looking for.

Dice takes the camera off the wall and follows the cable across the room. It's tucked right into the corner of the wall. The mortar has been ground out and replaced with new over the top of the cable, and as Dice gently tugs, it goes into the wall behind a brick. Dice takes a knife out and slides it into the mortar surrounding the brick, and gently teases it till he can remove the brick. There's a black box connected to the end of the cable.

"I need to get this back to my laptop."

"Do we need anything else?" Dice takes one more look around the room, shakes his head, and we leave with all the bags we've collected. Dice puts what he can into his backpack, but the rest we hand out between us, securing them under our jackets, and we head home.

Pulling up outside the clubhouse, Dice collects all the bags. I think I should go through these on my own first and tomorrow, we can go through what we've found.

"I'm coming!" These are the first words out of Steel's mouth. He's been expressionless since we entered that basement, and even now, it's like he's not really here.

"No!" I shake my head. "I'll go with Dice, but you're not watching any footage that we haven't vetted. There are certain things, Brother, that you won't recover from, so let us check it all first, and we can show you what we can tomorrow."

Steel sighs. "Ares!"

"Steel, please just let us do this."

He turns and walks away from us, storming back to the apartment. "Right, everyone, head home. We'll go through all this and see what's important and what's not. I'll call church tomorrow once we have something to share, okay?"

They all turn in as Dice, and I head to the tech room. I swing by the kitchen and grab some food and drinks as we go. I have a feeling it's gonna be a long night.

We start by connecting the box to the computer, and by "we," I mean Dice does while I stand there and twiddle my thumbs. He says it's encrypted, so he needs to run it through a programme that will, I don't know, make it not encrypted or some shit. Then we start sorting through all the paperwork and attaching anything of relevance to Ray on the wall with the other stuff we've found. To be fair, everything in the filing cabinets had to do with the surgery itself. Only the stuff attached to the wall has anything to do with Ray, but we hang it all up and destroy anything not of relevance.

It must be the early hours before the encryption is finally over, and we can start to watch. As we wait for it to load onto the screen, I freeze with bated breath. I'm not sure I can watch this. I know it's gonna be bad. I know I'm not gonna be able to sleep once I've watched it, but there's nothing else we can do now. We just have to see what the sick fucks have done to her and see what we can find to use against them and hopefully bring the fuckers down.

My breath stutters as the screen comes to life, "It's the night she was taken. She's still in her gown from the event."

She's strapped to the chair, and we can see shadows moving around the room, but none of them step into view of the camera. After a while, Ray starts to stir. Her eyes flicker open, and there's a gasp before she schools her features and then looks bored.

There's a voice that comes from the direction she's looking. "Surprised to see me, Reaper?"

She shrugs one shoulder but doesn't say anything. A hand strikes her across the face the next second, and a familiar voice spits at her. "Dante asked you a fucking question, bitch!" Roach steps forward and grabs her around the face. "Answer him."

A feral smirk slides across her face, and her gaze shifts over Roach's shoulder.

"Even after I taught him to fight, he still slaps like a little fucking bitch."

Roach gets right in her face and starts cursing at her, but her gaze never falters from Dante.

"So what do you want B— "

She's slapped again, but by Dante, this time as he shoves Roach out of the way. He gets right in her face and spits, "Don't you fucking dare!"

He grabs her around the throat and squeezes. "I swear to Hades himself you dare say that name, and I will fucking kill you right now!"

She grins up at him. "Ah, come on, B – "

She's gripped tighter around the throat so the words won't come out.

"You'll fucking pay for that, Reaper. You will join me one way or another, you were supposed to be mine, not theirs, and you will join me, or I'm going to destroy everyone you fucking love, including that cunt of a thing you call a husband! How dare you get in the car stinking of him? The smell was vomit-inducing."

"Do you want me to tell you what he did to me before I left? How he fucked me over the back of the sofa and then pushed his come back inside me and sent me to the ball dripping? Is that what you could smell? The other guy seemed to like it. His raging boner and dilated pupils were a dead fucking give away!"

She's slapped again. "Shut the fuck up, you dirty little whore!"

187

"He's still inside me now. You wanna see? Can you smell him on me?" She tips her head back and groans. "I can still fucking taste him."

Next thing, he walks away and gets a needle, injecting her with it till she's out again.

"Roach, cut that fucking dress off her and clean her up. I want every inch of her clean. I want every lingering smell of him fucking gone. You hear me?"

Dante pushes past Roach and out of the basement.

"It's him, Ares, Dante. He's the driver," Dice rewinds and pauses the screen, and we take a closer look.

"She clearly knows him. He knew her as Reaper, but did you hear him say, 'I swear to Hades'? Ray says that all the time, she never swears to god, always Hades. Cade does the same."

"Fuck, let's just keep watching. I don't know how much I can take, so let's just push through while we can." We skip through Roach taking her dress off and cleaning her as the dirty little perv clearly has depraved issues with the way he touches her and slides his hands over her.

When Dante enters the room, Ray's already awake. It's the next day, and Dante tells her about the screens and fires them all up. Her arms are strapped to the chair, and she's totally naked.

"You look and smell so much better than yesterday. Let's start again. I'm sorry for slapping you. Roach!"

Roach walks over to her with a scalpel, grabbing her arm.

"No! Not the tattoos," Dante says. "They're for me."

Roach grabs her other arm and slices into it. She doesn't wince. She doesn't take her eyes off Dante. Roach might as well not be in the room. He's clearly frustrated by her lack of acknowledgement, and as he goes to cut again, Dante stops him.

"No! She gets one there for every day those fuckers don't come to find her, a reminder of how long it takes them to give a shit."

"Fuck," I spit at Dice. "That's what those marks were on her forearm, a cut for every day we didn't look for her."

"Shit!" Dice scrubs his hands down his face. "I... Fuck... "

"Come on, let's carry on!"

Roach unties her wrist from the chair and ties it around her neck so that her hand is on the back of her neck and her elbow is up in the air. He takes out a blow torch and starts heating up a cross-head screwdriver.

"I'm gonna ask you some questions, and every one you refuse to answer, you will be punished."

Dante asks questions, and every time she refuses to answer, Roach pushes the hot screwdriver into the underside of her arm. She grits her teeth, and her face contorts, harsh breaths past her lips, but she doesn't give more than a grunt at the pain. She never answers a single question, and after he puts a neat row of holes in her arm, she passes out.

Dante throws a bucket of water over her, and she wakes with a start before sliding that mask firmly back over her face. "Okay, you won't answer questions about the MC. Let's see what you have to say about The Armoury. Everything you refuse to answer, you lose a nail." Roach comes back with some pliers and unties her hand. She yanks it from his grasp and manages to punch him in the face before he wrestles her arm back to the chair.

He removes every nail, finger and toe, and she still says nothing. "Fuck... she's one tough-ass bitch." I shake my head.

We watch footage after footage of Roach slicing her arm every day and asking questions and her ignoring them. We skip through all the stuff when she's left alone and focus on what we can learn from Dante and Roach. She's been there for days, and she hasn't eaten. She sleeps and sits in that chair. They allow her a few sips of water throughout the day, but she just pisses and shits in that fucking chair. There's a hole in the seat and a bucket underneath, which Roach empties every day. Still, the smell must be horrific.

We skip through more torture, and it turns out it's Roach who gives Dante the location of our armoury. He was away at Carmen's, so he didn't know we had moved it when we met with The Armoury. In fact, everything Dante had on us comes from Roach. Ray never says a word other than to taunt them and ridicule Roach when he tries to rape her while Dante's not there. She ends up with a beating instead, as with all her taunting, he just can't get it up. Thank heavens for small mercies and all that. Even when he beats her, she just laughs at him till he gives up and storms out. As soon as he leaves, her demeanour changes. She sags against the chair, and tears roll down her face.

"I don't think I can watch any more of this," I say to Dice as I get up from the chair. "If I knew where Roach was, I'd go and do everything he did to her to him. I want to rip him and Dante apart."

"Come on, let's take a break, get some sleep. We're only about halfway through, and I've got a feeling it's only gonna get worse."

I crawl into bed in my old room. We've cleaned everything up from when Ray had her little tantrum, and now I'm sure that's all it was. She could have actually destroyed everything if she really wanted to.

I only manage a couple of hours of sleep at most. The images floating around inside my head are fucked up, to say the least, and needless to say, Steel will not be watching any of that footage.

I meet Dice back in the tech room, and Viking joins us. We trawl through day after day of footage of the same thing: Dante asking, Dante getting no response, Roach torturing, and Ray just barely having any reaction at all. She must be in fucking agony. She's never been cleaned since that first day, other than when she passes out and they throw water over her. We can physically see her wasting away, but when Roach isn't there, Dante starts to come in and clean her face and feed her some bread, almost like he's playing good cop to Roach's bad.

"Just say you'll join me, Ray." He strokes his hand down her face. "We can rule the world together, you and me, like it was supposed to be all along. It was always supposed to be you and me."

She smiles at him. She must have been there about two, maybe three weeks now. She leans into his hand and closes her eyes. "Fuck, is she giving up?" Viking asks, "Don't give in, Ray, please don't."

"You always hated me, Bas!" Why the fuck would you want me to join you?"

"Wait... go the fuck back!" I spit, "Did she just call him... Bas?"

"Bas... as in Bas, her fucking brother?" Viking scratches his head.

"Fuck I think you're right, here." Dice plays it again. "Fucking Bas, that's why it's always been Ray. He's gone after her. He wants to destroy her relationships with everyone else. That's why the video of Steel getting his dick sucked and setting him up in prison to fuck the doctor. He knew Ray wouldn't stay after that, so she has no one but him. That's why he turned us all against her, and we fucking let him."

I shove out of my chair and punch a hole in the wall, putting my fist through the photo of Dante, who we now know is Bas, who's clearly not dead! "Do you think they knew he was still alive?" Viking stands, too, and starts pacing.

"Dane will have searched everything I did from the night she was taken. He would have seen the traffic cam footage, so yeah, they would have known the minute she was taken that it was him and he was alive."

"Motherfuckers!" I start pacing, too. "That's why she faked her death. She's going to join him, bring him down from the inside. He has to believe she has no one else. He has to believe we've all given up on her. Fuck!"

"So what do we do now? What do we do to help?"

"I don't think we can. Like Dane says, we need to not get involved. It will only make things worse. We need to stall Steel. If he knows she's alive, he will rip this world apart, trying to find her. We can't let him know!"

"You want us to lie to our brother, to let him believe she took her own life rather than be with him. Are you really okay with that, Pres?" Viking shakes his head. "No, I can't do that to Steel. He deserves to know she's alive and what she's doing!"

"What if we're wrong, though? What if she is dead after all?"

"Dice, this is fucking Ray. If anyone's alive after all this, it has got to be her. We have to keep this between us. We need to keep him occupied and away from wherever she is. He needs to grieve because if she's doing this, I don't think she believes she's coming out of this alive, and we can't let him lose her all over again."

"Fuck!" Viking punches the wall, putting another hole in it. "I can't do that to Steel, I won't, I need to leave. I'm going back to Carmen's. I can't watch him fall apart and not say anything."

"You do what you have to, Brother, but this stays between us. That's an order!"

Viking nods, then leaves, just like that, gone.

"Fuck, this is so fucked up. He's gonna want answers. He's gonna need something. What do we do? What do we say?" Dice asks me, and right now, I'm fucking winging it.

"Firstly, we watch the rest of that footage, then you fry the thing. I want it so that not even Dane can put it back together. Then we burn the stuff he hasn't seen, and we pretend we got nothing. Back to the drawing board, and we keep him on a wild fucking goose chase till either Bas is dead or they both are!"

"Fuck, Pres, you sure about this? This is Steel. He'll never forgive you for this if he finds out!" Dice claps me on the shoulder.

"Let's make sure he doesn't find out. We need to make sure we refer to Bas as Dante, we need to make sure we talk about Ray past tense, and we need to make sure that this stays between us."

Dice nods at me, and we lock the door and carry on. The footage gets worse. Dante never lays a finger on her, always Roach. He's trying to break her to prove he's stronger than her, but she won't let him win. She's wasting away before our eyes and refuses to back down. The day she gets the scar on her face is a day Dante isn't there. It's another day Roach is trying to fuck her, but she ridicules him, so he can't even get hard, and he loses it.

"You think you're so fucking brilliant, don't you? He doesn't want you, no one does!"

"Really? Is that why you keep trying to stick that pathetic thing you call a dick inside me? Firstly, I'm dryer than the Sahara looking at your ugly fucking

194

mug, and secondly, that thing wouldn't even touch the fucking sides."

"You take that back, you fucking whore. You think Steel's so impressive? He's fucking nothing. You saw the way he fucked that doctor. He didn't give a shit about you!"

"Maybe, but at least he could get it up. The only person you're gonna injure with that limp fucking dick is yourself!"

"Maybe I should shut you the fuck up and stick it in your filthy fucking mouth!"

"Be my fucking guest!" She opens her mouth, and he starts to undo his jeans, grabbing and yanking at his dick, trying to get it out of his boxers quick enough. He grabs the back of her hair, and she opens her mouth wider; he slides his dick between her lips and groans a split second before he screams. Next thing, he's punching her in the head, and there's blood coming from her mouth.

"Fuck, did she just bite his dick off?" Dice asks, but I can't make out from the footage. She's laughing, but her teeth stay firmly clamped. He punches her again and again, and he's still screaming. Next, Dante is running down the stairs, grabbing either side of Ray's jaw and prying it open. Roach drops to the floor, cupping his junk, and Ray throws her head back and spits a mouth full of blood at him.

"I'd think twice if I were you, sticking things where they don't belong."

Dante helps Roach up and carries him out while Ray spits the blood out on the floor, cursing like a sailor.

It's a while before Roach comes back. His hand is shaking as he gets hold of the scalpel. "Let's see how great you think you are when I carve up your pretty little face, bitch."

Smiling at him again, she says, "Ah, Roach, you think I'm pretty?" She laughs, and as he carves down her face. She holds so still while he cuts.

He grins at her. "See how well life works for you without the use of your fucking eyes." As he goes to carve the other one, he gets punched by Dante, who slams him to the floor. "You motherfucker!" he roars, and he punches him again before he gets to his feet and grabs some towels and tries to clean Ray up. "Reaper, hey, can you see me? Ray."

She opens her eyes and nods before closing them again as the blood runs down her face. Dante rushes off, and Roach gets up from the floor and starts beating the shit out of Ray, punching and kicking at her till she's covered in blood and wheezing for breath, her head lolling, and she's barely hanging on now. "Fuck, this must be before he dropped her back here. Roach really beat the shit out of her."

Next thing, Roach is running off, and it's a good ten minutes before Dante comes back with supplies to fix Ray up, but when he sees the state of her, he unties her from the cuffs and carries her out of the room, checking the date and time stamp. It's three hours before she was dumped back here.

"Fuck, does anyone come back?" Dice speeds through a few more days of footage, but nothing, "Destroy it!" I bark. "Now, Dice."

He nods, and we get to work getting rid of everything that will lead them to Bas and Ray. Fuck, this is all going to shit. What the fuck do we do now?

Ray

I take a deep breath as I enter the club. This is the last place I want to fucking be, but this is where my no-good brother is, so this is where I need to be. I need to find him. I need to join him and play nice while I figure out everything that's going on with his organisation, then I'm gonna burn him to the fucking ground.

"Bas," I rasp, my voice has barely been used in weeks. I left Steel a month ago and haven't spoken to anyone since I shut myself away in a safe house. I got fit and well. My injuries are almost healed, well, my external ones, anyway. We're ignoring the internal ones. I can worry about them if I make it out of this alive; then I might have a little breakdown. Till then, though, everything's getting shoved back down and sealed away tightly.

As I walk up to his table, they're playing poker. Some things never change. Bas always had an issue with drugs and gambling, which is how he ended up fake dead in the first place. Turns out he cut the fuckers a deal. They dumped someone else's body in that ditch and set fire to it, then Bas used Timothy's fucking passport to flee. He set up here as it was near to our operations, and he's slowly been trying to cause trouble and build an empire to take us down. If only you had paid more attention to me, big brother, you would know I'm here to take you down, but I'm playing the long game.

"Bas!" I shout over the background noise. Two guys rise from their seats with guns trained on me. "Oh, sit the fuck back down. I could have shot you all before you even knew I was here."

"Ray!" Bas gestures to the men to sit back down, and I step up beside the table. "What a lovely surprise. To what do I owe this pleasure, dear sister?"

"I'm in!"

"I'm expected to believe that just like that, you're in?"

"Yep!"

"What about the club?"

"They think I'm dead."

"And the pas? Dane? Bran?"

"I've not seen them since they left me at the hospital. They believed your version of events. It's just me now."

"So you're here because you've got nowhere else to go, not because you want to be?"

"Fucking hell, Bas."

"Don't fucking call me that!"

I bite my tongue because I'm sure as fuck not winning any popularity contest right now. "I'm… sorry … Dante, look, I'm here, aren't I?"

"What do you have for me? I want to hit their main base tomorrow!"

"Don't be a dick. We need to take out a smaller one, scatter them and once we've done that, hit another smaller one on the other side of the country, scatter them far and separate them. That's when they're at their weakest."

"So, which one do you have in mind?"

"Well, I'd prefer to talk about this in private."

"Fine." He gets up from his seat, and we leave the table, walking upstairs and to the furthest end of the corridor. "So, is this where you run everything from?"

"Ah, little sister, you need to prove yourself before you see behind the curtain. I'm not showing you how I do things so you can screw me over. All good things come to those who prove themselves loyal!"

"Have I not done that? I burnt down the Reapers, destroyed the Hellhounds, made my husband and brothers believe I'm dead, and the others have turned against me. It's what you wanted. Now it's you and me against the world, so come on, Brother, let's talk business.

"You say all the right things, but time will tell. I have a job for you. An initiation, if you will. I want Cade dead!"

"Cade?" I shake my head. I've just found out he's my dad. I can't lose him now. I need to repair my relationship with him, and he's target number one. Maybe I can just kill Bas—fucking Dante—right now and worry about the next bit later. "Why?" is all I say out loud while my mind is racing.

"He gave my life for yours. He tossed me aside like I was trash. I was his son, too. They looked at me like I was shit on their shoes."

"That's because you were a dick!" I shrug. I'm not lying.

"I thought you were coming over to my side. This is not a very good first impression, little sister."

"If you want a yes-woman, you've barked up the wrong tree. I'll tell you the truth, and the truth is our whole lives, you've treated us all like shit, especially me, Bran, and Dane. We were your family, Bas. We loved you, and you were a vile piece of shit!"

He grabs me by the throat and slams my back against the wall, spitting in my face. "You were supposed to be mine, my other half, something for me to cherish, and you chose them, you loved them, it was always Bran and you till Dane came along, then you made room for him but never me. I had to watch the other piece of my heart leave me behind for people who didn't even share the same blood."

"Are you forgetting that while I lay in that ditch dying, you were laughing and telling them to take what you owed out on me? You thought my pussy would pay your fucking debt. Do you know what, *Bas*? Fuck you. I'm out. Take them down on your own because you, Brother, are a fucking cunt of the highest order, and if I have to stand here and listen to any more of your fucking 'woe is me' storyline, I might fucking puke. Fuck you, Bas. Burn in hell on your motherfucking own!"

Well, that didn't fucking go as planned. I'm definitely not the right person for this job. I'm gonna

201

strangle this twat in his sleep and fuck this whole operation up. I just can't listen to the fucking drivel he's spouting.

He relaxes his hand, his eyes never wavering from mine, and he takes a breath and a step back. As I storm out of the door and down the stairs, I reach the front door, and two guards step in front of me. "Mr Crane says your meeting isn't over yet!" one says, standing there trying to be intimidating with his massive, meaty arms crossed over his chest.

"That so?" I reply as I punch him in the throat and drop and take the other one's legs out from under him. As I step over them and through the door, I turn to the camera, flip it off and mouth, "Fuck you" at it as I reach the bike I stole.

I climb on and peel out of the parking lot and into the night, mentally berating myself for not being able to stay in a room with him for more than half an hour. "Motherfucker!"

As I pull up at the safe house, my phone blings. No one should be using this number. When I open it, it's a gif from an unknown number. It's a stork with the words "It's a boy" flashing over it.

Fuck. Skye. I dive back on the bike and head for the clinic. I take all the back roads and alleyways that I know don't have cameras, and I park two blocks away and run. When I get to the clinic, it's teaming with fucking Reapers. They're everywhere. I catch a glimpse of Steel, my breath catches in my throat and my heart breaks all over again, even though I know this is for the best. I sneak in through the back and to the staff room, throw on some scrubs and a mask, hide my hair in a hat, grab a trolley, and walk through like I belong. Fake it till you make it.

As I get to the corridor, I can see Ares outside the door and Blade and Priest talking further down. Fuck, how the hell am I supposed to get past them? I need to see her and Tray just once. I know I shouldn't, but she feels like my responsibility. She feels like my daughter; I know it's weird, and she's older than me, but I love her like she's mine.

I push past and into her room. As I walk in, I keep my head down. She's asleep on the bed, and Tank has Tray in his arms, rocking him backwards and forwards. As I turn, his gaze looks up to meet mine, and I hold my finger to my lips and remove the mask, clicking the lock on the door.

The relief that spreads across his face makes my heart ache as he strides across the room and sweeps me into a hug. "Thank fuck!" he breathes against me.

"Hey, Brother." I smile at him as I hug him back. "How are they both?"

"Amazing!" He grins at me. "Tray, I want you to meet your favourite aunt." He hands him to me.

A tear streams down my cheek as I crush his little body to mine. "Tank… he's fucking perfect!" I hold his little hand, and his finger grips around mine. He has the most perfect little button nose and rosy cheeks, and I know I will die for this boy. He is the reason I'm doing this. Well, he and Skye. Fuck it, and the rest of the fucking cunts, too.

"Are you okay?"

I screw my nose up at him.

"Ray?" he whispers.

I reach out and take his hand. "I'm doing this for them, Tank." I look at Skye and then Tray. "To keep them safe. If I manage it, then yes. If not, they won't know I'm not around. They think I'm already dead."

He laughs. "Skye knows you're not dead!"

"How?"

"She knows you and that you wouldn't choose to leave her!"

I shake my head. "Too smart for her own good, that one!" I rub my thumb across Tray's cheek, and he gurgles at me. "Keep them safe, Brother, keep them close, and cherish every moment. Give her a kiss from me when she wakes up, okay?"

"You can give it to me yourself," Skye's raspy voice comes from the bed, and I smile at her.

"Skye, he's perfect." I walk over and sit on the bed, pulling her into a hug. "I'm so proud of you. I love you. Don't ever forget that, okay?" I lean over and kiss her on the forehead and kiss Tray on his. "I have to go!"

"Will I see you again?"

"I don't know, kiddo, I honestly don't!"

"Wait. Promise me one thing?"

"For you anything!"

"You'll try and live and come back to us; you'll try harder than you ever have before, and when it's all burnt to the ground, you'll come back for me. You won't leave me."

"Kiddo! I will burn this world down for you I promise you that, and if I can make it home, I will. I'm just not sure that's an option." I shake my head. "I love you. I love you all, and those twats out there. Be safe, okay!"

As I pull the mask back over my face, Tank walks to the door, lifting Tray from my arms. "We'll be the distraction." He smiles at me and kisses me as he passes. "Ready?"

I nod, and as he pushes out of the door, I head in the other direction. As I come round the corner away from the guys, my heart breaks, and I'm not watching where I'm going and bump into a solid body with my cart. "Sorry," I grumble and push past, but as he turns, it's him, my heart, my soul. I push my head down and scurry past.

"Wait!" he rumbles after me, but I keep moving. "Ray?"

Shit, shit, shit. As I round the other corner to the staff room, I abandon the cart and run, pushing through the door. I rip off the scrubs and launch myself out of the window I left open, climbing to the ground and crouching in the shadows. Fuck, it was stupid of me to come here, fucking reckless. My heart's pounding and thrashing against my chest, and it's not from running and throwing myself out of a two-storey building. No, it's from seeing him, hearing him, smelling him. He's all-encompassing, and those eyes... I can't bear to see the heartbreak I left in them.

Steel

I'm standing at the vending machine, trying to breathe. I'm excited for Tank and Skye, truly, I am, but it also makes my heart rip out, knowing that I'll never have that. *Bang*. A cart clips me as a nurse in scrubs comes around the corner.

"Sorry," she grumbles and pushes past, but as I turn, it's her. I know it is. I can smell her. I can almost taste her, my heart, my soul. She pushes her head down and scurries past.

"Wait!" I rumble after her, but she keeps moving. "Ray?"

She rounds the corner, and I take off after her. As I come round the corner, I collide with the cart she was pushing, forcing my way past it. The staff room door is swinging, and as I push in, the scrubs are thrown on the floor, and the window is open. I run to it, screaming out into the night, "Ray!"

There's no one, not a soul around, and my heart breaks again. It was her. I know it was. I lean back inside and pick up the scrubs, smelling them, and I slide down the wall. It was her. I can smell her on them. I would recognise her smell anywhere. She now smells like hope. As I push off the floor, I stalk back to Skye's room.

Pushing through the door, I say, "She was here, wasn't she? It was her. She's alive."

Skye looks away, but no answer is as good as an answer, in my opinion.

"Is she okay?"

Skye looks at me, then away again. Fuck… that means no.

I turn to walk away. I have to find her. I need to. I feel so empty without her, so lost. I'm not whole when she's not with me.

"Steel," Skye's small voice shakes as I turn to make eye contact.

"You need to let her go!"

"Skye… I can't breathe without her."

"You need to learn to, Steel. She… she needs to be alone. She'll come back if she can."

"You believe that?"

"She loves us all, she said, and whatever's happening, she's keeping us safe. You need to stop looking."

"Who's keeping her safe?"

Skye just shakes her head.

"Exactly, I need to find her, to help her." I turn to exit the room again.

"Steel!"

I turn, part in shock. I've never heard Skye raise her voice, and the authority that drips from her tone is all Ray's influence. A slight smile spreads to the corner of my lips as I school my features and turn again. "Will you do as you're told for fucking once?

I've just had a baby, I can't kick your ass to make you listen, but I would if I could right now. For Tray's sake, you need to leave this alone."

"What's Tray got to do with me going after Ray?"

"She told me she's staying away to keep us safe so that whoever she's going after won't come after us. That's why she's burnt all her bridges. You need to stop. You need to think of the bigger picture. Please, let this go."

"I can't, Skye. If it was Tank or Tray, what would you do?"

She looks away again.

"I'm sorry, Skye." I turn and leave to chase my heart to the end of the world and back if I have to.

As I walk into the waiting room, where all the scary bikers are cooing over baby Tray and passing him round for cuddles, everyone turns to look at me, I'm still gripping the scrubs tight in my fist.

"Congratulations, Tank, he's beautiful!" I clap him on the shoulder, and he sees the scrubs, and a look flashes across his face before he replies.

"Thanks, Brother."

"I'm heading back to the clubhouse." I shake the scrubs, and he grimaces. "I have work to do."

"Steel!" Tank pleads.

"It's okay, Tank!" I give him a half smile. "I'll be careful."

I turn to leave, and as I reach the door, Ares steps in front of it, blocking my path. "You need to stay, Brother!"

I glare at him. "Why?"

"Just trust me, you need to stay!"

"What the fuck are you not telling me?"

Dice steps up beside me. "Steel, please?"

I glance between the three of them and then at Tray. My shoulders sag. "You know she's alive?"

They all look away, and I have my answer. I push through them and out of the door. Motherfuckers knew she was alive and didn't tell me. Looks like I'm on my own. I head back to the clubhouse to the tech room to find what they've been working on. I'm sure I'll find the answers there.

I take in everything on the walls as I push into the tech room. It looks the same, but there are a few more pin holes in the wall, as if someone has pinned more things but removed them and then the two holes that look like someone has tried to punch their way through the wall don't go unnoticed. I check the desk and nothing. I check the shredder, and it's empty. I flick the computer on. I know enough to get by, so I can wing it. As it fires up, the screen comes to life, and a box for the password pings up. "Fuck!" I turn the fucking thing off and head back to the apartment.

As I walk in, Dane's on the sofa. "Where the fuck have you been?" He hasn't been back for days. It might even be weeks, who the fuck knows anymore. "Does Dice know you're home?"

"Only got back ten minutes ago. Where is he?"

"Clinic!"

Dane dives up from the sofa. "Fuck, why didn't you say, is he okay? I need to go!"

"Calm the fuck down. Skye had the baby!"

209

He sags back to the sofa. "Fuck, you scared the shit out of me!" He takes a shaky breath.

"You know she's alive, don't you?"

"Steel."

"Don't, Dane. I saw her at the clinic. I know it was her. What's everyone keeping from me?"

"Steel, you know I love you, but you gotta let it go, man. She's gone."

"I refuse to believe that Dane and the way you lot acted when I told you, you knew it wasn't true you would lose your shit if anything happened to her."

"Look, just leave this alone. Trust me when I say it's better you don't go looking for ghosts."

"What the fuck is that supposed to mean?"

"It means, let the dead stay dead, Steel."

"She's not fucking dead!" I bellow. "I've seen her. I'm not gonna stop till I find her!"

I turn to storm off. "Steel, sit the fuck down. We need to talk."

My chest is rising and falling rapidly. I'm gripping the scrubs in my hand like a lifeline, and I'm losing my grip on everything around me. All I can focus on is her. She's… everything.

"Sit down, Steel!"

I calm my breathing, close my eyes and ground myself on the feeling of the scrubs in my hand. I sigh as I slide on to the sofa and grip the scrubs tight to my chest.

"Clearly, keeping you in the dark will turn into a total shit show, so I need you to listen and listen well. You need to believe she's gone! You need to act like she's gone, and you need to start right fucking now, or you're gonna fuck things right up!"

"What the fuck, Dane?"

"Listen, I'm not supposed to tell you this, so this is between you and me. It can go no further, do you understand? I will tell you everything, but you have to admit she's gone and play along till the end, got it?"

"Dane?"

"Steel, I'm fucking serious!"

"Okay! Okay, Dane, I will do it. Just please tell me she's coming back?"

"I can't promise you that. Steel, if things go wrong, none of us will be coming back, okay? But trust me, if she does this, I will make sure she comes back. I can't promise she will stay. I will get her to come back. That's all I can offer."

"I'll take it."

"Right, this all started about four, maybe five years ago. You heard the story of Ray getting stabbed and nearly dying in place of Bas and Pa trading Bas's life for Ray's?"

I nod as he continues.

"So the three guys who did that, then killed Bas. They were called Edward Lee, James Lewis and Timothy Spent. They killed Bas and burnt his body in the ditch where they had stabbed Ray. It went to court, and they got off with it. Ray exacted her revenge on them, killing them all and burning the house down around them before coming out here.

Fast forward a few years from that night, give or take, and a new name popped up: Dante Crane."

211

"We already know that. Either Ray didn't kill Timothy, or someone stole his identity, and he was the driver when Ray was taken, and his wife is the one who framed me and pretended to be Ray." We know some things and have been putting bits together ourselves, but clearly, they have more than us.

"Yes, well, Dante has been trying to create a power surge and not gaining much. He's been on our radar for a while. That's how we convinced Ray to come out here to help us with our Dante situation, so when Ray arrived here and got taken by Miguel, that's when things started to ramp up. Dante stepped in to take Miguel's place with the Hellhounds. He had found out about Ray being here and used Tali to get Ray to take out the Hellhounds. Roach has been Dante's inside man, and that's why he got so close to Ray. He's been working with Dante all along."

"But why would Ray being here make a difference to Dante?"

"Well, if you stop interrupting me, I might be able to tell you!"

"Sorry, carry on."

"So Dante stepped into the gap Miguel and the Hellhounds left. Roach had started dating Tali, so he was also informing on Carmen to Dante, too. Dante was able to take advantage of the power vacuum they both left and recruited what was left of their organisations. He's been trying to find a way to unseat The Armoury from our position within the country; he wants to take it all over, and he sees Ray as his way of doing that, and he feels she owes him."

"Why would Ray owe Dante anything?"

212

He sighs and shakes his head. "Dante wants Ray on his side, to himself. He wants her to join him. He was going to use you, Dice, and Dozer to do that. He was trying to split you and Ray up by making it look like you were playing away. He thought she would see the video, flip and leave so he could swoop in and propose that she could join him. Ray didn't believe the video, swooped in, saved you all and killed his men.

Dante then set up this event. The guy was just some half-rich wannabe who Dante paid to play the part of getting Ray alone. But my dad would never send anyone on a job alone, so he had a security team follow them. Ray was drugged in the back of the car, and the security team disappeared. They were later found murdered. We tracked the car and found the picture of the driver. Till then, Dante hadn't made much sense. We didn't know him, didn't know why it seemed so personal. But that picture of the driver… and then when we pulled the driver's licence and found the name Timothy Spent, it all fell into place."

"You lost me."

"The night Bas was killed, he wasn't. Bas never died. He used Timothy's passport. He must have come up with some kind of deal with them or something, but he fled the country as Timothy and set up a life here."

"Bas? As in Bas, Bas? Ray's Bas?"

"Yes. Bas never died. He's Dante. And Bas or Dante or whatever the fuck we're gonna call him, wants his little sister back! He always hated how close we were. He's burning Ray's bridges, so she has nowhere to go other than to him. That's why she set fire to this place and fucked us off at the clinic, because she's playing into his hands. She's joining him and letting him think she's turned against us all, especially you.

Turns out his plan was rushed when Ray got in the car. All he could smell was sex, the smell of you on her. He lost it and took her then. He's jealous; he wants his sister back. He thinks she's his other half, and she should feel the same."

"So I need to pretend I've turned my back or believe she's dead so he believes what she's selling, and she finds out all his secrets and takes him down from the inside?"

"By Jove, I think he's got it." Dane claps me on the shoulder.

"So… what the fuck do we do now?"

"I'm on call. We have to play our part when they hit our bases. We have to let them get away with so much while still being a formidable presence, so he thinks they're winning. You, you need to organise a fucking wake." He grimaces at me. "You need to bury your wife and make it look fucking convincing!"

"How long do we have to play along?"

"Weeks, months, years, fuck knows till we're told otherwise. We have no contact, so we're just watching our usual channels of communication for the go signal or any form of update at the minute, mate. That's all we've got."

"Fucking Bas? How bad is he really?"

"The majority of his training is similar to ours, although he never went on a mission again after the

214

epic cock-up of a first mission we all did. He was left out and bitter. He hated that Ray was our sister and we her brothers, when he was the only one actually blood-related. He had this twisted view that she was his. It was the twin thing. He believes she's always meant to be his, to be his other half, his heart. That's why he went after you. He set you up in prison." He shrugs. "He made her watch day after day on repeat of you fucking that doctor."

"Dane, I can't…"

"Hey, If she returns, it will be for her to forgive. It's not up to me, but honestly, although I never believed it would be something you would do, it was definitely extenuating circumstances, and I can see how you were pushed to the limits and snapped. Hopefully, she will see that too and not that you just fucked someone else because you wanted to get your dick wet!"

"Dane…"

"Let's just worry about all that if she comes back, okay? Now, you need to do your part. You need to sell it and make them all believe she's gone. No one can look for her, Steel. He needs to believe you've all given up. She's doing this to keep everyone safe. If he thinks she still has ties here, he will burn the place to the ground with you all in it. Ray will not let that happen to Skye and the baby."

"What about the inner circle, Carmen, Demi, Scar and Skye? They should all know the truth. Especially Skye, or does she already know? Ray went to see her tonight. I'm sure of it."

"The more people that know, the more dangerous it is for her. If she did see Skye, she would have ensured she didn't let on."

"Fine, as long as you keep me in the loop, no matter how small the information I want to know. Deal?"

"Deal."

I rise from the sofa and shake on it before heading into my room. Then, I notice I'm still clutching the scrubs, and I pull them to my face. I lie on the bed, and I break. Why the fuck is this happening? Why the fuck does she want to stay gone? And why can't I help her? I mean, I fucking know why, and that makes it worse, because she's doing all this to protect us all, and I'm scared that I'm going to truly lose her.

Ray

As I pull up outside the house, there's a truck parked there. It's him; I fucking know it. I slide off the bike and slip my gun out of the back of my jeans, tapping on the window.

The window rolls down slowly, but he continues to stare out of the windscreen. "Thought you'd be home a long time ago, little sister. I've been waiting!"

"Needed to blow off some steam. You still seem to be able to piss me the fuck off just by breathing. I'm wondering if I should just save us both the hassle and put a bullet between your eyes right here, right now."

He slowly turns his head to face me. "Not the way to make me believe you're all in, little sister!"

"Believe what you fucking want, Bas. I burnt my home down, and my family thinks I'm dead. I don't really give a flying fuck what you believe." I turn and storm up to the house, and when I hear the truck door open and close, I grin to myself as I push through the front door, leaving it open behind me.

As he enters, he pushes the door closed behind him and follows me into the kitchen. He's screwing his face up at the place. I mean, it smells like an old lady

217

that's been fucked by mothballs. And the furniture and decor are grim, to say the least.

"Nice place." he murmurs as his jaw grinds while he schools his face.

"Well, like I said, my family thinks I'm dead, and I burnt my home, so I'm not really swimming in options right now. The Ritz was slightly out of my price range of… " I dig into my pockets. "Four dollars, fifty cents, half a packet of chewing gum and a piece of fluff!"

"You give me the information I need, and when my team pulls the job off, I'll give you a place to stay."

"No!"

He grabs me around the face and shoves me against the wall, skittling the stool across the floor as he drags me off it. "Little sister!" He cocks his head to the side and turns my face so he can see the scar. "Although I didn't authorise this, I won't hesitate to give you a matching one, only this time I'll be happy to take your fucking eye out with it!" He turns his back and walks back to the counter. "Now, sit the fuck down!"

I pick up the seat and slide back into it.

"Good girl."

That makes me wanna puke. I'm Steel's good girl, not fucking his, and it makes my skin crawl to hear those words come out of his mouth.

"Now, you will give me the information I want on how to get into the main base, got it?"

"I think—"

"I didn't ask you to fucking think, did I?" Then the feeling of the sting from his back hand makes me

218

hiss. "Now, if you don't want the fucking hairy side again, I suggest you start talking. Main base, now!"

"It's too heavily guarded. We need to start with the smaller ones, draw their defences out, then hit the big one while they're second-guessing which small base we'll hit next." I spit out before I get another backhander. Bas was always quick to think with his hands. It's a shame he didn't get to see me grow into the person I am now, but I will let him think it will get him his way for now.

"Hmm, interesting. But if I wanted your opinion, I would fucking give it to you!"

I nod and look down. He likes to rule with an iron fist, but he also likes to win, and I know I've planted a seed of doubt, so now, I wait.

"Be at the club tomorrow night at 10 p.m." He turns and walks away, shouting over his shoulder, "Don't be fucking late!"

Fuck, his dickishness hasn't even mellowed. The guy is still a total fucking douchecanoe. As I walk to the freezer and grab a bag of peas, resting them against my face, I turn the TV on and slump on the sofa. This is gonna be harder than I thought!

Pulling up outside the club, I'm early, not because he told me to be, just because I find it a real chore to not be on time. Dad always said if you're on time, you're already late. I guess somethings stick, although I suppose it's Pa, not Dad.

As I get to the door, the two security guards scowl at me as they step aside. As I stride to walk through them, one of them grabs my arm and yanks me towards him. "Watch your back. That stunt you pulled yesterday got our friends a bullet between the eyes."

Looking down at the hand that grips my wrist and then back to his face, I whisper, "Then you might wanna remove that before you share the same fucking fate!"

He steps back like he's been shot, and I carry on walking without looking back. Clearly not making any allies here. As I reach Bas, he nods to the stairs, and I follow him up to the same room as before.

"Little sister, sit!"

I flop into the chair and throw my leg over the side.

"I see your upbringing didn't improve after I left."

"Yeah, my attitude didn't either. Why am I here?"

"You're here because I fucking told you to be, you're here because, like you always do without supervision, you create one epic shitshow after shitfight, and you're here because you burnt all your bridges, so you've got nowhere fucking else to go."

"Ah, that." I chuckle.

He flies up from his chair, smashing his fist into the desk. "You think this is funny? You're only still fucking alive as I need something from you. When you surpass your usefulness, then I will fucking end you myself. Do I make myself fucking clear?"

"Fuck's sake, Bas, chill."

220

"Call me that fucking name again!" He slides his gun out of his jeans and leans over the desk, pushing it between my eyes. "I will fucking end you right here."

I slide my arms out to the side, push up and forward into the gun, and stand in front of him, arms spread wide, and I smile. "Do it! Like I give a fucking shit, you need me more than I need you right now, so have at it!"

He relaxes the gun back before slamming it into my forehead. I feel the trickle of blood, and I drop back onto the chair. I don't wince, and I don't make a sound. I just flop back down and throw my leg back over the chair again.

"So, where are we hitting first? What's your plan?" I ask as I look down and pick at my nails.

"What's their weakest base?"

"Erm… King."

"King? Where the fuck's that?"

"Cedarwood."

"Then where?"

"Then Pawn, Ridgeway Heights."

"They're across the country from each other."

"Yep!"

"So we hit King first." He stands and starts pacing. "How many men do we need?"

"How many men have you got?"

He grins. "Like I'm gonna share that with you."

I shrug. "Your funeral if we don't pull it off. There's about forty people on that base at any time, give or take."

"So we take fifty."

I nod. "Do you have a laptop?"

He slides it out of the draw and fires it up. "I'm fucking watching you, little sister!"

I grin as I start typing and pull up a map. He's come around to stand behind me, clearly not trusting me. Smart move, big brother. I'm gonna play you like a fucking fiddle. Hold on tight.

"This is the base." I list the buildings and what they hold. It's next to nothing, really. I know we've already moved all our good stuff; the stuff left is shit, and we can afford to lose. The people there are skeleton staff, at best. They're not even proper Armoury. We've moved everything according to the order we're gonna hit. "If we hit at 3 a.m. there will be less people around. The main shifts have already left, and the next ones won't be arriving for hours. We can breach with minimal contact, therefore minimal casualties."

"How soon before we can hit?"

"I think maybe three days, four at most."

"I'll put a team together. We'll set up a meeting for the rundown in two days. You'll have the specifics ready for then!"

It's not a question; it's an order, and I nod. "I will need access to the laptop and a printer. Also, I will need some background on the teams so I can see who to use where."

"You can use the laptop while I'm in the room, same as the printer, that's it, you don't get any information until the… mission."

"Seriously? How the fuck am I supposed to put all this together when I don't know what skills I'm working with?"

"You don't need to know skills. You will have fifty bodies. Use them as you see fit."

"Bas—"

As my head whips to the side and I wince, "I fucking warned you. Do. Not. Fucking. Call. Me. That!"

"Shit B—fuck, Dante, quit with the fucking hitting, yeah? It's gonna take some getting used to. I'm fucking trying, okay?"

"Just get fucking on with it. You've got an hour now, then you can come back tomorrow at 11 a.m."

"Fine!" God, he's a bigger arsehole than I remember. I much preferred him when he was fucking dead.

After an hour, I've done as much as I can right now. I need to get him to trust me, and I need five minutes alone with his laptop to download the software Dane gave me, which is currently stuffed somewhere I'd rather not fucking say, but it's uncomfortable as fuck and pinchy.

I leave for the night and head back to the squat I'm staying in. As I throw myself down on the sofa, I let out a frustrated sigh. "Fuck." I yell as I throw a cushion across the room.

I want to be at home. I want to be in bed with my husband, with his dick buried as far inside me as humanly possible. I don't care about the fucking doctor. I totally understand the position he was in, and although it hurts, I love him more than that. I never thought I would forgive him, but I just feel so emotional at the minute. I don't know what the fuck's going on. All I wanna do is cry, fuck and kill my brother. I can't do any of those things. It's been nearly two months since I've seen Steel, and I'm agitated, to say the least. My skin's itching to be touched. I'm so fucking grumpy.

I stalk to the freezer, grab the ice cream and a spoon, and head back to the sofa. Flopping down, I rest the ice cream on my belly. Fuck, I've been overdoing the ice cream, but fuck it, there's only so much ice cream a girl can eat, and I ain't there yet. But I'm horny and irritated at best. There's also only so many times you can violate a cucumber before you question your sanity and life choices. At this rate, I'm gonna break into home and fuck my ex-husband. Well, I suppose still-husband, because if I don't get laid soon, I'm gonna end up the size of a house. But for now, I recline with my new boyfriends, Ben and Jerry. Fuck my life.

It's the night of the raid, and we're at the club gearing up. The team turned up an hour ago, and I went through what was needed. We have thirty-seven, and I was working on fifty, so I'm having to think on my feet. I've managed to chat with at least half of the men here, and honestly, they aren't anything other than street rats. They have no training, and the majority of them are questionable as people. Morally grey is an understatement, so I will be more than happy to put bullets in a few of them tonight. I can't help but wonder if Bas—Dante—has spread

224

himself thin with so few turning up or if he's luring me into a false sense of security, making me think he's not got the support. The jury's still out on that one.

I split the men into four teams: three teams of nine and one team of ten. Dante refuses to lead a team that I'm not on, so I sort through the team leaders and give them their orders while Dante waits and watches. He's letting me run with this, but I can see he's testing me, so I must be extremely careful and prove myself.

As we roll out and pull up at the base, I send the men to their positions. Most of them are outside the fence, and they're here just to raid the base after. Our team of ten are the ones going in.

Pulling out my bolt cutters, I turn to the men at my back. "Ready?" They nod as Dante stands at the back. My eyes meet his, and he just stares. "Ready, big brother?"

He nods, and I make the first snip, tripping the silent alarm that will warn everyone we're coming. Obviously, Dante doesn't know that. All the people here are sporting bulletproof vests with blood packs attached. We already agreed on the tactics for the attacks. When I talked to the men beforehand, I told them to aim for the largest mass, body shots only when they shoot, and our people are instructed to go down and play dead, and we will hopefully get out of this unscathed.

Pushing through the fence, I gesture for the guys to follow me. There are mines around the perimeter. Oops, I may have forgotten to mention that little gem. I smile to myself as I know the telltale signs of where they are. Before we get to the edge, two of the guys trip the mines and blow up, skittering us across the ground.

"Motherfucker," I grunt as I try to stand, pushing a body off me. "Well, there goes our element of surprise. Fucking with me, now!"

I push to my feet and start running. Three bodies rush from behind the buildings, and I double tap each to the chest, and they drop as instructed. Running past them, I push into a hangar and wait for the remaining men to join me. Some of them shake their heads. Their ears must be ringing if they were close enough to the explosion, but the remainder of us are bruised, nothing more. The mines weren't massive, but enough to kill the person standing on them and damage those a few feet away.

Doing a headcount, there are seven of us. "Fuck." I spit. "We need to be more careful, I said to stay behind me. Why the fuck were they so far away?"

"This best not be a set up. little sister!"

"Dante, I told them to stay with me and to stay close. Those fuckers were over twenty feet away. The rest of you listen and listen fucking good. They know we're here now, so do as you're fucking told! With me, now, stay fucking close!"

Pushing back through the other side of the hangar, we can hear shouting and gunshots coming from outside. The Tower guards will pick off the guys outside the perimeter and hopefully thin the numbers. As we reach the middle of the base, "Now spread out, clear the base. You have zip ties. If you can take them

226

alive, do so. If not, bullet to the largest mass. That way, you dumb fucks shouldn't miss. No heroes, okay? We all want to go home."

We split into groups, and I scream, "Stay in the area around the buildings. Don't deviate from that. There must be other mines, now fucking go, go, go!" I rush out from behind the truck and toss a grenade onto it, creating as much carnage to replaceable objects as possible. Dante is right on my arse, and I'm fully aware that he's behind me with a gun and can clearly just end me right here. We happen upon two more men from the base, and I shoot them both, taking them down, turning and grinning at Dante. "It's like old times, big brother."

"Don't get too excited, little sister. I still don't fucking trust you!"

Grinning at him, I pull out another grenade and toss it toward a building. Again, causing maximum chaos but minimal actual damage to anything important. Dante's eyes light up, and I let out a maniacal laugh as I jog through the base. When the gunfire steadies, I shoot up at the towers, clearly not gonna hit anyone, but making it look like I could, and the shots cease. There are a few more shouts and shots, but the chaos is dying down, and we gather again near the centre. We have five prisoners, and the men say everyone else is dead. We secure the prisoners in one of the outer small buildings and leave them. Dante radios to the men to come through the front gate with the four trucks so we can start loading shit up. I head to the office blocks.

"Where the fuck you going?" Dante spits at me.

"You want the equipment. I want the intel."

As I stride towards the office block, Dante slides up beside me. Of course he fucking does. "You've done good. But I'm still watching you."

"Shock, gasp, fucking horror. Was that an actual compliment? Well, fuck me!" I laugh as he scowls at me. "Come on, we need to be over here." Dante starts pushing into the rooms. "Don't worry about them. There's nothing in there. We need the pas' office, top floor, last room." I take off up the stairs, and he's following me. I could just turn, kick him down the stairs and put a bullet between his eyes, but that won't help me. So I bite my lip and mentally berate myself for the thoughts of the bloody murder I will bring to my brother.

"Grab what you can carry," I say as I push through the door. "Do you have a tech guy?"

He nods, so I swipe the laptop off the desk. It's actually a dud, and Dane has put a lot of time and effort over the last month creating false information across all our platforms. Dante is rifling through the filing cabinets and pulls out a file. "What's this?" I turn, and he has a file with his name on it. Well, Dante Crane's name. It's a file Dane's put together to antagonise him.

I snatch it off him, "It's a file on you dipshit!" I shake my head at him, and he snatches it back.

"What the fuck?" He flicks through the pages. There aren't many. And most of it is derogatory, to say the least. He starts to pace as he reads, and I can't help but have to fight the smug grin that wants to spread across my face. "Fucking bastards, they'll fucking regret the day they swiped me aside as an inconvenience rather than a formidable opponent. I'm gonna fucking destroy them."

"Come on, let's get out of here before they send reinforcements." I turn and leave as he kicks over the desk before following me. As we reach the trucks, we load up and head back to the club. It seems dodgy to me that everything seems to be happening at the club, and I wonder if he really has the backing and standing he's crowing about or if it's all bravado and fake it till you make it. Unfortunately, only time will tell.

"Reaper!" he screeches out across the room and nods towards the stairs, and like the good little sister that I am, I smile and internally roll my fucking eyes and follow like the good little lapdog he thinks he's getting.

I grimace as I push through the door and take what's become my usual seat. "How many did we lose?"

"What?" His eyes reach mine from the document he's reading.

"How many men did we lose?"

"Sixteen, maybe eighteen?"

"What we don't know?"

He shrugs. "Not important, there's more where they came from."

"What now?"

"How long before you can put together a plan to hit Pawn?"

"Pawn's gonna be harder. We will need more men."

"Like I said, it's not a problem." He gazes back down and continues to read. He's frowning, and his jaw ticks as he reads. "You can read, can't you, big brother? You act like you're trying to figure out the secrets of the universe while playing Twister."

He screws the paper up, throwing it across the room. "Those fuckers have written me off. They've known for years it's me, and none of them reached out; not one of them looked for me. Fucking bastards never gave a fucking shit. They're gonna rue the fucking day they helped murder me, Cade's gonna pay last, I swear to Hades himself, I'm gonna destroy every last one of them. They're all gonna be fucking sorry. I'm gonna rip the adventure centre apart. I'm gonna destroy Daniel and Steven, and then fucking JJ, then I'm gonna destroy everything Bernie has here, and finally, I'm gonna rip Cade's heart out and stomp on it!"

"Dante… it's gone, they're gone!"

"What?"

"The Adventure Centre burnt to the ground, Dad's dead, Steven and JJ… they're both dead, there's only Bernie and Cade left."

"Get out!" he screams at me as he picks up his chair and launches it over the desk.

"Dante."

"Get fucking out!" He kicks at the desk, and I jump out of the chair before the fucking thing hits me. I make it to the door as a bottle of whisky or tequila, or something explodes at the side of my head as it hits the wall. I don't look back. I just push through the door and slam it behind me. I rest against the wall, listening and smiling to myself as the fucking tantrum carries on. He's smashing the whole room to bits, he's unravelling, and I can't help, but mentally fist-bump my fucking awesomeness.

I stroll down the stairs, and I'm met by a goon. "I need to see the boss."

"Yeah, I'd give him a wide berth for a few hours if I were you. He's having a… moment!"

"What the fuck's that supposed to mean?"

I smile and tap my ear, and as he pushes closer, you can hear the faint roars and smashing followed by ranting and cursing.

I clap him on the shoulder, "He knows where I'll be when he calms the fuck down. Good luck with that!" I nod back in the direction of my big brother and grin like the motherfucker that I am as I sashay out of the main door and into the early morning sunshine. It's a beautiful fucking day.

Dane

I flop onto the sofa. Fuck, it's been a rough couple of months. They've hit four bases, we've taken minimal casualties, and I'm grateful Ray's on our side, as she's really looking after everyone.

Steel pushes out of his room, "What time did you get back?"

"Fuck knows. I don't even know what fucking day it is." Wanker just grins like the twat that he is.

"Ray?"

"She's kicking our butts, and I'm exhausted and fucking sore and fucking relieved she's on our side as fuck… if she was against us, she would single-handedly be able to take us down and fucking crush us."

He laughs, fucking full-on belly laugh and grins. "That's my fucking girl."

"Well, I'm glad my misery is bringing you so much enjoyment."

"What can I say? It's the only thing keeping me sane right now. I'm trying not to burn the world down to find her, and the fucking wake nearly broke us all, but knowing that she's still a force to be reckoned with makes it bearable." He grins like he's lost in memory before adding, "Have you seen her?"

I shake my head. "No, nothing. She's sticking to the plan. She's doing everything she said she would, so she's still on top of everything, but no one has had eyes on her yet other than that first base they hit. They've been cleaner, more organised. We think Bas sent cannon fodder in on the first job, which is why it was sloppier, but he's upped his game since. We still keep dwindling his numbers, but we've heard nothing. She got me into his laptop, though, so we have some information, but we're still waiting to hear from her."

"I thought I heard your voice. Why didn't you come to bed?" Dice pushes through the door, looking fucking delicious in his boxers with his sleep messed hair, and I bite my lip and sigh.

"Because I'm dead on my feet, and this was as far as I could manage." I flop back on the sofa and sigh again. "I'm too old for this shit."

Dice chuckles. "Yeah, you're such an old man, so gross." He walks over and kisses me over the back of the sofa. "Shall I run you a bath, babe? I love you, but you kinda stink."

I pull my T-shirt to my nose and sniff, groaning, "Ergh, fuck, that's grim!" I rip it off over my head and push up from the sofa.

"Fucking hell, did you get shot?" Dice rushes to my side, grabbing at my arm.

"It's just a flesh wound, it's fine."

"Fine! It's not fucking fine. You could have been killed."

233

"Nah, I'm pretty sure it was Ray that shot me, so I was never gonna get truly injured."

"I thought you said you hadn't seen her?" Steel spits as he comes around to grab my arm, too.

"I didn't. Bas shot at me aimed for the head, Ray shot me in the arm, which made me lean over, and the bullet whizzed past my ear, so all good."

"I'm worried that you think being shot by your sister and bullets whizzing past your ear is all good. Maybe you took a hit to the head. Shall I get Doc to come and check you over?"

"Dice, it's sweet that you're worried about me, but trust me when I say I'm fine. We've got this."

"How can you be sure? You said it yourselves: you've had no contact with Ray, no one's seen her. You don't actually know if she's okay, and what if it's gone to shit? No one's seen her for over two months."

Steel clenches his fists and grinds his jaw.

"What you mean is you've not seen her." I reach out and pull him in for a hug. "Steel, she's fine. She's doing everything to plan. She would deviate if she wasn't fine, and we would know something was wrong. While it's all going right, we have to believe she's got this."

"Three months, three weeks and five days. That's how long it's been since I've seen her, nearly four fucking months. I'm trying, Dane, I really am, but I'm balancing on a knife edge, and I don't know how long I can hold on for."

I sigh and hug him tighter. "Just give her time, okay?"

"Fine. But please fucking shower, you smell like roadkill."

I push him away. "Arsehole." I head to the bathroom and dive in the shower.

The door opens after a few minutes, and Dice walks in with some clothes for me, stripping off his boxers and kicking them aside. He walks over to me, grinning. "I haven't had you to myself in weeks."

"Dice, it's been four days."

He steps up to me in the shower.

"Four"—he slides his hands down my chest—"long"—he slides his hand around my dick and rests his lips against my neck, nipping at me and stroking my length in his grasp—"long"—sliding his other hand around to my arse and gripping my cheek tightly squeezing and tugging me against him—"fucking"—he licks up my neck and nips at my jaw before devouring my mouth while he pulls me to him and pumps my dick, making me groan—"Days." My head falls to his shoulder, and he pushes me back against the shower wall.

"Dice."

"I know you're exhausted, so let me help." He grins at me, sliding down my body and dropping to his knees.

My eyes flutter closed, and my head rocks back to rest against the wall as he slides his tongue down my length before opening those beautiful lips of his and sliding me between them. My hips thrust against him, and my hand reaches and scrubs into his hair, gripping tightly. He winces but groans around my dick as he reaches up with his other hand to cup my balls,

235

and I sag against the wall as he sucks down my shaft, taking me all in as I bottom out. He groans, sending a shiver through my body as I groan back. If I were to die right now, I couldn't think of a better place to be than pulsing between his beautiful lips. Actually, thrusting between his beautiful cheeks would be so good right now. I yank my hips back, and my dick pops out of his mouth, and he gasps and sulks as I drag him up by his hair, stepping to the side and pushing him over. I slide up behind him, still with his hair in my grasp and push him further forward as he grimaces. I'm not being gentle, but right now, I need to be balls deep, and that's all I can think of.

Pushing my tip to his tight entrance, he's tense, "Let me in, babe."

I grunt at him as he relaxes against my intrusion. I push my hips surging forward as his hands fly up to rest on the wall so I don't smash him into it. I stop as I bottom out and groan as I give him a second to stretch to my size. He's gasping for breath as he tries to breathe with the water hammering down on his head. I slowly pull back out before slamming into him, and I lose my god damned fucking mind. He's like a drug, and I'm a total junkie. When I feel his arse clench around me, I'm done for. I let go of his hair and grip on tightly to his hips as I go to town, just pounding away. All I can think about is the feeling of him around me as I groan out and slam into him harder over and over again.

"Fuck, Dice!" I roar as I come in his tight hole, sagging over him and panting. I reach forward and grab his hair, pulling him up flush with my body as my dick pulses inside him, and I bite down on his shoulder before turning his head to mine and kissing him.

"You're a fucking animal." he murmurs into my mouth.

I grin at him. "You fucking love it!"

"I fucking love you."

I slowly slide out of him and turn him so his back hits the wall, devouring those lips, nipping and pulling his bottom one into my mouth. "I fucking love you too."

"He grins against me, and I slowly caress down his body and take his dick in my hand, pumping in time with my tongue in his mouth, slow and languid, taking in every shudder of his body as I hold mine against his, kissing and licking till he gasps his release over my hand, rubbing my thumb over his head. I bring it to my lips and suck it into my mouth before kissing him back. I don't know how long we stay like that, just kissing and being with each other before there's a knock on the door.

"Dane, your phone's going nuts out here."

"Fuck." I quickly shower off, throwing the towel round my waist, and storming into the living room. Picking up my phone, it's Pa. There are missed calls and texts. "Shit."

Calling him back, he's frantic. "Pa, calm down, what the fuck?" I can't make head nor tail of what he's ranting about. He's lost it. "Pa!" I yell down the phone. "Calm down, I can't understand you." He starts to talk, and I freeze. He lays everything out for me. "Shit." he carries on. "Hades, how far along?" I'm panting and

237

can't catch my breath as I start to panic. "Bran, my dad?"

I look round, and Steel and Dice are standing shoulder to shoulder together, just watching. "How long?" he starts getting frantic again. I turn to Steel, "Get Ares here right fucking now!" Pa's still talking, and I cut him off. "How long before you're ready to roll?" I ask. "I don't give a fucking shit. I said how fucking long before you're ready to roll." I turn as Ares pushes through the door.

"What the fuck's going on?"

I lift my finger to him to hold that thought. "Roll out in thirty minutes. We'll swing by The Tower on the way. We fucking end this today!"

I hang up the phone and turn to the guys. "I need a team. How many guys will come with me? I'm going after Ray. Shit's gone fucking sideways."

"What the fuck's happening?" Steel steps up, panic all over his face. "Fuck knows, all I know is she needs to come home, right the fuck now. Pa will be here in thirty minutes. I need as many men who will lay down their lives for my sister, as we're walking into a fucking shitfight, and fuck knows how many of us are coming out of this alive."

Ares pulls out his phone and frantically taps at the keys, sending a group message, "Whoever's in will be out front in twenty minutes armed and ready."

I nod and fucking run to our room and start throwing clothes around. Steel's shouting from his room, and as I pull my shirt on, I run into the dressing room at the back where he has the mirror slid back and a fucking mini armoury. "Fuck, Steel, you and my

238

sister really are perfect." We start loading up, and fifteen minutes later, we're pacing the parking lot, waiting for anyone to show up.

The first to arrive are Blade and Priest, followed by Tank and Dozer.

"Tank, man, I love you, but you should stay. Tray, Skye... they need you." I clap him on the shoulder.

"And what kind of role model would I be to my son if I stayed here safe while everyone else I love dies for the sister I would die for myself?"

"At least you'd be here to be a role model!" I grimace at him as more and more men turn up. I hear a tiny cry and turn to see Skye coming round the corner; Tray held tightly in her arms and tears streaming down her face.

"Tank, you need to stay and look after your family."

It's Skye that surprises me when she speaks. "Ray is my family; she saved me, and you all need to save her, bring her home, and just be safe. Will this help?"

"What's this?" I ask as she hands me an old phone, talking like before smartphone times, an old black brick. "Skye, what is this?"

"Ray gave it to me when she left. She said if there was ever an emergency, life or death, I could call her on this, and she would always come for me. But maybe you can get her a message, or she could get one to you if she knows you have it."

"You've had this all along?" Steel asks as he shakes his head. "Of course she wouldn't leave you alone. With no way to contact her." Skye smiles at him but hands me the phone.

"Thanks, Skye." I grip the phone to my chest as tyres screech behind me, and Cade jumps out of the truck.

"Just bring everyone home safe, yeah." Skye wipes a tear from her face as she looks at Tank and turns to walk away.

He runs over to her and sweeps her up in his arms, kissing her. "See you later, love."

She smiles at him and then at all of us. "See you all later!" We nod as we set off running for our trucks.

"Just follow us. We need supplies!" I shout as I dive into the passenger side of Pa's truck. Steel and Ares pile in the back, and we ride out as a convoy. Heading straight to The Tower.

Pulling up in the parking lot, we head inside. There are fucking trucks everywhere, six in total, and twenty-seven of us. Fuck, this is gonna be one hell of a shit fight.

"Where's Bran and Bernie?" Steel asks, and I shake my head.

"They don't want us to pull her out. They think she can complete the mission, then kill Bas."

"Why are we going in then?" He grabs my shoulder to stop me from walking off. "Dane, what aren't you telling me?"

"Steel, just trust me, we need her out of there, and that son of bitch dead, okay?" He nods, and I know he wants to push, but I can't tell him, he needs to have his head in the game, and I can't throw him off. We need him.

We load up and into the armoured trucks and head for the abandoned town. It's where they've been operating besides his club, and we've had eyes on them in the old church on the outskirts, so that's where we're going. Every truck has a map, and we're all heading to different sides of the town before we gatecrash as one. We want to come at it from all sides so no one gets out alive. Well, hopefully we do. We want them all dead, and now the bikers are suited and booted, all with vests, earpieces, and ammo. We stand a good chance of pulling this off.

Once we've got everyone in place, I give the order. "Heads on a swivel! Take everyone down, kill them all. Only us and Ray get out alive!" I look at my team. "Got it?" They all nod, and we draw our guns and make our way to the church. We're about a block away, so everyone we come into contact with we drop, double tap between the eyes. Our intel tells us he has around fifty to sixty men, so we're outnumbered, but we've got one thing they don't: a reason to stay alive, and that reason is counting on us even if she doesn't know it. I sent her a message on the phone we got from Skye, and hopefully, she will understand we're coming for her.

UPS: Your parcel is out for delivery and will be with you between 9 a.m. and 7 p.m.

"Two down!"
"One down!"

241

"Three down!"

"One down!"

"One down!"

"Two down!"

"One down!"

The reports ring out from the teams. We're nearly at the church; they're already eleven men down. Everyone who gets shot takes a bullet to the head. I'm not risking one of them sneaking up behind us and taking a potshot. So we're thorough, we're cautious, they'll know we're coming by now, but there's no way for them to get to us. We left a small team in one of the armoured trucks, and they're slowly driving in as we clear. Anyone with any medical knowledge is in there with enough supplies to patch up the Titanic. If things go sideways, we need them close but protected. Nothing safer than an armoured truck, am I right? Not being here would be safer, but that's not an option, so an armoured truck it is!

There's a screech of tyres, and I spin to look over my shoulder, and Doc has just flattened a guy.

Tatts gets out and puts a bullet through the mangled head of him.

"One down!" He grins at me as he jumps back in the truck. I flip him a two-finger salute before heading back towards the church.

"Team One in position!"

"Team Two in position!"

"Team Three in position!"

"Team Four," then a grunt. "Fuck, it's just a graze," as we all hear gunfire before, "Team four in position!"

"Team five in position!"

"Breach in, three, two, one." Teams one to four are on either side of the building, and Team Five are the guys in the truck. We all kick through the doors to the front and rear and windows at the side as we come face to face with a shit tonne of guns. We have them pinned, so it's just a matter of keeping our heads down and firing inside, hoping we hit them. Cade pulls out a tear gas canister and lobs it through the window.

"Fuck! Cover your faces!" I bellow as we keep firing, we should be okay. We're still on the outside of the building, but it's gonna sting like a motherfucker when we have to make our way inside. The gunfire slowly steadies as we deem it fit to head in. One of our guys, fuck knows what his name was, takes a bullet to the skull, stuck his head up too far and paid the price. One takes a round to the shoulder, and Priest is fucking lucky as one bullet skims along the side of his head and ear. There's blood all over him, but I'm informed that it looks worse than it is.

"Cover your faces, anyone in there, shoot in the head, even if they're already dead. No fucker is coming away from this!" As we push through the doors, there are a few people coughing and spluttering, hiding behind the pews, and taking potshots. There are a few left near the confessional booths, and as we surge in, they are taken out. Savage takes a bullet to the leg; Tank was the one who got grazed before we were in position, but seeing him inside, he's fine. As we take our positions and clear the floor, a single shot rings out, and the guy just behind me crumbles to the floor!

"Fuck!" I drop as I spin and see the head popping back. "Behind the fucking podium thing! Take that fucker out!"

Cade's up there and pops him once in the shoulder before walking over and putting two bullets between his eyes. I mean, fucking one would have done it, but at least he was thorough.

As we advance toward the stairs at the front, there's a rain of bullets that come from the mezzanine level, and we all dive for cover.

"Motherfuckers," Cade spits as he gets caught in the shoulder of his left arm.

"Pa, you good?"

"Yeah, son, through and through, hurts like a bitch, but I've had worse."

We take another round of fire. As the bullets slow, I jump up and run as I hear Dice bellow my name, but I don't stop until I'm under the mezzanine level and skid to a halt. Savage has taken cover near the stairs, and I look down at him. He's fucking bleeding everywhere, so I cut the bottom off my top and tie his leg up. "Better?" He grunts but nods, and I take off for the stairs. There's the main floor, a mezzanine level which looks out over the congregation facing the pulpit and what looks to be another smaller enclosed floor above that probably leads up to the bell tower at the top. My bet is that's where they are.

As I round the top of the stairs, I take three twats by surprise as they're looking over the edge, trying to pick our guys off. With three shots to the backs of their heads, two fall over the edge while one

244

slumps over the bannister. I clear the floor before walking over to him. He's dead, so I toss him over before heading to the second flight of stairs. I have Steel, Tank, Pa, Priest, Dice, Blade, Viking, and four other guys by the time I get there. I've no idea who the fuck they are. Apparently, they're called Irish, Razor, Snake and Dave. I don't have time to ask why Dave is called fucking Dave. I mean, they all have biker names, then he's called fucking Dave. But right now, I need to focus.

"When did you join the party?" I ask Viking. Last I heard, he'd fucked off back to Carmen's when he found out about Bas, and the guys wanted to keep Steel in the dark.

"Tank called on route, got some of Carmen's men outside. They are helping with the clean-up and the wounded."

I nod, and me and Pa push up the stairs first. It brings us to the back of the floor with the big stained glass window; well, what's left of it. It's all smashed bits, missing and broken, pretty much like the rest of the town. With the rest close behind, watching our six, we push to the next floor, we take a jump back when we're met with a round of gunfire. Laying down on the top step, I quickly poke my head around before pulling it back. Bas has Ray in front of the window with his back to it, using her as a human shield. He has a gun and a knife trained on her, and five other guys are with him.

Leaning back, I take out my spare gun and reload my first, whispering to everyone about their positions. I nod to Pa, and he takes a few steps back.

Grabbing my ankles, I nod when I'm ready, and I tense my legs. He thrusts me out along the floor as I slide I quick-fire two rounds before he yanks me back, and then we hear two thuds, and I grin as I get up off the floor. "Then there were three! Well, five if we count Ray and Bas."

"It's over, Bas!" Cade spits, "Give it up, son. There's no one left to help you."

"Don't call me fucking Bas, and I'm not your fucking son!"

"Dante." I try to reason. "You don't wanna hurt her. You know you love her more than anything in this world." I try to reason with the resident psycho as he believes in his twisted mind that he loves her. and she loves him. I stand close to the wall, and I nod to Pa. He reloads and pulls out his spare, and we run in before anyone can stop us. I hit one guy in the leg, and he goes down. Pa takes another out, bullet to the forehead, and we have our guns covering them all as we stand there in a Mexican standoff.

"Tell your men to leave." Pa tells Bas.

"You're outgunned, Dante." I grin. There's one dead, one with a nasty leg injury, and the other already has his hands in the air and has tossed his gun. He skirts around the edge of the room.

But Dante turns the gun on him and shoots him in the back of the head. "Fucking coward!" he spits, retraining his gun on Ray.

"I want him dead," Dante spits out, pointing at Steel. "The motherfucker who knocked up my sister. I want him fucking dead."

I glance at Steel, and his face pales. Yep, that's why we were in such a rush to get her out. We found out that Ray is pregnant. That was the only information we had.

"She won't take your fucking side if you kill him, dickhead." I spit back, but Steel steps out in between me and Pa anyway with his gun tucked back in his waistband.

"Let her go, and I will come quietly."

"Don't you fucking dare!" Ray spits at him, but Dante has a blade to her throat and a gun to her stomach. There's a slight line of blood running down her neck where the blade is digging in, and she has various colours of bruising around her eyes and cheeks. Fucking Bas, Dante, whatever the fuck he wants to be called, always slapping her around.

"Steel, please, go!" Ray's resolve is shifting; she's losing it at the thought of him being hurt, so I subconsciously take a step in front of him.

"Ah, little parasite thinks he can save him! He fucking defiled her, he's fucking ruined her! Look at her!" he yells, and Ray closes her eyes. Her hands are shaking as she holds them out to the side. She has a bump, a fair-sized one. She must be at least five, maybe six months. Could she have gotten pregnant while she was captive? Did Roach manage to do that? Did we miss it? My stomach churns at the thought, but Dante clearly thinks it's Steel's.

"I'm pregnant, you fucking dick, not ruined!" She winces as he applies more pressure with the blade.

"Don't." Steel steps further forward, and as he does, the others step from the top of the stairs to stand behind us, all with their guns trained on Dante. "Don't!" Steel says again as he steps forward with his arms out. "Let her go. You can have me. I'll come with you. They'll let you go if you have me. Leave her there and take me." He drops to his knees with his arms out at the side.

"I don't fucking want you. I want you dead, and your fucking bastard parasites the fuck out of my sister."

"Steel turns to look at me, but as he does, Dante lifts his gun and fires a single shot that rips through Steel. It goes into his shoulder, but that's fucking bad news when you're wearing a fucking vest. He gasps as he drops to his hip, his eyes shooting back to Ray. He coughs as he drops onto his back, and blood comes out of his mouth. There's a fucking almighty death-curdling scream, and we're simultaneously trying to get to Steel and watch Ray at the same time. Still, she forces her way out of his hold, rushing towards Steel, but we're already there. She turns and kicks Dante in the chest, making him stumble back nearer to the window.

The fucker's laughing, actually fucking laughing, but she runs, launching herself at him like a fucking rugby player, shoulder to his stomach, hitting him with everything she's got, and the next thing, they're both smashing through what remains of the fucking stained glass.

"Doc, get up here now!" Ares barks down his mic. "Steel's been fucking shot! Bring everything. It's fucking bad, Doc, hurry!"

248

Me and Tank are already running to the window, and as we peer out, Dante is impaled on the weather vane that sits on the peak of the roof of the entrance to the church, eyes wide and blood pooling, gasping for breath. Ray is straddling his body with his head in her hands, screaming and smashing his head repeatedly into the roof.

"Ray!" I scream. "Ray!" She turns to glare up at us but loses her balance and topples off the peaked roof. "Fuck, Ray. Do you see her?" I look over at Tank, his pale face shaking his head. We're three stories up, three high fucking stories at that, and the roof below juts out. As Doc and the guys burst into the room, I turn and run, but Tank's already ahead of me, and fuck, he can shift for a dude as wide as he is tall. Bursting outside, she's there on the floor, unconscious. Cade is crouched beside her.

"Don't move her, don't fucking touch her!" Tank says as he crouches beside her and turns the side of his face to her cheek. She's breathing. He sits back on his knees. "She's fucking breathing!" I pull my phone out and call my dad. "We need two med units now. Steel's been shot, and Ray took a dive out of a three-story window!"

I cradle my head in my hands as we wait. Dice finds us while the others stay with Steel. He slides his arms around me. "Hey, she's gonna be okay. Steel's gonna be okay, and the baby will be okay."

"Babies!" I say as I close my eyes. "I think she's having twins."

"Fuck!" is all we can say as we sit around her and wait. I hear the choppers in the distance, and as they come into view, I stand. A crew comes running towards us, and we step back, unable to do anything but just watch as they try to save my sister and her babies.

"She's pregnant!" Tank rasps. "Can you save them? Can you save them all?"

"We'll do our best," the doctor says as the other crew runs towards us. "Upstairs, third floor," I grit out but don't move to follow.

I have to stay with her. They run past and upstairs. Next thing, a guy with a stretcher goes running past, and as they bring Steel down, I'm pretty sure he's still breathing, but they pile him into the chopper with Ares by his side, and they fly off. They fit Ray with a collar and then attach her to a backboard, and once strapped tight, they lift her and take her to the chopper. I climb in next to her as Cade shouts over, "Where are you taking them?"

But we lift off and fly away, too, leaving the guys in turmoil behind us.

Tank

We stand and watch them fly away into the distance, turning to head back inside. "Where the fuck you going?" Dice questions.

"To check everyone's okay and get those out that need medical care. Someone's gotta check on the others." As I storm back into the building, I'm met by Savage trying to hop his way out. "Wait out front with Cade. I'm going to get everyone else out!"

I head through the church and find a few guys banged up a little and Dozer slumped against the podium. "Dozer, can you hear me?" He must have passed out. He's lost a fair bit of blood. Looks like he took a bullet to the hip and one to the shoulder.

As he comes around, the first word from his mouth is, "Ray?"

"They've taken her and Steel to the hospital. Come on, let's get you out front, and when I've got everyone, I'll take us to the clinic to get sorted." He leans against me as I pull him to his feet, helping him outside and sitting him against the front of the building.

251

Viking's out there ordering Carmen's guys to fetch the armoured trucks and kill anyone else they find. I walk back inside, up the stairs, and into the room where everything went to shit. My brothers and Doc are covered in blood and in total shock. "Guys, we need to get out of here. I don't know if they called reinforcements, but we must all leave now. The helicopters have left and taken Ray and Steel."

Doc tries to get to his feet, but he's shaking. "It's bad, Tank. I tried with everything I had… the bullet went in under his vest and just ricocheted through him. This blood… it's all his. It's all his, Tank. I tried."

"Doc… was he still breathing?"

"Yeah!" he rasps.

"Then we need to go." I help him to his feet, and he staggers a little. "You okay?"

"Yeah… it's just shock. I'm fine."

"Priest, you need to get to the clinic."

We get everyone downstairs, and those that are good head back to the MC. Those that need attention will come with me to the clinic. I look around, and no one moves, "Move it the fuck now!" I yell, and it shocks them all to get up off the ground. We lost a few good men tonight, but not as many as we could have lost. We did good.

As we head outside, we split into groups. Eleven of us need medical attention. The rest, Doc can patch up later. I take those and load them into the armoured truck. The others make their way back to the other trucks and head home. Before getting in the truck, I call Skye, and she answers straight away.

"Tank?" she gasps.

"Yes, love!"

"Thank fuck. Ray…?"

"Her and Steel have been taken to hospital somewhere. Ares and Dane are with them. Some of the guys are wounded, so I'm taking them to the clinic. Then I'll be home, okay."

"Okay… Tank, I love you."

"I love you too, love."

As I hang up and head to the clinic, I thank my lucky stars I didn't get more than a graze.

After some of us are patched up, the ones that are able to head home, it's a sombre return. The girls are gathered together in the coffee shop. Skye comes running out and throws herself into my arms. I melt into it as I hold on tight, thanking whoever was looking after me that I made it home to my family.

"Where's Tray? I need to hold my boy!"

She grins at me, grabbing my hand and pulling me along. "The girls are looking after him."

As we walk into the coffee shop, they're all there: Scar, Demi, Carmen, Beauty and Tali. Tali's rocking Tray in her arms and brings him over when she sees me. "Hey, what are you guys doing here?"

Carmen smiles. "When Viking rushed off to help you find Ray, we wanted to be here when she got back."

"Have you seen Viking?"

"Yeah, he told us the news. We're gonna stay till we have an update on where she is and how she's doing. Then we'll see. Dice says we can stay at the apartment till we hear."

I nod as I hug my little boy tighter, and he wriggles in my arms, grabbing my thumb and holding onto it. Fuck, I love this little boy more than anything. I close my eyes and breathe him in.

"You okay?" Skye asks, and I smile.

"Just tired." I kiss her on the cheek. "I'm gonna head home. You wanna stay for a while? I can take Tray with me if you like?"

She looks over at the girls and back at me. "I wanna be where you are. Just give me a minute to say bye."

Walking back up to the lodge, I sigh. "What did they tell you about Ray and Steel?"

"That Steel got shot, and Ray went through a window."

"It's bad, love!" I turn and take her in my arms and hug us all together. "Steel took a bullet which went in under his vest, so it hit him pretty badly, and Ray…" I shake my head. "She fucking lost it when Steel got shot and threw herself at Dante, taking them both out of a three-storey window. Dante ended up dead, impaled on the weather vane, and Ray, well, was unconscious on the floor when we got down to her. Ray's pregnant, but with the fall… we don't know what's happening or where they even are. They were medevaced away. They could be anywhere."

"Are you okay…?" She reaches up and cups my face.

"I am now!" I lean in and kiss her. "Let's go home."

Cade

Tank took us all to the clinic, and a couple of us needed surgery, so we had to stay in. Tank must have gotten word to Bernie and Marie as Marie's turned up at the clinic. I'm in a foul mood. I don't have my phone, I can't call anyone, and I'm stuck in fucking hospital, and I've no idea what's happening to my fucking daughter. I keep trying to clench my fists, but the pain I get through my shoulder is excruciating.

"Cade, oh my! Are you okay?"

"Hey Marie. Have you heard anything? Where's Ray?"

"When Dane sent Ray a message to say they were coming for her, she sent an information dump straight to us. It contained everything Cade, Bernie and Bran took, all the teams, and they're destroying the rest of Sebastian's organisation. They say they will be home tonight. She did it."

"Great, but where is she? Is she okay?"

"They medevaced her and Steel to the med centre at the main base. She took a nasty bump to the head and has a broken arm, but she's gonna be okay. They're keeping her on bed rest for the foreseeable future to monitor the babies."

"Babies…? As in more than one?"

"Yep!" she squeals. "We're gonna be grandparents to twins."

"Fucking Hades!" I shake my head. "I've only just found out I'm a dad, and now I'm a grandad." I sigh as I try to get out of bed. "I need to see her, Marie. I need to go to her. How's Steel?"

She shakes her head. "He's still in surgery. Bernie sent a clean-up crew in, and they pulled a few guys who were still alive out, but we don't have IDs yet. They're in surgery, too. The others that were dead, they brought back for funerals to be arranged or disposal of those that aren't ours."

"And Bas?"

"Tank and Dane said he's dead, but not confirmed yet."

"Can you take me there? I need to be near them." I start to get out of bed, but she pushes me back down and then presses the buzzer for the nurse.

"Let's just make sure you're good to travel, then I'll take you straight there, okay? I wanna be there too."

I nod as the nurse comes in and quickly leaves to fetch the doctor.

After giving me the lecture about resting and taking my meds, then saying I will need physio, I sign myself out, and we head over to the base. Marie gives me her phone while she drives, and I call everyone I need to.

Bran, Bernie and Dane don't answer, but I'm not surprised. I call Demi and give her all the information I have on Steel and promise to call her when I arrive and see him for myself. The girls have convinced her to stay with them, at least until they have more information. I call Ares, and he answers the first ring.

"Marie," he rasps.

"It's Cade. How are they?"

He takes a deep, stuttering breath, "Ray's banged up, but okay, babies are strong, but Steel…! He's still in surgery, and they said it's gonna be hours, but they'll let us know as soon as they know anything." I hear him slump into a chair. "Fuck, Cade, she's…"

"Let's not think about that right now. Ray's strong, and those babies, they have to be okay."

"Fuck Cade, are they even his?"

"I have no idea. We don't know what she's been through; if they're not his, it certainly wasn't through choice. We just need to tread carefully, okay? I'm coming there now, should be there in a couple hours, okay? Let me know if anything changes."

"Will do."

As we get to the base and head inside, Ares and Dane are there by the waiting area. They both look like shit. I make a call to stores to send us some sweats and trainers over as I'm back in my bloody clothes, too. I leave Marie in the waiting room and take the boys through to the staff showers to get cleaned up. When we get back to the waiting room, there's a commotion going on. Nurses are running everywhere and screaming and shouting, and one nurse is holding Marie by the shoulders and not letting her through the double doors. When I walk in, Marie just looks at me and sobs. "It's Ray."

I shove past everyone, and Dane's hot on my heels. Ares gets in between the nurse and Marie and hugs her while we follow the commotion. As we push into Ray's room, a bedpan comes flying across the room. She's stood in the corner screaming as she throws things with her good arm, and the room is chaos. She's flipped the table, and the chair that was at the side of the bed is now near the door, along with the bin and the bedpan she's just launched. A doctor is standing in the doorway, shouting for security and a sedative.

"Back the fuck up." I yell as I push through into the room. "Ray, it's okay."

Her voice comes out wrecked. "They won't tell me what's going on, where he is, what's happening. I need to know where he is. Dad, please?" She sobs as she drops to her knees, and I run over to her, scooping her up in my arms as Dane helps her up from the other side and hugs us both.

We stay like that till she calms down, and I turn to face the doctor, "Tell her what's fucking going on with her husband."

"She doesn't need any more stress, the babies—" The doctor starts, but I interrupt him.

"Tell her what's happening right the fuck now, or I will fire your fucking ass and find someone who will." The doctor looks confused till security arrives.

"White Knight, Black Queen, Black Rook." One of them nods.

258

"Sirs, ma'am, what do you need?"

The doctor pales as he realises who we are.

"Sorry, sir, of course." He nods. "I will retrieve his chart and update you." He scurries out of the room.

"You can stand down, gentlemen. Thanks." They nod and leave the room, and Dane pulls us both tighter.

I hold her as tight as I can, and when I finally let go, she looks up at me with her beautiful blue-grey eyes and sighs.

"You called me Dad." I take a deep breath.

"I did." She half smiles at me.

"I love you, Squirt."

"Love you, Dad."

The door pushes open, and Dane steps back as I wrap my arm around her, and we turn to look at the doctor. "He's still in theatre; he's stable, for now, but if he survives, he's going to have a long recovery ahead of him. We're doing everything we can, and someone will be along to update you as soon as we know anything different."

She scrubs a hand down her face, "If I lose him… I left him… What if he thinks I don't want him?"

"I told him everything. His stupid arse wouldn't stay home. He was still looking for you. It was the only way I could get him to be patient." Dane tugs her out of my arms. "Back to bed, dickhead. You threw yourself out of a three-story building while fucking pregnant. You should have been born a cat."

She smiles as he shoves her back to bed. There's a knock at the door, and as it opens, Ares and

259

Marie are standing there. Marie runs straight to the bed and hugs Ray that hard. I think she's gonna pass out from lack of oxygen.

I drag her a chair next to the bed, and she sits in it. Ares is still hovering near the door. "If anyone wants a coffee…" Dane and Marie nod.

"I think I need a tequila, the whole fucking bottle!" Ray grimaces.

"Well, you can have water and pretend it's tequila. How about that?"

"Fine." She grins at me.

"Ares, can you give me a hand?" He nods and steps back out of the door. We head to the staff room, as the vending machine coffee sucks balls. "You okay?"

He sighs and shakes his head. "What the fuck do I say to her, Cade? I mean, I wouldn't blame her if she hates me. I mean… I fucking hate me."

"This is Ray, mate." I clap him on the shoulder, "She'll probably punch you. You'll take it as you deserve it, then you'll be fine."

"Really?"

"Yeah. Word of warning, though, she punches like a freight train. The last time she punched me, I was out cold. When Bernie woke me up, she was gone." I shrug. "You'll be fine… once it's over."

He grimaces but nods as we raid the staff room for snacks, too, then head back to the room.

As we push into the room, Ray's asleep, and Dane has fetched some of the bigger, comfier chairs and some blankets so we can at least be semi-comfy.

"Marie, do you want to stay in one of the rooms we have, that might be more comfortable for you?"

"I'm not leaving her side." I nod and give her a kiss on the head before sliding into a chair myself.

I'm not sure how much time passes as we all doze off, but I hear the door click open, and Bernie pushes his head through. Standing up, I walk over and meet him in the corridor.

"How's things?"

"Bas's organisation, everything's gone. We burnt it all to the ground… there's not a single person or building left… the fucking intel she sent at the last minute, fuck… she's good." Pulling me in for a hug, I wince.

"Hades." I mutter under my breath.

"How is she? How's Steel?"

"She's Ray, broken arm, concussion but good. Steel, no news yet. Still in surgery, last we heard."

"Once they're stable, we will transport them to the clinic so they can be closer to home."

"Where's Bran?"

"Sent him to be with Demi. She's freaking out and I thought there's no point in the whole fucking club being here. I said I'd get her to FaceTime them when she's up to it. Demi's gonna gather everyone in the coffee shop so they can all see her."

"Fuck. We were fucking lucky this time, Brother, we could have lost her."

Nodding, he hugs me. "I know, Brother. How's the baby?"

I pull back from him, grinning like the twat that I am. "Babies." I grin. "Fucking babies!"

Barking out a laugh. "Fucking overachiever, she couldn't just save all our asses and be pregnant with one baby; it had to be two. Wait, tell me it's only two?"

"Yeah, it's only two." I chuckle. "Fucking grandparents, Hades, can we actually do this again? Kids, I mean. We barely survived them fuckers."

"I cant fucking wait!" He laughs.

"You're a fucking sadist, that's why."

"It'll be a breeze. We know what we're doing this time."

"She called me Dad." I blurt out.

"It suits you."

Grinning, we slide back into the room. Dragging in another chair, Ray grumbles as we enter before her eyes flutter open. "Pa," she rasps. Her voice is wrecked. It sounds sore when she speaks. Bernie walks over and hugs her. "It's all gone, Squirt. You did so good."

She nods and smiles, and he hugs her like he's never gonna let her go again, and I smile now that the family's back together. We just need Steel to pull through; otherwise… fuck knows what she'll do.

Dane steps out of the room to call Dice, and we all just sit, wait, wish, and hope. That's all we can do right now.

After a bit more sleep and a few hours later, a doctor comes in. He looks like he's come straight from surgery. "He's stable, for now. He's lucky the bullet went through his shoulder then in under his arm but at a downward angle. It ricochoted off his vest, puncturing his lung, liver and kidney. We had to remove the kidney and the damaged liver, we repaired the lung, he needed several blood transfusions, and we've placed him in a medically induced coma."

"So… what now?" Ray sounds scared and frustrated.

"Now we just wait. We've done all we can for him now. It just depends on how strong he is."

"I need to see him."

"You need to stay in bed to rest yourself." the doctor snaps.

"I'm sorry," Ray grits her teeth, "I don't remember asking for fucking permission. I need to see my fucking husband right now."

The doctor lets out a frustrated sigh. "I'll get a nurse to take you. You must go in the wheelchair, though. You're on bed rest, and if you want those babies to be okay, you need to take it easy."

She just nods.

"I'll send someone shortly."

Ray

The nurse takes me through to see Steel. He's so pale. He's lost so much fucking blood. "Stay in the chair," she insists as she wheels me as close to the side of the bed as she can get. Before putting on the brake and leaving.

I take his hand in mine and kiss the back of it. "Hey, beautiful." I sigh. His hand feels cold in mine. I close my eyes, rest my head on his hand, and contemplate what life will look like now. What if he doesn't make it? What if I'm left alone with the babies? I don't even know how to look after a baby, let alone fucking two. This is gonna be a shitshow of epic proportions.

I remember hearing somewhere that if you talk to coma patients, they can hear you. "Steel, baby, I love you. Please come back to me safe, please make it back. If you can hear me, don't give up, okay? I need you. Our babies need you. I'm so sorry I left you at the cabin. If I had known then what I know now, I would never have left. I would never have let you believe I was dead. I did it for you all. I didn't realise... the cabin... that's where we would conceive our children. The doctor says that when I was tortured by Roach, and he burnt me with the screwdriver under my arm, he actually damaged my implant, so technically, it's Roach's fault. I know you said you wanted kids, but I hope to Hades you still do after everything we've been through. I just want to be a family. Do you think I deserve to be happy? I hope I deserve to be happy. I don't want to not be with you. I love you. I need you to come back to me, Steel. Baby, please, don't leave me." I rest my head on his arm and sob. Everything just gets the best of me, and I can't help but let it spill out. I don't know how long I'm there, but I must have cried myself to sleep as I feel a gentle nudge on my shoulder. I jolt upright, but it's just the nurse.

"Come on, we need to get you back to bed."

I nod and kiss the back of his hand. "Goodnight, my heart, my love. See you soon. Don't leave me, okay!" I kiss his hand again before I'm wheeled back to my room. We can barely get the wheelchair in as there are too many chairs dotted around. They said only two to a bed, but when you own the place, I suppose no one wants to be the one to say you can't do anything.

"Ray." Ma smiles as her eyes flutter awake. "You okay, child?"

I nod. "I'm fine, tired." She nods as she helps me into bed while the nurse takes the chair away.

"Do you need me to do anything for you?"

I shake my head but grip her hand, looking at the guys sleeping around us. "Will you stay with me, Ma?" I grip her hand tighter and lean in. "I'm so scared." I close my eyes, sigh, and feel the bed shift as she climbs up next to me.

She wraps her arms around me, and I snuggle into her chest like I used to when I was little and first lost my mum. She used to hold me till I fell asleep, so none of the boys knew, and I was so grateful. I didn't want them to see me as weak.

As my breaths even, I relax against her. She whispers into my ear, "I've got you, my child. I always will. Sleep, and take care of yourself and my grandbabies."

I take a deep breath and hold onto hope as it's the only thing I have left right now. Hope that the twins will be okay, hope that Steel will be okay, and hope for a future which is more than I had a few days ago.

It's been just over two weeks since my world was flipped on its head. I still feel like I can't breathe, eat, or sleep. I'm still on bed rest, and it's driving me insane. I'm done. I sling the covers back, take a shower and pack up my things. I'm still in the hospital, but that's only because we own the fucking thing.

I head past the nurses' station, and Sharon pushes up from the chair. I glare her away, "Not to-fucking-day, Sharon!" She nods and sits back down.

I push into his room, pull the chair to his side, and take his hand. "You need to hurry the fuck up and get well. I'm not done here. We're not done yet. Do you hear me? Listen and listen fucking good. I'm here. We're. Not. Fucking. Done!"

I keep pulling and twisting at his fingers, pinching the back of his hand, anything to get him to wake up. The doctors come in for morning rounds, clearly not expecting me to be sitting there. Flicking me a stern glare of disappointment. "Mrs. Ste—"

I cut him off with a glare of my own, to which he apologises.

"I'm sorry, Black Queen, you really should…"

He trails off as I fix him with another glare. "How long? Before he wakes up? I want to take him home."

"We're monitoring him, and he's slowly starting to respond. He should wake up any day now. We won't know until he wakes up what the situation will be."

"Throw everything you have at it, Doc. I want him fit, well and home as soon as possible." I stand and turn to face him. "That isn't a request. That's an order."

The doctor nods and scurries out of the room. I know I'm being unreasonable, but I'm done waiting. I'm itching, and I know what I have to do. I just need to focus. Get. Him. Home.

The rest of the day is uneventful. I know they will come for me tomorrow, I haven't forgotten what day it is, but I hate him, and I refuse to go to his fucking funeral. So I pull my phone out…

"VERIFICATION."

"Sierra 8674463," I recite.

"VERIFIED! …IDENTIFICATION?"

"Black Queen, Delta 1."

"CONFIRMED! …REQUEST?"

"Patch to Dispatch!"

"Patching now, please wait."

"Dispatch."

"Dispatch, it's Black Queen Delta 1. What teams do we have available within my area for immediate dispatch?

"Bravo 8."

"No."

"Delta 6."

"Hades, no!"

"Foxtrot 5 or Echo 9."

"Foxtrot 5, why didn't you lead with them? Send them now. Transfer orders: I want them under my command and mine alone. Immediately."

"I'll need confirmation."

"Black Queen Delta 1, consider it fucking confirmed. I'll ping my location."

"Yes, ma'am."

As I slide my phone back into my pocket, I sigh, awaiting the shit storm tomorrow will bring. I take his hand in mine. "You need to come back and hurry the fuck up about it. I need you to come back to me. Do you hear me? Stop being a selfish prick and open your goddamn motherfucking eyes!" I scream out in frustration, and a nurse comes barrelling through the door, wide-eyed.

"Sorry... I thought... sorry!" She says as she backs back out of the door.

A few hours later there's a knock at the door.

"Come in." I shout, and the door cracks open. Foxtrot 5 walk through the door. They've filled out since I last saw them. As I rise from my seat, they survey the room warily. "Black Queen," Black Rook nods. "We were given instructions to report to you."

"That's right, you're under a new assignment permanently. You will answer to me and me alone, regardless of what Dad, Pa and my brothers say. Do you understand?"

"Yes, ma'am." They all nod.

"I need this room under constant guard, no one in or out other than me, the nurses and the doctors."

Black Bishop steps forward. He's the hot head. The fiery one, over-opinionated. "You pulled us from active duty to be security guards?" his voice like butter with that southern drawl he has going on.

I take a step forward. "Yeah, I fucking did. Do you have a problem with that?"

"No, ma'am." He sighs, shakes his head and steps back.

"Black King, are we gonna have a problem here?"

"No, Black Queen, there's no problem here, just making sure we're all on the same page."

"No one in or out. I don't care, you hear me? You answer to me and me alone, am I clear?"

Choruses of, "Yes, ma'am," ring out from the burley men as I push past them into the corridor. I have work to do. I need to get things ready to take him home.

"Stand down. Black King, that is an order."

"Respectfully, sir, we have new orders, and our team has been transferred to the command of Black Queen, who has requested no one other than herself and the medical staff to enter the room."

"Ray...Ray...! Ray! Do not make me kill my men to get to you."

I can hear the commotion in the hall, but the guys are standing their ground. Pa is losing his shit, and I can hear Dad pacing, well, more like stomping as we do when we are thinking.

"Squirt, please?" Dad asks much gentler than Pa's methods, but still, I crack the door and glare through it.

"Save your breath, Dad. I'm not going, I... I'm not going."

"Please, you'll regret it if you don't. You need closure, you ne—"

"Let me stop you there. What I need is in this room. What I need is to concentrate on getting him

270

home. I'm not trying to be difficult, but I know what I need, and this is it. Give my best to everyone there, but I won't be leaving this room." I step back, closing the door, and I can hear mumbled whispers before a loud crash. That will be Pa. He's either punched the wall or lobbed a chair. Either way, not my problem.

The next few days are uneventful. Dad and Pa stay away. Ma has been by, but I explained that I needed to be here, and she understood. She didn't like it, but she understood.

So Hades knows how many days later there's a twitch in his fingers when I'm pinching and pulling at them. My eyes flick to his face. His eyes start to flutter, and his fingers twitch again. Leaning closer to him, I say, "I'm here, it's Ray, I'm here, come back to me."

His eyes continue to flutter before opening and resting on mine. He tries to talk, but I shake my head. "Don't, you're okay, you're in the hospital. Don't try and talk just yet. Let me get the doctor."

As I go to move, he grabs my hand, grips gently, and shakes his head. "I'm not going anywhere. I'm just gonna press the button, okay?" He nods again, and I press the call button.

The doctors enter the room, and I step to the other side of the bed and hold his hand. It seems like the right thing to do. He's confused; that much is

271

clear, but the doctors check him over and say they'll monitor things to keep him calm and let him rest.

A few more days, and he's more coherent, starting to talk and ask questions. He wants to come home with me, so they're trying to make that happen. I assure them I have all the care he needs sorted, and then I can take him home in a few days. They don't want me to; they want him to stay here, but when you own the place, they really have to do what you say.

"Black Queen, I strongly implore you to revise your decision. I don't think it's wise for him to leave. He should be here with the medical staff."

"I don't need him fully fixed, Doc. I just need him well enough to go home. He will get all the care he needs there. I have everything in place now. You just need to say the word so we can leave."

"I don't like this, Black Queen. He's still not out of the woods. We still need to run more tests to see if there's any lasting damage."

"Is he well enough to travel?"

"In an ambulance, yes!"

"Is he well enough to be looked after at home? He's not gonna die if we move him?"

"No, he's not gonna die if you move him. We just nee—"

"You need to get him ready to leave. Give me a day and a time to arrange the fucking ambulance, then we will go. I have everything he's ever gonna need, so you just worry about making sure he's strong enough to make the trip home. Then, you're done. We don't need anything else. Do I make myself clear?"

"Yes, Black Queen. Friday… We will arrange the transport, and I will send a nurse back with you for a home visit to make sure you have everything in place that you need."

"Won't be necessary, just arrange the transport. I have everything else under control."

"Black Que——"

I step forward. "Doctor!" I square him a look as I cross my arms over my chest. I'm nowhere near as intimidating now with my bump protruding out from me, and my arms just kinda rest on my stomach rather than against my ribs, but I suppose that's the joy of being pregnant, something I've not really had the time to enjoy. I need to get him home before I get much bigger, before I'm useless.

"Friday." He nods, then scurries back down the corridor.

"Black Queen?"

I turn to see Black Rook standing there, not my brother, the one under my command. When The Armoury was set up, the initial group of my dad and pas were Alpha 1 and named after the white chess pieces as white always goes first. They were White King, White Queen, White Bishop, White Knight, White Rook and White Pawn. From there, every team was given a name: Bravo, Charlie, Delta, etc, and a number between one and nine. Me and my brothers are Delta 1, and these guys are Foxtrot 5. Then, there are three to six members in each team. Black King, usually the leader, Black Queen, some forgo this if they're an all male crew and there are less than six of them, sexist bastards, they can pick which name they have from those confines. My dad well, my pa Daniel—he was White Queen and rocked it. These five guys kept the Queen, and I respect that. They split into two shifts, three in the day and two for the night shift. Black Rook is here now, along with Black Bishop and Black Queen.

"Yeah, what do you need?"

"You're taking him home?"

"Yeah."

"Is that wise after everything? I mean, we heard the stories."

"You don't need to worry yourself about that."

I turn to leave. "Ray," he whispers out. I turn and glare at him. "We've known each other for a while now, and I owe you. I thought we were friends. I'm just worried about you."

I sigh. "Look, Rook, I appreciate it, but I need to do this. I picked your team because you're on it, and to be honest, I needed someone I could trust to follow me blindly. Will you do that for me..." I step forward and touch his arm. "Elijah?"

"Fuck, Ray, you're pulling that card, huh?" he chuckles and shakes his head. "Fine."

"Is that guy fine or girl fine?" I smile back.

He shakes his head. "Guy fine."

"Awesome." I turn to walk away.

"Ray?" I turn back as he steps forward, "are you ok?"

"I'm fine."

"Is that guy fine or girl fine?" He smiles back

"Girl fine!"

He sweeps me into his arms and hugs me. I stiffen at his touch but then sigh.

I whisper into his ear, "Thanks, Elijah."

"I've got you, you know that."

I take a step back.

"So, Black Queen, what are our orders?"

I smile at him. I appreciate the not lingering on the sensitive situation, and I appreciate that he will have my back. I also appreciate him not treating me like I'm going to break or have a mental breakdown after everything.

"We will transport him out of here Friday. I will need you all. I'm expecting some issues at the club when I arrive back. They're not gonna be happy about this. I need to get him set up and settled. It's gonna be a long few weeks. I've got everything set and don't need to leave him for about four weeks. You five are the only ones who know what's happening, and I want to keep it that way."

"You sure about this? You sure you can do this in your condition?"

"I'm doing this for them. I'm more determined than I've ever been. I can do this. I need to do this."

He nods. "Okay, then. I'll let King know on shift change, and we will make a plan for Friday."

I nod and turn away. Friday… Friday can't come soon enough.

It's Friday, and only me and Foxtrot 5 know what's happening. We're all outside the room as the doctor arrives. I give the boys a nod. "You know what to do?"

They all nod back. They're in full tactical gear, armed and ready. I hope I don't need them, but it pays to be prepared. My brothers don't know we're coming, but as soon as they see us, they will scramble, and I need to get where I'm going before they get in the way.

I step into the room with the doctor. "Hi." He smiles from the bed.

"Hi, ready to go home?"

"Home?" His voice is still scratchy from the tubes and lack of use.

"I just need to go through the next steps of treatment with you," the doctor interrupts, "and then you're good to go. I'll just need the forms signing, and then you're ready."

After listening to the doctor, I pull the wheelchair and blanket to the side of the bed.

"Hop in."

"Shall I get dressed?"

"Nah, you'll be fine. Let's just get you home."

He slides into the chair, and I wrap him up tight.

"You ready?"

"Yeah," he grits out.

I walk to the back of the chair, sliding my hand into my pocket and pulling out the syringe. I lean down and whisper, "See you on the other side, big brother." as I slide the syringe into his neck.

"What the…?" He grabs at his neck as he tries to get up out of the wheelchair, but I wrap my arms around him, holding him in place. "You took everything from me. It's only fair I return the fucking favour, Bas!" I spit at him.

His head lolls, and I grin against the side of his face. "Payback's a bitch, big brother, and that bitch is me. Karma's a bitch too! You'll get yours, and when I've destr–"

He sags in my arms, and he's out, fuck. I had a whole speech ready and everything.

As I wheel him out, the guys form a circle around me. "Front doors," Queen instructs.

I nod as we exit the hospital. There's an armoured truck, the ambulance and a second armoured truck at the rear. We load Bas into the ambulance, and me and Rook climb in. Queen and Bishop head to the back truck, and King and Knight head to the front. "You know where you're going and what to do?" They all nod, and we pull away.

"Just follow the truck." I smile at the driver, sliding a brown envelope onto the front seat. "You've seen nothing, you know nothing, you remember nothing."

He nods as he slides the money into his jacket. There are also a few pictures of his pregnant wife and daughter in his house and the daughter's kindergarten with the money just so he knows what I'm capable of if he forgets his place. That will be a nice surprise for him when he opens it.

As we near the club, I slide towards the driver. "Stay close to them, and when you see the barn, they will open the door. I need you to reverse in, but do it quickly. Do you understand? We don't have much time."

"Barn? I thought–"

"Don't think, just do as you're told, then you leave and never look back. Okay, John?"

His eyes shoot up to meet his hairline. Yeah, fucker. I know all about you. He just nods and carries on. As we fly through the gates at the club, the siren's going. The guys are scrambling out of the club, and Dane and Dice are flinging the apartment door open, but we're going too fast. We sail past and straight up to the barn.

Carrying Bas down to my office, I leave King, Queen and Bishop at the door. I can hear my brothers yelling and running towards the barn as the ambulance peels away.

"Just throw him on the table, then head back to The Tower. I will call you once I'm done!"

"What about your brothers?"

"They can't get down here once I shut myself in, and I've got supplies to last four weeks. Just stay put, okay?"

They nod and leave. I can hear the commotion outside as the door slides into place.

Ares

As we run towards the barn, there are three guys, fucking The Armoury by the looks of it, guarding the door. I slide my gun away. This has fucking Ray written all over it. "What the fuck's she up to?" I bark out as Dane pushes through the crowd.

"King, What the fuck, man? What's going on?"

"Just following orders, sir." He grins.

"Okay, then stand down, that's an order." Dane barks as he reaches them and goes toe to toe.

"No can do, sir." one of the others sings out in a southern tang to his voice.

"Bishop." Dane barks.

"We're under her command, and she took us over. We only answer to her now."

"She can't fucking do that." Dane spits.

"She can, and she did. She changed our contracts, NDAs, orders, everything. We are still The Armoury, but we're the Black Queen's Armoury now. Sir." King chuckles.

"You think this is fucking funny?"

"Guys, come on, let's not do this. You know it's not gonna end well," a guy says as he exits the barn with another guy.

"Might have known you'd be on her side, Rook." Dane spits, and the guy he called Bishop laughs.

"Why do you think she picked us?" Bishop nods to Rook.

Rook grins. "We should go, we're done here."

They step around us and head to the truck "Rook." Dane barks, and he stops and turns to look at him, "What's going on down there? Is she okay?"

"Payback!" He shrugs and they climb into the trucks. They peel out.

Shaking his head, Dane heads over to the control panel, and there's a beep. Then he tries again, and there's another one. "Fuck." He kicks at the hay bale. "She locked me out."

"So what do we do? How the fuck do we get down there?"

"Honestly? We can't go down unless she opens the door." Dane shakes his head.

He pulls out his phone. "Dad, what the fuck's going on…? She what…? So what now…? What the fuck do you mean? Dad…? …Fuck!" he bellows and ends the call. "She's fucking lost it. She's taken over Foxtrot 5, discharged Bas from the hospital, informing them she's going to take care of him at home, and then she's locked herself down there. Wait? Tank, where's Skye? Does she still have the app for the cameras?"

He pulls out his phone and calls Skye. "Hey, love… No…? What do you mean…? Okay, love."

"Ray called her an hour ago and made her delete the app and then told her we would call and ask for access to it and to make sure it was gone."

"What the fuck is she up to?" I spit out.

"Nothing good," Priest says, "if she's down there with him. She will have to come out soon to eat and sleep, so I'll wait for her."

"We'll all wait." My inner circle nods. We're all here, and I send the rest of the guys away.

"Is this why she nursed him back to health? So she could fucking kill him herself? We all thought she betrayed Steel's memory by siding with that fucking parasite, but we underestimated her again, didn't we? Who saw her last?"

"We all kind of gave her... space after she started going to Bas's room. So I haven't seen her since then. It's been weeks." Priest hangs his head and shakes it.

"We all did the same. Dane says Dad went to get her the morning of Steel's funeral, and she refused to go and said she hated him and wasn't leaving Bas's side. We all thought... Fuck, I don't know what we thought."

"Hey," Dice says, stepping forward and hugging Dane. "None of us saw this coming. We all thought she had taken Bas's side when Steel died, but we were all grieving too."

"He's right. After Steel was shot, he underwent massive surgery for hours and hours. It was touch and go for a good week, and then two weeks after arriving he just died... just couldn't hold on any longer. Ray broke. She smashed up her room, screaming, shouting, she wouldn't let any of us near her. She was still supposed to be on bed rest, but the way she threw that bed over... it was like she was possessed. They kept her on bed rest for the next two weeks, and we all arranged the funeral. We asked her opinion on things, but she didn't speak. It was like she wasn't even there, just empty, gone. Then, the day before the funeral, she packs up and goes to his room to get him well to bring him home. She told us, and we all flipped and left her again.

"I thought she would change her mind and come to his funeral, but when she didn't, I washed my hands of her again, and I never went back, but I should have. Steel wouldn't want us to leave her alone. He would want us to help her raise his kids, and we left her alone again. Fuck, why doesn't she just tell us what she's fucking doing? We all turned our backs on her again, and then she goes and proves what assholes we are."

"So what do we do now, Pres?" Blade taps my shoulder.

"I'll be fucked if I know." I shake my head.

Scar

It's been a few weeks since the shitshow that happened, happened. Steel is dead, Ray's off her rocker, and I fucked up. I let her down, and of all people, I should have believed in her, but I didn't. I believed the worst, and I don't know that she'll ever forgive me for that. Dad pulls me close. "It'll be fine. Worst-case scenario, she'll punch you, and you'll take it and move on."

"Dad, that really doesn't help. I would probably end up in the hospital bed next to fucking Bas."

"That's the spirit!" He smiles at me.

"It's like waiting to be hung." I whisper to Dad.

"Or shot." He grins.

"You're really not being fucking helpful, Dad."

"What if she's on Bas's side now and takes us all down?"

"Have you learnt anything? Ray has a reason for everything. You all think Steel's death has tipped her over the edge, and maybe it has, but she wouldn't just toss you all aside and join him after everything she's been through and lost. She must have an angle, something. This is Ray. I just want my girls happy and back together."

I smile at him, as his girls might be back together soon, but one of them might be missing a fucking head.

My phone blings with a message, and I open it.

Ray: I'm gonna call you. Don't answer it. Let it go to voicemail, then gather everyone at the barn and play it for them.
Scar: Ray, please, can we talk?
Ray: Just do as I ask. You owe me!
Scar: Okay.

My phone rings, and I ignore it. I climb into my car with Dad, and we head towards the club. Dad calls Uncle Bernie and Uncle Cade on the way, and they're gonna call Bran and Dane and meet us there. Dad tries Ares, but there's no answer. When we get to the clubhouse, it's empty, so we head to the barn. Pulling up, they're all there. "What are you doing up here?" I ask them all.

Ares just says, "Ray," and points to the hay bale.

I hear the truck pulling up outside. "Bernie," I say.

"Ray left me a message asking me to play it for you all."

Demi shakes her head. "I can't right now. I just can't."

"Demi, we need to hear what she has to say. She lost everything, and most of us didn't help her."

"I did, Scar. I had her back, and she couldn't even go to my brother's funeral. Where was she when I needed her?"

"We just need to listen, then we can decide how to proceed. Maybe it will be enough insight so we can make an informed decision," Dad says. He's always the voice of reason when it comes to Ray. He always believes in her, and she never lets him down.

We all gather closer. Cade, Bernie, Bran, Marie, Dane, Dice, Demi, Blade, Skye, Tray, Tank, Priest, Viking, Ares and me.

"Ready?"

We all nod.

I hit "Play".

"Hey, so if you're listening to this, then things have taken a turn. Firstly, I want to say I'm sorry, Demi and Skye. I'm sorry I wasn't there at the funeral to support you, but I was being selfish, and I knew if I went, I would break, and I can't afford to break right now! I fucking miss him so much, and every time one of the babies moves and kicks, it tears out a piece of my soul, knowing he's never going to see them be born or grow up. But I can't think about that right now. Ares, I know you never trusted me, and I'm sorry I made you feel like that. Tank, Skye, and my favourite little man, Tray... you supported me through everything. I'm sorry I let you down. My brothers, I love you all. I just can't be with you guys anymore."

"Wait, pause it!" Ares says. "Fuck... the message is she saying goodbye to us all? Is that what this is? She's gonna do something fucking stupid. Shit, we need to get down there now. How the fuck do we get down there?" He turns and runs to the hay bale, kicking and smashing at it, throwing the hay everywhere. Guilt finally kicked in and did a real number on him. "Ray!" he starts shouting. "Ray, let us in! Ray, please." He drops to his knees, trying to clear the last bits of hay before finding the solid steel trap door and pounding against it. "Ray, I can't lose you too!"

Viking steps forward and crouches down, taking Ares's hands in his, looking down at his bruised and bloodied knuckles. Ares takes a shaky inhale, and Viking pulls him to his feet.

"Carry on, Scar. We need to listen to everything. We need to hear her out this time instead of assuming the worst." Viking reasons, and we all look sheepish. That's what's gotten us into all this trouble: jumping to conclusions and assuming the worst. So we all take a breath and listen.

"I know you all hate me, and I don't blame you. I hurt you all, but most of all, I hurt myself trying to protect you from my brother. He threatened all your lives if I didn't come back to him. When Steel… when Stee—" You hear her take a deep breath and release it shakily, stuttering it out before taking another. "When Steel was shot, I knew I couldn't live without him. I knew I had to kill my brother, and I genuinely thought I had on that roof, but when I woke up in the hospital, and you told me what happened, and then the team that went to clean up found a few people still alive, I never imagined one of them was Bas, and in that moment, I knew I couldn't let him die. He needed to wake up. How could I get us revenge, retribution or

286

justice for what he'd done if he just died in the hospital? He needs to pay, and that he will.

I fought to keep him alive so I can kill him in the most painful ways I can think of. I want him to suffer, I want him to plead, I want him to beg, and when it's finally over, and he's gone, this time, I will make sure he's gone for good. Only then can we have true peace and rebuild and start again. I will pack up and leave once I've done what he deserves. I will start again somewhere else, me and the babies. I know I can't repair what's happened between us. We're fractured, and the parts will never fit again; I am truly sorry for the part I played in this, but know I will always love you all, and if I don't see you again in this life, I hope we find each other in the next. I love you all. Goodbye."

"What the fuck? Dane, you need to get us in there," Cade spits. "Now!"

"Pa, I can't. She locked me out of the system."

"Then find a fucking way back in. Now!"

Dane nods and takes off, running Dice hot on his heels. "We need to stay here. Someone needs to stay here so she can't leave. We need to guard that door twenty-four-seven," Cade says.

"Demi, can you, Skye, and Marie come and help me at the coffee shop? We will sort out a schedule and grab food and drinks," I say.

We don't need her to do that, but I just want to feel useful. We all suck at the minute, and we need to make sure Ray doesn't slip out without anyone noticing, like the slippery little fucker she is.

Ray

As I wait in the office, I look around. I have a fridge with enough supplies for four weeks. This shouldn't take longer than that. I installed a shower and a toilet down here after dealing with Skyes thing, so I'm good in that department. I brought an air mattress down here as I need to be able to rest. I know I have to look after myself and the babies and can't lose myself down here. I'm dragged out of my thoughts by groans.

Walking to the side of the metal table, I have my brother strapped to it naked. What's good for the goose is good for the gander and all that.

"Where am… where am I?"

"You're home."

"H… H… Home?"

I laugh. "Well, as home as you'll ever be again. You'll never see the outside of this room, big brother," I spit at him.

"Ray, I can't move."

"No fucking shit, Sherlock! You're strapped to my torture table. Why the fuck would you be able to move?"

"Ray, we're fa–"

"Let me stop you there before you make an even bigger twat of yourself. You and I are not and will never be fucking family. You destroyed my family, you took my kids' dad away from them, you destroyed my brothers' trust in me, and now I'm all alone down here with you!"

"Blood's thicker than water, Ray!" he coughs out.

I bark out a laugh, causing him to flinch. "Blood's thicker than water?"

"Yes, yes, Ray. You and me, we could be good. We could rebuild, we cou—"

"Let me stop you right there. You, big brother, are and always have been a cunt of the highest order, the cunt of all cunts, the King cunt of Cuntsville. You are a right royal cunt! But blood's thicker than water just proves it! Do you know what the actual saying is?"

He shakes his head, well, as much as he can with it strapped at the forehead to the table.

"Blood is thicker than water. You're referring to that because we are blood. We're actually a team. We should have each other's back."

"Yes, it's you and me against the world!"

I laugh again. "The actual saying is 'the blood of the covenant is thicker than the water of the womb.'" I shake my head. "It means, arsehole, that chosen bonds are more substantial and significant than family ties. You've been saying it to me all this time, and it means the total opposite of what you're preaching. Like I say, a cunt of epic proportions!

"Ray!" He gasps. "Whatever you think you want to do, you don't really. This isn't you. This isn't right. We're family."

"The family that offered up my fanny and my bloodshed as payment for your debt. The family that faked his own death only to plan and plot our demise. The family that destroyed mine and left my children without a father and me without a heart. Ray's left the fucking building, Brother! You're shit out of luck if you think you can find any love left for you. You will pay with your life, but it will be slow, and it will be painful, and I will make sure you get to see every drop of that so-called thicker blood as I spill every single cell of it. I will destroy you, and I will make sure that what I do to you this time, there's no coming back from. You're not going to show up again. You will stay dead this time, and I will deliver you to Cletus's myself."

"Cletus's?"

"Ah, you missed so much over here, Brother! Cletus makes the most exquisite alligator products, and since you owe me a pair of boots as I had to toss my favourite ones, that's going to be my gift from Cletus for all the nutrition we supply him for his stock."

"You're not making any sense."

"Fuck, big brother, you got thick after you died! Cletus has an alligator farm. We supply him with the bodies of our enemies, and he repays us with the finest alligator products going. My favourite boots I had to abandon because of you, and Cletus is going to recreate them using the alligator he feeds your disgusting, nasty, deluded arse to. And they will make me smile every time I wear them, knowing your blood paid for them."

"Ray!"

"Firstly, we need rules. One, don't you go bleeding out before I've severed everything I can imagine. Two… Well, one should do for now. We will come back to them later if we need more rules."

"Ray, you don't want to do this. You're my little sister. I love you."

"Funny, the arsehole who was beating me and allowing Roach to torture and try to rape me didn't love me, didn't care enough to stop. What makes you think I give a shit about you?"

"I'm your brother. I know how much that means to you"

"No. Bran and Dane are my brothers. Ares, Dozer, Priest, Viking, Blade, and Tank are my brothers, and I love them with everything I have. That's why I joined you, to protect them from you. You, big brother," I grit out at him, "are nothing to me, and every bit of pain you've inflicted on me over the years, you're about to receive tenfold. You labelled me Reaper as a slur, as something pathetic skulking in the shadows. But you're about to meet her, the her you helped create, and trust me, you will shit yourself.

You removed the last piece of humanity I had left, and I thank you because I will now get the opportunity to bring her out. I kept her and Ray separate for so long, then I met Steel and could actually be them both together, and I'd never been happier. Now, Ray's definitely gone. I can't even hear her faint voice of conscience in my ear. All I can hear now are screams and shouts of 'make him suffer,' and suffer you will!

"Ray, please."

"Fuck, you really are a pussy! After everything you and Roach did, you didn't once hear me beg. I haven't even started yet, and you're wanting out!" I shake my head. "You're such a fucking disappointment, Sebastian!"

I turn and walk to my toolbox, done with this conversion. "Ray, Ray, please, Ray, we can sort this, Ray."

"We're done talking." Holding the scalpel in one hand and the tweezers in the other, I walk back over to him.

"Let's begin, shall we? Oh, and feel free to scream all you like. No one's coming for you, big brother. I don't need a TV screen to prove that. You know it, and I know it, which will make this so much sweeter."

I walk down to the soles of his feet, and start to slowly remove the skin from them, and toss it into the bin. He screams and pants and cries, and I've barely got started. Next, I remove his toenails with pliers. I just rip those fuckers out. "This little piggy went to market," I squeeze his bloody big toe between my thumb and finger. When I release it, he's gasping, so I grab the next one. "And this little piggy stayed at home." I squeeze down on it. "This little piggy had roast beef." I squeeze. "And this little piggy had none." I squeeze again. I grasp my tin snips from the drawer. "And this little piggy cried…" I squeeze the snips around his toe, and the crunch makes me groan.

Fuck, that's satisfying. Grabbing a spoon and the blow torch, one of those cute little ones for making crème brûlée, I cauterise the wound.

Once the screaming stops, I move to the next foot. And then I go through the toes again until I've removed every single fucking one, tossing them all in the bin.

The only time I take a break is when he pisses himself, and I have to take a step back so I don't get covered in it.

But now I head over to the freezer, grab a lasagna ready meal, stick it in the microwave, and lay down on the air mattress while I wait for my food. I tune out the whimpering and calls of my name. I mean, I could end this and be done, but where's the fun in that?

DING! The sound of the microwave startles me awake, and I slide off the mattress and grab my food. I walk over to Bas and sit beside him. I cut a fine slice of the piping hot lasagna and move it along his skin between his top lip and his nose, making him scream out from the burning sensation. "Good to know!"

I flop back into my chair and start to blow my food. It's clearly too hot from his reaction. It's late after I finish my food, and I'm exhausted. I take my rubbish away, and I come back with some eyelid clamps, fuck knows what they're called, the ones they use to keep your eyes open. I lean over him and quickly slide them on from either side. "Get some shut-eye, big brother. Tomorrow's gonna be a long day." I laugh.

Dane

I've been in Dice's tech room all day, and I'm working like a dog trying to hack into Ray's system. Fuck knows who she's had help from, but they're good, and I can't find a way around it. Dice rubs at my shoulders. "Babe, let's go home. You need to get some rest."

"I can't. Wait till I get to her. I need to get in there and make sure she's okay. If I lose her, Dice… if she does something stupid… if he gets loose and kills her down there… I can't." I rub my eyes and lean back into him, and close my eyes for a second.

"Let me help," he mumbles, walking round to the front of me and sliding to his knees. He slides off my trainers and pulls my sweats down. "Fuck, I love it when you don't wear underwear." He grins at me.

"I thought you hated it?"

"I hate it when we go anywhere, and people can see what's mine."

"Oh yeah, and what's that?" I grin down at him.

He grabs my dick and licks it base to tip. "This." He grins at me before taking me in his mouth.

"Fuck," I groan, sliding my hands into his hair.

294

His tongue swirls around my shaft, and his teeth graze up it. Licking along my slit and diving in for every drop of pre-cum he can, my head lolls back. "Fuck, Dice, like that, baby, just like that."

It's not rushed or hurried as he slowly fucks my dick with his glorious mouth. He pops my dick out of his mouth but continues with his hand, and he sucks my balls into his hot mouth. "Fuck, baby," I gasp out. Damn, his mouth makes me want to do filthy things to him.

"Dice," I gasp again, and he sucks on one of my balls, nipping with his teeth and groping and tugging with his hands. "Fuck, baby, I need to fuck you so bad." He stands and undoes his shirt, throwing it on the floor behind me, and then he slides out of his jeans and boots, standing in front of me with nothing but his boxers on. I could come right then and there. I step up towards him and kiss him, groaning into his mouth as our dicks rub together. He grabs them and rubs them up and down in one hand. I groan and slide my hand around him, and rub at his tight hole.

"Fuck, baby," I grit out. "I need to be inside you so bad. Do you have lube in here?" He shakes his head as he kisses my neck. "Fuck," I grit out again.

I spin him around and slam him down over the desk roughly with my hand on the back of his neck. I slide down to his arse.

"Stay!" I bark as I open his cheeks and dive between them, tonguing his puckered hole like I'm auditioning for a job. I pull back and spit against it, and he groans.

295

"Ah, you like that, huh?" I spread his cheeks and spit again, sliding my finger straight in, and he bucks as I reach the knuckle, pulling my finger out. I spit on him again, and he groans and melts into the table. I spit one last time as I stand up and slide straight in balls deep. He clamps down hard on my dick, and I gasp. "Fuck, baby, I want to tie you down and do unspeakable things to this arse, fuck." I pull out and slam back into him. "Hades, Dice, I'm losing my fucking mind."

I pull him back off the table slightly so his dick isn't pinned anymore. "Hold on, baby, this is gonna be fast and dirty."

He stretches his arms up and pushes back off the wall, grinding into me. "Give it to me, babe, make it fucking hurt like only you can. I want you to fill me up and slam into me so I know who owns me."

"Fuck, Dice, I love your filthy mouth. Hold on, baby!" I take a breath and pull out, only to slam back into him. I have one hand wrapped around his dick and the other kneading his arse cheek and pulling and pushing it against my dick as I slam inside.

"Dane, fuck, there, right there. Ah, like that. Fuck... Dane, harder, babe, harder. Jesus, Dane!" He gasps and groans as I thrust harder, tugging on his dick with a ferocity that's making my teeth grind. "Fuck, Dane. Fuck me like you own me, babe, yeah, like that, there... there." He's panting and slamming back into me. "Fuck! Dane, that's... that's it... that's... fucking It! I'm gonna come, I'm gonna... Fucking Come."

The ribbons of come shoot all over my hand and onto the floor as I pump him for every drop. "Fuck, baby, hold on." I grab onto his hips and crash into him over and over, pulling him back into me as I slam myself against him. "Fuck, baby!" I grit out. "I'm. Gonna Come. Fuck!" I roar as I shoot my load into his tight hole, filling it up so hard. I sag against his back as my dick softens inside him.

"Jesus, Dane, I fucking love you." He turns his face and kisses me.

I slide my hand up to the back of his neck and hold him down, and I gently rock my soft cock in and out of him. I can feel the come sliding between his arse cheeks, and fuck, if that isn't hot.

"Dane!" He gasps. "I can't."

"Yeah, you can, baby, I'm gonna fuck this arse slow and steady till my dick is rock solid again, and then I'm gonna fucking ruin you for every other man."

I lazily slide in and out of him as he shudders against the desk, kneading his cheeks and grinding into him, pulling him back against me. He feels it at the same time I do, my dick thickening, hardening, solidifying and fuck, what a glorious feeling, as I feel the goosebumps spread across his skin and the shudder of his legs I start to speed up. I reach around him and rake my fingers over his dick. "Fuck, Dane, you're gonna be the death of me!"

I kiss down his back as I pump his dick with one hand and hold him down with the other. "Ah, death by dicking if I remember rightly." I grin against his skin. I start to speed up, and as I do, I hear the door click and swing open. I grin to myself, and I feel Dice tense under me and try to pull away. We're both naked.

"Fucking hell, that's hot!" Scar says before schooling herself and backing out the door.

"You can stay and watch if you like?" I grin, and Dice grumbles.

She nods, walks in the door, and closes it, leaning back against it. I mean, Scar's fit as fuck, but I've never looked at her like that, but being watched by anyone always has my heart pounding.

"Fuck my life!" Dice grumbles, and I kiss his back.

"Let's put on a show for Scar, baby!" I wink over at her, and she licks her lips and slides her hand down her front, sliding her dress up and her hands inside her pants. "Fuck." I grin at her, and she winks back.

"Show me what you got, Dane." And I do. I kiss Dice's back and stand back up, rolling my hips against him, and he groans. I grip his hips and slam into him as I tug against his dick. I turn to look at Scar, and she's rubbing her clit resting on the door. She rolls her fingers around her breast and hooks it out of her dress, pinching at her nipples.

Dice groans as he makes eye contact with her, and she bites her lip. "Fuck, guys, you two are so god damned hot, ahh, fuck," she exhales on a moan. As I pound into Dice, Scar's flush rises across her chest and cheeks. Dice is mesmerised. It's not about wanting to fuck Scar, it's about the way we're making her feel by fucking in front of her, and she's loving it.

Dice gasps as I hit that spot he loves and shoves back against me. Scar gasps again against the door.

"Fuck, Dane, don't stop, please don't fucking stop!"

"I got you, baby." I grin down at him, but he doesn't take his eyes off Scar. She licks her lips.

"Fuck, tell me how it feels, Dice," she whispers out.

"So fucking good, he so fucking big! I feel like I might lose my fucking mind, Scar." He gasps her name as I slam into him. "Fuck, and his rough hand around my dick... it's making my skin dance. I can feel his come from before sliding around between us, and every time he bottoms out, my skin feels like it's on fire.... I'm fucking.... gonna come... if you keep looking at me like that!" he grits out.

"I wanna see that," she purrs, "I wanna see that so bad, Dice."

I ramp up my speed, and they both gasp, "You gonna come for us, Scar?"

"Yeah." She grits out. "Yeah, I'm gonna come. You fucking guys are so sexy together... fuck, I can't... I can't stop it... I'm gonna... fuck..." She gasps as she comes, and Dice's arse tightens around me as he comes over my hand and on the floor again, and I spill inside him. I collapse on his back, watching as Scar's heart pounds in her chest and as she pants, staring at us both.

"Fucking hell, Scar." Dice shakes his head as I stand, pulling him with me. He rests his head against my shoulder. "You're definitely gonna be the death of me." He grins, and I laugh. Scar's sorting herself out and straightening her dress as I slowly pull out of Dice. We all groan as we try to right ourselves and clean up the best we can.

"What did you need other than that?" I chuckle, looking at Scar.

"Shit, fuck. Yeah, I came to say Demi had made food for everyone in the coffee shop."

"We'll be there in a minute, okay?" She nods and steps through the door. Dice walks toward me, still shirtless. You really like being watched, huh?"

"Yup, you really like it when I spit on your arsehole, huh?"

"Yup!" He grins at me and kisses me like a starving man, and I'm the best thing he's ever tasted. Pulling apart and finishing getting dressed, we head to the coffee shop.

Ray

I don't know how long I've been down here. I eat when I'm hungry, drink when I'm thirsty, sleep when I'm tired, and stab, maim, and torture when I'm feeling murdery. There seems to be more of the murdery feeling going on than the other stuff, but with it being underground, I've no idea what day or time it is, and it doesn't really matter. My job is to make his life, what he has left of it, as miserable as possible, and if they were handing out gold medals, I would be getting gold in every single event. I've removed the toenails, the toes, the fingernails, and the fingers. He's passed out a few times. I've removed a lot of skin, so much skin, I could give the guy from *Silence of the Lambs* a run for his money. I reckon I could make myself a new dress, not that I'd want to, that's just fucking sick, but I could, and that's what makes me smile. "Lady Gaga's meat dress is so last season. Skin is the new meat." I chuckle to myself, but then realise it's out loud, and then I laugh harder.

Fuck, it feels good to laugh, even if it's at the thought of me wearing my brother's skin like a dress. Fuck, I think I'm losing it. I actually think my cheese has slid off my cracker, and after all this, they're gonna come get me and sit me in a padded cell for the rest of my life. Damn, that's a miserable thought.

Bas groans, and I think to myself there's no rest for the wicked. Then I think, *fuck, I must be awful*, then realise I'm slowly removing parts of my twin brother's body to exact my revenge on him for killing the love of my life. Yeah, not your average fairy tale. "Wakey wakey, rise and shine, motherfucker. Today's a new day, or maybe not, who the fuck knows? You ready for some fun?"

"Thirsty," his voice scratches out.

"Shit, sorry." I turn and walk away and come back with the hose, turn it on full blast in his face and laugh. "Let me know when you're not parched anymore, big brother." After he's sputtered and choked enough, I turn it off.

"Please. Let me go?"

"You're such a fucking pussy, Bas. Did I beg, did I plead, did I cry?" I shake my head. "You're such a fucking disappointment. You really should have been put down at birth."

"Ray, please?" His voice is tight from all the screaming. I'd say he screams like a little girl, but that would be offensive to little girls everywhere. "You're my sister."

"Yeah, that doesn't really fly, Bas. You know, the whole trying to let me get killed, the offering me up to be raped, then torturing me and letting your henchmen try to rape me? Luckily, he wasn't capable. Oh, and don't forget killing the love of my life and the father of my children, all because you were fucking jealous of Bran and Dane. All because I was your toy, and you didn't want anyone else playing with me. Fuck you, Bas. You're no brother of mine. You should have stayed fucking dead. Let's help you along with that now, shall we?"

I look down at my handy work. Nails gone, toes gone, fingers gone, ears gone, teeth pulled out, nipples gone, skin majorly gone. The only skin left is his face and his back. I will be fucked if I can be arsed to turn him over. Maybe I could call the boys. I pull out my phone, and it's dead. Fuck, when did that die? I shuffle around, looking for my charger. Damn it, where the fuck is it? I thought I had one. Nope, nope. "Fuck!" I roar. Damn it. I'm gonna have to sneak out and grab my phone charger. Fuck, fuck, fuck. I take a good, hard look at myself. Damn it. If it's daylight, I'm gonna scare the shit out of someone. I decide to take a shower and at least change my clothes.

Sliding the trap door open, the sunlight burns my eyes. Fuck. I wince as it opens, and as I step into the barn, three faces are glaring down at me. "Erm, Hey guys!.

"Hey, guys? That's what you got? You've been down there nine days. Nine fucking days, Ray and you come out with fucking 'Hey guys'?" Ares starts pacing. "Jesus fucking Christ, Ray, we've been worried sick with the situation and the message you left Scar. The babies... fuck, Ray, are the babies okay?"

I nod. He storms towards me, and I back away. "Don't." I bark out, and he steps back like I've shot him, and he looks hurt. Crushed.

303

"Ray?"

"I just need my phone charger. I still have work to do."

"Work to do? Ray, what the fuck?"

"I'm sorry, Ares. I would love to stay and chat, but I'm kinda in a hurry here."

"Ray, you need to grieve, you need to give yourself time, you need to be around people who care about you."

"Well, when I find those people, I will be happy to stay around them. For now, I need to get my phone charger so I can call my team."

"Your team?" Blade asks. "Who the fuck are 'your team'? I thought we were a team."

"We?" I shake my head. "There's no we, Blade. When I needed you, you weren't there."

"Ray, that's not fair. We didn't know where you were."

"That's the thing, though, Blade, it wasn't that you didn't know where I was. It was that you thought I had done those things, and you didn't care. Excuse me, I have pressing matters to attend to, and I need to get on those urgently, and as soon as I'm done here, I will head off and find those people who what was it you said oh yeah , care about me."

I push through them, and Priest grabs my arm. "I always believed in you!"

I sigh. "I'm sorry, Priest, that was unfair of me. I'm sorry." I go to walk away.

"Don't leave Ray, please."

"I'm sorry, Priest, I don't belong here. I'm not welcome. I got your brother killed." I swipe a stray tear that runs down my face. "For that, I'm truly sorry, and I will never forgive myself, but I'm not staying where I am not wanted or even liked."

I walk away, leaving them standing in the barn, bickering amongst themselves.

Rook

We've been holed up in The Tower for nine days, and we're all going stir-crazy. King's phone bings. "Thank fuck for that!" he says as he reaches across the table for it where we're sitting playing poker. "Fuck's sake!"

"What's wrong?"

"She wants us to go there to turn her fucking brother over so she can start on the back. She's run out of things to carve!"

"Carve?"

"That's what it says." He tosses me the phone.

I grimace. "Fuck, that's graphic!"

"Yep, I gave you the abridged version."

"Do you think she's okay?"

"She's your fucking friend," Queen spits.

"Its technically your fucking fault we're sat here right now with nothing to do but play with our dicks." King groans.

I waggle my eyebrows, "I told you I could help with that!"

"Rook, why would I want your rough, scratchy beard near my cock? Start looking after the thing or shave it off, and I might let you." King grins at me.

"Fucking tease!" I wink at him. King's not gay or even bi, but I know if I shaved the beard, he would totally let me suck him, but then I would look like a twelve-year-old girl, so I probably shouldn't.

"Come on, stop flirting and let's go!" Queen nudges me as he walks past.

I jog to catch up with him. "Ah, don't be jealous, sweetie. You know I'll fuck you good when ever you want." I sling my arm over his shoulder. "King can even watch. You know how much he likes that."

Queen grabs my face with his whole hand and pushes me away from him, rolling his eyes at me, but I see the smirk on his face. He fucking loves it when I fuck him, and King watches. And we all laugh as we head out to see what shit show we're gonna find at the office.

"Fuck, I don't know if I can look at burger meat the same again. I need a fucking drink after that shitshow." I grimace.

"She's your fucked-up friend," Bishop spits out.

"Yeah, and she's been through a lot, okay? So don't judge, and she's fucking talented. Did you see the state of him? And he's still alive. Fuck, it's been nine days, and the fucker's still breathing. And did you see the fucking size of her? She looks fit to burst. All that and being pregnant with twins. I know whose side I want her on."

"Damn fucking right." King grins. "Right, let's get shit-faced. She said she wouldn't need us again for a couple of days, so let's let loose."

"Are we staying here or going to the club?" I ask hopefully. "We haven't been dancing in so long, please, King, please?" I whine.

"Fine, but you're driving!" He laughs.

"Damn it! I'll take it, let's get ready!" I whoop as I head to the shower.

We end up at the gay club, which is my absolute favourite club around here. I am the bi one of the team. Queen is gay, but King, Knight, and Bishop are straight as an arrow. Well, King has a voyeurism kink, so maybe his arrow has a slight bend, but he never touches. Well, he does himself, which is so hot. We spend a lot of time together so we have become extremely comfortable in each other's company.

As we dance and the guys drink, Queen becomes the flirt that he is, dancing and rubbing his ass into my groin. I slap it. "Queen, fuck off, man, you're driving me nuts." He chuckles as he turns and nips at my neck. I groan. "Fucking hell." I scrub a hand down my face. "I need some fresh air."

"Hey, what's wrong?" Queen grabs my hand as I walk away. "Nothing, sweetie. You have fun, okay?"

He pouts, but he turns and starts dancing with the others. We're not a couple. We fuck occasionally because it's convenient, but I don't know, the lines keep blurring for me, and although we said it was just a fuck, and we're free to do what we want with other people, I'm just not into that anymore. I kinda want someone, something more, but I know he doesn't, so I keep pulling away from all the other stuff, the lingering looks and soft touches, the kisses he tries to give me when no one's around. To be honest, I've been avoiding him as much as possible, but fuck, it's getting harder to.

I step outside and lean against the wall. I grab my smokes and light up, tilting my head to the sky and breathing out a puff of smoke.

"Hey, beautiful," a feminine voice breaks me from my thoughts. He's a tall, thin, wiry-looking guy, definitely wearing guyliner and lip gloss, totally not my type. "Fancy some company?"

"What kind of company were you thinking about?" I keep my position, blowing the smoke into the sky.

"Maybe I could blow you and bum a smoke after. You could buy me a drink and see if you wanna take all this back to your place." He gestures to himself when he says all this.

"I mean, it's rude not to, but there will be no coming back to my place!" I say firmly.

"Oh, okay." He steps in front of me before lowering himself to his knees. He runs his hands up and down my thighs as I continue to smoke. I know I said I wanted something more, but I also want to stop thinking about Queen twenty-four-fucking-seven. He starts to undo my zipper, and I hear a roar as I exhale.

"You must be fucking shitting me right now!" I turn just in time to receive a punch to the cheek, knocking me sideways.

"Motherfucker!" I grumble and shake my head from side to side, trying to shake the sense back into me, but as I look up, a hand grabs me around the throat and slams me into the wall. "Queen," I gasp, grabbing at his wrist and forearm to get him to release me. The wiry dude scrambles to the other side of the alleyway we're in and stays there, his heart almost pounding out of his chest. "Queen," I croak out as my eyes start to roll into the back of my head, and I start to sag into his arms.

"Queen!" King snaps. "Fucking release him." He lets go as I drop to the floor, coughing, spluttering, and gasping for breath.

I try to talk, but nothing comes out. I'm clawing at my own throat, trying to see if I can gulp some air down, but I can't. I'm gasping, and I see him turn and stomp away. "Queen?" I croak out after him, but he storms off. Bishop takes off after him. King and Knight pick me up one either side, and I sag against them, grasping at my throat.

"What the fuck was that all about?" King asks.

"I don't fucking know," I gasp. "I was having a smoke, and that guy offered to blow me, I thought—"

"You fucking dipshit!" Knight spits.

"What?"

"Don't tell me you haven't noticed?"

"Noticed what?"

"Fuck's sake!" King shakes his head.

"He's fucking in love with you, ya twat!"

"What? Who? How?"

"Fuck's sake." Knight shakes his head, "For a fucking intelligent man, you're thick as shit sometimes!"

I stare between them both, rubbing at my throat. "What the fuck are you talking about?"

"Come on, let's get back. I think we should call it a night," King says as we head back to the truck.

Queen and Bishop are nowhere to be seen, and King checks his phone. "Come on, they're heading back to The Tower. They'll meet us there."

Parking up and heading inside, my stomach turns. What if they're right? Could Queen really be in love with me? I mean, I haven't fucked anyone else since we first hooked up, even though it was just supposed to be convenient. We've been in this team since we were eighteen, three years, and I've been fucking Queen for at least half of that. Could he really like me, like... really like me? Fuck. I head up to the roof to be alone and pull my phone out, calling the one person who will always tell me the truth.

"Hey."

"You good?"

"Yeah, I know it's a shit time, but I need some advice."

"And you thought the girl locked in her office carving bits off her brother for sport was your best option." A soft chuckle comes through the phone. "Hades, Elijah, you're fucked!"

I sigh, "I know, but I have the guys and you, and that's it, and it's… it involves one of the guys, and I don't know what to do."

"So you're finally gonna admit you're in love with Queen, huh?"

"What? I'm not. Shut up."

"Dude, you so fucking are!"

"Well, he doesn't even like me. He tried to choke me."

"Ooh, in a sexy way?"

"No, not in a sexy way. Is there even a sexy way to choke someone out?"

"Fuck yeah, there is, dude, damn it!"

"Why did I even call you? You're no help."

"Whatever you did, apologise and suck him off. He will forgive you."

"That's your advice? You don't even know what I did."

"Yeah, blow him. That will sort it all out. I gotta go, dude. I'm up to my nuts in blood and piss. Catch ya later."

"Cheers, Ray." I hang up on her for being no help whatsoever.

"Hey, can we talk?"

"Queen," I gasp and step back. "I'm sorry whatever I did to upset you. I'm sorry."

"You don't know?"

I look him in the eyes, then down at the floor and shake my head. He steps towards me, lifts my chin, and turns my face backwards and forwards. No doubt he's looking at the bruise on my face and finger prints around my throat.

312

"You've no idea what pissed me off?"

Again, I shake my head. "I'm so sorry, Queen. You're the last person I want to upset."

"You can't think of any reason I would be pissed at you?"

"I thought we were having a good night. I thought we were great, and I went out for a smoke, and then you punched me."

"Rook, you dumb motherfucker. You were about to get your dick sucked."

I frown. "Yeah."

He sighs like I'm the thickest cunt he's ever encountered and pinches my chin tighter. "By someone who isn't me."

"What?"

"Fuck's sake." He shakes his head again. "I don't want you to let anyone who isn't me suck your dick. Ever. Again."

"What?"

"Fuck's sake, Rook!" He drags me flush to him and crashes his lips to mine. He is not gentle about it as he steps into me, pushing me back against the wall.

"Queen," I gasp.

"I don't want you to be with anyone else ever again." He smashes his lips back against mine and rubs the palm of his hand over my dick, grinding into me. "Do. You. Understand?"

I nod.

His hands slide up my chest, unbuttoning my shirt before tossing it on the floor. Taking the buttons of my jeans in his thick fingers, he undoes them and shoves them to my ankles. My dick springs free, and I groan at the cold air that brushes against my overheated skin.

"Queen. Please," I gasp.

He drops to his knees and takes me to the back of his throat as my head falls back against the wall. I slide my fingers into his blond hair, and his bright blue eyes gaze up at me as he swirls his tongue and takes me into his throat again. "Fuck!" I grit out, "Queen!" I tighten my hold on his hair as he stares into my soul, and he winks at me, deepthroating me into oblivion, I stutter and come down his throat. Once I've finished, I sag against the wall, and he slides up my body, reaches up and scrunches his hand into the back of my hair. Eyeing me, he grins.

"How many people have you fucked since we started fucking?"

"None," my voice comes out hoarse and breathy.

"How many have sucked you off?"

"None."

He nods once. "How many are you gonna let do anything to you again?"

"One!" I grin breathlessly. "You, sweetie. Only you!"

He crashes his lips to mine again, and I groan as I can taste myself on his tongue. He tastes like a future I didn't know I could have.

Ray

I'm so tired. I'm struggling now. This has become a chore rather than the retribution, the revenge, the closure I thought I needed. There are more parts of my big brother in the freezer than there are still attached to him, yet the cunt's still breathing. "How are you not fucking dead yet?" I spit at him. There's nothing really left of him anymore. I destroyed him, and now there's only a shell. I take out my circular saw. I double bag the bin and start by removing a foot, then the other, then I cut at the knee, then the other.

I look at his limp dick and nearly barf. Huh, so blood and guts, I'm fine with. The limp dick of my soon-to-be-dead brother? Not so much. Good to know. He is bleeding out profusely now as he dies a horrible death, so I just continue to chop off limbs. It's gonna be much easier to transport him to Cletus's in bits. So I take off his arms and the rest of his legs. I remove his head and hold it up. Grabbing out my phone, I stick my tongue out and take a selfie before tossing it into the bag. Fuck, I'm gonna have to call the guys to shift this lot!

"King!"

"Yes!"

"I need you lot at the office. I'm done, and I need you to make a delivery for me."

"On our way!"

I start trying to chop the rest of my brother up, but the saw just won't go fucking through. Its blade isn't deep enough, so I have to toss him over and do him in sections motherfucker difficult till the fucking end!

I bag everything in manageable bags, grab all the smaller extremities from the freezer, and then I leave the bag with his head in on the side open with his face staring out! "Don't want you to suffocate motherfucker!" I laugh out loud to myself.

My phone rings, and I answer. "Yo. What up?"

"Black Queen, it's King. We're outside, and your guard dogs won't let us in. How many of them can we kill before you get pissed?"

I climb up the stairs, literally looking like a horror movie, and as the trapdoor opens, all eyes turn to me as I climb out.

"Holy fucking shit, Ray." Dice comes running over to me, stopping a foot or so away. "Are you okay? Are you hurt?" He reaches for me, but I pull back. "Get Doc. Someone call Doc."

"Dice, shut the fuck up, I'm fine. Now, can you lot shift and let them in? I've got dinner reservations, and I need to get cleaned up."

"She's fucking lost it!" Ares shakes his head as he moves to the side, and the team drives the truck in

316

and opens the boot. Bishop gets out and lays a tarpaulin out in it.

"Down here, fellas." I lead the guys down and show them the bags, then I joke about leaving the bag open. Tough crowd.

"Hey, you good?" Elijah walks me to the far end of the room.

I wrap my arms around myself and look up at him. I shake my head once. He nods. "What can I do, Ray?"

"Just deliver him to Cletus's. He's expecting him."

"Then what?"

"Once I'm cleaned up, I'm leaving. I need to grab my clothes, but that's it. I don't have any transport, so…"

"I'll take the guys back to The Tower, and I'll come and get you, yeah?"

"You will?" I say with a shaky breath.

"Always!"

I nod, and he smiles, and he turns and walks away, taking the bag with the head in, tying it in a knot and hitting it against the wall as he walks up the steps. As I hear them pull off, I drop to my knees, nothing holding me together anymore, and I just sob.

When I can physically cry no more, I grab the hose and clean everything down and climb into the shower. I take a bin bag with me and shove my clothes into it. Once I'm dressed and packed up, I head out of the office, leaving the trapdoor open. I won't be needing it anymore. It's been a couple of hours, at least, since the team left. As I climb out, they're all standing there: Ares, Dice, Bran, Dane, Dozer, Blade, Viking, Priest and Tank.

"Hey." Tank steps forward. "You good?"

I nod and step around them, walking out of the barn.

"Where the fuck do you think you're going?" Ares yells at me.

"The apartment."

"That so?"

"Look, Ares, I know you've probably got a whole speech planned to rip me a new one, and while I probably deserve it, I've literally just bagged all my fucks to give up with the severed parts of my brother and sent them on their merry way, so while I appreciate you've got stuff to get off your chest, I just really don't wanna hear it. I'm grabbing my things, and I will be out of your hair. I'd like to say it's been a wild ride, but most of you can actually go fuck yourselves." And with that, I stomp past them, leaving them all open-mouthed and in shock.

Ares

"What the fuck was that?" I spit after Ray leaves. "Why the fuck does she make my blood boil every time I fucking see her! Good fucking riddance, the sooner she leaves, the better. I'm done. I'm over it. Let's move on."

"Go on then!" Tank laughs.

"Go on then, what?"

"Move on, walk away, be done with her, go on then!" He laughs again.

I fold my arms over my chest. "I will! I am!"

"Sure you are." Priest grins. "Just like the rest of us, we're all so done, and our lives will be so, so, so much better without her and those babies in it. We can all go back to how it was before she even came here, right?"

"Yeah, exactly!" I nod. "Yeah… we will… it will … Fuck's sake, why does she get under my fucking skin and drive me insane, and why do I not want that to stop? What the fuck's wrong with me?"

"You love her! Like we all do, and we've been shitty brothers, and we need to stop her," Blade says. I glance at Bran and Dane, who are standing shoulder to shoulder, arms across their chests, not saying a word.

"How do I fix this? How do we fix it?"

Bran laughs. "You act like Ray's so complicated. She's really not."

"Just tell her you're sorry, you will try to be better, and take the punch," Dane adds.

"Take the punch?" I shake my head. "Nope, no, someone else can go. I've made my peace with her leaving. Everything will be fine!"

"Pussy!" Tank laughs as he walks off.

"Easy for you to say, she's not gonna punch you!" I shout after him. But then we all follow him out of the barn anyway and head towards the apartment. I hang back. What the fuck do I say to her? I know everything is actually my fault for not trusting her, but fuck, how do you admit that to someone who gets under your skin so much that you wanna rip each other's throats out before you hug it out?

As we reach the bottom of the stairs, the door opens, and a bag comes flying out over the bannister, thudding to the floor. A minute or so later, another one follows it. Then, after a lot of cursing, Ray appears, rubbing her back.

"Motherfucking babies kicking me every goddamned fucking second of the fucking day!" she grumbles as she closes the door, turns and sees us all standing there. "Fucking hell, guys, do we have to do this? I'm going. My lift's on his way; just give me ten, fifteen minutes tops, and I will be gone. You don't have to see my fucking ugly mug again! Okay... please... I just can't anymore!"

320

She hangs her head as she walks down the stairs, her eyes not meeting any of ours as she pushes through us. I'm at the back, so I step in front of her and cross my arms over my chest.

"Ares, please don't! I'm done, okay, just please let me leave. I can't argue anymore. I'm drained."

"I know." I step forward and wrap my arms around her. She tries to push me off, and I hold her tighter. "I'm sorry, Ray, I'm so sorry. Please stay. I can't lose you, too, or the babies!" I feel her shudder in my arms, and I pull back slightly, but she pulls me to her harder and just sobs into me while I rub my hand up and down her back. "I love you," I whisper for only her to hear.

After a few minutes, she pulls back and scrubs a hand down her face. "I can't stay, Ares. There's nothing left for me here anymore. I lost my reason for being, my reason for breathing, I lost my sister, I lost my brothers." She turns to look at all their faces, and their eyes are all red-rimmed and glistening. "What do I have left? A club that hates me? What kind of life is that for my children?"

"None of us hate you, Ray. We love you. You can't leave. Please don't leave me. I'm lost without you!" Dice says.

Stepping forward and crushing her into his chest, she starts to sob again, muttering, "It's the babies making my hormones all screwy. I'm not really crying."

"Sure it is." Dice teases. Pulling her closer and whispering something in her ear, she nods. He squeezes her again and steps back. She looks up, glassy-eyed, and takes us all in.

"Does this mean you'll stay?" I ask hopefully.

She shakes her head. "I just need to be alone for a bit. I need... I don't think I can stay here. I just need some time."

"Ray, please. I step forward again. Give us a chance to make this up to you. Just let us try?"

"Ares, I... I..."

One of the guys pulls alongside us all in an armoured truck and gets out. "Ray, you ready?"

"Yeah." She nods, resting her hand on my chest. "Not forever, just for now."

"Promise?"

"I promise!"

I step away and grab her bags for her, throwing them in the truck. "Call me and let me know where you end up, Ray. Please don't go too far, okay?"

She nods as she steps into the truck, and they drive off. I can't help feeling like we've failed her, and in return, we failed Steel and the babies. "Does she have anything for the babies?"

"What?" Tank asks.

"The babies, does she even have anything for them with everything that's gone on? Surely she hasn't been shopping. That's how we make her see she belongs here. We babyproof the fuck out of that apartment and set up a nursery and... fuck, everything. She's gonna need everything. Dozer, get Beauty to give me a call. I need her organisational skills. Boys, get your hand in your pockets and let's buy some shit!"

"You do realise Ray is loaded and can just buy this all herself?" Dane chuckles.

"Don't you piss on my sorry! This is what we're doing to show how much we care and shit like that. We're gonna make sure those babies have a home here and never want to leave. I lost my brother. I refuse to lose his children, too." I clap my hands. "Let's get to work!"

Everyone groans, but we all head to the bar to decide on what we need, as I'll be fucked if I know what babies want or need, but I have decided on mini cuts; those are a must.

Rook

As we pull out of the club, I take a quick glance at her. She's clearly not coping very well, "Where do you want to... Ray? ... Where do you want to go?"

She sighs. "I don't know, maybe a hotel somewhere. I don't really have anywhere to go... kinda burnt all those bridges, well, beds, same difference." She looks out the window and just stares.

I reach over and rest my hand on her leg, and she flinches, "Wanna talk about it?"

"About what?"

"Steel, Bas. The babies, your new scars, any other shitshow I don't know about."

"Not really."

"When did you last sleep or even eat?"

She shrugs, and I shake my head. "Ray, you need to look after yourself... those babies..."

"I know, I will... I just... fuck, Elijah, what the fuck do I do now? No home, no family, no friends—"

"What the fuck am I?"

She turns to face me. "Sorry, my emotions are just getting the better of me. I don't know if I wanna

324

eat fuck, or fight, and I'm in no position to do two of those things, so I don't know what the hell to do."

"Well, in that case then, seeing as I'm the greatest friend ever, let's go somewhere and fuck. I wouldn't do it for just anyone, only you, you understand?" I turn and wink at her as she barks out a laugh.

"Thanks, I appreciate that, and that would probably lead to a fight as Queen would want to kick my arse or try anyway. Maybe I should get some food first just so I can hold my own."

"Come on, I'll buy you dinner. What do you fancy?"

"Fuck, everything I eat just tastes like ash. I don't even care. In fact, just drop me at the next hotel. I'm probably better on my own."

"Okay," I say, but fuck it, I'm taking her back to The Tower. She's got her own room there, at least, and we're all there till she fires us or finds us something else to do.

As we pull in and I turn the engine off, she startles. She's been asleep for the last god knows how long, "Shit." She gasps. "What are we doing here?"

"You're not staying on your own. We're here, so you're here till we figure out your next move."

As the elevator doors open, I'm greeted by the rest of the team. "Hey guys," Ray says as we get off.

Queen cocks a brow at me, and I shrug, following her to her room and putting her bags down. "Shower, rest. I will make you a sandwich, okay?" She nods and sags onto the bed, just staring off into space. She looks so fucking lost. I've known Ray for nearly four years now, and I've seen her wear many faces, but never this one.

"Hey, it's gonna be okay, you'll see."

"I wish I believed that I really do."

She grabs a towel from the drawers and heads towards the showers. I turn and head to the kitchen. The guys are sitting around the table, "Hey, where's Queen?"

"Went to take a shower, why?"

"Shit, Ray just went in there."

"Queen will be fine. A pair of tits and a vag won't startle him too much." King grins, and they all chuckle.

"You're all fucking dicks, you know!" I tut at them all. "She's fucking devastated, she's just lost her husband."

"Don't forget she skinned and filleted her brother." Knight shudders.

The door swings open, and Queen walks in, looking physically sick. "Hey sweetie, you okay?"

"I need a fucking drink." He grabs at King's beer, chugging a massive mouthful. "Shit, I need something stronger."

"What's wrong?" I rest my hand on his shoulder.

"I saw Ray in the showers, naked…" he trails off.

"I take it back. Clearly, a pair of tits and vag have traumatised him!" King laughs, but Queen shoots him a glare.

"Not fucking funny, man. She's carved to fuck, and I mean seriously. I know we were told her brother

326

kidnapped her and held her, but dude, he fucking tortured her. She's a fucking mess. I know her face looked bad, but fuck!"

I storm out of there and head to the bathroom. As I shove my way in. I can hear the shower still running, and as I get closer, she's hugging herself on the floor of the shower cubicle, pools of red running around her. I drop to my knees. "Shit, Ray, what did you do?"

Her eyes flick to mine, and she shakes her head, "Nothing, I didn't do anything. They just haven't healed properly yet. They keep opening up. I just need to keep them clean. They're fine."

"Fuck, Ray, they're not fine. Stand up." I take hold of her hands to pull her up. That's when I see her nails, or lack of them. I look at her feet, and they're the same pink, crumpled skin where nails should be, and as she stands, I notice the carved patch on her hip and over her heart. I rub my thumb across her hip. "What the fuck happened to you, Ray?"

"Bas happened, Elijah, Bas happened."

She's covered in scars and cuts every single piece of skin that isn't tattooed is carved, stabbed, punctured or damaged in some way. I wrap a towel around her and lead her into her room. "Knight, I need medical assistance," I shout down the corridor, and he comes rushing out of the kitchen with the first aid box in his hands.

"Shit," he utters under his breath when she drops the towel and stands there in front of him, blood seeping from her wounds.

"Sexy, huh." She shrugs. But I can see the discomfort at having us there looking at her. She's clenching her fists by her side, and I look at Knight. He nods.

"Ray?" he says, using the softest voice I've ever heard him use, and I'm thankful for that. "Can I come closer and take a look?" She closes her eyes and clenches her fists tighter. She lets out a shaky breath. "Just don't touch, okay? I can sort it myself."

"Ray, some of these need restitching." He says, stepping towards her but stopping and resting the first aid kit on the bed.

"I can do it." Her eyes open, and she finds both our gazes. "It's fine, I can do it."

"Ray, just let me help you, okay?" Knight takes another step, and she flinches.

So I stride straight over to her and take her hand in mine. She initially flinches but then relaxes. "You trust me, right?" She looks between us and then nods. "And I trust Knight, okay? I need you to trust us, can you do that? Let us look after you, please, Ray. Let me help you."

Knight goes over to her bags. "Don't." She rushes over and snatches the duffle handles out of his hands. "Not those." She goes to the drawers and pulls out some underwear and a T-shirt.

We both look at each other again and nod. I take her hand and lead her back to the bed. "Slide them on carefully." I nod to her underwear as I lay the towel down and pat it. "Let's get you fixed up, and I can get you some food." She nods, and I kneel beside her and take her hand in mine. "It's gonna be okay.

328

I've got you." She stares at my hands and her eyes well. Her lip trembles, but she never takes her eyes off my hands engulfing hers.

As Knight touches her skin, she grimaces. "Did I hurt you?"

She shakes her head, "I don't like being touched." Knight nods, removing everything he needs and cleaning and dressing the wounds with as little contact as possible. Once he's done the front, he gets her to roll onto her side and tends to the wounds on the back of her leg. We glance at each other over her, so much destruction on every inch of bare skin but not a single mark on her tattoos. Knight patches her up and goes to leave.

"Knight, thank you." He nods and leaves the room.

"Here, put this on." I hand her the T-shirt, and she pulls it on, sitting up and crossing her legs. She sighs.

"Let me grab you some food, okay?" I pull the covers back, and she slides in. I head to the kitchen, slide straight into a chair, take a deep, shaky breath, and scrub the palms of my hands into my eyes.

Queen rubs my shoulders, "You okay?"

"Fuck, man, she's a mess."

"Hey, she's strong. You know that better than anyone. It's early days, but she's gonna be okay." Queen rubs at my shoulders some more before taking a step back. "Has she eaten?"

"No, I was gonna make her a sandwich." I stand and take a shaky breath before I make my way to the kitchen. I make her a sandwich in silence and then take it to her. When I open the door, she pretends to be asleep, but I can tell she's crying, so I turn the light off and crawl into bed at the side of her.

"What are you doing?"

"Shh, get some rest. I will stay here with you." I wrap my arms around her and pull her to me, and she screws her hand in my T-shirt and whimpers. I cry for her, and we fall asleep in each other's arms.

Ray

There's a slight knock at the door, and it cracks open, then it opens all the way, and I squint my eyes and screw my face into Elijah's chest. "Hey, are you two awake?" Queen takes another step inside. "I brought you some breakfast."

I turn to look at him and go to sit up, but Elijah's hold tightens on me, and he grumbles something.

"He sleeps like the dead." Queen chuckles.

"How long have you guys been together now?"

"Erm, we're not... I suppose we kinda, I don't know that we are." He shrugs.

I smile at him. "It's been a while that I know of."

"He told you?"

I smile. "You sound surprised."

"I mean, I knew you guys were friends, kind of. I guess I just didn't realise you were *friend* friends."

"We play it cool at work. He doesn't want to seem like a suck-up or like he gets preferential treatment."

"Does he?"

"Don't answer that I will deny it all." Elijah's raspy voice cuts through the room, and I laugh.

"No, he doesn't get preferential treatment." I wink and nod, mouthing, "Yes, he does," and Queen laughs.

"Bitch!" Rook pushes me away from him, "Sweetie, come hug me. She's being mean."

Queen's eyebrows shoot to his hairline, and I laugh and shake my head, pushing Rook in the face and further away from me. Right, I need to call a meeting. The guys both groan. "Go let me eat, then I will be with you. I'm literally wasting away over here." I rub my large belly, which is getting so large I can't remember what my vag looks like without the help of a mirror.

After eating and showering, I head to the kitchen, and the guys are all sitting around the table. "So, what's this all about?" King grumbles.

"I know I was a bit of a twat commandeering you like I did and changing your orders, but I'm blaming the hormones for the whole incident. That being said, I appreciate you not being dicks and going along with it, even against my dad and Pa. What I want to know is… do you guys wanna go back or stay with me? I can't promise there will be as much work as you had before, but you will still be able to pull missions from The Armoury, as, in theory, I fucking own part of it, anyway. I'm gonna go make a call, but I need you to decide what you want to do. If you stay with me, it will mean relocating this way, as my family won't let me and these babies too far out of their sight, so the choice is yours." I go to leave, but King stops me.

"You're giving us a choice?"

"Yes, no repercussions either way. You either stay under my command while still being part of The Armoury, or you go back to being The Armoury, no harm, no foul." I nod and leave the room, and head to the roof.

I pull my phone out. "Hey, Dad."

"Squirt, where the fuck are you? Dane said you took off with Rook!"

"Don't make out you don't know where I am right this second."

"Okay, so I know you're at The Tower."

"Floor?"

"Roof."

"See, you knew I was here, and he picked me up in an armoured truck, so you would have been tracking that too. I'm not five anymore, Dad. I know all your tricks."

"I know, Squirt. I miss you. How are you doing?"

"Like I was kidnapped by my deranged brother, beaten, tortured and abandoned, tracked down by my husband, knocked up, pretended to be dead, joined my psychotic brother, who then murdered my husband, only for me to torture, mutilate and chop him up, sending him on his merry way to Cletus's... Yup, that about sums it up... oh, and I'm pregnant with twins, so there's that."

"Squirt."

"I'm fine. I'm in denial, so it's all good if I stay away from the club. I can pretend he's still there; that way, I won't know he's actually gone."

"Why don't you come home, well, to Bernie's, and we can be together? I can look after you. I will look after you, you know that."

"I know, Dad. I just need to sort out my next move. I'm kinda flailing at the minute, and Hades knows what the hell I'm doing, but I think I'm numb, and I don't know what to do for the best, so I'm doing what I should have done to start with, and that's hiding out in The Tower with snacks."

"Well, it seems like you have a whole plan there, Squirt, so what's happening with Foxtrot 5? You know you can't keep them. They're one of our best groups of operatives."

"Yeah, about that, Dad… So, you know, after all I've been through, I think I need to be with the team, and I've told them they can choose to stay with me or come back to you guys. I'm waiting on their decision now."

"Is that so?"

"Yup."

"You know you're avoiding, right?"

"Yup."

"We gonna talk about it?"

"Nope, I'm gonna stay here as long as I can before I have to deal… Dad, I don't think I'm strong enough to really process everything. If I think about it, I might just lose my mind, and I can't afford to do that while I'm pregnant. I think I can finally try and process it all once the babies are here."

"Squirt, that's not healthy, you need to grieve."

"Well, I will schedule some time in between the babies being born and their tenth birthday, okay?"

"Sunshine."

"Don't, Dad, please… he used to… just don't, okay."

I hear him sigh. "Okay… for now."

"Love you."

"Love you, Squirt."

I hang up and pace the roof. I have no idea what I'm doing. I'm over half way through this pregnancy. I'm totally on my own. I've got no husband, no family… well, I've got Dad, Pa, Ma, Bran and Dane, but if I go back to my brothers, how long before I break and fuck knows what will happen then? I mean, I could take out a small fucking country with my hormones alone, but is it hormones, or is it grief? Either way, I'm going to do what I do fucking best: compartmentalising and shoving that fucker into storage so I can stay in this town I've named Denial, population one. Well, I suppose population three.

"Hey," Rook says as he comes out on the roof.

"Hey."

"You good?" I shrug. I mean, what the fuck do I say to that? No, my heart got ripped out and stomped on. No, I watched the other part of my soul get ripped away. I was so lost and lonely I convinced myself that I hated him so I wouldn't have to go to his funeral. I say what I think will work best in this situation,

"I'm fine."

"We'll stay on one condition."

"That is?"

"We want a base."

"Deal."

"Wait, I didn't finish."

335

"Okay."

"We want our own base, a place we can call our own with a bit of land for training. We wanna be close to where you're gonna be based, and we wanna have some down time and do a place up. We have savings, and we still wanna do what we do, but we want a home."

"Deal."

"Deal, just like that?"

"Yep, however…"

He crosses his arms over his chest. "Come on, then hit me with the unreasonable bit to make this totally suck."

"I'll buy you a place, I will give you a budget, anything over that you pay yourselves. I want it to be close to the MC. I think I will end up back there, maybe. I will also need it to act as a home base, so while you have your own space, there will need to be a command centre. But that's negotiable. I will transfer the money now into the team account, and you can purchase somewhere ASAP, but I need to see it and have a say, too. Also, there will be babysitting involved."

"Deal, you have a deal."

He picks me up and spins me around, making me scream, and the other guys come barrelling through the door.

"Fuck, dude, we thought she threw you off the roof." Knight chuckles.

"You did not think that scream was me. You didn't, right?"

"Sure." King laughs.

"So, care to fill us in on what's happening?"

"We get to babysit."

There's a chorus of groans. "What the fuck do we know about babies?" Queen cocks a brow and looks at us all.

I walk toward him, pat him on the shoulder, and grin. "About as much as I do, so we're all fucked."

Ares

I'm pacing in the bar, my fists clenched by my side. Scar is sitting at the table with the laptop, working away on a case, and I just continue to pace.

"Ares, you're gonna wear a hole in the floor at this rate. Come sit down and talk to me."

"No one's heard from her. It's been weeks. Where the fuck is she?"

"She's been gone five days, Ares. She'll come back if and when she's ready, but we need to let her come back on her own. You can't force her, or she will just leave for good."

I scrub my hand down my face. "What if she chooses not to come back? What if she decides she doesn't want to be here and she takes them away? I can't lose them and him. Scar, they're all I have left of him. I need her to know I'm sorry."

"We all need her to know we're sorry, but we're just gonna have to be patient, okay?"

"Yeah, I suppose, but I have an idea. I'm gonna go. Thanks, love you."

"Ares, don't do anything stupid, okay!"

I wave as I rush to the med room, snagging a bottle of tequila from behind the bar on my way past.

"Hey guys, I thought we could have a drink." I push into the apartment. It's about … fuck knows. It's dark outside, anyway. Dice and Dane are curled up on the sofa, looking all cosy.

"Hey, Ares," Dane says. "Come in, make yourself at home, why don't you?"

"Thanks guys." I slide in between them. "I got booze."

"I can see that." Dice chuckles. "We were kinda gonna watch a movie."

"Great, I love movies." I shuffle between them, making more room. "Dane." I hand him the bottle.

"Nah, I'm good, man." He shoves it back.

"I got it special. Come on, don't be a party pooper."

"Ares, you're acting weirder than normal. If I have a drink, will you fuck off? When we say we were watching a movie. We meant we were gonna watch porn. Hot gay porn."

"Fine, a quick drink, then I will leave you to all the porn, okay?"

"Fine." Dane takes a big gulp, but just as he goes to remove the bottle from his lips, I push the bottom up again, forcing another big gulp before he splutters.

"What the fuck, Ares? You trying to drown me, you twat?"

Dice reaches to grab the bottle, and I put the lid on. "I thought we were having a drink?" Dice says, and I just shake my head.

"Ares, what the fuck?" Dane goes to stand up but blinks and shakes his head. "Did you put something in that?" he slurs.

"What the fuck, Ares?" Dice stands to grab Dane as he sways.

Sitting him back down, he rushes to the kitchen to grab Dane some water, but he's out cold.

"Grab his legs and keys. We need to go. Priest and Blade are waiting outside. We're going to get Ray back."

"So the one person who knows where she is, you fucking drugged, and now you're kidnapping him. You have finally lost it, Pres!"

"Just grab the keys. We're going to that place where they live, you know the one."

"Bernie's?"

"No, the one where they went after all that shit happened at the airfield where you found Ray, that's where she'll be."

"The Tower?"

"You don't know where The Tower is, so how do you think you're gonna get there?"

"Well, Steel told me you needed Dane and his truck to get in, so... now we have both. Get the keys. You'll have to drive. I don't know where it is."

"You know he'll skin you alive, and I will hand him the knife for this."

340

"Fine, whatever. Now grab his keys and his legs, and let's go fetch her home."

Actually, I'm gonna tell Ray, and she will skin you alive. Rook said she kept Bas alive that whole time down there while peeling all his skin off, so you, my friend, are her problem."

"Fine, but just hurry up and lets go. I don't mind if I end up looking like Deadpool. It will be totally worth it. Tell her to leave the face alone, though, okay?"

Dice gets us into the parking garage and drives towards a wall. "What the fuck are you doing?"

"Ares, shut the fuck up. I know what I'm doing."

As he drives towards the wall, it moves in, and we find ourselves in another parking garage. "Wow, that's so cool. I want one!"

Shaking his head, Dice pulls up and gets out of the truck and Blade and Priest climb out of the back with Dane.

"You sure you wanna do this, man? She's gonna flip when she finds out what you've done to Dane." Priest shrugs.

"She's at least gonna have to come see me, so I'm taking it as a win."

"Twat." Blade nods towards me.

"Right, now what do we do?"

"Retinal scan and fingerprint near the elevator." We carry Dane across to the scanner and scan him.

Beep. Nothing. *Beep*. Nothing.

341

"You're doing it wrong," I curse at Dice.

"Am not."

The intercom buzzes. "This place is a fucking fortress. Do you think I can't lock it down from the inside because you have a key? Fucking amateurs. Now what the fuck have you done to my Brother?"

"Ares did it," They all speak at once.

"Bring him up. I will be pissed if anything happens to him." The doors open, and we step in.

As we reach the floor they're on, we don't know what it is as Ray must control the buttons in the lift. The door pings open, and we're greeted by the five guys. Who now appear to be Ray's bodyguards. They're all built like brick shithouses, around six feet tall, and seem to be nearer to Dane's age than Ray's.

"When did you stop to pick up the *Magic Mike* boys, or is it dream boys? Or are they the Thunder From Down Under?"

"Why do you know all those?" Ray pulls a face, and I shrug.

"Can we talk?"

"Look, we're talking. Rook, can you and Queen take Dane to our room and ensure he's okay?" They step into the lift, dragging him from our hold as we step out.

Ray walks up to me, looks me up and down and punches me straight in the dick. As I double over, she hits me square in the chin, and I slam onto my back, panting. "Fucking hell, Ray, a bit of notice would have been preferable."

"Did Dane get notice of being drugged?" She steps over me and sticks out her hand.

342

"No."

"Didn't think so!"

As she pulls me to my feet, she pulls me closer and then punches me in the gut, knocking the "Oomph" out of me as I fall back on my ass.

"That should do it." She nods behind us and then stalks off in that direction while I'm left sitting on my ass, dick, and balls in one hand and the other arm wrapped around my ribs while I pant for breath.

When I finally catch my breath and climb off the floor, I head in the direction they all went, pushing into a large kitchen, where they're all sitting around a table.

"Take a seat, Ares." She nods to the seat opposite. I slide into it, linking my fingers onto the table.

"Ray, I'm—"

Raising a finger, she cuts me off. "Firstly, Ares, I said I need some space, and here you are in my space; secondly, you drug my brother to break into my home."

"This isn't your fucking home!" I snarl as Priest digs me in the ribs. "I'm sorry." I clench my hands, then relax them and slide my fingers together. "I'm sorry, Ray, please continue," I say through gritted teeth.

"What do you want, Ares? I really can't be arsed, so say what you want to, then fuck off, okay?"

"I want you to come home. I need you to come home. As you can see, I'm clearly not thinking straight without you, and I need you and those babies safe. I can't lose them, too, Ray. I've lost him, and I can't lose you and what's left of him."

"And what about what I want, what I need? Do you think I can be there right now? You think I didn't lose fucking everything?"

"I know you did, and that's why I want you home. He would never forgive me if I didn't look after you and those babies, so please. I'm not above begging. Just come home."

"I don't know if I can. Me and the boys are gonna get a place near the family, so we—"

"I can find a place. What do you need?"

"Ares."

"Ray, what do you need?"

"The boys are coming to work for me. I need a house or somewhere big enough for them all. I need some land for training. It needs to be private and big enough to build on if we can't have what we want. I need it to be self-sufficient, solar panels or space to build them."

"Okay, pack up then. I have just the place. It needs some work, but it's yours, you can have it. Just come back with me now."

"And what if I don't?"

I lean back and cross my arms. "I will stay till you do."

"Fuck." She turns to look at them all, and they shrug. I don't know which ones which other than Rook and Queen as they're with Dane.

"We will come and have a look at the place, and then we will decide. If I choose to leave, then you

344

have to let me go till I'm ready to come back on my own, okay?"

"Deal." I smile. Come on, let's go.

"No, we go in the morning. There are plenty of rooms here. Hunker down, and we'll go tomorrow."

"Ray."

"Don't test my fucking patience, Ares. I swear to Hades, you got off fucking lightly."

I nod. "Okay, let's get some sleep, and then we can head out tomorrow."

"This way," one of them says as he pushes through the door. "Well, you coming or not?" He pushes through and lets the door spring back into place. As he shows the guys to the rooms, he steps into the room for me, and I follow him in. He turns and closes the door. "What the fuck are you playing at?"

I square my shoulders. "I'm getting my sister back home by any fucking means necessary, and if that means playing nice with you lot, I will for now. But don't fucking cross me or her. I will destroy each and every one of you."

He smirks. "Back at ya, bitch!" he says as he storms out of the room.

Ray

We pull up in a convoy back at the club and slide out. Dane storms up to the apartment, and Dice sighs, glaring at Ares, who just shrugs. I had to stop Dane from going to The Armoury and grabbing his gun so he could shoot Ares this morning, and I'm kind of on Dane's side with this one. But if this gets me what I want, then so be it.

"So where are we going?"

Ares points up the lane behind the clubhouse. "You've seen the old compound, military base, doomsday prepper paradise, whatever you want to call it."

"Yeah." I look at him, confused.

"It's yours, theirs, whatever, if you want it, it's yours. It's closed-in, large enough for building on, room for training, self-sufficient or could be. Give me a second." He wanders around to the garage and comes back with bolt cutters. "There must be an entrance somewhere, but we've never found it, so knock yourselves out. Be careful. We don't know what's in there. We've always just left it well alone."

He tosses the cutters to King. "I'll be in the clubhouse when you're ready to talk." Then they turn and walk away.

I climb in the driver's seat, wince, and get back out. Fucking hell! "Come on, let's go look." climbing back in the passenger side.

Rook drives up there, we do a perimeter check, and the boys fan out, trying to find an entrance. We find the best position for the main entrance and cut a hole, I step through. "Fuck, this place is massive!" King grins.

We've driven between the gym and the barn and come in to the right of the buildings. There are three massive aircraft-like hangars; a large fence surrounds it all, almost eight feet, with rusty razor wire circling all through the top. As we all push through the fence, you can see a lake, and the three massive aircraft-like hangars have eight large barracks, maybe lodges. There's a large open space between the buildings and the lake. As we push inside the nearest hangar, it's just an open storage area, totally empty apart from debris, but the bones look good from here anyway. We step into the middle one. This one has a trap door on the floor right in the centre of the thing.

"Let's come back to that!" I say as we head to the next one. This one is like our stores back at the base, racking everywhere with stockpiled tins and rations, bottled water, clothing, and blankets. The guy before was probably a doomsday prepper. It's a shame everything's rubbish and out of date, but the racking's good and it would make a good stores. There is also a row of offices, but again, we will venture into them later when I know roughly what we have.

Heading to the barracks, the first six have a large open room with ten bunk beds on each side with a large bathroom and toilet area at one end. The other two have a kitchen on one end and tables and bench seating. It's set out like our armoury summer camps, very military base style, and then there's the lake.

"Well, boys, what do you think?"

"We could use the first one for vehicle storage. The trap door may be a good gun store. We will need further investigation. The last hangar goes without saying that it'll be the stores. The six barracks with plumbing could be an apartment each, the last two, one could be a communal room, and the other could be a tech room. That way, Dane could work from here, too. It will need securing and a lot of work, so it depends on what it's gonna cost," King says, and we all nod.

"Ares will give us this for me and the babies to stay. I know that's what he's thinking." I shake my head. "I just don't know if I can live in that apartment, but I also don't know if I can be away from it. That's all I have left of him till these guys make an appearance."

"So if Ares is giving us this whole compound, we should have enough savings to make a dent in the renovations," Rook says.

"I've already transferred the money to the team account, so if you wanted to bulldoze the place and build a mansion, you could."

Bishop pulls out his phone and logs in, waiting a few seconds, then his face drops. "Holy fucking shit!" He turns the phone to the boys, and their faces drop.

"Is this a joke…?" King asks.

I shake my head. "I thought you would need an incentive to hang around, and I feel like keeping you close, so that should cover everything you need for a while."

"Ray, there's over a million in here!" Queen looks at the numbers again.

"It was Steel's… I have more than enough of my own, then I inherited Steel's, and I gave some to Skye and Tray and the rest for you guys. I don't know what the future will look like here but I'm hoping having you around will make it… bearable."

Reaching for my hand Rook grabs it and pulls me in for a hug."

"So, no preferential treatment or anything like that, hey?" Queen grins at Rook.

"Shut it, okay?" Rook chuckles back.

"Wait, Rook gets preferential treatment?" Bishop looks between us all.

"You don't think all those cushy money jobs just come to you guys because you're fabulous do you?" Ray laughs. "It pays to have friends in high places and Rook does." I wink at them. Right, are we in or not?

"We're in!" They all sing out together and crush me between them. "Right, let's go and iron out the negotiations with Ares."

"I thought it was a done deal?"

"Yeah, but I need to make him sweat, and also, I need some assurances, and I might see if I can squeeze in a little extra."

"Like what?" Knight winks.

"I haven't decided yet, but I wanna make him squirm."

Scar

I'm sitting in the bar with Demi, Skye and Beauty as Ray walks in the back door with five guys all six feet and built like Bran.

"Make yourselves at home boys, I need to speak to the girls for a minute."

Before Ray can turn to head towards us Tank scrapes his chair across the floor as he stands holding Tray in his arms. "You replacing us?"

She turns and looks at the guys and then laughs, "Never brother! Now give me my nephew, come on, hand him over."

Tank grins and walks towards her handing him over and she smells his head and groans " Fuck they should bottle that smell."

Ray Brings Tray over and sits with us.

"Firstly we're not doing this here and now, I can't, I just don't have the energy right now but I love you all even you Scar but you hurt me the most," She nods to the guys, "I can kind of understand them but you? That broke me, it's just gonna take time ok. We will talk and we will sort it all out but for now I just need to call a truce."

351

I start to cry, and she reaches a hand for me and grips it. "I'm so—"

"Some other time, yeah? Please."

I nod. I know she will give me a chance, but I also understand how raw everything is, so I put my big girl pants on, nod and wipe my eyes. Ray kisses Tray on the head and hands him to Skye. "We need to see Ares. Is he in the office?"

I nod, and just like that, she's gone again.

"I can't believe she's acting like my brother hasn't just died," Demi says with an element of disgust hanging in the air.

I sigh. "She isn't, Demi, she's just so fucking lost right now. If she breaks, she won't make it out alive; she needs to process and, knowing Ray, that will happen behind closed doors on her own, and she will either get over it or she will implode, and then we will have to wade through the aftermath and try and piece it back together. She is far from fine. All we can do is watch for the cracks and try and hold them together as well and for as long as we can until she heals… or explodes."

"And what do we do if she explodes?" Demi sighs.

"Run." I shrug. And we all take a drink and contemplate the very outcome that if it happens, we will all go up in smoke for real this time.

Ares

I'm in the office, and the door swings open, and in she walks, almost like she hasn't got a care in the world, and to most people, that's exactly what it looks like, but now I really take the time to look at her, I can see it in the tightness of her jaw, the pinch of her brow and the tension in her shoulders.

She stalks in, followed by them. She throws herself down on the sofa like she normally does, but with less grace now she's pregnant, closes her eyes, and throws her arm over her stomach. The guys close the door and line up across it like statues, legs apart, hands behind their backs.

"Make yourself at home, Ray."

"Thanks," she mutters and sighs. "So, Ares…"

I clench my jaw at my name on her lips. I hate it when she calls me that. It means business, and I want the easy banter back. "What's the catch?"

"Catch?" I ask.

She lets out a big breath. "Yeah, Ares. Catch, you want something from me, you know it, and I know it, so what is it? That's a mighty fine set-up you're willing to give, and I know it's gonna cost me dearly, so what will it be?"

"You!" is all I say.

"Me?" She laughs. "Nah, what do you really want, Brother?" She spits the word 'brother,' and I internally wince.

"Do they need to be here for this?" I snarl.

One of the big fuckers takes a step forward. "Too fucking right we do!"

"Now, boys, let's save the pissing contest till later, shall we?" She swings her legs off the couch and sits leaning back on it, taking a deep breath, rubbing her stomach, taking a massive inhale, and then wincing."

"You okay?"

"We don't have the time, and I don't have the energy for that question. Just tell me what you want, and we will head back to The Tower for a meeting."

"No!" I shove up from the desk. "No more fucking leaving, you stay, we sort this out, you go back to being my Enforcer. Second chance, do over, restart, whatever the fuck you wanna call it, but no more leaving."

"In case you haven't noticed, I'm heavily pregnant and due to give birth in a couple of months, so I can't see myself being of any use as an Enforcer, can you?"

"Are you fucking kidding me right now? Even knocked up and ready to drop, you're deadlier than most of the men I have here. So, my terms: one, you stay put. Two, you become my Enforcer again. Three, you can have whatever the fuck you want, I don't care, but you don't leave, and you don't take those babies away from me."

"That's it?" She never takes her eyes off me, and I'm starting to sweat. I berate myself internally for how she makes me feel and how I allow her to make me feel.

"We sort it out, everything and move on."

"Easy as that huh?"

"Well, no, but yeah."

"And we can have the compound?"

"Yes, I will have Pops draw up the contract separating the land and the external roads from the club and put it into your name."

"Our names." She nods to the guys.

"All your names, got it."

"And to make it up to me, the whole club will help with the work I need, whatever I need." She phrases it so I know it's not a question. I nod.

"Oh, and the dealbreaker Ares..." She rises from the sofa. "Get Barbie back, or the deal's off." She walks to the door. "I will return when he does."

"Ray." I gasp. She stops and turns to look at me. "No one knows where he is. No one has heard from him since he left."

"Well then, Brother, best look fucking harder. When he returns, give me a call." And with that, she leaves, and the guys stay there for an uncomfortable minute before turning and leaving with her.

"Fuck." I pull out my phone.

Pres: 911

355

I put the call out to the club. Fuck, this is gonna be like looking for a needle in a haystack, and when I find him, I know I'm gonna have to grovel. Shit, this sucks. What happened to blood in, blood out? We've all got fucking soft since she arrived. Barbie should have been dead for fucking leaving, yet we let him stroll right out the front fucking door. Now it's time to drag his ass back, kicking and screaming if I have too.

Six days, fourteen hours and twenty-eight minutes till we found Barbie. Me, Dozer and Viking head out to see him while he's being watched and stalked so we don't lose him. It's a three-hour fucking ride, and it's stupid o'clock, and he's in some ratty shit hotel in the middle of bum fuck nowhere, population more cockroaches than people.

Pulling in, we get off the bikes and check out the area. There is no back way out of the room, and no way to escape. I walk to the door and knock.

"Who is it?" Barbie says from inside.

"Fucking housekeeping." I grit out.

He swings the curtain back on the window, and we just stare at each other before he closes it again. "What do you want?"

"You've had your fucking vacation. I've come to take you back."

"What if I don't want to come back?"

"Have you forgotten who I fucking am, Barbie? Blood in, blood fucking out. Now, either we can do this the easy way or the fucking hard way, but whatever you decide, you're fucking coming back tonight. Now just pack your fucking stuff, and let's go!"

"You're not gonna kill me?"

Viking laughs. "He couldn't if he wanted to."

"Dick!"

The door cracks open. "What's that supposed to mean?"

"Can we come in? You've missed a lot!" Dozer adds.

After we explain everything, Barbie is a whirlwind, gathering all his stuff and stomping around. "Why the fuck didn't you just start with Ray's back? Would have saved the last forty minutes of shouting through the fucking door" He slams stuff into his saddle bags. "Well, come the fuck on, then." He grumbles as he shoves through the door.

"Fuck's sake." I scrub a hand down my face; why the fuck didn't I just think of that? Viking slaps me on the shoulder. "Don't you fucking dare. Right, last one back to the clubhouse is calling Ray."

We all dive on our bikes and ride out of there.

Fuck knows what time it is, but I grab my phone

"What?" an angry, sleepy male voice comes down the line.

"Who the fuck is this and where the fuck is Ray?" I spit back.

"Who the fuck's that?" She grumbles and I can hear her rolling over. "Tell them to fuck off its the middle of the fucking night."

"You heard her," he mutters.

"Put her fucking on now. It's Ares."

"Ray, it's your brother," he says.

"Which one?" she grumbles.

"The cunty one!"

She sighs, grabbing the phone off him. "Ares this best be fucking good!"

"Ray! Are you fucking... ready to come home? We have Barbie." I start spitting out. Is she fucking him? Then rein it in at the last minute. Fuck, I need to be really careful here.

"You do?"

"Yeah Ray I do."

"I'll be back first thing... Ares?"

"Yeah?"

"I wouldn't do that, I wouldn't be fucking someone else."

"I'm sorry, Ray... I just, I shouldn't have, just come home, okay? See you in the morning."

"Boyband?" As she whispers it over the phone, I slide into my seat. I close my eyes at hearing her say it again, as I never thought I would.

"Yeah?" I sigh.

"Tell me everything will be okay," she whispers.

"It will when you come home. I promise."

I hang up the phone and clutch it to my chest as the lump appears in my throat and the clenching in my heart intensifies.

"She's coming home, brother. I promise I will look after them all. I will love them for you every day and never let them go again." A tear rolls down my face. I let it be followed by another and then another, and I just hug that phone to my chest. "They're coming home." I sigh, hoping wherever he is, he can hear me and know I will die for them all.

It's been a whirlwind of a few months. Ray came home, Barbie settled back in, the boys have been working non-stop since they got back. Turns out the entrance to the compound was behind one of the panels in the "office," or kill room as we now all think it should be called.

They've reinforced the tunnel and electronic doors and ramped up the security system. The barracks were stripped out and turned into nice, real nice apartments. There's a tech room that Dice is practically wanking over on the daily and Dane is just as bad. Their stores is amazing, too, and I may have helped myself to a few little bits while I was "helping" load it up. The hanger with the stores in had a hidden panel in the wall in one of the offices with stairs leading to an underground bunker, which they're turning into The Armoury. Ray says I can't have a rocket launcher, but I've been the best of her brothers since she came back.

Scar and Ray are almost back to normal, but Scar is still eaten up with guilt and, some days, is so hard on herself. Ray slapped her the other day, telling her to stop being a little bitch and get over it already. Only time will tell how that pans out.

But right now, we're here in the clinic pacing, Ray's in labour and Marie's in there with her. We were all kicked out as we all wanted to be with her. We haven't let her out of sight since she got back, always ensuring at least one of us is with her at all times, even when she sleeps. Normally, Dane slides in with her or Bran, but this last week, she kicked them out and said she needed to get used to it now the babies are coming. And so here we are, waiting, pacing, drinking shit coffee. Bernie and Cade are the fucking worst, constantly pestering the nurse for updates, to which they keep saying they'll be here when they're here. It's been fucking hours, and we're all really worried. They keep assuring us this is normal and everything's going well, but…

A doctor pushes through the doors. "Are you all the family of Ray Steel?"

All standing as a unit, the doctor takes a step back, and Cade steps forward. "I'm her dad."

"Well, Grandad"—he smiles—"we have two healthy little ones, a little boy born first, then a little girl born twenty-eight minutes later. You can go and see them now, but not all at once." He looks at us all. "Maybe in twos, but mom and babies need to rest, so don't stay long, okay?"

Cade and Bernie go first, then Bran and Demi and Dane and Dice, and as me and Scar go in, I take a breath at the door.

"You good?" Scar asks, and I just nod, but I'm starting to feel the pressure.

I can't let them down now they're here, I can't for a single second drop the ball, and I know that's unreasonable, and it's not true, but for him, I would burn the world down for them, and as I step into the room and look at their little sleeping faces, I know I will die for them. They both look like him, like Steel. I can see it already. The little girl has his raven black hair, and it's so thick already, and the little boy has hair like Ray and Cade.

Walking over to the bed, I stroke my big, meaty paws down their delicate features. "Fuck, Ray, they're fucking perfect." I lean down and kiss her, whispering into her ear, "He would be so proud of you, you know that, right?"

She nods once and closes her eyes and takes a deep breath. Meeting my gaze, she smiles. "You see it too, don't you?"

"Fuck yeah, I do." I chuckle, "They look like him, even this little."

"Fuck, guys… how am I gonna do this?" she says.

"Are you fucking kidding me? You literally have an army out there, fuck. I don't think you will ever have to change a diaper."

She chuckles and the babies stir. "Shit," she mutters.

"Hey, get some sleep. I will fuck them all off, they can come back tomorrow."

"Boyband, you may be the president of the club, but do you really think you're gonna keep my brothers from their niece and nephew?"

"Yeah, you're probably right. We will go so you can get through them quickly and get some rest. I've got a feeling we're all gonna need it."

Ray

It's been a fucking roller coaster of epic proportions. I've tried so hard to do everything for the twins myself, River and Storm. River has my hair colour, but he looks so much like his dad; they both do. They have his grey eyes, and Storm has his jet-black hair. She's going to be a handful, I can tell. She's so strong-willed already, and my baby boy River is so chilled. She's going to be the ringleader, and I know I'm in for it, and while I love them fiercely, it breaks my heart every day looking at their faces and seeing his staring back. I know Ares sees it, too. The others say it's too soon to tell, but I'm not so sure.

Things have been quiet around here since I killed Bas. Word got out about the psycho Reaper Enforcer and to steer clear. There will come a time again when I know it will change, and I will have to resume my position, and I'm itching to get back to it. I'm living every day as it comes, pushing the feelings down and stomping on them till I can no longer feel, rinse and repeat. I know it's not healthy, but with night feeds and nappy changes, it keeps me from thinking too much. When I'm alone in the dark, that's when it's at its worst, and now the babies are a few months old, they are sleeping longer through the night, and the memories are starting to come back. The longing, the loneliness, and the emptiness seep in with the shadows. I'm on a downward spiral. I know I can feel it, but I can't stop it. I've stopped breastfeeding now, so the tequila I consume at bedtime isn't harming anyone. It helps me sleep, it helps me forget, and most of all, it keeps the nightmares away.

Dane

Ray's done so well. She's fought it off for as long as she can, but now the grief is taking over. I see it in her eyes and how she looks at the babies. She loves them more than anything, yet can't seem to let herself be happy. Now, the twins are six months old. They're sleeping through the night, and this is when she struggles. She started drinking a few months ago after she stopped breastfeeding. It started as a tipple to take the edge off and help her sleep. Now, it's getting worse; it's not helping anymore. We have tried to talk to her, but she's so adamant she's good that we don't know what to do.

"Dane." There's a small rap at the door. "Hey, can you look after the twins? I'm gonna head out for a bit.

"Out? Where?" I ask as I sit up in bed. It's not massively late, but still, she's never left them before, not this late anyway.

"Just to the bar, gonna have a game of pool and darts with Priest and Blade."

"Sure, give me the—"

She waggles the baby monitor at me. "I'll turn it off in there when I get back." She heads out, and I stare at the monitor. It's set up so I can see them both. They're in separate cots now but still next to each other. Hopefully, they will have the bond that Ray and Bas should have had.

I smile down at the little screen, and warm arms wrap around me. "Wanna practise making one?"

I bark out a laugh. "If one of us could, we would be minted, we could sell our story, and fuck, just think of all that money. Let's do it." I grin over my shoulder at him."

"As if you need the money." Dice grins. "You could do with the practice, though, so come here."

He slides himself around to my front and straddles me. We're both naked, and I groan as our cocks rub together. I slide the monitor to the table and I hear Storm grumble and we both freeze. She settles down and Dice slides his arms over my chest and nuzzles into my neck. Nipping and sucking at my neck, I groan, and he grins against me, licking over the bite he's just sucked into his mouth and nipped. Pushing me back, he slides his legs between mine, grinding himself against me.

"Fuck, Dice, baby!" I grind out through my teeth. He sucks his finger into his mouth and then slides it between us, pushing at my arse, and I groan and relax again as he works a finger in, slowly making me gasp. "Fuck, baby, so good, more, give me more."

He grins and pushes his finger in further, and I buck as his finger is as far as it will go. I push down onto his hand, loving the feel of him on top of me. He pushes slowly in with another finger, and there's a grumble. Our eyes shoot to each other, and we freeze. Storm again. We wait it out, but I can't help it. My arse clenches around his fingers, and he grunts at how hard I clench down on them.

"Fuck, babe." He grins. "Easy, you nearly broke my fingers," he whispers as he starts up again. It's torture, absolute torture, as he pushes three fingers in as far as they will go. "Fuck, babe… I need you inside me now."

Slipping his fingers out, he spits into his hand and slides his hand up and down his cock. Fuck, why is that so hot? I spit onto my hand and slide my hand over my own. He groans and spits again onto his hand, coating his dick one last time and pushing inside me. As he bottoms out, we both shudder and stop for a second, breathing heavier now as I accustom myself to him. The grumble comes louder this time.

"No, no, no!" I mutter. "Shh." We freeze stiller than still and hold our breaths. My arse clenches again, and Dice groans as there's another grumble, then a whimper.

"Shit, shit, shit. Don't move," I grumble at Dice but he shakes his head and pulls out, slamming into me and then again. "Dice, fuck, what the hell?" But he just pounds and pounds.

"Babe, I'm getting as much as I can. If they wake up, we're fucked, and not in a good way." I hold on for dear life and yank at my cock as fast as I can. We can hear the grumbling getting loader. Setting Hades off whining outside Rays bedroom door "Fuck,

367

hurry up." I throw my head back and furiously wank myself off while Dice pounds into me like he's trying to push me through to the garage. He shudders against me, and just as he flops onto me, I come, shooting up his chest and mine as he drops onto me. As we pant for breath, they start to cry. Hades starts to scratch at the door.

"Fuck, quick." Running into the living room. "Hades, bed." We run to the shower and scrub as quickly as possible before heading to the twins. "Hey, hey, it's okay, little man," I say as I bend down and pick up River.

Dice grabs Storm and grins down at her. "Fuck she's so god damned cute."

"You wouldn't have said that twenty minutes ago."

"True, but now she's cute."

We pace and rock until they're finally asleep and we put them back to bed. "Shit, have you seen the time? Where the fuck is Ray? She should have been back by now."

"Go look for her." Dice nods towards the door "Go, I've got these two."

I throw on some clothes and my trainers and head out the door. Ray's hanging over the bannister, puking onto the concrete. I rush down the stairs to her.

"Fuck, Ray... you okay?" She turns to look at me, and there's blood on her face. Ray, what the fuck happened?" I turn her and look her face over but can't see anything. I take her hand, but as I grab it, I feel the wet, slightly sticky feel of blood running down her wrist, "Shit, Ray… What the fuck did you do?"

She looks up at me, unfocused and swaying. "I wanted to feel something more than numb," she slurs.

"Fuck." I pull her up the stairs. "Come on, let's get you cleaned up."

I mean, I knew this was coming, the drinking. It's how we always used to cope. It's what we did after missions, but she hasn't been able to with the twins, but now they're mostly sleeping through. I fear she's only gonna get worse. She throws herself at the bannister and pukes again. I know she's been using drink to get through these last couple of months, but not like this. Not to this extent, and self-harm. What the fuck am I supposed to do with that? I hope it's that and not anything more serious.

Walking in through the door, Dice comes to meet us. "Shit, what the fuck?"

I shake my head. "Can you stay with the twins? I'm gonna clean her up and stay with her to make sure she doesn't choke on her own vomit." Dice scrunches his face up as I walk into the bathroom. "Can you grab some pants and a T-shirt? It's gonna be a long fucking night," I grumble.

Ray

I wake up with a warm body next to me and I sigh, then I freeze. "It's just me, dickhead."

"What the fuck died in my mouth?" I question, but I know what it was: it was Jack... and tequila and definitely vodka.

When I try to move my arm, it pinches, and I look down, and there's a bandage wrapped with tape around my forearm.

"Are we gonna talk about this?"

"I need coffee and a shower before the twins wake up." I move to leave, but Dane grabs my arm. I wince as he holds onto the bandage, gripping tight so it stings like a motherfucker. I sigh. "Let me get cleaned up, and then we'll talk, okay? But I'm okay. I'm just working through some shit."

After getting out of the shower, Dane and Dice are feeding the twins in the living room. "Hey, why didn't you shout me?"

"Because you've been trying to do it all on your own."

"Look, I appreciate it, but it's not what you think, okay? I just... since Bas, I just don't feel, and then to

370

lose Steel... I'm angry, hurt, and betrayed, and I hate him most days, but I feel numb. I just want to feel something that isn't misery, and after all the torture, I only seem to feel when I cut. It's like a release. I can't go out and kill. I have the twins. I can't go out and fuck, who the fuck's gonna want me looking like this? so I cut. it helps, and the drinking... I just really missed tequila, but I mixed it with vodka and Jack, which made me puke, okay?"

"Ray, let us help more. Let everyone help more. How about you go back to work part-time? Maybe just let people help by looking after Storm and River for you. Everyone's chomping at the bit to get their hands on them. You don't have to do it all alone, you know."

I sigh and flop on the sofa. "I just feel like I'm letting him down. I wanted to be so great at this, but I feel like a fuck up."

"Come on, let's have breakfast, take these two out, see what's happening, and think about returning to work. You were never gonna be a full-time mum, Ray; you're too... much to be cooped up. You need to find a better way of releasing whatever it is that you need to release."

"Yeah, I just don't know what that is. Look, I will watch the drink, but the cutting helps, and I'm scarred to fuck. What does it matter? At least these ones are my choice.

"Fine, but maybe you should talk to someone!"

"What, like a shrink? Fuck, Dane, you know they'd damn well have me committed."

"True but maybe a grief counsellor, we lost Pa Daniel, then Pa Steven, and Pa JJ, then you found out Pa Cade was your dad, and Bas was alive, then got kidnapped, then lost Steel, then killed Bas."

"I do not regret that one bit. If it wasn't for all the other stuff, I would sleep soundly at night over that fucker."

"What are your nightmares about then?"

I sigh. "Steel. I relive him being shot over and over again, and I never quite reach him. The more I run, the further away I get, and he dies anyway, and there's nothing I can do to save him."

"Fucking hell, Ray." Dane hugs me tight, and Dice hugs me from behind. The twins gurgle.

"Come on, let's make a move. I need to head up to the compound, anyway."

Walking outside, Dozer is hosing down the concrete. "Sorry, Dozer."

"Don't worry about it. We've all been there."

"Fucking hell, the old Dozer would have punched me in the gut and made me clean it up myself."

"Yeah, well, new Dozer"—he laughs—"has a fucking horny as fuck wife since those babies came along and, well, let's just say I don't have time to be grumpy much anymore if you know what I mean?"

"Ew, Dozer TMI." I shake my head and walk behind Dane and Dice, who have the pram, and I can hear Dozer whistling while he cleans up my puke. "Hey, Dozer." He looks up at me, "Two weeks, yeah, and I will be back at work. Give me two weeks."

"You sure, Ray?"

"Yep, two weeks, but if you fucking whistle near me, I will cut your dick off!" I laugh as I turn and jog back towards Dice and Dane, pulling my phone out. "Hey, can you guys watch the twins to—"

"Yep," Dice cuts me off.

"I was gonna say tonight, I wanna start back at the gym and see if that helps too. I'll do bath and be—"

"We'll do it," Dane cuts in.

So I send a text to the group chat asking for a gym buddy, and Priest answers straight away.

Ray: Need a gym buddy tonight, who's free?
Priest: 6 p.m. work?
Ray: Bring it on!
Priest: 'laughing emoji' 'thumbs up emoji'

As I get ready, I grab my bag and head up to the gym. Priest is already up there as I push through the door, and he's warming up. "Well, aren't you a sight for sore eyes?"

I grin, walk up to him, hug him and sigh in his arms.

"Hey, you okay?"

"Yeah, I just kinda… miss it, ya know?"

"Yeah I know what you mean." As I pull away, he grabs my arm. "What happened?"

"Nothing, come on let's get going. Gloves?"

"Come on, show me what you got." He laughs.

"At the minute, nothing." I laugh after gently sparing to warm up. We ramp it up a bit. "Fuck, I'm gonna hurt tomorrow." I laugh, and he grins. "Let's see if we can make it hurt everywhere."

I groan. "Do we have to?"

373

"Baby." He laughs, but I freeze for a split second.

I feel his hand rest on my arm. "Hey, where did you go?"

"Sorry." I shake myself out. "Come on, let's do this."

"Hey, you good?"

"Yeah, just… nothing. Come on."

"Ray?"

"Hey, it's nothing, just a small trigger, that's all. He… Steel used to call me baby. I know it wasn't in the same context. Sometimes, I'm okay with the word. Other times, I space and get lost. I'm good, though. Please just treat me like you normally would. I need things to go back to normal." Things aren't normal, though, are they? I'm not the same person anymore. I'm damaged goods now, no fucker's gonna want me. I look like a fucking two-year-old tried to do dot to dot, for fuck's sake, and failed miserably.

Priest puts me through my paces, and I groan with aches and pains in places I forgot what it felt like to have. And I like it. "Again," I say as we ramp it up again.

"Hey, don't overdo it, Ray, you're bleeding." He grips my arm in his hand.

"It's okay, Priest, it's just a nick."

He peels the tape off and looks down at my arm. "Did you do this yourself?" I sigh and nod. He pulls it closer to his face, gripping my arm tight. His eyes flash with something I'm uncertain of, and then he looks at me and back at my arm, taking a step closer. "Why?"

374

"I wanted to feel something."

"Did it help?"

"Yeah."

"You know it was risky cutting there?"

"Yeah, it was just easier for me."

He pulls me closer again till our chests are almost touching but he doesn't take his eyes off my arm, his chest rises as he breathes deeper.

"Priest?"

And just like that, whatever spell he was under is broken, and he takes a step back, blinks and then inhales a deep breath. "Shall we call it a day?" He lets out the breath shakily before bending to grab his bag.

"I'll catch you later. I need to do some… stuff."

"Oh, okay." I step towards him, but he's already heading for the door. "Tomorrow?"

"Yeah, sure." He waves his arm before heading out and leaving me alone.

Priest

I can't get out of there quick enough. I can't let her see me like that, like some sort of feral creature with a boner. Something about blood makes my dick hard, and damn, it was straining in my shorts. If she'd have looked down, she would have seen, and the fact that she did it to herself makes me shiver. I can't start looking at her like that. She's my sister, and she… she… I sigh. I've always been like this. I like cutting while I have sex. I like them to bleed while I have sex, and just thinking about it… I need to head to the shower and take care of my straining hard-on that feels like it's gonna explode out of my shorts.

As I slide into the shower, I run my hand down my body and shudder. I close my eyes, but it's her face I see now. I shake my head, trying to rid myself of the thoughts of her. But now that I've seen it, I can't go back. She's changed since she came back and I've tried to ignore it, tried to push the feelings down and it worked till I saw the blood. I sigh and resign myself to the fact that this is inappropriate. My dick feels like it's gonna explode on its own.

I take it in my hands and groan as I imagine sliding into her. I haven't had many partners, I just can't seem to get there without the blood, and there aren't many people out there who want to be cut up during sex. If anyone would be up for it, it would be Ray. I mean, not before, but this Ray… This Ray is a darker creature altogether, and she's never been more beautiful.

As I slide my hand down and twist, I lean my shoulder against the wall and slide my hand around, tugging slightly at my balls. I groan as I quicken, but I'm not gonna last; this is the most I've felt in years. I feel alive as I grunt into my hand. She's lit something inside of me now, but how can I compete with a dead guy? My dead brother? I think as I shudder my release into the bottom of the shower. I shake my head. Nope, this is my secret, and I will take it to my grave.

Ray

Today's the day. First day back at work. Demi is taking the day off from the coffee shop and looking after the twins while Skye is working there part-time; she's loving it. Tank comes sauntering in with Tray attached to his side. "Hey, what you doing here?"

"This one wanted to come and see his favourite aunt on her first day back." He shrugs and grins.

"I'm sure he did." I laugh, "Gimme a squidge. How's my favourite nephew?" I coo at him, and he babbles away.

"He's crawling now, and I don't think he will be long before he's walking," Tank informs me.

"Shit, are we all ready for this? I mean, what the fuck are we even doing, Tank? Kids? This place… it's like I've been dropped in an alternate reality. I wouldn't change them for the world, ya know… just wish he was here to see them grow up."

He nods, pulling me into a hug. "Don't worry, they will know who he is. They will hear our stories. He was never truly happy till he found you, Ray. But you deserve to be happy now, you know that, right?"

"I know. I just can't even bear to think about that… it's too soon."

"There's no limit to grief, Ray. Just don't let it swallow you whole." I nod and grin, handing Tray back.

"Come on, let's get some work out of you. I've been hanging out my ass for months." Dozer laughs from the doorway.

"Come on, old man, let's get this show on the road." I kiss my nephew and my brother and crack on. Fuck, I've missed the place, the smell of fuel, the grease in my hair and fingernails, the smell of the leather on the bikes, the grumble of the engine as they start and the sweet purr of the open road…

I glance back into the corner, Hades is laid asleep and behind him there she is, covered with a tarpaulin. Dozer fixed up my bike for me, but I can't bring myself to ride her. Maybe I should. Maybe it would make me feel closer to him. He's slipping away. I can still smell him, still feel the ghost of a touch when I'm alone, but it's fading. How can someone have such an impact on your mind, body, and soul when, in reality, we weren't together long? But I can't push myself to move on either.

I've been back at work a couple of weeks. Rook and the guys are all set up on the compound and they have started coming to the club for drinks in the evening, socialising with the guys. Everything is calming down, but my heart's only beating faster. I've been good. I've not overdone it with the drink. I've been working and looking after Storm and River. I've allowed myself to accept help and most days, I have to wrestle my children back from Dice and Dane. They're so cute together with the kids, and now things are calming down; they're starting to plan their wedding. Beauty's helping, of course.

I head home, and there's a note on the counter.

Ray
Taken the kids for ice cream
Uncle Dane

I yank my phone out of my pocket. "Dane, what the hell? They can't have fucking ice cream, you twat!" He barks a laugh at me.

"I know that, we're in Ravenswood, we're having ice cream. The kids are fine, don't wait up."

"Dane, Dane…" Motherfucker stole my kids and hung up. I get cleaned up and pace the apartment a bit. I don't like it here on my own anymore, though. I pick up my Kindle, but nothing holds my attention any more. I loved dark romance books, but when you've lived it, it doesn't quite hit the same, and the morally grey men never quite live up to my morally grey husband. I sigh, tap out a message, grab my bag, and head to the gym.

"Hey, Priest!" I shout across the room as I walk in. He looks around, startled for a second, before he schools his features.

"Hey Ray, I am just finishing up."

"Ah, come on, stay and spar with me. I need some kind of release, wanna make me ache? Dane has stolen the kids, and I'm home alone and bored."

"I can't stay long. I have an … appointment."

"Ooh. Hot date?" I laugh.

"No." He snaps back and looks at me weirdly. "No, it's nothing, really. Sure, let's spar."

"Priest? Hey, you okay?"

"What happened to Roach?"

"He's alive-ish. He's in one of our prisons if you like, for lack of a better word." I chuckle. I need to finalise everything, just haven't had time. You wanna go with me?" I smile up at him.

"To do what?"

"His days are numbered, Priest. Let's go end the miserable fucker's life. I need supplies, though. Meet me on the field at the back of the clubhouse in thirty minutes."

"Wait, on the field? Where is he?"

I tap my nose. "That's for me to know. Now go get ready. Wear something suitable." I laugh over my shoulder.

Priest

I mean, what do you wear for a murder date? I suppose it's not a date, but the way she looked at me made my palms sweat and my dick twitch. She's awakened something in me that I thought I'd shoved far enough down that it would never resurface, but clearly not.

"Well, don't you look cute!" She grins at me as she walks towards me. We're wearing almost the same outfit. Black combats tucked into black boots and a hoodie, she's sporting a black cap and a backpack.

"So why here?"

She grins, tapping her ear. I frown. "Listen." She grins back at me. And I do.

"Helicopter?"

She nods and smiles. I don't say anything else. I just wait, my hands in my pockets to stop me from doing something stupid, when she rolls her lip ring through her teeth. It never bothered me before. Now, I imagine biting her lip and blood pooling around it. Licking across her lip and sucking it into my mouth.

"You okay?" she snaps me out of my thoughts. What the hell is wrong with me?

"Erm, yeah, I'm good."

"Come on then." We jog up the field to the helicopter and climb in, nodding to Rook And King. "Thanks for this, boys." King flies us off, and Rook turns in his seat.

"Sooo… whatcha doing?" He smirks. "Couples costumes for date night are pretty cool." He winks at me, and I shake my head.

"Not a date!" I snap out my tone lost over the hum of the helicopter though which I'm glad of.

"You good?" she asks as she rests her hand on my leg, and oh, how I want her to slide it up higher. I stare at it, willing it to move, willing it to take hold of my dick and slide it into her mouth. My hands clench at my sides, and I flinch as she slides close.

"Don't like flying, huh?" She starts to rub my leg up and down, and I can't take my eyes off her hand.

Rook coughs from the front, and my gaze jumps to meet his. He has a shit-eating grin on his face. He glances back to Ray and then to me. She's looking out the window but is almost sitting in my lap; she's that close and still rubbing my leg. My eyes shoot to Rook again, and he's still watching me, grinning. So I glance out the window but find myself looking into the window at her reflection as she turns to talk to King and Rook. I'm mesmerised by her animated conversation with these guys, but I can't take my eyes off her. I watch her every move, and as we land on an oil rig in the middle of the ocean, only then do I turn and meet Rook's knowing gaze.

"Well, let's get date night underway, shall we?" Rook laughs as he jumps from the helicopter, throws his arm around Ray's shoulder, and kisses her temple, never taking his eyes off me. I'm not sure if he sees my spark of jealousy. I'm lying. I know he does. The smirk is back on his face as he turns and walks off with Ray. I'm frozen to the spot when a clap on the shoulder jolts me from my thoughts.

"Does she know…?" King asks.

"Know what?"

"That you're in love with her?"

"I'm not in love with her."

Barking out a laugh, he throws his arm around my shoulder. "Of course you're not!" He grips me tighter as we walk, and he leans over to my ear. "Women like her are like unicorns. When you see one, you better ride it and ride it hard. You never know when it will disappear!"

"That makes no sense." But he laughs anyway

"Come, we don't wanna miss the show."

"Show?"

"Yeah, let's say Ray is fucking talented, twisted and inspiring when she works. She's the most beautiful creature you will ever see."

"Sounds like you're in love with her." I chuckle.

"Dude, show me a man that's met that woman and doesn't love her in one way or another." He laughs. "You can't, can you?"

"Bas," I blurt out. "Look what he did to her!" I spit. "If he was alive, I would kill him myself."

"Wrong, he loved her. It's what drove him crazy in the end. Don't end up like Bas. She won't be alone

384

forever. Make your move, or you'll have to stand back and watch someone else step in."

He lets me go and continues to walk. I fall in a step behind him and stick my hands back in my pockets, reeling from our conversion. I know he's right, but she'll never love me, love anyone after Steel. Could I play second fiddle to my dead brother? I could if it meant having her, even a small part of her.

Ray

Rook wraps his arm around me and pulls me to him, kissing my temple. I feel him grin against me as he pulls me away. "What are you up to, Rook?"

"Up To? Me? I don't know what you mean."

I laugh. "Okay, Elijah, you know you'll tell me one way or another."

"How long has he been in love with you?"

"What?" I try to push him off, but he pulls me harder. "Priest? He's totally in love with you. The way he's looking at you has changed. Has something happened between you guys? Oh my god, it has, hasn't it? You're fucking him."

"No, I am not fucking him. Keep your voice down. He's been acting a little off since we started training again, maybe a few weeks or so."

"You did something with all that, didn't you?" He gestures up and down my body.

"All what? You mean all this scarred, damaged fucked-up-ness? I look like a fucking Picasso, Rook, and not to mention the stretch marks, which actually aren't as bad as the scars, but still, and there's that flabby, what do they call it... apron? Yeah, that's it.

That just hangs where my six-pack used to be. Yeah, being tortured and having twins was fucking fun. I've never looked so fucking sexy, and don't get me started on my motherfucking face."

"Just calling it as I see it, something's shifted, and that man there, is no longer wanting to be your brother."

I dig him in the ribs. "You're an arsehole, you know that?" but as I go to turn and look for Priest, Rook pinches my chin and slides my gaze forward. "Don't wanna seem too keen. Let him watch you at work and see if he still feels the same."

"Rook, don't be stupid, he's my brother. And totally not my type."

Rook barks out a laugh. "That man is totally your fucking type, a little more clean cut than the normal ones, admittedly, but definitely your type."

"Fuck… what if you're right? What do I do?"

"Well, do you like him like that?"

"I don't fucking know. My dead husband is still fucking warm, for Hades' sake. I don't think I could ever love someone like I love him."

"Love doesn't have to be the be-all and end-all, Ray. You're not the person you were then after everything. You're darker, more feral, if anything else, and it's been nearly a year, Ray!"

I sigh.

"Just allow yourself to feel. You don't love him any less if you love someone else and you don't owe him anything. He would want you to be happy, wouldn't he?"

"Not with his brother," I mumble.

"All I'm saying is, he's been gone longer than you were together. Don't forget, but allow yourself to move on, at least try."

We reach the end of the platform, and I wait for Priest. "Are you coming in?" I nod.

There's a walkway out over the sea, and there's a single cell at the end. There are twenty of these cells here, all isolated, all as cold as what's left of my swinging brick. They're filled with the worst of the worst excuses for human beings, but people we need information from. They all snap sooner or later. No one's talked to Roach in months. They feed and water them, and that's it. When they give up the information, they get released into gen pop. I chuckle to myself. They think it's the general population, but gen pop is what we call the ocean. They get a bullet between the eyes and released into gen pop, the ocean, destroying what's left of them.

Turning to the guys, I say, "Ready?"

King and Rook Grin, but Priest looks at them both and then back at me. He just nods but doesn't look so sure. Maybe he shouldn't watch this. He will never look at me the same again once I start.

"You don't have to." I reach out and grab his hand, stroking my thumb over the back of it. He looks down at the contact and freezes. "Hey, King, will you take him back to the chopper?"

"Wait, no. I'm staying." Priest steps closer. "I'm staying."

I nod and pull out the bandanas from my pocket. I tie mine around my face and then pull it down. I'll bring it up to cover it when needed, but for now, it just swings around my neck.

"So I may be a little unorthodox here. If any of you have any problems, please just leave." They all nod, and we step through the door, locking it behind us. Roach is laid on his bed, well, cot, bunk, whatever you want to call it, in the thin scrub-type uniform with a threadbare blanket wrapped around him. His teeth are chattering. As I step in, I can see my breath drift through the air in front of me, and his eyes widen.

"Well, hello, Sixteen." They're given a number, just the cell number they're in when they arrive.

"R… R-Reap-per?"

"Today is your lucky day, Sixteen. If you're good, you'll get released into gen pop."

"R-r-eally?" he chatters, and I smile.

"Really. Before we do that, though, we need to have a little chat."

I drag the metal chair over to the side of his bed, and he sits up, wrapping himself in his blanket. He's skinny, real skinny now. His sunken eyes and defined cheekbones stand out like carved marble through his thin, pale skin. He's lost the muscle he'd built, and he now has a lollipop head, which makes his bug eyes even more prominent. He's covered in bruises, when the guards come to check the cells and leave food they are not gentle with the inmates, for lack of a better word. The only criterion: don't speak to them. That's it.

"So, Sixteen, I have someone who wants to speak with you." I reach into my backpack and pull out a telescopic tripod. I set it up at the side of my chair and pull out the iPad, making the call.

"Hey, beautiful."

"Ray, it's so good to see you. I've missed you!"

Roach hears her voice and winces.

"Hey, Tali." I smile. "I've missed you too, kiddo. You sure you wanna do this?"

She nods, so I step in front of the tripod with my back to Roach and attach it, stepping back and sitting down. "Can you see okay?"

"Yeah, is that really him?

"What's left of him." I laugh out loud, and she chuckles.

"So, Sixteen, before your release, is there anything you want to say?" He shakes his head but hasn't once looked at the tablet. I lean forward, pinching his chin between my fingers. "You will fucking look at her before we leave, Sixteen," I spit. I turn his face towards the screen, and he closes his eyes. "Fucking look at her, or I will remove your fucking eyelids."

His eyes flutter open, and he gazes in her direction. Something flashes across his gaze as he looks back at me. "C… can I go now?"

"Not quite, Sixteen. There are some formalities, a matter of payment for your stay, if you will. You have nothing to say to Tali before you leave?" He shakes his head but refuses to look at her; she sighs. "Tali, is there anything you want to say?"

"Yeah, I hope he burns in hell!"

"I can do one better than that." I grin. As I nod to King, he and Rook grab Roach from the bed. He tries to scramble, I take a remote out of my pocket, and a neck collar slides out of the wall; wrist and ankle brackets follow. They drag him to the brackets and clip him into place, securing him at the wall with his ankles, legs spread, and his arms wide palms up. I turn the tripod so Tali gets a good view.

"Is that Roach?" I hear Carmen gasp.

"Shush, Mom, he's called Sixteen now. Sit and watch. This is gonna be fun. I wish I had popcorn."

"Ah, I thought that, too." I rummage in the bag, pulling out a bag of kernels, and shake it at the camera. Tali laughs, and Carmen shakes her head. Walking over to Roach, I place a handful in each hand. "Don't drop it, Sixteen. I don't want floor on my popcorn, got it?"

King and Rook have taken their place on either side of Priest, and Roach's eyes keep flicking to him, but when I look, Priest's eyes have never left mine. His face looks bored, almost impassive, but we shall see.

"It's no good looking at Priest. He isn't here to save you." I take out the Swiss army knife that's Tali's and wave it at her, and she grins. She made me promise to stab him with it at least once. I jab it into his gut and step back while he screams. It's up to the hilt, just hanging in there. Tali squeals and claps with delight.

"You two really need to spend less time together." Carmen chuckles.

"Never!" We both say at the same time and burst out laughing before both screaming, "Jinx!" and laughing again. I squirt the lighter fluid all over his scrubs and then some around the kernels.

"You sure you don't want to say anything other than the squealing like a pussy that you're doing right now? And… Ah, fuck, and pissing yourself. Tali, when you were kidnapped, did you piss yourself?"

"No, Ray, I didn't! You know why?"

"No, kiddo, I don't. Why don't you fill us in?"

"Because I knew you would come for me. Who's coming for you, Sixteen?" She grins, and I wink. "I will always come for you!"

As I pull my matches out of my pocket. A good Enforcer always needs a box of matches. They're so handy, am I right! Tali wanted you to burn in hell, But fuck you, Sixteen. You—"

"Wait!" Tali yells.

"You don't have to look, Tali."

"No, Ray. I want my knife back!"

Roach is still screaming and pleading, but we're all just ignoring him as I yank the knife from him, and he screams again. Well, I say yank, there was mild sawing.

"Don't clean it. I wanna see his blood on it." I nod as I strike the match and toss it at him. *WHOOSH!* He goes up in flames and screams constantly. His hands are held in place, and as we all stare at the flickering flames, we ignore the blood-curdling screams until we are broken out of our daze by loud popping.

"Holy shit," Carmen laughs out through the screams as I step closer and as the kernels pop and fly in the air. I catch one in my mouth before spitting it straight back out.

"Ow, that motherfuckers hot!"

I hear King and Rook chuckle, but as I turn to Priest, the flames are shimmering in his eyes. A slight curve to his lip appears, and I give him the same in return. I catch a couple of kernels and cool them before making a spectacle of tossing them up and catching them before the screams stop, the gurgling quiets, and the body sags. I pack away my things and say bye to Tali and Carmen, heading out the door.

"What do we do now? With the body, I mean?" Priest asks, genuinely curious.

"We leave the cell door open for a few days, and the wildlife will take what they want, then what's left will be released into gen pop."

"So what do we do now?"

"Head home and get shit-faced."

Dane and Dice are watching the twins. I told them I wouldn't be back for a day or two. They know what I'm doing, so we head for the clubhouse.

Before King and Rook take off, Rook grumbles. "I need to get the smell of terrible BBQ off me before it ruins it for me altogether," he kisses me on the cheek. "You did good!"

They walk away. I smell myself and frown. Priest reaches over the bar, grabs a tequila bottle, and then reaches for my hand. "Come on, you can get cleaned up in my room." He doesn't wait for a reply. He just takes off down the hall, dragging me behind him.

He chugs the tequila as he backs into his room but never breaks eye contact. It feels different, he feels different. When he hands it to me, I do the same. I only turn to look away as I rest the bottle down. He steps towards me. "You were fucking magnificent tonight."

I give him a half smile as he steps forward again. "Are you okay?"

I nod, giving him another small smile. He steps closer still, and now his chest brushes mine as we both breathe heavier. "Priest," I say quietly. I close my eyes. He reaches up and cups my face. "I'm not sure–" I sigh as I relax into his hand. "I'm so fucking lonely, but I'm not sure I can do this. I'm not sure relationships are for me anymore. I'm not the same person."

"Ray, look at me." He pushes my chin up so I'm facing him. "Steel once told me, he told you, when people are made, they're made in pairs, one single heart and mind split into two and sent off into the world. Maybe they'll find each other, maybe they won't. He... he said you were the other half of him."

"Priest, don't... please."

"I truly believe that Ray, that you were made for him. However, after everything you went through and survived..." He slides his hand over my hammering heart. "You were reborn in the fires of hell. Reshaped into a new being, a superior being, a phoenix rising from the ashes. What returned, this devastatingly beautiful creature before me I believe, is the other half of me, the other half of my heart and the other half of my soul!"

He moves slowly towards me, giving me an out, but as his lips reach mine, gentle but firm, I melt into him. The kiss is relaxed and unhurried. His tongue slides against mine, and he steps into me, pushing me back against the wall. I slide my hand up over the back of his head, pulling him in closer, but he steps back as my heart hammers in my chest.

"I will put the shower on for you." He steps back, and I'm confused.

"Priest, I'm sorry... Did I do something wrong?"

"Not at all, but I'm a patient man, Ray. I want you to be one hundred percent ready for this, whatever this is, and for that to happen, we need to have a talk. I have very specific tastes... and we need to make sure that is something you're comfortable with. But you must shower first because that smell is confusing."

"Confusing?" I ask, cocking my head to the side.

"Yeah, I can't decide if I'm hungry or horny."

I actually laugh and can't decide when I last laughed like that.

As I step into the bathroom, Priest steps out; a part of me is disappointed, and a part of me is relieved. I don't look... how I used to. My body is not the same. It's been abused and broken and reborn... I just don't know if I know who I am yet.

Priest steps back in the bathroom while my back is to him, and I freeze and start to breathe heavily. Fuck, I can't think straight. I'm panicking at the thought of him seeing me naked, but the door clicks open, and he slides in behind me, wrapping his arms around my waist and kissing slowly down my neck.

"I want to take this slow with you and want to make sure you're ready. I will wait for you, but I can't play second best to a ghost, Ray, so you need to be ready. That being said, knowing you were in here, I couldn't stay out there."

He spins me around so I'm facing him, and I look up into his eyes. He's not that much taller than me, only a few inches, and as I meet his eyes, he steps back, raking his gaze over every part of me. I suddenly feel self-conscious. I start to cover my stomach, and he takes my hand in his and pulls the small scar to his lips that I left on myself, and he kisses it. He drops abruptly to his knees before kissing across my stomach, every place where there's a stretch mark or a scar not caused by Bas and Roach. Then, rising to his feet, he kisses me slowly. Then he takes a step back, causing a shudder to rain over my body.

"You're the most beautiful thing I've ever seen, and I don't want to scare you off... maybe we should talk before we... can't put the lid back on Pandora's box."

He steps back again. "I'll wait. No rush. I just need to take a step back till we've talked."

I nod, and he leaves. When I climb out of the shower, there's a T-shirt on the sink for me, so I dry off and slide it on. This all feels too familiar and not quite different enough. But I step out of the room, and he's on the bed, ankles crossed, a long, lean body covered by only a pair of boxer shorts that are doing little to help hide the situation.

I pull at the bottom of the T-shirt, stretching and tugging it down. "I can't say I've seen this look on you before, Ray. It's adorable. I don't think I've ever seen you so unsure about something."

I take a deep breath. "I'm unsure of everything these days, Priest, especially my body... I'm... self-conscious. My body isn't what it used to be. It's tattered, torn, defiled, and ugly... you're laid out with barely a blemish, and the only tattoo you have is the Reapers' one. Priest, we are a million miles apart."

He clenches his fist beside him and takes a swig from the bottle. "Sit down, Ray." He pats the bed beside him. Taping his temple. "I got this scar the day we came to rescue you. I have plenty of scars, Ray just most of mine are internal. I never found you attractive before. I mean, I could see you were beautiful. There was no doubt about it, but you did nothing for me, not in that way anyway.

"What changed?"

I cross my legs and shove the T-shirt between them, as I'm not wearing any underwear.

"I have a kink or two, shall we say... I'm into knife play and have a kink for... blood."

"The day at the gym..." I smile.

"Yes, the day at the gym, Ray, I struggle to... Get interested. To perform without it when I'm with someone. I need to cut and see, feel and taste the blood to... get me going. To feel close, to feel a connection" He shakes his head. "I know it's fucked up, but the minute I saw your blood trickling out of that

397

wound and knowing you'd done it to yourself… was so satisfying and such a turn-on. I just don't know what that looks like with anyone, no one's ever really allowed me to show that side. I've had a few partners, and I tried to be normal, but I just couldn't fake it, and then I gave up, but with you, I'm not sure if that would be something that you would be into?"

I lean forward and run my hand down his body. "And yet barely a mark on you,"

"*My* blood does nothing for me… it has to be someone else's… it has to be during sex or leading up to it, and…" He sighs. "I just haven't found anyone for such a long time that I thought I'd given up. You caught me off guard."

I smile at him. "So, basically, you want to cut me while you fuck me, and that will get you off? I mean, I get it. Something about torturing a scumbag gets me really hot." I crawl up onto my knees and take the T-shirt off as I straddle his legs so we're eye to eye.

"Are you willing to give it a shot?"

"Yeah, I think I am, but can we keep this between us? I don't need the added pressure and want to see where it goes in private." I lean over and open the top drawer to find a blade.

"How did you know that was there?" he asks.

"Where else would it be?" I shrug. I take the knife and slide it over the skin between my breasts, and he groans as he reaches for my hips, rubbing me over his solid dick that's straining to get out of his boxers. He pulls me forward as he runs his tongue up the trail of blood and fuck me, if it isn't erotic. His eyes flutter closed, and the sheer look of pleasure on his face makes me smile. He opens his eyes, and his pupils are blown. He never takes his eyes off the blood slowly seeping from the new wound. Once there's a steady trickle again, he pulls my hips closer and groans as his tongue slides over me.

"Fuck!" he whispers with a sigh. He never swears; it sounds so foreign coming from him. He pulls his legs up, kneels up with me on him, and then lays me down on the bed. "I think I've just found my own brand of heroin," he groans as he takes the knife from my hands. "Do you trust me, Ray?"

"Yes," I breathe out as he slides his boxer shorts off and lays with his chest between my legs. I'm breathing heavily. I know I am. The anticipation is going to kill me, and as he lays the blade of the knife against my hot skin and drags it along the sensitive flesh of my breast, I shudder underneath him and try to grind myself against him for a release. I close my eyes and savour the feeling of being touched again, of feeling anything but misery.

"Ray." His voice is so soft my eyes flutter open, and he kisses me so gently, the complete opposite to the slice of the knife. "Stay with me, be here with me."

I know what he's saying. *Please don't close your eyes and think of him.* And I smile, cupping his face. "I'm here. With you. Me and you."

He nods, sliding the blade again and resting the tip on my collarbone as I pant heavier, my breaths coming in raspier. The tip of the knife cuts deeper each time, making me gasp and grind against him. The more I grind, the more I gasp, and my eyes start to roll as I'm about to come. He bites down on my

399

nipple, and I scream out as I come undone for him. His name rolls off my tongue as he continues to bite down and suck my nipple between his teeth, but he never takes his eyes off the blood. Once I've stopped panting and my breaths return to normal, he slides up, and his thick, rigid cock nudges at my opening. His eyes meet mine for a split second before his mouth covers the wound, and he sucks so deep and slams into me at the same time. I scream out, not prepared for the onslaught. The sensations are all over the place, and my mind is reeling as I feel him suck over my collarbone and slam into me. I reach down and grab onto him, holding him against me till I'm coming again, and as he spills inside me, he steadies his pace and licks at the wound till we both find our breath.

As his dick softens and he goes to slide off me, I smile. "I kind of have a thing." I grin up at him and start to roll my hips.

"Oh fuck," he grits out as I take hold, hold him where I want, and rub myself under him. "Shit, shit," he gasps, and his eyes start to flutter while I start to build.

"Shit, Priest!" I grind out as he takes over and slides over me, making me grit my teeth. He flicks his hips, and I see stars as I scream his name. He collapses on top of me.

"Fuck," he gasps as he slides off and flops on his back, and we both just pant.

I wake up wrapped in strong arms with a leg over my hip. I kiss his chest. "Hey." He looks at me and strokes down my scar as my eyes flutter closed, and his thumb passes over my cheek. I open my eyes straight into those intense, dark, almost black eyes, and my breath stutters as I exhale.

"Hey." I smile back, and he kisses me. There's no rush with this man. He's gentle, kind, and patient, but the knife and the blood… such a contrast. I'm actually excited for the first time in a while that he could be something special. But then my gut twists. Is it too soon? Should I have waited? What will my brothers think?

"Hey."

"What?"

"You left me, you're overthinking, you're thinking about him, aren't you?" He's not pissed, but a flash of hurt passes across his features, and I smile.

"No, I mean… kind of, but mainly about them, about my brothers and my family. Will they judge me?"

"Do you regret it? No one knows. We can just pretend it never happened and go back to normal."

"No, I don't, and no, I don't want to. I just want to see where it goes for a bit first… I don't want to tell people if this is just gonna fizzle… I don't want it to be awkward if it doesn't work out."

"How long?"

"How long what?"

"Do you want me to be your dirty little secret?"

He moves to get off the bed, but I throw my leg over him and pull myself on top of him. "Hey, don't you ruin this for me. This is the first time I've felt anything but broken in over a year. You don't get to feel hurt because I need this to be just me and you for a while. I've got too much to lose, Priest. I lost Steel, I lost everyone, and now I'm back; I'm waiting for the other shoe to drop, for you all to realise you were better off without me and abandon me again."

"I never abandoned you, Ray. I was here, and I believed in you."

"Do you believe in me now?"

"Of course."

"Then just give me some time, okay? I need to sort out my feelings. I need to see where this goes, but most of all, I don't want any outside pressure. If this fails, it will be because it wasn't meant to be, not because someone else had an opinion. That patience you said you had… I need you to extend it right now, okay?"

"Okay, I'm sorry."

"I'm gonna have to go soon. Dane's expecting me back."

"Yeah, sure."

He goes to slide off the bed. "Where are you going?"

"You said you had to go."

"Soon, I said soon, now fuck me real good before I have to go home. I want to feel you everywhere when I'm on my own tonight."

He grins down at me. "Now, can you be a good girl and open those pretty little thighs for me?"

As I do, he slides my arms above my head and slides to the side of me, holding the knife. He slides the handle over my pulsing clit and rubs it. As I gasp, he slips it down and slowly slides the handle inside me, and I buck against it.

"Fuck, Priest."

He grins. "Lift your leg up."

And I do. He slides the handle in and out before pushing between my cheeks and forcing the handle straight into my arsehole. I grunt, and he lets the knife go. "Keep those legs open." He grins as he rubs around my clit, pushing two fingers inside me and rubbing my clit with his thumb.

"Priest, fuck. Shit."

"I think I like you at my mercy, Ray." He smiles, and then he drags an orgasm out of me as my arse clamps down on his knife. I'm dying to buck against him, but keeping still is torture. He slides the knife in and out a few times before tossing it, clattering to the floor, before he slides straight in between my cheeks, thrusting into my arse and making me gasp out. He flicks the other hand over my clit, thrusting his fingers inside me. Pushing down over my clit harder with his thumb.

"I thought you couldn't come without the blood, the knife?" I gasp as he continues his assault on my arse. Burying himself as far as physically possible as he forces me further up the bed with every thrust.

"I can at a push but I haven't wanted to before, and I still love it, want it, crave it, but now it seems like it wasn't the blood I love, I crave I need," he grunts out as he stills inside me, continuing to push me over the edge, coming hard around him, as he comes deep inside me, he groans, "I think I just need you." And in that moment, I know I need him too.

Epilogue

4 years later…

My phone goes off, and as I pull it to my ear, it's Ares. "Ray, 911. Emergency in the bar. I need my Enforcer."

He's gasping and sounds out of breath. I can hear Hades barking in the background. "Ares!" But the line goes dead. I take off running and shove into the bar.

"Fuck's sake! Seriously?"

"Reaper?" he gasps. "Help me!"

I look up, and Dad sits at the bar, facing the carnage, grinning from ear to ear. Hades sitting beside him barking at the situation playing out in front of them

"Storm, River!" I bark at them. "What the hell are you doing?"

Storm looks up at me with her daddy's raven black hair and swirling grey eyes. "Mummy!" She lets Ares go; he's lying on the floor in some kind of chokehold that the twins have got him in. She runs at me, throwing her arms around me as I lift her to my hip. She's too big to be picked up, but I still can't resist. "Why are you trying to kill Uncle Ares?"

"Mummy, he said I can run the club when he dies!"

"Ah, he did, did he?"

Dad chuckles from his seat at the bar. "He did. I heard him myself."

"Well, maybe Uncle Ares should learn to watch his fucking mouth!"

"Mummy, you said a bad word." River looks up at me.

I smile down at him. "Mummy's allowed. I'm the Reaper, after all, but if I hear you say a bad word before you're eighteen, I will typewriter you till you stop."

River grins, jumping up onto Ares' chest, causing an "Oof" to fly from his mouth as he starts to typewriter Ares. I shake my head.

"Hey, I called you to help me!"

"I did help you. I halved your problem!" I grin down at him as River sits on his chest, shouting "Ding!" and slapping him around the face.

He has my dirty blonde hair but the greyest eyes, and he has his dad's dimples. Looking at both of my children, they're a gift from the gods, and I don't know what I did to deserve them. My heart swells then breaks all over again, knowing he will never see any of this. I stroll over to Dad, placing Storm down and slapping her on the behind. "Go help your brother!" Ares "Oofs" again as Storm dives on him.

I shake my head. He and Scar never wanted kids, but he's definitely the fun uncle. Scar took some time to come around. She would look, pat the babies on the head, say "Cute," and walk off, but now they're older, she dotes on them. Ares always says he's glad I had kids, as until that moment, he was totally on the fence, but now my children are growing up, he knows he made the right decision in not having any. Arsehole!

Tank pushes through the door with Tray following. Tray's always been a quiet kid, but the minute he sees Storm, he just lights up, and she can get him to come out of his shell.

"Tray!" Storm shouts. "Help us. We need to drag Uncle Ares over there!"

They all pick up his legs, and he starts thrashing. "No, someone save me!"

"You're such a dick!" I laugh at him as the kids have his leg in a death grip and are trying to drag him to the back door while he tries to scoot along, helping them. "Where are you guys taking him?"

"Your office," Storm informs me. And my eyes shoot around the room. "Why my office?" I grimace. I mean, the kids know I work in an office, but they've never seen it and don't even know where it is or what I actually do.

"I heard Uncle Blade say it's where you take people you want to kill." River informs me.

"Uncle Blade said that, huh?"

"Yeah, and Uncle Viking said it's in the barn!" Tray tells me.

"Well, fuck! My brothers are fucking idiots!"

"That's a lot of bad words, Aunty Ray!" Tray nods.

Tank and Cade laugh behind me, and I glare at them both. "Not helping, guys!" I thought it would be years before they knew what we did. I know they don't really understand, but my brothers need to be more careful. The door opens, and ruckus laughter fills the air as they all walk in.

"Mummy, it's those fucking idiot brothers of yours."

They all freeze in shock at the words that have just come out of Storm's mouth. "You're in trouble!" Tray points at them.

"Run!" Cade shouts, and they don't ask why. They turn and run out of the door, and me and the kids take off after them. They run around onto the grass and pretend to trip while Storm jumps on Viking and Tray dives on Blade. Priest gets on his knees and surrenders, holding his hands out, and River runs right past him, going after Dice.

Once they're all restrained, the kids sit on them. River says, "Mummy, do we need Grandad, Uncle Tank and Uncle Dane to help us take the idiots to your office?" I run my hands down my face and shake my head. This is my life now.

"Tell you what, kids, you can deal with them right here. How about that?"

"Typewriter!" Storm yells, and the rest of the guys come to stand beside me as Blade, Viking, and Dice receive their punishments.

"Looks vicious!" Priest slides his arms around me. "Maybe you should implement it in the office!"

I dig him in the ribs as he kisses my neck.

"What are you doing to my husband?" Dane's voice rings out from behind the guys."

"Argh Run. It's the monster!" Storm shouts, and they all tear up the field as fast as their little legs will carry them while Dane chases them all. He throws Tray over one shoulder and grabs Storm by the back of her jeans, lifting her off the floor and running after River, making stupid monster noises while Dice comes to join me.

"Fuck, I think if I had ovaries, they'd be clanging right about now."

"No! No more kids in this fucking club, it took me years to control most of you, some I've given up on!" Ares glares at me, and I smile at him. "But those three are fucking feral." He shakes his head, drops to his knees, and clasps his hands together in front of Dice. "Please, Brother. I beg of you. No more!"

I punch him in the shoulder. "You're such a fucking dick."

We stay out there and watch the kids run around, and I fucking love my life. I am happy; in a way, it was a hard road to get here, but now, at this moment, I'm lucky to still be here, even though I thought I would die without half of my old heart. I've gained half a new one. I'm lucky to be so loved.

THE END

Acknowledgements

For those of you who have made it this far, thank you for taking a chance on an unknown author releasing this, the fourth and last book in my debut series. I've poured my swinging brick and little black soul into this series, and my swinging brick thanks you from the bottom of it for your support. I couldn't have done it without you all,

My mum and son,

My boozy book club Bestie,

My queen.

My besties,

The girls at United.

My new author/bookish besties for being there through my rants and the chaos.

To my ARC and Street teams.

 I LOVE YOU ALL!!

To anyone who's read my books, liked/shared a post/video, no matter how small you think the gesture, I appreciate you all!

This is the last book in this series, so if you loved this as much as I loved writing it and can't wait to see what fucked up brain can come up with next get ready to ride this rollercoaster with me. This is only the beginning and I promise it's only gonna get crazier!

Buckle up, buttercup and let's see what I can come up with for you next!

Books by Harley Raige

The Reapers MC, Ravenswood Series

Reaper Restrained 1 Aug 23
Reaper Released 1 Oct 23
Reaper Razed 1 Dec 23
Reaper's Revenge 1 Feb 24